Praise for James Ha

Didn't Nobody Give a Shit What Happened to Carlotta

"Razor-sharp...A hilarious, righteous transgender remix of *The Odyssey*...Carlotta's bold voice hooks readers from the beginning, making them willing ride-or-dies...Hannaham hasn't merely given the classics an update; he has given readers an unforgettable glimpse into the injustices the carceral system heaps on women like Carlotta—and deftly made space in literature for a distinctive voice that deserves a place in the modern literary pantheon."

—Paula L. Woods, *Los Angeles Times*

"Lovingly linguistic and equal parts Zora Neale Hurston, Chester Himes, and the now mythical Stagg R. Leigh, this refreshingly cool look at the new New York through old eyes is the Blackest book I've read in years. Carlotta is more than one to remember, she's a treasure."

—Paul Beatty, Booker Prize–winning author of *The Sellout*

"Captivating...Hannaham's bumper-car narrative astonishes... Carlotta is irrepressible. No matter how much the prison system has abused her, regardless of the cold-blooded stipulations of her parole, she is brave enough to be guided by the woman inside her tireless heart...At a time when families with trans and gay children feel persecuted by state governments, Hannaham makes Carlotta heroic. Don't let the title of this wondrous novel fool you. Hannaham cares deeply about Carlotta. From a mash-up of perspectives, he writes like a guardian angel." —John Irving, *New York Times Book Review*

"Borne along by a riotous current of verbal ingenuity, James Hannaham's new novel is—like its endlessly vibrant protagonist—a marvel of invention. There wasn't a page that didn't surprise me. By its end, this book had conjured a depth of identification with its heroine that I was not prepared for. Utterly brilliant."

—Ayad Akhtar, Pulitzer Prize–winning author of
Homeland Elegies

"A bon vivant of a book that makes you feel like you're at a party from the minute you open the front pages...It's manic, colorful, riotous, and filled with energy."

—Neda Ulaby, National Public Radio

"A remarkable novel...The hilarity, the sharpness, and the wild lyricism of Hannaham's *Delicious Foods* resurface in *Carlotta*, along with an interest in racism, community, family, love, the possibilities of language, and the preciousness of the freedom to be who you are...The rhythms, the vocabulary, the barbed observations and flashes of insight, strike us as flawless transmissions of the voice Carlotta is hearing inside her head...It's a daring move, paraphrasing a masterpiece [*Ulysses*], but Hannaham shows us why a writer might do it...He makes us see that his heroine could be the prodigal Blatina daughter of Clarissa Dalloway and Leopold Bloom—and that modernism has been waiting, all this time, to welcome Carlotta home."

—Francine Prose, *New York Review of Books*

"Maybe the comic novel is the best way to explore some of the least funny aspects of our society. Maybe the justice system is so immoral, the forces of capitalism so relentless, the treatment of some of our citizens so indefensible, that we have no choice but to turn heartbreak into hilarity, to laugh. *Carlotta* is a beautiful, unsettling book. The title is a trick; James Hannaham gives a shit, and so should everyone else."

—Rumaan Alam, author of *Leave the World Behind*

"Hannaham's buoyant sophomore novel introduces us to the unforgettable Carlotta Mercedes, an Afro Latinx trans woman released from a men's prison after serving two decades…Over the course of one zany Fourth of July weekend, Carlotta descends into Brooklyn's roiling underbelly on a quest to stand in her truth. Angry, saucy, and joyful, Carlotta is a true survivor—one whose story shines a disinfecting light on the injustices of our world."

—Adrienne Westenfeld, *Esquire*

"James Hannaham's *Didn't Nobody Give a Shit What Happened to Carlotta* is an astonishing act of empathy and identification, which will shake readers out of their torpor and remind them that fiction at its highest is a form of metempsychosis. Carlotta steps off the page and into your room, and stands there, implacable, educating you on her terms."

—Lucy Sante, author of
Low Life: Lures and Snares of Old New York

"Carlotta, the bold, brash, and bitingly hilarious protagonist, seeks to come to terms with the Fort Greene, Brooklyn, that she left behind. Hannaham's novel has drawn comparisons to *Ulysses* with its style, specificity, and snapshot framing."—Laura Zornosa, *Time*

"Hilarious and heartbreaking, with language that reaches for your throat…With an unforgettable voice, Hannaham takes on gentrification, the prison and parole system, and more."

—Xochitl Gonzalez, *The Atlantic*

"As if by means of some mash-up of Hubert Selby, Darius James, and Bruce Wagner, James Hannaham's trip-wire provocations and dazzling verbal fireworks give way to a fathomless tenderness and remorse. His Carlotta is spectacularly Brooklyn and devastatingly human all the way down to the bone."

— Jonathan Lethem, author of *Motherless Brooklyn*

"An exuberant odyssey...Carlotta's passion for life is unstoppable. Her story beats on, the narrative third person regularly bursting open into a surging stream of consciousness."

— Lindesay Irvine, *The Guardian*

"Timely, gripping, and compellingly written...This book had me from the first page...Hannaham introduces us to the distinct narrative voice of Carlotta, who's willing to cut through all the noise to tell her truth in her own distinctly hilarious way...This is a book that deserves to be read by anyone who's interested in how public policy affects the everyday lives of marginalized communities in America."

— David Vogel, *BuzzFeed*

"This is the fastest, funniest, and most furious novel I've read in ages. In James Hannaham's blistering prose, his heroine's return from the American gulag to gentrified Brooklyn becomes an odyssey through the absurd, cruel, and sometimes miraculous condition of being poor, Black, and trans in a system and a city determined to erase the Carlottas of this world. The book is a tour de force of a spirit undefeated by this journey."

— Adam Haslett, author of *Imagine Me Gone*

"As a creative dynamo, Hannaham is the real deal...*Didn't Nobody Give a Shit What Happened to Carlotta* is his most tender and tenacious novel yet, with the ear, soul, mouth, and swagger of a real New Yorker."

— Kalup Linzy, *Interview*

"We were big fans of James Hannaham's previous novel, *Delicious Foods*…The long wait for his follow-up is finally over, and it's a doozy: a raucous social comedy that takes on our carceral system, the poor treatment of trans people, and capitalist failings in one unmissable package."
— *Chicago Review of Books*

"Hannaham's latest novel is at once irreverently funny and devastatingly sad, a quixotic tale about the queerness of missed time; how, for the most marginalized, the shackles of the past and uncertain promises of the future make dwelling in the present seem impossible."
— Michelle Hart, *Electric Literature*

"Engrossing…A brash, ambitious novel carried by an unforgettable narrator…In its day-in-the-life framing, hyperlocality, and rhetorical invention, *Didn't Nobody Give a Shit What Happened to Carlotta* is also an homage to *Ulysses*…Carlotta deserves a lot of things society rarely provides to women like her—among them, a role in great fiction. Hannaham gives Carlotta her due."
— *Kirkus Reviews* (starred review)

"Carlotta is a vision to behold as she attempts reentry into a now-unfamiliar world. In Hannaham's hands, this theme shimmers with humor, pathos, and that kind of queer energy that readers love."
— Jim Piechota, *Edge Media*

"*Didn't Nobody Give a Shit What Happened to Carlotta* expertly balances the seriousness of the criminal legal system with the irreverence, absurdity, humor, and healing connections of Carlotta's world."
— Sarah Neilson, *Them*

DIDN'T NOBODY GIVE A SHIT WHAT HAPPENED TO CARLOTTA

James Hannaham

BACK BAY BOOKS

Little, Brown and Company

New York Boston London

For Brendan

Back Bay Books / Little, Brown and Company
Hachette Book Group
1290 Avenue of the Americas, New York, NY 10104
littlebrown.com

Originally published in hardcover by Little, Brown and Company, August 2022

First Back Bay paperback edition, August 2023

Back Bay Books is an imprint of Little, Brown and Company, a division of Hachette Book Group, Inc. The Back Bay Books name and logo are trademarks of Hachette Book Group, Inc.

The publisher is not responsible for websites (or their content) that are not owned by the publisher.

The Hachette Speakers Bureau provides a wide range of authors for speaking events. To find out more, go to hachettespeakersbureau.com or email hachettespeakers@hbgusa.com.

Permissions for song lyrics have been granted by the following:

Genius Of Love
Words and Music by Tina Weymouth, Christopher Frantz, Adrian Belew and Steven Stanley
Copyright © 1981 METERED MUSIC, INC.
All Rights Controlled and Administered by UNIVERSAL - POLYGRAM INTERNATIONAL PUBLISHING, INC. All Rights Reserved   Used by Permission
Reprinted by Permission of Hal Leonard LLC

Birthday Cake
Words and Music by Robyn Fenty, Ernest Clark, Marcos Palacios and Terius Nash
Copyright © 2011 Annarhi Music LLC, Sony Music Publishing (US) LLC, Viva Panama and 2082 Music Publishing
All Rights for Annarhi Music LLC, Sony Music Publishing (US) LLC and Viva Panama Administered by
Sony Music Publishing (US) LLC, 424 Church Street, Suite 1200, Nashville, TN 37219
All Rights for 2082 Music Publishing Administered by WC Music Corp.
International Copyright Secured   All Rights Reserved

Little, Brown and Company books may be purchased in bulk for business, educational, or promotional use. For information, please contact your local bookseller or the Hachette Book Group Special Markets Department at special.markets@hbgusa.com.

ISBN 9780316285278 (hc) / 9780316286282 (pb)
Library of Congress Control Number: 2022936661

Printing 1, 2023

LSC-C

Printed in the United States of America

And whoa, where did all those yesterdays go?
　　　　　　　　—Odyssey, "Native New Yorker"

ONE

wo decades and change into her beef, Carlotta Mercedes braced herself for audition number five with the New York State Board of Parole. She knew her many years in the SHU — 23-7 with no TV, no radio, no books, and no good touch — would probably blow her case this time too. With so many box hits, she couldn't finish any of the A&D programs the knuckleheads like to see. But solitary overkill wasn't the worst of her shots Them sonofabitches said I had bad behavior, but they definition a bad behavior's if you scream when a CO whupping yo ass like a Betty Crocker fudge cake. Why did she keep getting hit? Sometimes she thought her case grossed out the panel, other times she blamed her mini-beefs — the LOMs, the LOCs, the LORs, the LOVs. She knew the bosses were pretty much Klansmen, and at some point she always went apeshit.

"Those motherfuckers better let me out this time," she told Frenzy, the new man she was riding with, out in the yard the day she heard. "Who is they to judge *my* ass?"

"Shut up, bitch," he soothed. "You think you special? Don't expect nothing. You got nothing coming."

Her eyes rolled behind her lids and she whacked her arms closed. "I *been had* known not to spect nothing forever by this time. Fifty million motherfuckers already done told me how much nothin I got comin. So let's see it! Where my nothin at? And who's more of specials than I is?" Her tongue had slipped a little out of fear that he didn't really have eyes for her, or big enough ones, anyway. She felt like some kind of monkey-mouth even before she'd shut her trap.

"If you want out, you better learn to talk right," Frenzy said, flashing a dimple. "Folks be talking proper out there."

"Oh yeah? Since when?" She gave him face and flipped her hair so it grazed his nose.

In 1993, Carlotta's cousin Kafele had shot some old lady who sold little bottles of Thunderbird to the skels of Bed-Stuy and put her to sleep for a month. Carlotta was in attendance, showing off her talent for bad timing. The lady woke up again, but the bullet lowered her IQ to a chimpanzee's and she could hardly brush her own teeth anymore. Kaffy landed in Attica, doing all day and a night. Mama must've stopped saving his supper. Carlotta turned state's evidence and still got 12½ to 22. The public defender called that "getting off with a reduced sentence," but to Carlotta that didn't sound like getting off in any way, shape, or form. "The robbery or the aggravated assault with a deadly weapon could have gotten you twenty-five each!" the judge whined. "You're lucky to be doing them concurrently" That's luck, then fuck luck.

Sleeping Beauty's daughter, Noreen Green, always dragged her bitter puss up to the hearings, and she made no exception for this sequel in the franchise. She dug harsh sentences — she thought that if you croaked before you killed your number, they wouldn't dump your carcass off-site. When she shouted, "I want their bones to turn to dust in the prison cell!" she meant it literally. She had spat that oratory at the public defender, a pale mousy girl with big glasses who looked like a PhD candidate in macramé. Made the poor thing spaz and knock her coffee all over her papers Which show you how good the bitch had her shit together not at all.

Even before Carlotta's time on the catwalk that day, they'd kept her in the SHU, and of course the COs tried to yank her out before her toilette. She hadn't finished drying her sink-washed locks and massaging mess hall margarine into her scalp when they banged on the door, barking like Dobermans selling wolf tickets about an upcoming beatdown Ise like, Ho-hum, another? Cause I knew they wasn't gon do nothing to me right before no damn parole hearing. Or maybe they was gonna but I din't give a fuck. Part of her wanted to risk an ass-whupping, but the minute she clocked the reality—getting scalped with a bare hand, a Doc Marten jammed in her rib cage—animal fear took over. Her body cashed a check at her memory bank and she could feel the fists and boots of yester-year colliding with tender body parts. One time a CO belted her in the face and she almost made a meal of her own tongue Ise talkin like Daffy Duck for two fuckin weeks. And of course they punished her for getting punished. Against her will, her mind snapped back to the worst of the worst, a scumbag called Dave, and something inside her gave way like a noose going slack after doing the Strange Fruit swing.

Carlotta pushed her paws through the bean slot and let the COs cuff her. But she hadn't finished her face—she only had the blue pool-cue chalk (smuggled in from the juvie wing) on her left eyelid This gon look bad. It *do* look bad! If they got no kick from paroling what some of these jerk-offs called "he-she things" with painted faces, no way would they spring a freakazoid with just *one* blue eyelid. The minute she saw her chance, she leaned over and smudged her blinker with the one chalky finger she still had, trying to keep everything clear of her headlights, because that might juice her eyeball like a lemon Or maybe I *should* do like a fountain if that gon get them on my side.

They didn't let her shower either. As she swung past the cells in the cinder-block alley, she could smell her funk through her prison grays; she hoped nobody else got a whiff Prolly can't nobody smell nothing over the stench a this joint nohow. Let's just say her look did not kill, but the peanut gallery whooped it up regardless, all piercing whistles, *Hey, mami*s, and *Do-fries-go-with-that-shake*s. Up at Ithaca, a lady din't always had to bust her sparkle. These lusty hustlers weren't faking the flattery either, no way, José. Some could take a mocking tone, but if she shook the tree, Carlotta knew she'd get a real nut Oh, honey, at this point they'd fuck a mop. She beamed at the guys and wiggled her fingers as she passed, letting the handcuffs and chains stand in for the rocks and bling she'd've preferred. She couldn't call these suckers *suckers*, but why not gloat now, knowing the spotlight of parole would never beam down on such luckless gangstas, the same spider monkeys who'd bitten her like Rottweilers mauling a chew toy, passed her around like a spliff until the last tiny red ember in her soul almost winked out with a little puff of smoke Fuck these guys, they'd never even get a hearing, let alone five! My ass be the Susan Lucci a parole! If any of this crew did get parole or even release When hippos fly they'd probably leap back into their hustle toot sweet and boomerang into these same cells. Carlotta's hellos took on the saccharine taste of scorn Goodbye, Beezus! Goodbye, poor little Stinkbug! Ciao bella, Glitch, you cold-blooded motherfucker! But who could tell if they'd finally boot her out of the joint? Carlotta knew what time it was, she wasn't bumbling around in Pampers But a bitch gotta dream.

After the whole *Get Smart* routine with the halls and gates and checkpoints came to an end, the COs pushed open a green door Green like Frankenstein and there sat three poker faces from the NYSPB See Evil, Hear Evil, an Speak Evil fingers poised on padfolios stuffed with the details of every beef they'd give a shot that day Look at them smug-ass faces, think they some kinda gods sittin at a tribunal gon decide my fate, which I guess they kinda are, uh-oh, fuck me.

The second their prisoner made it in, the COs whipped the metal door back and locked it—*clang!* The clang rang out in the room like a pipe hitting a lamppost, but Carlotta had heard this noise so often that to her, it could've been a butterfly fart. In the back left of the room, a few yards from where the guards plopped Carlotta into a standard-issue government chair, Noreen Green sat squinting, crinkling her hand inside a plastic snack bag of—was it pretzels? Or popcorn? Popcorn? Like my suffering is fucking entertainment for your stupid ass? Unlike most victims, Noreen had some sort of special dispensation that allowed her to be in the room More like a cousin who a judge or some shit and had dragged her malfunctioning parent with her, this time in a wheelchair—maybe she thought some extra visual oomph would get Carlotta buried under the jail the way she wanted. The mom, Dorothy, sat silent, lolling her head side to side, grinding her teeth. In any case, she looked cranky. The lights were on in that noggin, but somebody had locked the door—Kaffy, specifically. She seemed worse off than last time, season 19, episode 4 Oh shit, she brung her again? This fucking sucks. Why do I even bother?

One of the panel's poker faces, none of whom Carlotta recognized This must be a new crew, maybe they gonna see my beef different belonged to a white guy with a baldy bean, round and rough as a basketball. He had on a too-tight suit, probably from a discount outlet; his giant biceps puffed out the sleeves. So much for tailoring. Dead center sat a fiftyish white lady in a black blouse rocking frosted highlights and oversize bifocals; she could pass for a daytime talk-show host from the '80s Maybe she'll spring me in exchange for some style tips. The woman kept twisting her gold rings like Gollum or somebody. Off to the right, Carlotta felt judgment pouring from the stink eye of a Black woman with tiny rectangular glasses and a conservative hairdo in the shape of the Liberty Bell, wearing a suit the color of a grape Popsicle. She had a more mysterious look about her than the other two, and that sparked fear in Carlotta She don't look like the type who gon give you no racial break, she look like the type who give you a hard time cause they think you gonna try some nigga trick they already know, bein a nigga theyself. Try to catch you out when you ain't even frontin.

The tribunal got the ball rolling by stating their names: Demodocus Johnson Demodocus? He Black? He look too light to be a brotha, but you never know…Helen Alcinous, and Malea Thoon, but the names vanished from her head in no time Damn, I can't never remember nobody's name, not even when my life literally depend on it! COs musta knocked my memory clean out my head. Sometime I wish they had. The drab chair had a green seat with a rip down the middle, a hole that seemed, like every hole did now, like a good place to stow a shank or stash some molly. Moving her fingers between her legs, she probed the opening to see if someone else had gotten there first and left her a present. She almost forgot to react when Basketball Head piped up.

"Can you please state your name for the record?" he asked.

Carlotta had picked up a reflex for whenever a boss quizzed her. She knew she had to fake like mad, to knuckle under like a trained bear riding a unicycle and balancing a ball on its nose at some Ringling Brothers joint. You had to stuff your ego up your ass and kowtow to the COs and the other shitheads; you had to grind your attitude into a fine powder and try to look as tame as a Ring Ding, what with the mogwai raising hell in your skull all the time, making you so rowdy, so loco Sometime it just be them up in there too, my ass wasn't nowhere near that brain. She knew she couldn't tell him her name; an honest answer to even this Mickey Mouse question would bring down enough drama to keep her on ice until she hit the half-century mark. She jammed her frustration into her stomach and took a gander at Basketball Head again. He reminded her of one of those Chinese dogs with the smushy muzzles What they call that?

She could *not* say Carlotta Mercedes, and she knew it. She pushed her fingers deeper between her legs, careful not to disturb Señora Problema, and tugged at the strings hanging off the sides of the break in the vinyl. Could be every con who ever sat in this chair had done a little fraying. Frenzy had flopped seven times to her four, and he had the knowledge. "The board ain't gon axe you no questions they don't got the answers to right there in that jacket," he told her. "And don't be altercatin with how they spin your beef, okay? Cause if you tell em they wrong, specially when they *is* wrong, they just gon give you the heave-ho and bum-rush yo ass right back to D Block." It had slipped her mind to ask if her name change would rattle them, but now it seemed like, Duh. To call herself Carlotta right off the bat would be suicide. It would lead back to Dave—the thought hollowed her out.

She snarfed down a loogie, trying not to show off too much hate for her deadname, closed her eyes so she could roll them without the board seeing, and sucked in a big breath. "Dustin Chambers, sir," she said. Then she yanked her hands from between her thighs, raised her wrists, cocked her head to one side, and tried to push her hair back with both cuffed hands. Not easy, so she did it slowly, fanning out her fingers as she went, trying to kill Dustin Chambers again and shout Carlotta Mercedes with body language alone.

"I'm sorry, can you repeat that?" said Basketball Head.

Carlotta froze, dropped her hands back in her lap, and locked her jaw I know I said that shit loud enough, an I know you heard me! Frenzy had coached her on this too. "They gon try to get your goat," he'd said. "Provoke you to see if you gon freak out and fuck up, which make they job easier cause they get to send your ass right back to the joint. That shit you *definitely* gotta resist. Don't give em *nothing*."

Anger management, Carlotta thought. It was just a phrase, though—she had never had any real training Anger management. She squeezed her knees and counted down from ten in her head—she figured that was how people on TV kept from flipping out. In her mind, a song her mother used to sing along with in her Colombian accent took over—*Think about what you going to do to me*—but she gave no outward sign of inward singing. A little smile found its way onto her face, though—its fakeness felt like a layer of hot wax over her real face. She swallowed again and said the name again, at an almost mocking volume. She pretended he'd asked for her brother's name. "Dustin Chambers."

"Now, Mr. Chambers," he kept on, "I have here that you've served twenty years of a 12½ to 22 sentence on an armed assault and robbery?"

Carlotta nodded *Not countin the year in jail fore the sentencing, but I ain't gonna split no hairs,* and said, "That is correct" *How I coulda did the whole twenty-one an then some is I'm a fuckin bruja.*

Basketball Head softly wheezed, "Armed assault and robbery," all the time scribbling some note with a ballpoint pen, probably the thing he'd just said.

Ms. Thoon took over, like a script she and Basketball Head had to follow *I guess they kinda do got a script.* Her voice had a surprisingly smoky, luscious quality. Frenzy had schooled her on how you didn't need any real bona fides to get on a parole board, and that thought looped in her mind as she listened, trying to knock them off whatever pedestal they thought they were on *Miss Lady Day here could use that voice to be singing standards on Saturdays down at the local motor lodge.* But her voice also sounded serious, like a newscaster's. "Mr. Chambers, can you give us a detailed picture of what took place on that night, the night of August 14, 1993?"

This I could do. She concentrated on talking proper. "Saturday night. It was about sundown, around 8:22 p.m., and I was on my way to my best friend's birthday party. As I'm walking over there, I had the intention to hit the Sippy Sip liquor store, located at 726 Myrtle Avenue, corner of Walworth Street." She paused. "Shoot. I mean *buy* something from there, not hit it like rob it. I was gonna grab a bottle of André or something and then stop in at Gloria's Thrift Gifts, which is a shop just up the street, so I can get a present for my friend. They closed at nine cause Gloria didn't usually even show up till around three on Saturdays. She from Trinidad. And, lo and behold, I see my cousin Kaffy crossing Myrtle, and I'm like, 'Hey,' and like, 'Oh, are you also going to Doodle's party?' Her name is Deirdre but everybody calls her Doodle. He's like, 'No, I'm going to Sippy Sip,' and he points to it cause we're only a block away, on Spencer, and I said, 'So am I!'" She had rehearsed this saga maybe three hundred times, and her lawyer had coached her to curb her potty mouth and include small details like exact times and the names of streets and establishments to boost her cred. Nowadays it came more or less naturally, but she could rattle it off like something she had memorized Like shit that happened to somebody else ass.

Ms. Thoon rifled through the papers on her clipboard and stared at something written there. "Mr. Chambers, I believe the record states that at that moment, you were carrying a loaded weapon, were you not?"

"That is true, yes" *Were you not.* What the fuck, all this stupid language! Why they gotta talk like they in a Shakespeare play all the fucking time? Romeo, Romeo, wherefore art thou's ass in the hole?

"Are you the sort of person who carries a loaded weapon to a birthday party?"

What kinda condescending bullshit question is that? Who gon be fool enough to say yes to that? Like, Yes, ma'am, I'm so crazy I'd bring a flamethrower to a baby shower. As a gift! Now parole me or I'ma bite off your titty. What? But Frenzy had given her hell about telling them exactly what they wanted to hear "at every possible fucking moment you could." She thought about his full, wet lips talking, how the sneaky soul patch under them wiggled like a caterpillar, then the eyes in her mind found their way around his body to a tattoo of a phoenix spanning his entire back. "At the time, the record states that I was, ma'am, but since I've been inside I have done a great deal of work to change who I am. I have been a part of the recovery program even though I did not have a substance-abuse problem, I gained permission to do laundry duty through my years of good behavior, and I even briefly worked in the law liberry. I guess in Bed-Stuy in them days, there almost wasn't really no other type of person but one who was holding. Cause the other type was called dead." Carlotta widened her eyes. She saw the left side of the Black lady's cheek twist upward slightly Also, I spent bout six a them years in solitary cause a how much I got raped an beat up, an I quit them substances cold turkey, but fuck it, they don't wanna hear none a that. Plus that shit din't even help. It helped Dave. She heard the scenes in her mind again and the blood rushed out of her head *Rape! Leave me alone, you son of a bitch! Somebody help!*

"I'm concerned that you're making light of this situation, Mr. Chambers," Basketball Head barked, bouncing his ballpoint clicker on the desk. Noreen grunted from the peanut gallery.

She shook herself out of the starry-eyed dizziness for a second. "Oh, it ain't no light, don't worry bout that." Carlotta felt she had lost Basketball Head already, and since the vote had to be unanimous, the ladies would need to struggle hard against him if they wanted to grant her parole That din't look too likely. Nother day, nother hit. I only got a year an a half left anyways, so I mean, fuck it, maybe I should just kill my number an kick it with my man. Her hand went back to fiddling with the rip in the chair. Basketball Head sure had a brick wall for a body Hmm, do that cop attitude make him sexier or not sexy? Maybe sexy at some *other* bitch's parole hearing. Suddenly he pushed all the papers off the table, grabbed her by the shoulders, fucked her ass pussy silly, and granted her parole when he came Nah, he ain't really did that, that's just my li'l fantasy.

"I'm not, sir. I just felt at the time that I needed to be ready for pretty much anything?" I also adore guns. Damn, it's too fuckin easy to fuck this up. But I can't give up—maybe the women gon be on my side. My sistas. Sorta? The white lady with the frosted hair didn't ever say anything, but she smiled—not a big smile, but a steady one. Like the Virgin Mary. "So Cousin Kaffy and I walk in the store together. I start looking for the discount liquors—Doodle ain't that picky—and before I know what's happening, Kaffy had pulled a gun on the lady behind the counter. There was a bullet-proof cage thing for the cashier, but Kaffy always been cute, he don't look threatening, even though he actually a real dangerous dude. He pretended to have a question about a bottle of Malibu rum or something—like, he deliberately chose a sweet type of liquor so she wouldn't get suspicious—and he got Mrs. Green to come out the cage. And that's when he pulled out the piece—the gun. She tried to go back in, but he yanked her out." Everyone heard Noreen sniffle and then blow her nose, making a sound like a broken trumpet. People turned for a second to look at her and her mother until the image got too sad.

"And what did you do?" Ms. Thoon asked, tugging down a purple sleeve.

She know what I did! She seened the damn videotape! This complete bullshit. I'ma tell her what I *said* instead. "I said, 'Kaffy what the—what the F are you doing? We not about to rob this joint. If you need money, I will lend you money, we will find you money somewheres, but don't do this, and don't drag me into it neither!'

I said, 'Ain't you apposed a be getting a GED? Din't you wanna be a engineer?' But he didn't pay me no mind. Later I heard he was doing it for a promotion in his gang. I was like, *Gang?* What gang he could join at his age? The Little Rascals? He knew I was holding, so he yelled at me to cover him while he went into the little room and jacked the register."

"Did you cover him?"

"No, ma'am, I did not. But that's part of what caused the problem. See, Kaffy pulled Mrs. Green into the room by the neck and made her take the money out the register. But somehow she got away and start to stumble out the little room. That's when Kaffy shot her. For the life of me, I do not know what possessed him to aim at her head. He had a very difficult upbringing. We all did."

"You guys have had a rough time," the Virgin chimed in. "He's serving a life sentence."

"Yes, that's correct" An prolly won't never get no parole, given what happening to me.

"It should be longer!" Noreen yelled at nobody with stabbing anger.

Longer than life? Like they gon put a jail cell round his grave? Honest to God, honey, he ain't going nowheres.

"How do you account for the fact that, on the surveillance-camera video, you can clearly be seen drawing your own weapon, Mr. Chambers?" said the Virgin, pushing her glasses up the bridge of her nose for the ninth time to rest in the kidney-shaped divots there. She had upped her angle, Carlotta suspected, because her previous comments had seemed soft You two-faceded ho! Y'all got my goat, m'kay? Y'all done *curried* my motherfucking goat!

"Around that same moment, I aimed my weapon at Kaffy, trying to get him not to shoot the woman, but it was too late. If you could hear sound on that video, you'd hear me shouting, 'Kaffy, don't shoot! Put the gun down!' I didn't never fire my gun neither."

Basketball Head came in for the kill. "You're aware, though, that it appears that you are aiming directly at the cashier?"

Here we go again. "Yes, sir, I *am* aware of that, sir. Mrs. Green was between the two of us, and that makes it difficult to tell. But y'all has seened the footage and y'all know that the 'cinematography' or whatever? It ain't that good." It was an old line. The women smiled, but not Basketball Head. "The ballistic evidence also had shown that I didn't fire no gun. Any gun" I'm a fucking dead duck. Like a Peking duck hanging in the window a the skankiest greasy-spoon joint in Chinatown.

Malea Thoon took over, her voice mellow and motherly, almost tender now. Perhaps Carlotta had misjudged her. "Do you have any regrets about your part in this crime?"

"Oh, gosh," she said, jumping at the chance to show remorse I got this. "Regrets. Talk about regrets. If you drilled a hole in my heart, right here," Carlotta said, jabbing her rib cage with her thumb, jangling the cuffs, "or anywhere, really, y'all would see all the regret draining out of me like Ise a aquarium tank and the water was regret. Then once all the regret had spilt out, my whole body would flop down like a empty garbage bag, because there wouldna been hardly nothing inside me *but* regret. I eat, sleep, and dream bout regret ever since this happened. My life became a path with a fork in it when all that happened, an there's nothing I wish I could do more than go back an take that other road, the one that din't lead to no twenty years in prison, to none a this" Cept getting with Frenzy. "I wish I didn't have a cousin Kaffy, and I almost wish I ain't had a best friend Doodle, especially one who had a birthday party that night. I wish I didn't have a gun on me" More like I wish I had left it at home, that shit was my favorite gun, a absolutely gorgeous Llama Micromax with a mother-of-pearl inlay, cost me fifteen hundred dollars I saved for two years, never gon see that shit again. "I ain't got nothing but regret." Frenzy had instructed her to play it up when they asked about guilty feelings. She wondered if she'd overdone it, but she had to admit that she actually felt about 80 percent of what she'd said. Just saying the words made her eyes fill with tears. Like the actress she'd named herself for, she whipped up the memory of her fucked-up past into a meringue of mostly real emotion.

"Boo-hoo-hoo!" Noreen shouted from the other side of the room.

"Uh," said Basketball Head, drawing out the vowel in Noreen's direction, careful not to ruin the flow of the meeting. "So at this time, we can open the hearing up to comments. Ms. Green, it sounds as if you have something to say."

Carlotta closed her eyes and braced herself I hope I could keep from punching out her fuckin pea brain. Guess these cuffs is good for that. I understand what it feel like for someone you love to get hurt bad, but what the fuck happened to mercy?

Noreen got up, whisked off her glasses, and chucked her handbag into the empty seat. She practically did a pirouette as she spun around to face the panel. She had no notes. Against all stereotypes, taking off the specs made her look like the smartest person in the room, and talking without notes let them all know she meant every damn word. Her eyes narrowed and she squared her shoulders. She planted her feet and folded her arms. She started talking almost in a whisper, which took nearly everyone aback. "It is my considered opinion that this individual as well as his cousin are very dangerous violent criminals, and neither should receive parole at this time — or ever. This crime was shocking, it was senseless, and it was incredibly brutal. The *two* perpetrators — I am not making a distinction, and neither should you — showed no regard for human life, certainly not the life of my mother, Mrs. Dorothy Green, who sits before you today in an extremely diminished state." For a second, she turned to nod at her mother, then pointed at Carlotta. She revved up the megaphone. "You, *Mr. Chambers*" — she emphasized the name probably because she figured it got up Carlotta's nose—"you deserve nothing even approaching clemency for destroying my mother's business, which she took over from my father after his death, God rest his soul, for destroying her quality of life, and for ruining my own life as well, as I have depleted nearly all of my own resources in caring for my mother without health insurance or financial support of any kind outside my administrative-assistant salary. Twelve to twenty-two years!" she scoffed, her eyes back on the panel. "For shame! Twenty-two *thousand* years wouldn't be enough time for *Mr. Chambers* to repent and contemplate the heinous nature of his horrible crime, and I think that from the bad attitude he has displayed here today, the panel can tell that he is still not at all ready to reenter society and still needs a very long time to pay his debt to society. Much longer" Damn, Meryl Streep, if I wasn't me, I'd almost buy what you sellin! Yeah, gimme twenty-two thousand years a all the shit been done to me that you don't even know the half of! I'on't think so, ho!

Carlotta turned her shoulders to face Noreen. She didn't say *Bitch, you got no idea what a bad attitude look like from me,* but she tried to make those words as clear as possible with side-eye alone.

Noreen took a pause and bent her knees to get her purse from the chair. She threw the strap over one shoulder, unzipped the bag, and rifled inside. "My mother can no longer speak for herself, as you can tell," she continued, "and she has a great deal of difficulty writing, but I'd like to share something she wrote down when she found out that Mr. Chambers would be going up for parole yet again, and I urge you not to grant parole this time either."

Holy shit, Carlotta thought. She pullin out all the stops. You can't win gainst no cripple factor, let alone some white cripples. Fuck me. Am I gonna die up in here? Motherfucking death by bunga-bunga.

Noreen pulled out a weathered piece of yellow legal paper and uncrinkled it against her thigh. When she lifted it again, Carlotta could see that something had been written there in black Sharpie and the ink had bled through to the other side. Noreen took one side of the paper in each hand and inched up to the table. "You see what that says? Can you read that?"

Through the paper, Carlotta peered at the reverse image of the words, sloppily scrawled in block letters perpendicular to the faint blue lines. She had a hard time making out what the short phrase said. Just as she figured it out, Noreen explained it to the panel.

"It says," she proclaimed, pointing to each of the three words as she read the inscription, " 'They shuld fry.' She left out the *o* in the *should*. But that's what it says. 'They. Shuld. Fry.' " She drew out the word *fry* extra-long when she said it the second time. At that moment, Mrs. Green rocked violently in her wheelchair and grunted to let everyone know how well the note expressed her views.

"Thank you, Mrs. Green," the Black woman said, her face suddenly glum. Noreen glared at Carlotta, moved her purse, and sat down, a look of satisfaction on her face.

Carlotta gave up, covering her eyes with her fingertips so that her handcuffs touched her chin I am toast. A burnt-up fucking piece a black toast.

Then, like sweet pruno pouring out of a Ziploc bag, she thought of how adoringly Frenzy would receive the bad news, that this setback would earn Carlotta more than a few hot bear hugs in those solid, veiny arms. But then terror carjacked her mind—she avoided certain areas of the pit where Dave lurked; she had sometimes fainted when she thought she heard him coming. She had a flight instinct to GTFO that made almost everything else shrink like a wool blanket in the prison laundry. Plus she had fantasized about getting parole for two decades, to the point where the ideas of heaven and leaving Ithaca had jumbled up in her mind, and she couldn't dump that feeling in the Hudson River for anybody. Her pictures of certain family members had creased and torn, but sometimes late,

late, she would pull them from the bottom of her stash and lay the pieces on her bed like a puzzle until she could look at their faces. If only she could put everything back together as easily. She still had Aretha's jam buzzing in her head— *"Freedom, oh, freedom!"*

After all the brouhaha and a little hush-hush consultation, Basketball Head sounded like he was about to unleash Carlotta on the free world again Freedom indeed. Color me surprised! Carlotta smiled like a fool, trying to hide her iffiness and doubt In who fuckin mind did that go so good? Do they need the beds that bad? How come din't some CO just gimme a ticket based on my gettin jumped before? Maybe that whole thing bout remorse got em. Frenzy always said that's what they wanna hear, that you had some "insights" after thinkin bout shit in your cell, that you ain't had nothin but regrets, even bout shit you ain't done. I know the governor office gon smack this one down but quick. Fear of success had her shitting bricks.

From the look on his face, Basketball Head Demodocus didn't seem to give a rat's ass, but the ladies showed bighearted smiles. Noreen, though, blew a gasket. She turned red and leaped up to yell epithets She almost to the color they used to dye them pistachio nuts. She turned and grabbed her chair, ready to wing it at the commission, but the COs, used to far worse, blocked her before she could get the chair too high or gain any momentum. In a sudden verbal blitz, she promised Carlotta she would find a way to overturn everything, including the chair, and implied that she might commit a crime herself. In the end, the COs pulled Noreen out of the room, still railing and thrashing. A CO came back to collect Dorothy, who snarled at the commission as he wheeled her out.

The panel would take another look-see, Basketball Head said, and the official notice of action would come in a few anxious days.

Frenzy didn't exactly whoop and holler when Carlotta told him three days later that she got sprung. He nodded his leonine head slowly and blinked those pretty eyes. For some reason, he wouldn't look her in the face. Everybody played their cards close to their chests in the joint, and just because Frenzy never took anyone on a tour of his emotional landscape didn't mean he didn't have one. But it made her cranky that whenever she did get past the gates of his heart, the ticket booth for the monorail was always closed.

"Spread your wings and fly," he said, like some kind of fucking oracle. He squeezed the back of his neck and squinted at the blank sky. Either he was fronting like mad or he truly didn't give a fuck; both possibilities corked Carlotta so hard that she decided to whack his bars with her own honesty The fuck his problem?

"Truth is," she said, "I'on't really wanna go no more." It wasn't the truth.

He turned and peered daggers at her If I ain't know better, I'd think he got some mockatory attitude goin on. But maybe I *don't* know better. "Yo, bitch, did you lost your fucking mind?" He could talk all kinds of smack, but in that velvety voice, everything sounded like an invitation to a hot-oil massage.

Carlotta sucked in her cheeks and passed her tongue over the front of her teeth with her mouth closed. She returned his stare You apposed to axe what changed my mind, an I'm apposed to say *you*. "No. Why you don't axe what changed my mind?"

"Aw, hell, I already know. Y'all females is all the same."

Carlotta thought of dressing him down for the sexist comment, but then she realized that he'd grouped her with women, and that made her happy enough that she decided not to confront him I'ma do feminism on him later.

Farther out in the yard, a hundred or so of their fellow inmates lumbered around in too-tight or too-loose prison garb. A few played double-deck pinochle at a metal picnic table cemented to the ground; others did pull-ups on the crude jungle gym. Frenzy threw his chin toward the 127-year-old prison and its 30-foot-high fence, decorated with razor wire like a psycho Christmas display. Slowly, he shook his head. "Look. If this shit was the fucking Disney Castle and Ise Prince Charming, like in your li'l fantasies and what-not, I could see you wanting to stay. But for reals, I don't gotta explain this shit to you. This ain't no place to *love* nobody."

"Love is love. The place don't matter."

"This place *don't* matter. Don't nobody matter up in this place. It's like you dead in here. It's like you could get killed while you in the hole and the world be like, *Did I hear some shit? Naaah.* I don't gotta tell *you* that." Seven months before, Carlotta happened to be in the shower area when an inmate they called Glitch raped and shanked a fish newly dubbed Brownsville. Yorkie was on look-out, but they didn't realize Carlotta was in the stall. Glitch popped the shank into Brownsville's right eye and blinded it. Somehow the COs pegged it on Glitch — for once they got it right. But rather than blaming Yorkie, the inmates all jumped to the conclusion that Carlotta was the snitch Hell, I done runned out the showers long before I seen somebody eyeball poked out. I scream when I gotta pull a hangnail, honey, I ain't stickin round for no gouge-outs. But you never could argue the finer points with a bunch of convicts. One afternoon in the laundry room, while she folded pants, Glitch the goddamn guilty party, tryna cover up his sin Yorkie, and a couple of other guys kicked Carlotta in the head enough that she nearly lost her own right eye, and like some sick joke, they ironed the sole of her right foot. The COs knew the real culprit, but they backslid to apathy and didn't back Carlotta up They be lyin and denyin, what else is fucking new. It looked like they would move her to solitary "for her own protection" again, but that kind of protection she didn't want They protected my ass by puttin me on harm's fuckin plate every time with that goddamn Dave. Ithaca didn't have a separate facility for people like her — hell, they had no *vocabulary* for people like her — so they let whatever happened happen in gen pop. By that time, though, she had already considered asking Frenzy, who had just been moved out of maximum security to D Block, for protection; once the bruises subsided and she could walk again, she felt sexy for a moment and used the opportunity, if you could call it that, to let Frenzy know her intentions I still look damn good for my forties an ravaged by a pack a toothy-ass prison wolves. Blatina don't crack, honey. Asides, Frenzy wasn't no spring chicken hisself, but the dude still built like a bank vault.

She poked his shoulder to make him look at her. "Things are so different for me now. I'm not sure I want the challenge a goin back out there. Not while you're in here, an I gotta leave you here, boo." Motherfucker don't you *love* me?

Frenzy crossed his arms tightly in front of him and looked away from Carlotta. "It ain't been that long," he said, shaking his head, pointing to the space between them, and then specified As if my ass coulda misunderstood "You and me."

"Five months could feel more real than five years sometime."

"That how long you was with your wife?"

"Jasmine? Oh, shut up! We wasn't married, she was my girl friend. Two words. Or I was hers, I din't ezzackly know. An din't hardly nothin—oh, forget it, that shit's not the point, Frenzy." Tears of frustration climbed up her voice. "Why you had to bring that up? Them people don't know nothin bout who I am."

"I'm just saying, Cee, life in here and life out there is two different lives."

"That's why I ain't so sure bout gettin out no more. Maybe they won't let me out anyways. I don't got but a year and a half on my beef. Parole is stupid."

He raised a finger to the end of her nose like a switchblade. "Don't even motherfucking think that shit. You got a son out there. Ibe."

He'd said the password. Now her eyes gushed like Hurricane Sandy hitting the Rockaways. Carlotta folded herself in half. "I write him every week but ain't heard from him since he turnt nine! I bet he's out there waitin to hear from me. His mama keepin him from me."

Frenzy gripped her by the shoulder as if to say *Get a hold of yourself* but didn't throw any more words on the fire. Instead, he watched their fellow convicts in motion for a while, bench-pressing, doing push-ups, walking together, playing cards, shooting the shit. Eventually Carlotta composed herself and joined him. B-Money had a prison tattoo of barbed wire across his Neanderthal forehead; Miguel "Basura" Guerrera had sharpened canines. The Aryan brothers, Beezus and Luke Duke, were pale, double-dealing men with frowzy beards (they said they had them for bullshit religious reasons) and veins all over their noses. Big Deano loved to show everyone the scar from the operation he'd had after he got shot four times—it looked like a king crab crawling across his chest These motherfuckers, some of em's as ugly as they crimes. Sweetums had a weird beef: armed assault and murder—he liked to admit, like it was funny, that he'd gotten so involved in the killing-people part that he forgot to rob the gas station. He kept saying *into the zone*—"I just got so *into the zone* that I forgot why I had went" Remind me to stay bout fifty miles out that zone. Then he would laugh extra loud. He was doing all day and a night—aka life. Stinkbug, a white dude, periodically blew up into rages without warning. He had tried to brain his wife with a golf club, then locked her in the garage with the Pathfinder idling, thinking the exhaust would choke her dead, but she lived, and he still kept trying to hire someone to snuff her from prison, as if the two of them lived on some cosmic plane outside morality, outside reality. Maybe outside mortality. "That's some Road Runner cartoon shit," Carlotta said when she first heard about Stinkbug.

She knew how she was *supposed* to feel about prison, and on a certain percentage of the days, say, 63 percent, her pain lined up with all the warnings she'd heard before and after she started doing time. But in that other 37 percent, the pigeon of perspective would shit on her temple, and the whole place would suddenly be…no, not a paradise, no one in their right mind could talk about it that way, but a kind of sanctuary where B-Money's barbed-wire tattoo, Stinkbug's pockmarked cheeks and forehead, and her own dorsal scars were all beautiful, where Frenzy's chivalry and even jealousy meant more than a hill of beans, and the flow of adrenaline and testosterone Other people testosterone, keep that shit away from me got her high, keeping pace with the other drugs. The way the joint controlled your schedule, the way that the COs whacked the bars of your house to enforce lights-out, the way that other inmates spent hours scheming to slam your head against a concrete floor without getting caught, all of it meant that she was cared for Not cared *about*, mind you. But for Carlotta, life inside had started to mean that people knew she existed An that's prolly the most dangerous part. Everyone had something to offer that cramped world, if only a cigarette, and even if she joined the ranks of the wildest, most uncontrollable problem children ever to get sent to the hole, *someone* would have to face her, *someone* would need to solve her somehow, by any method from tenderness to murder. Wasn't this what the majority of men here had lacked all their lives? They needed to feel that they mattered to someone, that someone was *required* to give a shit. Usually a man—men were famous for not giving a fuck.

Frenzy kept a tight lid on his beef, but the rumors had come to Carlotta before she'd even met him that he was the notorious criminal dubbed the Cheerios Killer by the *New York Daily News,* the perp of the violent 1999 rape and murder of Yolanda Willis, a young Harlem woman. According to the police report, after the killing, the murderer had sat himself down in the victim's kitchen and scarfed down a bowl of cereal, probably wearing gloves to keep his fingerprints off the utensils, the cereal box, and the milk carton. This grab bag of calculation and coldness sparked the public's wrath almost more than the murder itself, if the tabloids got the story right. The police grilled everyone who had ever looked at Ms. Willis. They figured only a lover or a relative would have the cojones to lollygag in the kitchen with her corpse like that. Frenzy and Yolanda had been romantically involved, and his violent history—in and out of juvie, fists of fury, a king-sized rap sheet including two armed robberies—had spoken for itself. His beef, though, did not arise from that case, for which he did not stand, but from possession of an unlicensed weapon and a gram of pot. Like a lot of dudes at Ithaca, he had gotten kicked upstairs to a max prison after some frighteningly bad behavior and back downstairs after some good behavior. Over the course of fifteen years.

During a flirtation a couple of months before, he and Carlotta had bonded over their mixed heritage. He was Black and Italian—the last name Franzi and his attitude made some cell warrior call him Frenzy and it stuck. She was Black and Colombian. He'd let his guard down slightly and spilled the beans about his beef. "Maybe I do belong in lockdown," he told her, "but I ain't no damn Cheerios Killer." He grimaced. "I *hate* Cheerios! I don't never eat nothing but Frosted Flakes or Cinnamon Toast Crunch. You could ask my moms. But ain't nobody heard that. And when they couldn't get me on the Cheerios, they got me on the AK and possession. Like the two of them things was the same! But to these folks, don't no logical sense matter." The system needs blood, he explained. "You build a whole buncha high-tech prisons, hire a shitload of COs, and it's like, can't no brand-new, state-of-the-art jails be sitting round empty, right? It's like *Field of Motherfucking Dreams*, yo. They built that shit, so somebody ass gotta come. And you and me know that's gon be you and me. Lucky us" Well, fuck luck.

TWO

Five months later, Carlotta did Ithaca like Usain Bolt. The day of, after the merry-go-round — as they dubbed the offloading process — they dumped her at the bus depot out of a taxi driven by Dave's pissy brother, Darren, of all possible slimeballs. They had rushed her through because the next day was the holiday observed.

At the strip mall, the car disappeared down the street and Carlotta caught her first unsupervised hour in years. She peeped left and right and then busted out into a Neutron Dance, waving her arms, swiveling her hips, clapping, twirling, and zigzagging through the rows of futuristic cars Who all cars is this? George Jetson? I'm like, Eep-opp-ork-ah-ah, motherfuckers! She did catch sight of a couple of tin boxes too, tricked-out Lincoln Continentals that some Aqua Velva polyester disco king would've driven in the '70s An it *was* a dude like that in one them cars too! I couldn't keep myself from pointing like I'm a kid in *Jurassic Park* or some shit, my mouth wide open like, Aaaaa! Good thing he din't see that.

The scummy COs wouldn't cough up any of her possessions or the clothes she'd had on when she got there Whatever — they was men's threads an they was twenty years outta date too, woulda had me lookin like Kadeem Hardison. Instead they'd foisted on her the stained white shirt and scratchy khakis every ex-con on the man side got on his last day if his duds didn't fit or got jacked Someway the pants fit. They was tight, but them legs was long enough for fuckin Yao Ming.

Carlotta rolled up the pant legs, unbuttoned the cuffs, shoved the sleeves above her elbows, and tied a sloppy halter top for herself My titties yelling, Free at last, free at last, thank God Almighty, we free at last! A thick, lipless man in the passenger's seat of a sedan gawked at her and then looked away, powering up his window—trying, Carlotta thought, to pretend he hadn't seen anything. "I don't give a fuck!" she sang, joyously off-key. "There's a lotta Carlotta in the car lot today," she yelled, gyrating and voguing. "Freedom is the shit!"

When she got bored with voguing, Old way, new way, vogue femme, vogue femme with *face,* vogue femme cray-cray with extra cheese, whatever, she did every dance she could remember from the old days—the Hound Breakdown, the Cabbage Patch, the Electric Slide, and the Wop, and taught a garbage can how to do the Bump, nearly knocking it over in the process Ise thinkin bout kissin the ground, like ev'body in the joint say they gon do, but that's just nasty, dogs an cats be shittin and pissin all over that ground. It be like kissing the can in my own house! She walked an imaginary runway back to the bus stop, where she did the Bus Stop I'm gonna be a star! Star a what, I don't got no idea. Specially in these "garments." Check out Miss Thing here, all y'all upstate grandmas ovah theah! Attention, Price Chopper shoppers! Stewart's customers, behold Miss Carlotta Mercedes, punishing in head-to-toe Ex-Con des Garçons! Work!

She only had 45 bucks cash and the check they'd thrown at her on her way out of the slammer—a whopping $537.83, which made her feel like Bill Gates until she thought about all the fees she would have to cover I tried not to never go to no hospital for the whole time Ise upstate, but I bet the whole thing gon get ate up by that or by some a that pay-to-stay bullshit where they charge you for the damn prison cell, like any motherfucker had a choice would go there, like it's a five-star hotel. If she could have cashed the check somewhere, maybe she'd've gone into Harriet's Consignment Shop nearby and bought a whole new outfit If I wanted to look like a seventy-year-old upstate dyke. Prolly for the best I can't cash it. The scratch needed to go to rent, food, real clothes My choice a real makeups! Not just whatever random smuggled-in shit, pool-chalk eye shadow, lipstick made outta melted M&M's and Vaseline. Gon be some Sephora, some MAC, talkin bout Ebony Fashion Fair, baby! My lip gloss gon be *poppeh*! Gotta be purty for all them job interviews that's gon just fall in my lap. Not. But I do wanna look presentable when I see my boy Ibe again.

In a drugstore a few doors down from the consignment shop, she took full advantage of a sample bottle of rose-scented hand lotion I'm goin all the way up these ashy prison arms! and bought her first outside makeup kit ever On clearance, $4.99! Then she got a three-pack of large panties and a few pairs of panty hose, sniffing her newly sweet skin the whole time I forgot what a fuckin rose even smelt like. She ducked into the bathroom at the bus stop — single-occupant, thankfully — to luxuriously upgrade her look I ain't puttin these hose on under no pants, though. Later, as she waited outside for the bus, she petted a dog and touched a tree, flipping out like Stevie Wonder checking out the world for the first time I'ma touch every damn tree! I'ma pet every damn dog! The owner had to tug the dog away from her I wanna say hello to ev'body! I ain't seen none a this in almost twenty-two years — I ain't seen no grass growing up through no cracks in no asphalt, I ain't seen no plastic bags stuck inside no bushes, I ain't seen no upside-down shopping carts, I ain't seen no fat-ass white woman carrying no babies an putting em in no minivan, I ain't felt the goddamn sun on my fuckin face, I ain't stepped in no goddamn gum on the ground, I ain't seen no flower shops, definitely not no banks. I sure as hell ain't never used no ATM machine. Every last second a this shit be crazy beautiful an I love life! She twirled in the street like Mary Tyler Moore and stopped short Is that a broken beer bottle on a traffic island, honey? I love it! That's me!

Because she hadn't opened a door for herself in so long, she stopped at the door of the terminal and swung it open and shut a bunch of times Practice make perfect, y'all. It felt paranormal doing things herself I'm all like *Firestarter* and whatnot. The hacks of Ithaca had given her a voucher for a one-way ticket, and when she turned it in at the booth, nobody gave her a hard time about it; they actually exchanged it for a real ticket How it could be that you wanna do some shit an it work on the first try? What? The outside be a magical land.

No one had her in their sights. No white guy's eye, robot or human, eavesdropped on her How that could even *be*? Did I really get away from Disgusting Dave? Yasss! No lights-out, no 2:30 a.m. count times, no COs frisking motherfuckers for contraband sandwiches, no warnings bout "no warning shots." She strode over toward the beer bottle and conversated with a couple of finches picking at a half-eaten muffin. "As a today, bitches, you and me got the same amounts a freedom," she informed them. "Don't be lookin at me like that. Fuckin chickadees!" Wonder should I snatch that muffin. It look better than that slop they serve in the chow hall. Ha, I crack myself up.

On the bus to New York City, Carlotta got good and drunk on possibilities. She couldn't actually get drunk—that would violate her parole. And maybe they would figure out how to turn the bus around and take her back to Frenzy and, unfortunately, all her attackers. With that thought she sighed for her boo, his long bid, and the fearful joy of escaping the horrible years in Ithaca. She daydreamed about her son, Ibe That chile round the same age I was when I went inside. I hope he not as nuts as I was then. I wonder what he gon think a me now. It been almost ten years since I heard a peep outta him or Jasmine. Maybe he gon hate me an not wanna see me. Or maybe he done come out too, an he go by, like, Halle Berry Judson-Chambers. Mama don't got no idea after all this damn time. The torn snapshot she treasured, the only image she had of her son, taken on a visit just before his fifth birthday, had faded like one of those haircut pics in a barbershop window and completely blued out his face. Putting the bits of that tattered, misty photo together on her flattress felt like looking at an actual memory. Did he look like she did on the Day That Ruined Everything?

The numbers of the highways the bus merged onto reminded her of birthdays Frenzy might have before he got sprung—79, 81, 80 Maybe even 380. Passing through two states and the Lincoln Tunnel, she rested her face against the window and smudged it with greasy makeup So much green stuff out there. Trees. Grass. An brown too. Dirt. Dead deer. Dead raccoon. So much rocks. Big rocks. Falling rocks. Huge-ass green mountains majestics. People who got two mattress tied to a side a they van with…is that a piece a string? Ooh, that broken couch musta fell outta somebody pickup. Look at all these sonofabitches drivin around goin wherever the fuck they want. I can't believe I'm one them people again! Goin wherever the fuck I want. Almost. Am I really? Shit, where the fuck I even wanna go?

When she thought about what would happen when she got to her mom's house, Hollywood visions flooded her head—happy tears, loving hugs, a total pardon from everybody. The giant pitcher of relatives in the four-story brownstone would pour their sweetness on her like condensed milk drizzling over a pile of cocadas de lechera. But this was rosy even for a fantasy. Two years ago, her mother had sent her a weird letter in handwriting squiggly as hair, and when Carlotta studied it hard enough, she didn't understand what her mother had to apologize for. Around the time she heard about her fifth parole hearing Five's the charm one of her half brothers, Xarles, passed through Ithaca. She hadn't seen him since long before she went inside. Xarles didn't know her as Carlotta; she'd grown into herself a year and a half after her prison bid got going. She figured everybody had heard; she knew how these gossip folks did, they'd blab about her to keep from fessing up to their own mess. When she made the scene in the dinged-up booth across from him, like a girlie in a peep show, he flinched and made like he didn't recognize her Xarles ain't had no clue whatsoever, looked at me like a Mack truck done run over both a us.

As they chatted, she could see him getting all bajiggity about it Don't know why, but I think I know why, he just plain disgustified by my beauteousness, the sumbitch. Xarles told her that Paloma had gotten sick and couldn't talk much but that he hadn't heard all the details from Thing 1 yet because Thing 1 hardly ever said much of anything. Even though he seemed uncomfortable, she begged him to cajole the judges so she could tell them she'd have a home plan with the family and maybe get to see Ibe before she dropped dead. "As you know, I haven't had much contact with the family myself over the years," he told her. "But I'll see what I can do." When Carlotta gave him an Aunt Esther face, he said, "C'mon, you know Frona. She'll either be fine with it or she'll pretend to be fine with it." Eventually, Frona did come through, but she hadn't had to do much—just respond to a brochure and be home when they visited—and she hadn't contacted Carlotta in the meantime Din't even tell me she said yes, it was the damn parole agents.

Carlotta hopped off the bus at the Port Authority Terminal and lingered by the pool-ball sculpture on the ground floor, the one where all the billiards used to roll happily past on a metal pathway like a mini roller coaster. But the balls didn't go anymore, and the mechanics inside the plastic box had crusty dust all over them. She considered this bad enough juju that she decided to peep outside and make sure 42nd Street hadn't gotten nuked out of existence. They'd come through the Lincoln Tunnel, so she hadn't seen anything but the skyline, now without the Twin Towers at the end, and she got bajiggity herself until she noticed that for her, the shock had come fourteen years too late Damn, how they even possibly did that shit? An then motherfuckers had to clean it up an breathe in all the asbestos an shit? Meanwhile I couldn't even keep my damn crib clean.

When she got to the doorway and saw the mudslide of humanity rushing down 42nd Street, she felt like a brain-damaged African elephant trying to jump into a game of double Dutch. Skyscrapers puked out Asians and Caucasians all up in their Executive Realness, oblivious to anything but their stock portfolios. Middle Eastern cabdrivers honked for her attention, maybe macking on her, maybe dissing her, maybe just trying to shoo her out of the way. Latin ladies and South Asian men jaywalked, and a Black kid with a gigantic afro blasted down the pavement, parting the furious crowd That brother don't give no kinda shits whatsoever, I love it. Way above, a monster crane's payload of bright red I-beams spun around unsteadily, twirling into the stratosphere.

Down at eye level, people rushed at each other, dodging rolly carry-ons and shopping carts. The stroller jockeys clomped along beside them, swerving around scaffolding posts, running over dog leashes, shoving their wheels into shallow brownish puddles. Out of SUV windows, Carlotta heard merengue, salsa, and bachata tunes, most of which she didn't recognize, though she tasted the flavors of older songs in them, and soon she had two rendezvous with the gut-punching bass line of the latest hip-hop summer anthem. The smell of warm pretzels and pralines flew her back to the womb I should just git me one a them pretzels, it smell like my whole life from before. It took a few near-accidents for Carlotta to fall in step, and even then she goofed it up. Walking the streets of New York City felt like doing the tango for two seconds at a time with every stranger in a crowded filthy ballroom.

At the corner, she peered across the street, knowing she should've caught sight of the crazy light bulbs on the Show World sign, even on this gaudy afternoon. She crossed the street and studied the building closely — no LIVE NUDE REVUE, no XXX movies, nothing Is this where it was at? Yes, definitely. The place had become a haunted house; the sign read TIMES SCARE Huh? So what is it now, like a *dead* nude revue? A vague memory of having heard that some puritanical mayor What his name, Adolph Giuliani? had cleaned the city of its adult booth-stores and nasty movie theaters floated into her head. The words of one marquee she'd seen around here as a child came back to her:

HORNY ORGY
DIRTY GIRLS
PINK BUNS
FRENCH SEX

Won't be no horny orgy round here no more. Only pink buns gonna be them cupcakes in that Cupcakes Only store over there. Cupcakes only? The fuck is that shit? I guess if you on a diet it's good, bet you eat one cupcake in the morning an can't afford nothin else all week She missed the booth-store around the corner, filled with the syrupy smell of edible lubricant and panties made of licorice, the head shop that sold six-foot purple bongs and self-published books with titles like *How to Steal Stuff from the Supermarket.*

Suddenly flipped out, still stumbling through the thick crowd and shaken by sudden movements at her sides — the piercing shriek of bus brakes, people shouting, and pigeons flapping up into her face—Carlotta hiked farther east on the north side of 42nd, trying to remember what she'd heard about all this redevelopment. The glittering mall she lurched through did not even compare to what she had heard about it. She didn't recognize the names of the twelve *Twelve!* movies playing in the multiplex Cept for *Terminator*! Yeah, I know that one!—some of them duplicates. Not even the names of the theaters sounded familiar. One of them looked like it put on productions for children You can't be bringing no kiddies to no 42nd Street! That's madness! Don't it be Drug City an Hookerville round these parts?

The brightest marquee on the block featured a flashy display of flickering lights that read MCDONALD'S, glitzier and more animated than the Show World sign had ever been McDonald's got a theater? What is it, a movie bout the Hamburglar playin in there? Oh, snap! That's a actual McDonald's. Oh my God. They don't all look like that now, do they? No, cause I seened one upstate. I seened a bunch of em upstate comin down 87.

Wow-fucked by the dazzling, chaotic video screens, the people leaning on their car horns, the stench of boiling pushcart hot dogs and sauerkraut, and cell phone arguments, Carlotta turned on her heel and rushed back to the subway Yo, this here New York Experience be too much a too much! How the fuck I did this twenty-some-odd years ago? Hmm, maybe Ise twenty-two stead a bein forty-four. How dare so much shit change an not wait for me! Slow the fuck down, Big Apple! Time is a chomo, honey, sure gon mess wit a kid, damage her for life.

The 42nd Street A/C/E station felt exotic too—cleaner than she remembered. But the uptown and downtown sides were still herky-jerky Like they don't hardly be the same stop. She also saw that she'd missed the chance to enter the subway from the basement of the Port Authority I can't member, you could do that before? The station don't got a token booth nowhere. Really? How that could happen at such a important station? People swiped yellow credit cards through the turnstiles and lined up at video machines sliding bills into slots with their fingertips. After a few minutes of panic, Carlotta grilled a hunchbacked Black woman in a shiny burgundy wig from the 1960s as she maneuvered herself down the staircase with a four-footed cane.

"Excuse me, ma'am," Carlotta said, pointing at the machines. "Do you know where could I get a subway token?"

"A *subway token*?" the woman growled. "1985!"

Okay, that was not helpful.

Eventually Carlotta convinced a different old Black woman with a sweeter disposition Meaning any other Black woman in New York City to explain that they discontinued tokens in 2003 Oh, snap, where the fuck my ass even been? Don't answer that and that now everyone used a different system. That woman helped her buy a single-use MetroCard, since that seemed cheaper and less complicated than other choices. The A train didn't come, but from the map, it looked like it still only skipped two stops between 42nd Street and Lafayette—the Brooklyn Lafayette, that is—so it made more sense to wait for the local Ridin the subway be like ridin a bicycle, you don't never forget what you hadda do to get where.

A pair of sparkling E trains visited the station one after the other, a red letter in their third eyes, and that knocked Carlotta out almost as much as the smoothness of the cornflower-blue seats in each car as the train blurred by, plus the bright interiors, TV-kitchen clean except for a single Coke bottle—half full of water—lolling wildly between everybody's shoes This train look like a Rolls-Royce compared to back in the day! She couldn't unglue her eyes as the giant robot worm disappeared into the tunnel.

Before she turned around, she heard something rumbling behind her and twisted her neck to get a look. After witnessing the total makeover of two once-familiar places, it cream-filled Carlotta with joy to see that at least one thing had not changed at all in the many years she'd suffered upstate—the C train.

It shuddered into the station like an old dog, covered in wavy metal like the roofs of the shanties in Bogotá, the snot-green C on its smudgy face almost covered with soot that had probably reached the legal drinking age. The brakes squealed, the train rattled to a halt, and it took about fifteen seconds for the doors to part. Once they did, they seemed to open a portal directly into Carlotta's past. She entered the gray gloom and stepped around a big sticky patch of something Prolly soda, but who know *what* that shit is? Her heart plumped up like an Oscar Mayer frank; she felt like a cartoon princess magically walking into her childhood bedroom. She found a seat beside an unopened copy of some thin rag she'd never seen before called *AM New York* and across from a cardboard box with several chicken-wing bones nestled inside it on a crushed piece of wax paper. The box, proud as any passenger, read KFC on every side. It didn't seem like the MTA had replaced the posters in the ad curve above the windows since 1993 That Zizmor motherfucker still at it! A blast of fuzzy noise rang out in the place where an announcement should have gone, the doors closed, and the train jerked forward. Before the next station it stopped, wobbled a little way down the track into the concrete purgatory between stops, stalled again for longer, and tottered off Oh, dag, ridin this bitch feel ezzackly the same's it always did! Singing, *I ♥ NY...*

Carlotta clapped her hands and crossed her legs even though that made her lose her balance and slide down the long gray bench Why ain't no other people bugging out inside this here time capsule? Everyone sat there stony-eyed, headphones on, staring at ingots in their palms, slumped over, maybe from overwork, maybe just dazed. As the train blundered through the tunnel, the lights went on and off and the thing hardly picked up any speed. The lurching lasted until Carlotta's stop, four into Brooklyn. Her ecstasy tipped into stupidity I am home, goddamn it! Who'da thought the damn C train woulda stayed the same this whole time? Like they saved some shit just for me. The train that time forgot!

She hopped off at Lafayette, a few blocks from her mother's house. She walked down Greene, staring at all the pale pedestrians, their babies, and their tiny dogs. Linen-white mothers shoved strollers over the concrete, and Black women pushed yet more white children in other strollers Dag, what happened, did they cancel Black chillun round here? A freaky hunch that a few of the ladies were grilling her like *she* didn't belong there poked her in the chest, so she started counting white folks. Then she lost count. She peeked into a gift shop window and pretended to buy hip furniture and scented candle I'ma take that white couch for 500, Pat?

A few minutes later, Carlotta rolled up at the building she'd lived in all her life until she left Or where that other person who was me used to live—whatever. A deli had moved in next door A motherfucking fancy-ass deli with a name I can't even read, let alone pronounce. She stomped up the brownstone steps and her chin rose naturally when she stopped at the high doors. The minute she got to the top, she faintly heard people talking and laughing inside, a set of footsteps slapping against the wooden staircases, shrieks of what she hoped was delight, and a PA system playing "September"—she clocked it from that jumpy bass line *Body-oddy-oddy-oh*. She paused to do another little dance and drink the wine of freedom again, slowly turning to soak up the view from the stoop. She'd spent so many of her days here as a chickadee, watching neighbors and traffic, gossiping, and waiting for all kinds of dreams, gifts, and people that never showed.

Her parents, Paloma and Joe, had bought the brownstone forty years ago, in 1975, back when "everything was going co-op and you could do Mitchell-Lama programs and there was incentives for low-income folks," as Joe used to gripe. In 1989, when Paloma and

Joe split up, neither one of them wanted to give up the house, and the divorce didn't get too ugly (their betrayals seemed to cancel one another out), so a lawyer suggested that they divide the place between the top and bottom two floors. Carlotta's mother went along with that plan — it seemed the least disruptive option for the family; they could pretend that nothing had happened, and if it could work, it might be like a sitcom.

For the next twenty-five years, Paloma had lived in the garden apartment and Joe in the upper two, and Carlotta had a big room on the parlor floor, where neither parent ruled. For a long time, the family had planned to jury-rig a wall on the parlor floor between the two apartments. Around the time Carlotta went upstate, the metal bones of that wall had gone up in the hallway, but it never got finished. Even before Carlotta left, the family got tangled up. Both Paloma and Joe found new spouses, and Joe's new wife, Odella, had a daughter, Makeba, in 1991. Even Xarles had lived there for a good long while. When Carlotta and her brothers had kids, they made a habit of living in the brownstone. She'd heard that for her brother David, his wife, and their three children, that period had yet to end. Jasmine and Ibe had burrowed into the third floor for a while right after Carlotta got taken into custody. The awkwardness and over-population in the house never fazed Paloma, or so she claimed. "I'm from South America," she would say, shrugging Like that esplained it all, like ev'body down there had the same weird-ass attitude bout family, like she ever gone back to Colombia even once since she left when she twelve years old in 19-fucking-58. Carlotta's mother hadn't even wanted the kids to learn Spanish. Carlotta once over-heard her telling David — always her favorite; she told him some of the secrets and pronounced his name the Spanish way — that she wasn't keeping it from them to make them more American. After all, she didn't hide the food or the culture. She hid the language away for herself, for when she needed to chill out or chitchat behind people's backs, including her husband's, or to unwind with relatives and girlfriends from back home. "You can learn it in school," she told David. "You can learn it in the street."

Honey, I din't know shit bout shit back then. The setting sun blazed against the side of the funeral home across from the brownstone and flashed in its windows. The Schiavone family had sewn up bodies in that same location for Carlotta's entire life. They must own the building and sit there waiting for ev'body else to die. The thought of death stole her breath, and suddenly the desire to spring Frenzy out of the joint gave her a jolt in the tail. How else could they share the rest of their lives? It would be hard.

She turned back to face the tall doors and bobbed her head to the music, figuring her folks had plotted a surprise party for her. But maybe they'd just gotten a jump on the Fourth of July—it was Thursday, July 2, after all, so the holiday weekend wouldn't truly start until the next day Could be they killing two birds. Why else they partying up on Thursday? By the time she had that third thought, she'd jabbed the bell more than a couple of times, but no one inside reacted to the old-fashioned ding-dong of the bell.

After a few more dings and dongs, she gave up on the button and jiggled the knob. The door was unlocked. Carlotta stuck her head in The fuck wrong with Frona an em! You don't leave no door open in no Fort Greene! This a dangerous-ass neighborhood! You gotta deadbolt that bitch! "Grandma! Where you at!" She pushed the door, hopped in, and twisted the lock behind her. That left her stuck in the dark entryway, feeling her way into the dim hall, following the sound of the music and the faint light rising from the stairs to the garden level. The floorboards grunted. Carlotta's back muscles tensed and she raised her fingernails slightly, like a lion showing its claws, assuming somebody would try to jump her—the normal level of terror at Ithaca. Up there, gut feelings and a hair trigger served her well I'm ready for you, motherfucker, whoever you are. Bring it the fuck on.

Still mostly sun-blind and confused, she bumped to the bottom step and felt something brush past her waist—maybe some fool trying to trip, grab, or mess with her. A flashback blew up her stress. She gasped, swung at whatever it was, and missed *The fuck was that? Somebody German shepherd?* She jumped the rest of the way down and slammed her hand on the door at the bottom of the stairs, causing it to whiz open and bang against the wall. Shaking her injured hand, she stumbled into the light, and when she got halfway across the downstairs living room, she realized she had just made a deeply embarrassing grand entrance in front of an audience *Oh, snap, this like a bad dream but it's real life!*

A couple of people turned their heads to mark Carlotta's arrival, but the hum of conversation kept up *Good to know I ain't the whole show!* They'd set up the room like a little auditorium, and it was jammed with faces, one or two of them relatives whose names she couldn't remember, most faces she didn't know at all. She tried to find Ibe's face and couldn't, but couldn't stop trying. On the wall, a fluttering banner made of multicolored metallic letters read CONGRATULATIONS, TAMEEKA! Off to one side, someone had taped a piece of wide-ruled notebook paper with the words AND WELCOME HOME, DUSTIN! scribbled across it in highlighter *They ain't forget me! Or I guess they din't forget that guy. It's something, anyway. How marvelous is family? Love it.*

The big animal turned out to be Tameeka herself, dressed in a pricey-looking shiny white frock. Carlotta could see her in the stairwell now, smoothing down her eyebrows and fluffing her hot-combed hair to prepare for her own much more elegant entrance. Once she turned, Carlotta spotted a free wooden folding chair toward the back of the room, next to her aunt Trixie, Kaffy's frosty-as-an-Astro-Pop mother, who would probably rather set herself on fire than kick it with Carlotta. Carlotta didn't see any other empty seats, though, and she could feel judging eyes all over her, so she skulked along the far wall to the seat, terrified of the shade she would have to stomach This apposed to be *my* day, my happiest day. The fuck happen? Congratulations, *Tameeka*? Damn, my hand still hurts so frickin bad! Is that Ibe over there? Is that? No. Where my baby *at*?

During the reentry-information session at Ithaca where they spoke about the importance of home plans and gave her a twenty-five-page booklet full of flowcharts, Carlotta had been asked to make a slew of resolutions before her release, including a pledge to meet uncomfortable situations and conflict head-on: to resolve tensions, make amends. Having to say a polite hello to Trixie first, before anyone else in the family, felt like some god's smart-alecky pop quiz If that's God, God actin like a CO. She could see at least one possibly sympathetic relative, her brother David, sitting too far away to get his attention. The empty chair sat four seats in from the wall, and that meant Carlotta had to squeeze by three people before getting to Trixie, who had on a bright white dress with a crimson pattern that looked like spattered blood All her previous victims.

The three others rose out of Carlotta's way, but Trixie just sat there, legs crossed, arms crossed over her legs, body wrapped around a black purse under her breasts that peeked out of the hole of the donut she'd made with her midriff. She stared like somebody cooking up a nasty scheme to off her archenemy That'd be me, the evil freak that put her beautiful, perfect, violent-ass criminal son away forever. Ugh. Here go nothing.

Carlotta pointed at the chair to Trixie's left, but stupidly, behind her back. "Excuse me, Trixie."

The sound of her name seemed to shatter against Trixie's attention. Without moving any other part of her body, she swiveled her head to face Carlotta. "Oh, of course, of course," she said, following Carlotta's finger to the chair. Relaxing her anaconda grip on the purse, she turned her legs sideways and pulled back her upper body to let Carlotta pass. As she squeezed through, Carlotta could now see that the pattern on Trixie's dress consisted of silhouettes of bouquets of roses, not a bloodbath, but that didn't put her at ease. She didn't think Trixie would take the time to peep her and register that sitting together looked like reconciliation. Carlotta couldn't imagine Trixie patching up the wounds, considering how many times after Kaffy's arrest she had said she never would and how many curse words and sprays of hot spittle had flown out of her face as she said so This lady was literally bout to slit my damn throat in broad daylight.

Since her son went inside, her hair had turned bone white — Carlotta bet the stress of Kaffy going upstate had done that — and Trixie had packed on a few pounds. Her face had seen better days Girlfriend got so much crow's-feet it look like some birds done opened up a disco on her face. An evil expression burned in her stony eyes Mama used to say if you make a ugly face an the wind change, yo face gon stay ugly. Hmm...sounds bout right. Carlotta settled down and tried to check Trixie's vibe, only moving her eyeballs to the right, but that started to hurt. "Trixie, I just—" she started in apology mode, but at that split second, Tameeka walked onto the living-room stage and set off a wave of applause.

"Ma'am!" Trixie whisper-snarled. "My grandniece bout to — do I know you?"

Carlotta halted. "No, I'm just — just...a fan." But then the Spirit of Prison Past took over, a thirst for violence caused by the fear of violence. In the joint she always had to leap headfirst into one disaster to avoid a worse disaster. She remembered one of those times when getting her ass kicked saved her from getting raped. Dave again. "You tryna pull some shit on me, honey? Fronting like you don't know who I am?" She was proud of herself for saying *honey* when she'd meant *bitch*.

Trixie reared back and scowled. "What on earth..."

"I know, you don't *wanna* know." At this point, the clash hadn't ramped up to a level where Tameeka would've had to cut her performance short. The kid, a shiny spokesperson for herself, curtsied to show that she was ready to sing, then shushed everyone and blabbed about coming up with the idea in a rambling monologue. She had helped to arrange the seating, found the correct karaoke CD, etc. The bodacious little chanteuse then attacked "His Eye Is on the Sparrow" with a spine-chilling lack of pitch control Ooh, chile, this some new kinda capital punishment? No no no no no no no.

Trixie eyeballed Carlotta. "First of all, you better watch who you're calling honey, honey," she snapped under her breath. "I ain't sure what's your issue, but you better have it somewheres else and at some other time, you feel me?" To diss Carlotta more, she turned her head away and stopped addressing her directly.

Carlotta shifted a little in her seat and raised her hand, waiting for a slap from the right, poised to punch Trixie out with her left. Then it hit her that Kaffy's mother actually *didn't* recognize her—these people from home had known only Dustin Chambers, not Carlotta Mercedes You couldn't look at no boring-ass caterpillar an recanize the gorgeous butterfly that it done become after, right? Her cheek twitched and her eyebrow rose. She doped out how oblivious or unmoved her family had been during all the earthquakes of her life story. They had just let time pass, not totally without caring, but most definitely without caring *enough* or not asking the right questions or saying anything directly to her. Despite everything she had told them over the years, despite their rare visits, which she figured meant a lot more to her than them, they had not just *tried* their damnedest to ignore all of it, they had *succeeded*.

Trixie, at least, had an excuse—Carlotta didn't expect her to give a shit because of all her blubbering over Kaffy, so Carlotta settled down and took a breath. When she muttered, "I'm sorry, ma'am, I thought you were someone else," Trixie didn't notice her sudden about-face or her brazen lie I called her ass by name an she still don't know it's me. Trixie sucked her cheek in Carlotta's direction and slid her chair away, then shifted her full attention to Tameeka's hurtful rendition of the gospel song:

> *I sing because I'm happy,*
> *I sing because I'm free!*

Feeling ridiculous, rolling her eyes at fate, Carlotta folded her hands in her lap to keep from covering her ears Look at this shit, I am actually folding my hands in my lap — such a proper lady. She smiled at her own expense, but she had to struggle to maintain the smile, because the child's singing soon reached such a crescendo of yelps and squeals that Carlotta snorted and then coughed to cover it up. In prison, shouting would've broken out like the Kool-Aid pitcher bursting through a wall. She threw her eyes left and right to see if anyone else was having the same reaction I wish I had a tape recorder so I could play this for Frenzy. He would lose his shit. It's so bad! She so bad! Am I on some other planet where people *like* this?

Still on the hunt for Ibe, she spotted Tameeka's parents, her brother Tom and his wife, Bliss, on opposite sides of the front row, their eyes glazed with sweet admiration Damn! I can't believe I'm the only motherfucker who want to call the hook on this li'l girl making this caterwaul! Chop huh! Guards, take huh away! Still smiling fakely, she grabbed one of her locks of hair and twirled the end into a tight cluster around her fingernail, examining the nail and pondering what shade of polish she should paint it to celebrate her release What would Frenzy like? Marvelous Mauve? Passionate Pink? Carlotta's smile, she knew, gave her the appearance of a parent beaming with pride, taking in the beauty of Tameeka's voice, approving, even though the girl sounded like a twenty-four-hour slaughterhouse full of pigs I thought Ise gettin outta prison an goin home, not landin on the hostile Planet Zarquon. Right then Carlotta remembered that people used the same term for coming home from prison and coming back from outer space: *reentry*. It made her smile a little through her aural agony. In the prison library, she had read a sci-fi book about an astronaut who reached the speed of light in a spaceship and then came back to Earth, and when he got back, for him it was a week later, but for everybody else it was twenty years later. Everything had changed, but he was still the same age, the same level of maturity, light-years behind them, which she thought might have been the title, *Light Years* They musta put that motherfucking book in the prison on purpose. They got theyself a cunty sense a humor up in that bitch. But I need to behave myself.

Tameeka, a pleasantly chubby eight-year-old whose eyes always threatened to toggle from ecstasy to misery, finished her routine and took in the crowd for a microsecond. Unbelievable jubilation broke out. Tom, probably thinking his daughter would fall apart otherwise, jumped up and cheered and whistled. Not to be out-parented, Bliss immediately stood too and threw herself into her ovation, joined by everyone else. Carlotta applauded with real enthusiasm I'm glad that shit is over! What the opposite a *encore*? Non-core! Non-core! happy for the opportunity to scan the crowd and see who else she recognized Wonder if anybody showed up just for me and not this here li'l banshee serving her banshee realness? Is that brotha Ibe? No. Where he at?

Tom had gone to dental school, but she couldn't remember if he finished, so she checked him up and down for anything dentisty He sure did gain a lot of weight since I last saw him. On the thighs and the ass, specially. What happened? He useta play ball and go to the gym and stuff, so maybe he don't do nothing now but sit in a chair and mess with people teeth and that's how he got big? To gain so much weight, he must have had enough money to eat a lot, Carlotta thought, so he *must* be a dentist now. She wrinkled her brow. Did the fact that he was standing across the room from Bliss mean that they'd gotten divorced? Oh, shit! Did I completely missed they entire marriage? We sure was on some different paths, wasn't we? Well, at least I don't gotta get em no present I can't afford. An it been too long anyways.

She scoped the room for Ibe again and thought of her other brother Joe Junior, who they called Thing 2. Xarles had reported to her that Thing 2 had become epically depressed and gained so much weight—more than anyone else in the whole family, all of whom seemed to turn getting big into a hobby—that he never appeared in public anymore, and that Frona, despite being eighty-six, cooked biggie-size meals for him and even sewed XXXL clothes for him out of duvet covers because she couldn't find anything that fit him, not even in the Big and Tall section at Jimmy Jazz, and that Thing 1—aka Joe Sr.—had stopped speaking to Thing 2, even though they lived in the same house I guess it couldn't be that hard to avoid somebody who don't never get out his bed.

Carlotta's adopted younger sister Amber had been eight when Carlotta went inside, and she had seen a high-school graduation picture of her in an orange and blue cap and robe, but by this time, she'd've gone through college as well and nearly hit thirty years old Is that her? Is that? Even so, she thought that if she saw Amber she would recognize her immediately by the birthmark on her neck that their father liked to point out to everyone had a shape like the border of Liberia, the country from which he and Paloma had adopted her, even though it did not. Once when she was six, Joe would then report, Amber had shouted, "No! It's more like Uganda!" and then Joe would laugh uncontrollably, as if the story were funny She African Black, like African blue-Black, but I'm not sure if it's that sista or that one. I bet it's her. Carlotta could count the number of times Joe had visited on one hand—his visits came to a skidding halt after Dustin blossomed into Carlotta—but she'd heard the story at least four of those times. Carlotta couldn't see anyone's neck clearly after they all stood up to give Tameeka the approval she expected and enjoyed. The longer it went on, the more the avalanche of praise pissed Carlotta off. Her anger heated up like pancake batter on a greasy griddle. But how stupid to get jealous of an eight-year-old girl's moment in the spotlight Stupid? Hardly. Fuck that shit! That li'l cricket ain't even begun to chirp, an I done had nine lives on the inside, gotta rebuild the tenth from scratch right fucking now? Oh, hell no.

Carlotta clocked her mother right then, and the fact that it had taken so long to notice confused her, because her mother had been sitting close by, behind and to the left. But she saw right away that Paloma had changed drastically, and the drop struck Carlotta like a cell door slamming on a pinkie Mama look like she sitting on the curb waiting for the garbage truck to take her away, shit. The garbage truck a death. Paloma hadn't gotten up to applaud, and that pricked up Carlotta's ears because she thought she might also have hated the shrieking, but she was still blocked by a couple of people, so Carlotta turned her head to gawk, politely. Nobody used to host a party like Paloma, but she sat there deflated, eyes empty, hunched over in her wheelchair, skin tone dulled to a moldy gray, the fantastic glow Carlotta remembered in it now wrinkly like a wadded-up plastic supermarket bag somebody had tried to smooth out. Paloma sported a wig so much like her old hairdo that it could've been a joke, and a multicolored housedress somewhere between gown and housecoat. A woman in a nurse's outfit—the whole deal, white cap and clunky orthopedic shoes—stood next to her, clapping for Tameeka with the rest.

Gradually, the audience scattered. Some clustered around to admire Tameeka's shiny dress and offer their highfalutin predictions about her future career; those farthest back found their way to the backyard and its dilapidated garden; and middle people, like Carlotta, glanced back and forth suspiciously, hemming and hawing about which group to join. She eyeballed Trixie's path in order to avoid her even as she displayed herself in different directions, testing her other relatives to see if they would recognize her I do not look *that* different from when I left on out this jwant, y'all. Is it the hair? The makeup? This outfit don't show off my best features, but come the fuck on. I'ma hafta stand on a chair an shout my name if don't nobody get it!

A pair of tiny hands shoved two adult pelvises apart to reveal the untalented cherub herself. Tameeka gazed at Carlotta for a second, her pupils dilating, then lunged at her, stomping like a show horse and letting out a high-pitched shriek She ain't seen my ass when I nearly housed her upside her head?

"Dustin! Dustin! Oh my God! Dustin!"

Carlotta braced her stomach, but Tameeka sent her stumbling backward into a gray plastic folding chair. Her hand still throbbed from their first collision. Tameeka fastened her arms around Carlotta's waist, and even though she got a thrill from human contact that almost made her burst into tears, Carlotta wished Tameeka hadn't used that name.

The two of them had literally never met before, so Carlotta found it weird that only Tameeka had recognized her What the hell wrong with all these folks? She expressed her gratitude by lying her face off.

"Tameeka, you darling! Girl, you got the voice of a angel!" Lucifer, to be exact. "You sung so good!" Why the hell I'm pouring it on like this? The novelty of human touch had already worn off.

Tameeka squealed. "I've been waiting for you to come home my whole life!"

Your whole life. Shut the fuck up. I been in the fucking joint bout three times Your Whole Life, you li'l cutie!

Tameeka took a huge breath, like someone about to blab forever, and then she did. "Oooh, I have to tell you how I know you're you! See, when I was little, my daddy had a pitcher of you that he put it in the garbage pail? But I saw it in there and went out to the curb and I fished it out and wiped off all the ketchup and taped the two pieces together and put them inside a big book to make the pitcher flat again, and I showed it to Daddy and I asked him Who is that? He said it was nobody, and Shut up shut up, but then I said But he looks like you, Daddy, is he your brother? And he told me No he doesn't and Go play in traffic, so I went out and played—not in traffic, though—but I asked again later cause I found the pitcher again in the book, and and I asked about you and he told me about who you were and the whole entire story of how you got sent to jail for years and years and had a baby that you couldn't take care of, my cousin, because of how long you would be in jail, Daddy said maybe you'd be there for the rest of your life or maybe forever, cause you kept doing bad things that made them keep you there, and I said, Daddy, what if *you* went to prison and you couldn't take care of me, and he said, That won't happen, pumpkin—he calls me pumpkin even though I don't like it because pumpkins are fat and orange, and I'm a little bit fat but I'm not *orange*, but I let him call me it because he likes to call me it—he said, I'm not going to rob a bank today, and I cried because he said not *today*, he didn't say not ever, and maybe he would rob a bank later, but I cry about *everything*—I cry about when someone hides the periwinkle crayon that I love more than any other crayon from the Crayola crayon box, and and the kids all know how much I love it so they do it to make me cry, or another time I cried when I heard that Ashley's cousin got shot even though I don't like Ashley at all and her cousin didn't even die from the bullet, and even though you weren't dead I was sad, so I kept your pitcher, half of it, in my scrapbook and looked at it a lot a lot until I memorized it, then I got so excited because Mommy told me that you might get out and then that you had got out and would be coming back to see your baby that you left here and and and who grew up to be my cousin who is over there outside, and I would get to meet you, and I made that sign saying welcome back to you and and and and are you a lady now?"

Carlotta looked toward the backyard and took a deep breath. Ibe was out there. She turned back to Tameeka and blinked Where we was at? "I go by Carlotta. Carlotta Mercedes," she said, thinking Tameeka would rev up her jaw again without taking a pause. She kept watching the back door, eager for the first opportunity to cut the conversation short and rush outside. Tameeka froze, letting go of Carlotta's waist and taking a step back—Carlotta stood and rearranged her clothes—then staring like a cat, her arms at her sides.

Carlotta filled the awkward pause by singing, *"I'm not a woman, I'm not a man / I am something that you'll never understand,"* pointing to herself with both index fingers and working her neck in a little dance.

In keeping with the song, Tameeka actually *didn't* seem to understand, but instead of trying to make sense of what Carlotta had sung, she jumped over the gap in her confusion back to her monologue More people should learn how to move along when they don't get shit. Go 'head, Tameeka.

Tameeka then told Carlotta many details of her eight-year-old life, but by that time, Tom had waddled up behind his daughter and performed a mime show of gestures and fake shock about seeing Carlotta again. But Carlotta remembered that Tom had never met an emotion he couldn't crush faster than a thief could snatch a gold chain off a neck Somewhere up in that dude, there's a actual person, but it's like it's twenty a them Russian dolls down deep. He had probably described Carlotta's bid to Tameeka by saying something with the word *camp*, like "Dustin has gone to sleepaway camp!"

It served him right that his daughter was a filterless motormouth who gave away all his private feelings *Do he really think I robbed a bank? That I wasn't paying no child support to Jasmine and Ibe? Because I'ma have to school him on all that.*

But Carlotta couldn't gnaw on her brother's slights for long. Her imminent reunion with Ibe had her twisted, fear and excitement rising and mixing together the more she imagined seeing him again. Was that him sitting at that metal picnic table, laughing? The scene was far away, the garden hardly visible.

All the speculation created a tangle of questions in her mind more complicated than the Cross Bronx Expressway interchange at the Major Deegan. Everybody knew from Tameeka's sign that Carlotta would be arriving, or at least a lady version of Dustin. Had Ibe really not looked forward to seeing her as much as she had to seeing him? *This ain't gon be good. No, maybe I'm being too harsh. How it could be bad to see one your parents after so many years? Reunited and it feels so good, reunited cause we understood…*

Tom nudged his way through Tameeka's stream of talk to give a feeble welcome and a nervous giggle. "Good to have you back, D—Carlotta! Carlotta, right?"

You could at least try to get some enthusiasm going, mother-fucker. I been in custody seven thousand nine hundred an seventy-four days an that's all you've got? Fuck your fat ass. No, on second thought, don't nobody have that much time. That'd be a all-day job. Tight as it is. Oops, I mean, I love you, brother! Boy, it been a long-ass time. I mean, damn, I wish I din't always hafta feel five different things at the same time an every one's real as the next!

"Yes, it's Carlotta." She threw a big fake sugary grin at him *This some Rue McClanahan shit right here.* He did get the name right, though. She tried to soften her reaction.

Tom reached out—his hand puffy like a new baseball glove—for a handshake that sickened Carlotta in most ways: its icky formality, the expectation of butch behavior it set up, his cold, slack hand. Tameeka had tried to tackle her without knowing her from a hole in the wall, but Carlotta's own little brother, the gawky kid she'd taught to tie his shoes, couldn't even bring himself to give her a hug after such a long time apart? Hostile motherfucking planet indeed. Feelings hardened again.

Tameeka's hurricane of chatter didn't subside while Carlotta navigated a lukewarm reunion with Tom. As soon as the adults' attention shifted away from her, the girl raised her volume until she got to shouting, unrolling Carlotta's shirtsleeve to tug on it violently, her questions growing harsher, pinpointing every worry that Carlotta had harbored about reentry since long before that day: "Carlotta, are you going to find a job? Can people get a job after they get out of jail? What skills can you do? Are you going to live here with Grandma Frona and Grandma Paloma and Uncle David and Auntie Dwayne and Cousin Max and Loris and Raphael and Thing 2, I mean Uncle Joe? Is Uncle Joe ever going to come out of his room? He's really fat, you know, he's so fat that he can't get out of his bed and the bed is about to break and I wanted to laugh but it's kind of sad, too, he's like a tree or a big giant rock that also can't go anywhere? You probably can't stay in that room. But I don't know if there's another room that's empty in the house. How long are you going to stay here? Do you have enough money to get an apartment somewhere else? Everyone talks about how expensive it is. Especially around here. You might have to move to New Jersey or to the Bronx or a bad part of Connecticut — is there a bad part, or is it all just horse farms?"

Despite Tameeka's alleged innocence, the questions cut; it felt like the child had run up the stairs to Carlotta's brain, picked the lock, found the giant cardboard box way in the back labeled FEARS, ripped it open, and chucked its contents in all directions. The questions came harder and faster and took on a singsong tone, like a whole choir of snotty kids. Tameeka didn't wait for Carlotta to answer any of them, certainly not with the kind of well-thought-out answers required. Carlotta began to suspect Tameeka of taunting her in a shady way, that sneaky tone she knew from the sarcasm of COs, the taunting of one particular rapist. Combined with her anxiety about finding the guy she thought was Ibe, the one person she really wanted to run outside and gush over, that feeling grew giant hands that pushed her away from Tameeka and made her lose control of her barely controllable manners.

"Oh God, shut up, shut the hell up you little—fuck!" Carlotta screwed up her face and exited the room backward, feeling proud she had stopped short of calling her niece a cunt.

In the small amount of pre-release counseling she'd endured, mostly just a PowerPoint presentation by a CO who'd emphasized how much you had to shut the fuck up, the CO had said, "You can't be on a hair trigger out there" (although she heard later that he was a CO because he couldn't be a cop anymore after he'd filled someone's chest cavity with lead because of his own hair trigger) Whew, I did good. I even said *hell* instead a *fuck*. But I guess I did say *fuck* after that. I'm gettin there!

But if, instead of congratulating herself at that moment, she had listened to the commotion in the room she'd just left as she dodged her way through the crowd in the kitchen to the backyard, she might have heard Tameeka wailing and screaming and her father consoling her in condescending tones using unpleasant words to describe Carlotta. "We're praying for him," Tom said.

At the back door, Carlotta loitered at the threshold and gazed at a guy she thought was Ibe. Across the broken concrete and neglected garden, he held court at a patio table by a tree in the far right corner. He and some other men sat under a tattered umbrella leaning at a steep enough angle that it looked useless He do favor Jasmine... he got her skin tone, an I think those her cheekbones, but aside from that, not much. Why the hell she ain't here? Okay, I don't got no time to be shy. Puffing herself up like Foghorn Leghorn, she crossed the yard and approached the guy, using all the tricks she knew to conceal her fear Breathe, bitch, breathe. Okay, grab your hip or some piece a furniture, like this here lawn chair. Here go nothing.

"Hey, brother. Is you Ibe?"

To her deep embarrassment, he laughed out loud, raised his eyebrows, took the toothpick out of his mouth with one hand and slapped the other on the table, continuing to laugh as he spoke. "Am I eBay? What the hell you talkin bout, lady — man? Am I a website? Hell, I wish I *was* eBay, I'd have a lot more damn money. Nah, I ain't no eBay!"

Carlotta recognized the behavior. This kind of bullshit jeering and shit-talking made up 95 percent of the jibba-jabba anyone ever stepped to her with in Ithaca An that's just the fuckin COs! Maybe this motherfucker had did time too, but with that smug attitude, he ain't got the shit kicked outta him nearway enough.

She leaned her palms on the table and stared directly at him. "Oh yeah? Ladyman's gonna cut your stupid ass if you don't come correct. This the happiest day of my life and I'll be damned if I'ma let you fuck that up, m'kay? I just got out the state pen to*day* after twenty-one motherfucking years, but don't you think for one Kentucky Fried second I'm afraid to go back, y'hear?" She raised her finger and scribbled all over the air in front of his face.

The man next to the one she had dressed down leaned sideways and threw his arm over the back of his chair. At orientation they had said not to bring up your prison record But fuck it. Even though I *am* actually scared out my fucking mind to go back. Except that I would get to be with Frenzy again. Prolly. Her bravado seemed to have baffled him enough to shut off his stream of contempt, but she knew not to wait for him to react.

"Nigga, I'm looking for my *son*. He spell his name I-b-e. Ibe.

That's a African name that mean 'friend' in the language a Nigeria. His other parent gave him that name when he born, in *1992*, long before any a these white motherfuckers thought up a stupid website called eBay, okay? He the *original* eBay, see? The OG eBay."

A dude sitting next to the arrogant guy whom Carlotta had barely noticed spoke up. "Hey, uh, ma'am? I might be able to help you."

He raised himself from the lawn chair behind his friend's and squeezed himself between the guy's broad back and the fence that separated their yard from the next lot over. "Just come with me a second." The kid had lighter skin than his friend—cherrywood as opposed to mahogany. Five thick cornrows defined his skull, each one ending in a stiff braid that curled up from his neck in defiance of gravity, like a Black male Pippi Longstocking. His big shiny tank top and tube socks were supposed to make him look taller, but aside from his clothes and his habit of leaning forward and dangling his arms in front of him when he walked, he resembled a jockey more than a ballplayer. Carlotta smelled the desperation in his attitude Now this a short pretty man tryna look tall an ugly so he could got power, an he *so* damn far from what he tryna be. Is he, like, Spike Lee nephew? I hate that he tryna be a big man but he ain't gonna do it. That's some sad shit. I feel bad for the motherfucker.

The guy's expression gave away his vulnerability, she discovered when they faced each other near the rosebush by the broken trellis. Since the old days, nobody had taken care of much in the backyard. The only upgrade consisted of a gas grill the size, color, and shape of a hearse dominating the far corner, pumping out smoke heavy with the aroma of burning beef over the ginkgo tree and out into the neighborhood Them li'l ginkgo fruits be smelling so nasty when they fall everywhere, I member that, like a giant baby out *The 4:30 Movie* done puked all over Brooklyn.

"Listen," the guy mumbled, his face turned like he thought he'd go blind looking at her. "I'm Ibe."

Carlotta's eyes got huge; she gulped, grabbed her face, and exhaled like a prayer, "Ibe..." Her lids fluttered closed. She felt feverish, anemic; she stretched her arms wide to hold him, but he didn't move toward her. When she looked again, he had raised his left hand and was waving it between them as if to reinforce the invisible barrier. She said his name again, and as her disappointment swelled, narrowed her eyes and let her arms drop.

"Yo, nobody even know that's my birth name, okay? I mean, my relatives do, but don't none a these niggas who ain't my blood know. Everybody call me Iceman."

For a while no words passed between them, and Carlotta drank in this Ibe, or Iceman, anyway, dumbstruck by how much about him she had missed—enough that she had not considered for a second that he was Ibe before he admitted it—and how different he had turned out from what she had dreamed of and who he was just before he turned five. Now she saw all the features they did have in common, starting with the rough texture of his hair and his brown irises—like two glass coffee mugs filled with pancake syrup—and his high cheekbones. He had Jasmine's heavy eyebrows Well...eye*brow*, really, but obviously they both be pluckin em a whole lot. She prolly taught him to do it. But them lips a his is Paloma's, or used to be her lips, an now he got em, an that look in his eye is pure Thing 1.

She wanted to ask why he had changed his name, his beautiful African name, but she figured she had just heard the answer from his stupid friend, and she didn't think she had a right to question anybody's decision to change their name Hey, we both changed our names! Like mother, like son! It started to feel pointless to try to stitch the two of them back together like that, but she had no other needle in her sewing kit.

Iceman looked everywhere except her eyes. "So this my dad, huh?" he said, like some tramp blaming a tricky god for his dumbass fate. He nodded to himself and smiled wryly, like he couldn't believe anything—not what had happened, not what was happening right then, not what would happen after—and had no intention of accepting any of it. Even Carlotta sometimes thought of him as a fluke, the miracle child of two careless queer club kids, the improbable blessing of an MDMA odyssey. Lord, Ise full a love an chemicals! I actually member thinkin that havin straight guy sex'd be *kinky*. But Ibe turnt out as my li'l Beanie Baby...

Wait, what he mean, "So this my dad?" Carlotta thought. Do he think he talking to somebody else bout me? "This your *parent*. Yes." She tried to inhabit the parent she meant by using a commanding tone she had never attempted in her whole life.

"And this is..." With a cupped hand, he pointed at her hair, then her body, slowly shaking his head. "Man, I don't even know, man."

Carlotta glared at Iceman If my ass was not on parole, you smug-ass little sonofabitch, who I guess is me that's the bitch you the son of, I would haul your ass over to that motherfucking gas grill, jam your neck down, barbecue the fuck out your face, and make your neck eat it with pickles and a side a curly fries lightly dusted with cayenne pepper. "No, you definitely *don't* know. But you gonna need to find out fast" Okay, I'm angry, but I don't wanna blow this. He still my boy, an now that I could do it, I gotta be there for him whether he get it or don't. That gotta be my new mission in life. 3...2...1.

"See, I—I had heard. But I thought—I didn't know you was gonna be here."

"Jasmine ain't tell you? You ain't read Tameeka's sign?"

"Mom specially don't tell me nothing bout you. Why you think I ain't seened you since Ise, what, four years old? She said you ain't want no contact while you up in the joint. Now you come back, and you like, you all a woman and whatnot, it's like, I been waiting on my *dad* this whole time, and here come...shit, I ain't never even had a dad for reals." He kept his voice low and glanced back toward the table, probably at his friend. "And I guess I still don't. Tameeka made a sign?"

"Hold up. Jasmine said *I* didn't want contact? She din't tell you that Ise paying your child support on thirty-three cents a hour? Oh, fuck that shit. I bet that's why she not showin her face, cause she knows I would call her lying ass out. Ibe—I mean Iceman. The only thing keepin me alive up in the joint was me hopin Ise gonna come back for this moment right here when I seen you. You din't get my letters."

"Letters?"

Carlotta rolled her eyes, slapped her thigh, and gripped her forehead. She didn't want to blame Jasmine for hijacking the mail—she had written at least one every week. She had always considered them a lifeline. But her mind instantly jumped to the conclusion that Jasmine had circular filed the letters, and at first she couldn't come up with another explanation. Had security at Ithaca destroyed every last one of her letters to Ibe, her *many* letters to Ibe, or had Jasmine done it, for mysterious but obviously malicious reasons But probably Jasmine? She thought about herself writing so passionately, so badly—*Dearest Ibe, son of my heart, my reason for living…* humbling herself by asking other people to help with her writing, not giving up when she didn't hear back from him or Jasmine, sending them to other relatives to slip to Ibe just in case. She must have intercepted them before they got to Ibe. How hard Carlotta had tried to write well More like how hard I axed ev'body else to help me write that shit. The best was Professor Brown at the law liberry, he was like, a real-ass poet.

The COs and the administration in charge of parole had told her not to use violence to resolve conflict on the outside, but three two-hour counseling sessions had no chance of balancing more than two decades inside I cannot believe this shit. I'ma kill Jasmine. I'ma kill her to death, I swear. They'll lock me up for good, but I don't give a damn shit. Carlotta remembered their conversations about Ibe:

Why don't he never write back?

He don't like writing.

Well, can't you put him on the phone?

You know how expensive these calls is.

Okay, but you assepted the charges, it ain't espensive to pass him the phone for two seconds.

Jasmine wouldn't reply or she'd change the subject, hoping the time would expire.

"Ask your mother bout my letters," Carlotta said now Fucking should have made carbon copies an saved em. Shit probably went straight to Fresh Kills. Seagulls on them garbage heaps been pecking my letters apart for years, didn't nobody read em. Fuck me. The fuck is wrong with me that I ain't seen this coming?

"Oh, okay. What did they say?"

"Nothing much" I just smashed all the emotions out my mother-fucking heart, soul, and brain for the child I loved more than myself is all. Tried to save you from my own fate, prove to you that my fate ain't even no fate an that you could have a different one if you did X, Y, and Z. Told you all the stories I could member from when Ise coming up. Told you your history. Esplained everything bout how prison works an why you din't never wanna go there, an how I became who I am now, Carlotta. Told you maybe a couple thousand times how much I missed you, how much I loved you. An Jasmine brainwashed you like snapping her fingers. No mother-fucking biggie. But maybe I could turn this mess around? Yeah! No. Yeah?

"Well…um…"

Carlotta could see, as badly as she wanted not to, Iceman pacing around inside the cage that the conversation had trapped him in. Only her body stood between him and the end of the conversation, when he would return to his friend's side I guess you could find a brontosaurus in Brooklyn before a straight Black man who'd take a surprise visit from his father-mother in stride. Why the fuck you making excuses for him, though? He a li'l shit. He really ain't rised above the kind of mentality a them DL rapist thugs that's up in Ithaca. Why I'm even wastin my time talkin to him? Just cause he my son? Cause I love this sonofabitch that's me more than my own damn self? Or maybe I loved a damn fantasy that's the opposite a this dude. Just cause you love somebody don't mean you gotta assept they abuse. Which what I oughta say to Thing 1 if he ever get here. Or the whole a New York State. Or the damn country. The motherfuckin universe, hello.

"Well, um, *what?* You gotta go? Where you gotta go that's so much more important than me? Back to yo friend?"

Iceman lost his cool. "Yo, I don't even know what to call you, yo!"

He gotta be shittin me. "My *name* is Carlotta Mercedes."

Iceman shuddered and ducked past her, torquing his spine like a limbo dancer, balancing himself by stepping into an area of garden dirt and risking a fall into the thorny bushes, one of which pinched his shirt for an instant and pulled a tiny thread on his tank top out of place Is he shaking his damn head?

Iceman turned sideways before departing completely. "Could you please, *please,* don't say nothin to my dawgs? Aight? See, they don't know me by that name." He launched a pleading expression at her, one she instantly clocked as a strategy for manipulating girlfriends, followed by a bright glint in his eyes. "If you love your son, do me that favor, okay?"

Carlotta's head went on lockdown; she was stunned that he had the nerve to ask her to keep quiet How rude! So ghetto! Plus he had said it with a disgusting charm whose fakeness should have canceled it out but magically blew it up instead. It shocked her so much that she accidentally gave him the silence he'd asked for. By the time she flipped out, Iceman had trotted back to the side of his dawg like the faithful bitch that Carlotta now judged him to be

That's some low-class shitty shit. But I'ma get through to you, just you watch. You gon live up to my dream.

She needed a break and decided to stand by herself near one of two stone benches that had sat on the patio for as long as she could remember. She almost literally kicked herself for believing that Ibe would accept her, for not anticipating any other possibility My stupid ass thinkin he gon be Halle Berry, ha! Of the two benches, both of whose concrete legs sported schizo cherubs, one now lay in several pieces, stained everywhere with moss. Paloma had used the broken bits as accents in the garden. The benches delighted Carlotta, who loved seeing familiar, unchanged objects Since I ain't did too good with people so far.

She bent down and ran her hands along the rough surface of the unbroken one, checking for wetness, before turning to drop herself there I can't be looking over at that fucking child of mine, na-ah. She straddled the bench, then swung both legs over to its opposite side to face the back door. This put her eyes at nearly the same level as her mother's. The nurse had wheeled her out onto the patio and sat beside her, wobbling sporkfuls of red Jell-O near her mouth. For a few minutes Carlotta observed them in sad silence, then she figured that she would have to get to know the new Paloma as well as her nurse. Her anger might lift, she felt, if she stopped worrying about herself for a hot minute, and she slowly got ready to interact with them, glancing over and failing to catch the nurse's eye.

Eventually she got up and went the long way to get to them, making a half circle around a table where a row of large aluminum food trays sat under tinfoil. One overdressed woman lifted a corner of the foil with two fake magenta nails, revealing a sticky-looking heap of baked chicken. Carlotta approached her mother from her left, over the shoulder of the nurse, thinking that Paloma might see her first. In place of an awkward conversation with the nurse, they could just hug.

Just as Carlotta got near them, her mother spat Jell-O and yanked her face away from the spork, trying to shout "No!" without opening her mouth. The word *no* came through primally, as if she had only that word left in her vocabulary, like she had both worn out her life and turned back into a baby. Carlotta waited for her mother to calm down before crossing into their space and kneeling in front of her, hoping that the nurse wouldn't have to operate as some kind of translator.

"Hey, Ma?" she began, partially to let the nurse know who she was.

The paper plate slipped off her mother's lap—or her mother gave it a push—and Carlotta grabbed for it to keep the Jell-O from splattering on the ground. She was only partly successful. She replaced the plate, but most of the food had flown to the concrete. Carlotta and the nurse cleaned up the broken cubes of Jell-O The fuck we doin this for? from between clumps of grass around and under Paloma's wheelchair and put them back on her plate. The nurse folded the plate and spork into a taco shape and chucked them into a garbage can a few feet away.

"I guess you took care a that Jell-O, eh, Ma?" Carlotta joked. Her mother stared back and smiled, blankly Is she smiling cause a what I said or somethin she thinkin? Do she know it's me? "Ma, it's me, it's Carlotta. I wrote to you an I ain't heard back in a while."

The comment did not seem to register. Carlotta felt like she had just screamed down an empty hallway and hadn't even gotten an echo back.

"Oh, she don' say nutting no more," the nurse jumped in, adding what seemed a rude chuckle, at a volume next door to shouting. "Jus' yes an no. Mostly no. Sometime it's all you need—*no!* But when I first come two year ago, Miss Paloma used to be all the time yap-yapping." The nurse made a talking motion with her hand and laughed openly. "Oh God, yes!"

Carlotta held out her hand and introduced herself.

The nurse's eyes glinted. She grabbed Carlotta's hand with both of hers and held it with almost as much gusto as Tameeka had hugged her waist earlier. "Oh yes! I heard all about you! Carlotta Mercedes! You de dawtah dat was de son! Fe long time I want to meet *you*. You soun like de mos fascinating person!" She let go of Carlotta's hand and glanced at Carlotta almost flirtatiously. "Welcome home, dear!" she announced, making it clear that she knew where Carlotta had come from and that she did not want to embarrass her, instead acting as if she had returned in triumph. "Oh, gyal, you must got some *stories*. De prodigal dawtah home from de man jail!"

"How it is you know everythin bout me? So who are you? Tell me, honey" Ain't too sure bout your daughter-son thing, but whatever. I'll take friendly.

"Everybody call me Pam, but between you an me, de name on de certificate say Valvondra McKenzie. I don' know where on eart' my parents fin' de name Valvondra, maybe on de side off a motorcycle someting, so I don' use dat, no nevah!" She raised her palm and pushed the name out of the air.

"I won't. Pam" Well, Valvondra, who wouldn't want to change that shit? Is you telling me this cause you know I changed my name too? And what the hell—where did Ma get the money for a damn twenty-four-hour personal nurse in the first place?

Carlotta imagined that she might get to have a long, pleasant conversation with Pam, the first since she'd left Ithaca, but then Thing 1 made his appearance on the patio along with David, directly in her line of sight, hauling a red and white plastic cooler so gigantic that it almost couldn't fit through the back door.

"Beer's here! Beer's here!"

They seemed to think that an eight-year-old's party and the homecoming of a parolee couldn't go on, at least not into the evening, without copious amounts of alcohol. Evidently they didn't know that Carlotta could wind up right back in jail practically *that night* if her PO discovered that she had come within fifty yards of a beer can, let alone a case and a half of Aguila Look like my first interaction with my dad since 2008, when Frona made him drive her upstate, gon have to be a big fight. But if I wanna make it on the outside, I can't be backing down on this kinda shit. She excused herself and pushed her way to her father and brother, hoping to arrive at the massive cooler before anyone could open it.

David tried to slip his hand in, but Carlotta thrust a heel down on the cooler lid and pushed away her father's fingers as he tried to pry it open. Without removing her foot, she spun to face David. "I'm sorry, David," she said. "An by the way, hello!" Thing 1 lowered his center of gravity, stuck his thick fingertips into the crevice under the lid, and tried to move Carlotta's foot.

"I jus' wan have a beer and watch the game!" he protested. He then repeated himself several times while trying to open the cooler, each repetition weaker and less intelligible than the one before, like a broken robot winding down.

"Daddy!" Carlotta shouted. They still practically lived in different dimensions; he acted like she hadn't said anything.

She bounced to the top of the cooler on the other foot and twirled, standing on it like a giant hood ornament that loomed above him. She realized too late that she had also made a spectacle of herself for everyone present Oh shit—but really, fuck it! This apposed to be my party too, regardless a the fact that don't nobody recanize my ass! She felt for a second like a knockoff version of Moses, standing on the holy beverage cooler about to deliver the Ten Commandments of Parolees Thou shalt not put no drugs nor alcohol before me. This must be what motherfuckers mean when they say *risin to the occasion*.

"Good evening, friends and family! Hey, y'all! Yo!" she began several times, raising her voice until she had gotten everyone's attention. "My name is Carlotta Mercedes! Many a y'all useta know me by a different name, a ugly man name that sound like somethin the maid be doin, but what's in a name, right?"

Thing 1 had crossed his arms. Carlotta felt that the brand of crabbiness in his face had nothing to do with her new self, her reappearance, her status as a former prisoner, or really anything except the fact that she had blocked his access to cold beer and sports An what game it even was? Basketball? Dag, do every fucking man gotta forsake his children less they like watchin a dumbass sport on a stupid couch with cupholders built in the arms? She stomped on the lid of the cooler to quiet the last few jabberers. Ibe had his back to her Is that motherfucker still talking?

"First, I wanna say congratulations to Tameeka, who a fantastic student an a superstar singer, definitely the next Whitney Houston!" Ooh, I shouldna said that bout Whitney, they did not like that comparison. I meant the first part a her career, not drowning to death on drugs in a bathtub, y'all. Actually I ain't mean none of it, Lord knows that poor chile couldn't hold a fuckin banknote. Tameeka herself now stood near one of the kitchen windows, moping. "Let's hear it for Tameeka!" Carlotta began the applause herself and surveyed the backyard, provoking the group into half-hearted claps, before moving on to her real point. "I also want to say a special thanks to Tameeka for membering this a special day for me too. Many a y'all prolly know that I been, um, out a town for twenty-one-ish years—which that's a long time to be away—an why."

Carlotta spotted Trixie in a corner of the yard, making a cranky face Ooh, check out the Sour Patch Kid over there! and possibly flinching forward Did one a her girlfriends just grab her wrist to keep her from tryna bum-rush me out my own motherfucking house? I believe I did see that happen. In her search for a friendly face, she saw Pam beaming at her as if Carlotta was her own dawtah dat was de son. David didn't seem hostile either, but like Tom, he had mastered the ability to say one thing with his face and another with his body or his words or both, so the jury remained out.

"Some a y'all may even know what it like to be away that long, an also what it like when you get back home, cause you under a *certain kinda supervision,* know what I'm saying?"

A few *ohh*s of recognition floated up from behind the hood of the gas grill near the small vegetable garden.

"Anyway, what I'm sayin is thank you so much for puttin this all together, an I want y'all to have a good time an everything, but if y'all start drinking up in here, I'ma have to leave. And I don't know if you want your guest a—one a your guests a honor gotta leave on out the party" On second thought I ain't sure I shoulda said that shit cause watch—somebody gonna use it as a excuse to throw my ass out my own party that's really Tameeka's party. An Tameeka got bout thirteen years till she hit the drinkin age.

Carlotta clapped again to let people know her speech was over and they should get hip to its overness. They mostly did. She lifted her chunky inmate-release shoes off the cooler and stood next to it, trying to pierce her father with a look. A tense lack of agreement electrified them. Thing 1 took a tentative step forward and opened his mouth more than once as if about to speak but couldn't complete the circuit.

During that standoff, David moved closer to the cooler and dropped his bottle back into it, saying, "Carlotta, it's good to have you—can I say that it's good to have you *back?* Because, I mean, when you left you were not—I mean, you have to admit you've changed!"

"For me, it is absolutely back. I'm more myself now than when I left."

David pouted and took another step forward, holding his arms out. For a second she didn't understand, then she snapped to. Only a fool would turn down an embrace from David, the anointed one. She hooked his shoulders and pulled herself toward him, resting her cheek against his warm stubbly jaw and neck, circling her hands around his sturdy back and cupping his shoulder blades. Regardless of what you or he wanted, gaining approval—or even phony affection—from someone at his movie-star level of charisma always felt like winning a prize. You could pay taxes on it later. And since nobody else had thought to do so Well, Tameeka did, but that don't completely count this particular hug felt promising. If the First Squeeze of Freedom had come from David Chambers, luck like that would surely start to ooze all over the rest of her life.

Thing 1 glanced around and took another step toward the cooler. "David, maybe you should take Carlotta upstairs and show him where he's going to stay. Her? She?"

David dropped the hug and they both glared at their father with low-key hateration His intentions is bout as subtle as 9/11. The two of them went inside, and as they turned the corner to the staircase, Thing 1 scuttled through the corridor into the downstairs living room, where the television cast jittery shadows all over the dark walls. He had a bottle in each hand and he moved backward, with his eyes fixed on the TV, toward the couch opposite the television. As they went up the stairs, Carlotta could hear the nasal voice of an announcer just beginning to wrap things up. Or get things started, depending on whether you planned to keep watching.

THREE

C arlotta woke up only twice that night—the loud party in the background felt just like bedtime at Ithaca, so sleepytime was normal Even left on the damn lights to get the upstate-prison flavor that keep you ugly all night. The usual nightmares—of getting eaten alive by a six-headed demon woman or flushed down a gigantic toilet—didn't roll in. A less violent dream, of wandering lost through a city all day, was somehow more confusing. But when she woke in the morning, she got a special delivery of caller-inside-the-house-level panic Like I had a one-night stand with Frankenstein. Fear pushed her out of bed Hadda get my hustle on. The training-session leaders had told her to make to-do lists like someone drowning. "Your freedom depends on it," the CO in charge of orientation droned But I ain't had no paper and pen or nothin so I just be keeping my list in my head. My head was a pocketbook, though, it'd have a hole in the bottom you could get yo arm through.

Carlotta had spent the night in a dusty narrow former utility closet. She remembered all the junk that had once piled up in that room—oil-stained cardboard boxes, a Philco swivel-head TV from the 1950s, dust bunnies nearly big as real bunnies, old coats and broken furniture that had made that room a great hiding place during her childhood. The old digital clock radio Frona left in the room for her said 9:30 Damn! Ain't nobody wakin me up at no 5:30 no more! The room didn't look any better in the present day—the old mattress she lay on was squashed into the room, curving against the floor and wall like a potato chip; a mop full of dark mold sulked in the far left corner; a glue trap behind a garbage bin memorialized a mouse—but it didn't make a difference given the place she'd just left That joint was ten times as filthy. The many sneezes she'd honked out after only a minute living there made it clear she'd need to find her own place It's just wide enough to got a window with *actual* trees outside. This time I could even *open* it. Appointment number 1 with the real world was at 11:00 a.m. with her PO. When Grandma Frona showed up outside the door shouting about coffee and breakfast, Carlotta absentmindedly blabbed about how she needed new threads.

After breakfast Frona strong-armed Carlotta into a quick wash and set with shampoo and conditioner she kept calling "expensive" Why she keep sayin it's espensive? Like should I pay her now? When Carlotta mentioned the meeting with her PO, Frona loaned her some things and offered to sew her an outfit. To ace that meeting, Carlotta needed to wangle some "nice" clothes Or at least somethin better than that frog suit on the chair. Carlotta said there wasn't time, but her grandmother shot back that she could make a drapey dress real fast You mean droopy. When Carlotta dilly-dallied Drapey? I ain't going to no cocktail party! I need a frigging suit! Frona blurted out, "You could borrow one of mines!" like a mad scientist having a eureka moment.

Carlotta took in her grandmother's figure—a farsighted fireman might try to hook a hose to her boob—and compared it to her own longer taller body Leggy, even. Proudly Frona displayed a loving smile with two vacancies, one on top, another kitty-corner on the bottom. Carlotta knew she couldn't turn down the offer Bitch, how you gonna diss your toothless-ass grandma? without snubbing Frona six ways from Sunday—first by implying that she was too fat and short, and second, judging from her ankle-length black house-dress, with a breastplate of little pom-poms and fringes, that her taste hadn't changed since the 1960s *It's so outta date it's almost up-to-date again. Like me!*

"I'm not sure I'd fit in anything a yours, Grandma," she managed to purr *Nor do I want to.* Her eyes dropped to Frona's feet. "Not even the shoes."

"Oh, I betcha I got something!" Before Carlotta could stop her going to her room *Oh, shit, Grandma, I don't got the time!* she ran out of the kitchen and turned at the doorway. "You know, I wasn't sure how this gonna go, but I actually like that you a woman now. I think you done it right. You had a child as a man and *then* you made the switcheroo. That was smart."

I am so glad I axed for your opinion on that. Do that mean it's time for you to be my grandfather? She got some nerve. Switcheroo? But I guess it could be worse. I mean, I wish Ibe coulda had that positive a attitude. Or Thing 1.

When Frona came back, Carlotta spent the next several minutes tugging on tight Old Mama wool skirts or ankle-length dresses exploding with orange, gold, and brown triangles, ersatz African patterns *She used to wore these things to church—in, like, 1979!*

If a garment didn't fit, Frona got downhearted as a Billie Holiday track, then bounced back and promised that the next one would. Eventually the time got so tight *Them threads too that* Carlotta almost had to run away.

"Grandma, thank you so much for your help, but I'ma just go downtown and get me somethin just for today. I got enough to get a nice suit" *If it's such a thing as less-than-forty-dollars nice.* She had only about that much left of the gate money since she hadn't cashed her check yet and couldn't figure out how to make that happen in less than an hour Supermarket? Check-cashing joint? What bank gonna do it for somebody without no account? Ha-ha, no account. That's me, no account.

"How you fixed for money, dear?" Frona asked, her hand diving in an apron pocket. She offered to cash Carlotta's check if she'd sign it over. "I think I got something somewhere, just not nough to cover that check. I'll get it when I go to the bank later, though, that I guarantee you. But in the meantime, here go a hunred?"

"I'm fine, Grandma" What the fuck wrong with me that I can't just take her money? Am I just too chickenshit to handle that much cash? Yes. No. Where'd all this stupid *pride* come from?

"You sure?" Frona rescued a crunchy C-spot from her apron Where the hell she get all this goddamn money? Is she gonna want me to pay it *back*? Cause that ain't happenin anytime soon.

"Yes, I'm sure" Who the fuck said that? While I'm staring Benjamin Franklin hisself in the fucking face? Take the damn money! Are you kidding? I can't skim my poor grandma out a hundred dollars prolly apposed to pay for her heart medicine or whatever. But knowing her, she gon spend it on Thing 2 an have a heart attack tonight. I'm sorry, I can't be taking none a her money.

"You *sure* you sure?"

"Yes, Grandma. I'm sure that I'm sure that I'm sure" Idiot. It's like I'm on the Bugs Bunny cartoons when somebody change to a donkey cause they did the dumbest shit possible on the earth.

"I'ma loan you one my purses," Frona said, "Cause you *can't* be out and about in this city without no pocketbook."

She ran to her closet and grabbed the first handbag she touched, a dull, black faux-ostrich shoulder bag with metal hoops for handles. Carlotta lifted it out of Frona's hands, spraying her with thank-yous, then brought the bag to her room and filled it with the few cosmetics and necessities she had bought, found, or borrowed already—seven pulls of toilet paper would have to do for facial tissue. She threw the hoops up her arm and hustled into the heat.

From deep in Frona's bag, stuck in a manila envelope stuffed with photocopied sheets about job programs and group therapy, Carlotta dug out the tear sheet the COs had given her with the PO's address on the top. The address, on Livingston and Nevins, sounded familiar from a bad date long ago. It was right near a hive of discount stores, and if she only did the thrift joints in that area, she might have enough time to yank the tags off and jump into the suit before 11:00 a.m. These people prolly gon be late anyhow, tell your ass one time an make you wait two motherfucking hours for shit, just like upstate.

Carlotta toured downtown Brooklyn with her jaw trailing on the ground Look at all these damn high-rises! What the fuck happen to the Albee Square Mall? I mean, it was a shithole, but wow, how it's all Armani up in here now? That's crazy. Mother is on Mars! The mothership reentering the atmosphere, and honey, it's thick! Junior's still here, but the Dime Bank gone? Guess motherfuckers round here like cheesecake more than money. Thing 2 sure do. Oh! The Fulton Grill gone. No more greasy meat. Watch out across the street, Mr. Fulton! Atlantic Dental—there go that crazy toothpaste, still on fire, chasing the toothbrush, and the foot lawyer be in that same damn building, you know that shit's doomed. Soon Carlotta rediscovered the discount dresses of Danice—Oh, Lord, this joint wasn't never no good—and avoided the Salvation Army in favor of the Goodwill Don't nobody need Jesus sellin em no broken bullshit. She shook down the women's racks until she found a lilac jacket and skirt that more or less fit It's tight up the armpits and kinda itchy, but I ain't got but twenty minutes. Twenty dollars? Sold! So what if it was un-her—she wanted to look like somebody else.

She bought the suit and marched into the dressing booth, where she bit apart the plastic connector on the price tag, tugged the skirt over her hips, squirmed into the jacket, and then, as the butterfly splits the chrysalis, mashed everything but her prison shirt into the bag they gave her at the register Now I'ma jam everything else in the first trash can I see outside. She didn't find any women's shoes that fit, but she considered a tight pair of open-toed pumps in basketball orange that clashed so brutally with the suit that they almost worked as a grand statement Against all fashion. Paying for them would've left her with seven dollars I don't gotta spend no money on no shoes for no PO appointment. Ain't no PO gonna be lookin at my fuckin feet through no fuckin desk.

Soon she got in the spot where she thought she'd see the parole office and found a construction site instead. The keys to the panic she had woken up with twisted in the ignition now; the engine revved and growled Can't *nothing* be in the same place it used to was? Can't they leave nothing alone in this goddamn borough? Shit is ridicalous! The developers of something called METRO FEAST had covered the windows in that chalky stuff they smear on glass to keep you from seeing inside and slapped up big sheets of brown paper with blue tape like that wasn't enough. Carlotta checked the address again, gawked down the street in both directions, took a trip to either side of the building, and then another excursion across the street. The office had maybe moved next door, or upstairs Fancy new hotel. Joint called Ms. Store, for all your hair-care, cell phone, and jewelry needs. Pizza parlor. Drugstore. Some highrise they callin "the Nevins." Ain't no PO nowhere. I hope they don't think folks at the PO could afford all this swag.

She tossed her hair back and wandered farther down Nevins Street, wondering if maybe all the government offices that used to run along Schermerhorn (and possibly still did) might've wanted Parole closer to Jobs or Labor or something Cept that would make sense, an ain't no gov'ment office motherfuckers gon do nothin that make no sense, like give you the right address a the place they want you to show up at.

She stopped in front of a building with the number 1912 over the door, which she figured meant the year they'd built it, not the address You'd have to go real far down Nevins to get up to 1912. The place had a real old-school New York–apartment-building look Damn, they got a crazy iron balcony up there, maybe they redid a hospital? but things felt off.

A grizzled Black man with problems leaned against the iron fence along the sidewalk out front This ain't no "the Nevins" over here. Carlotta decided the man's issue was mostly facial and figured he might know where the PO actually was That is fucked up that I even thought that. With so little time to waste, she asked him directly about the PO. He grumbled some jazz about keeping the harmness out of your cojoy Guess it's more than facial so she kept her distance and asked other unwilling people as they exited. One of them told her that the 1912 place was a halfway house in a tone that suggested she should go away if she didn't have any business there, but to Carlotta, *halfway house* meant that somebody definitely *would* know where they moved Probation and Parole. Eventually a beefy, eggnog-colored lady with a tight slick wavy hairstyle lumbered out of the building and told Carlotta that P&P had moved to someplace near the Gowanus Canal. She pointed a juicy finger down the street. "They been down there like a month," she said. "Just head down Nevins, seven or eight blocks?" Good thing I ain't buy them heels.

The economics of the neighborhood took hairpin turns as Carlotta jetted south, across Atlantic, then past a couple of blocks of jacked-up brownstones with a crumbling school on the left. But the candy coating of dumb luxury A hip clothing store I ain't gon be heading to later for no shoes soon melted into a parking lot, and then a monolithic, off-white high-rise housing project, a patch of

grass, more scaffolding You know, cities come and go, but scaffolding be up forever more parking lots each emptier and more remote,
one with a vine-strangled fence surrounding it, then What the
fuck—a whole city block that just be gravel an a barb-wire fence?
I'm like, somebody could live there! Like me—*I* could live there!
Just gimme a couch.

I can't believe I'm late for my first face-to-face meeting with my
PO for God's sake. That ain't no promisin start. An how I'm gonna
find a job? Well, I did work in the liberry up in Ithaca for a little
while. I heard some a them legal terms. Din't read none, but I heard
em. Professor Brown, who run the joint, done told me a whole bunch
of em, say he gonna help me write my memoir when I get back in
touch. I'm like, *Memoir?* Day 5,428: My ass still in solitary. Paint on
them concrete walls be the same color. Shit, they ain't even give me
a magazine up in the SHU till I literally slit my wrists an bled all
over the place. They so scared behind that blood, thought Ise the
fuckin AIDS Monster or some shit, gonna give em the Ninja, that
they done whatever I wanted for a hot minute. But you can't do that
every week. It's like Daffy Duck when he blowed hisself up and then
went, "I could only do this trick once," that shit was funny, I loved
being a little kid, wish I ain't never had to stop. I wish I coulda been
there for more a Ibe's childhood, we'da had ourself some *fun*.

She walked past abandoned factories with milky windows,
hopped over puddles of antifreeze and oily water reflecting the sky
and up her dress, a long low brick sanitation building Is that the
PO? No? Goddamn, where in the hell did they stick this place, in
frickin Tokyo? An why anybody need a handball court right there?
Garages, garages, garages, a mural and then the street ended at
an intersection. After looking around, Carlotta decided that she
would simply hope and pretend that the street continued on the
other side of the block, as if she could walk through the building in
front of her and come out the other side. She took a left and then

a right and another left and went to the center of the next block and asked a veiny, fortyish white man with a bushy beard hauling a pair of paper sacks with handles if he knew where the PO had gone. He thought she meant the post office No, I don't got no packages to mail, motherfucker, an it ain't none yo business if I did! and it took some doing to make it clear An the dude *still* din't know where it at.

Behind her, above a tin fence that ran almost the whole block before falling apart and giving in to weeds, a desolate power station loomed, a building that reminded her of the crack houses of her youth I didn't get into no truly hard drugs stuff but I knew where it was at right next to some glassy snazzy apartments under construction across the bridge. Painted graffiti across the highest bricks called for the end of a harmful police program. On the other side of the street Carlotta had already seen but only now noticed a ginormous supermarket, a chain loved by liberal do-gooders with deep pockets, powered by solar panels that sheltered the parking lot and windmills shaped like the blades of the rusty antique lawn mower Frona still used to cut the small patch of grass in the backyard at home with which Carlotta currently shared a space Gotta get outta that mother.

She took a more careful look at the supermarket Now *that* joint definitely *not* the PO. Where the fuck is this place? I'm already half a hour late. They gon put a warrant out on my ass faster than you could say RuPaul an I will be back with Frenzy tomorrow. Hmm, that don't seem so bad, but I need to get out this circumstance an I don't need nothing else that's up at Ithaca by a long shot. Not even shit I *forgot* do I need. Not even shit motherfuckers *stole* from my ass do I need from up there. Not even money. Well, okay—*some* money. They could have my pink purse, though.

Oh! I know! Maybe one the (prolly Black) sisters running the registers inside there gon know where the PO at. Carlotta crossed the street and entered the closest entrance, which opened into a wide produce aisle. Judging from the cars in the lot, she figured on high prices, so she strolled in with extra pride and peeped a pile of grapes in bags just to feel the outrage. She had no clue how much grapes should cost; she didn't remember what they'd gone for in 1993, so the idea that they went for $3.99/lb didn't surprise her even though it offended her I member when you could buy a whole record album for $3.99 an you'd prolly still own that bitch today! $3.99 for grapes you gon shit tomorrow? That's like ten cents a grape or somethin. She gaped at the customers I'on't get it, if they so rich, why they all look like hippies an don't nobody shave nothin? Y'all oughta just hand *me* that money, I'll grow you some damn grapes an buy y'all a razor.

A wide Black woman with flawless skin and a wavy weave stood behind a customer service desk explaining something to an exceptionally hairy white man in a purple tank top, cutoffs, and heavy black eyeglasses. The woman used a high, breathy voice. Behind her, a thin brown man who looked East Indian wiped off the counter with a rag, facing away. The woman's name tag said CARIDAD, which encouraged Carlotta, thinking they might share some heritage. The white guy kept trying to interrupt Caridad but she raised her hand and her eyebrows and lowered her chin until he clammed up. Carlotta leaned in to let them know she had a time issue, but they ignored her until the conversation came to an end. The man picked up a green shopping basket from between his athletic socks and turned back inside the store, shaking his head.

Carlotta tried to cop a high-class attitude, hoping that the Black woman would clock her meaning I know I'm stereotypin this poor lady but I'on't even care, I'm late. "Excuse me, ma'am, but I have become lost. Might you direct me to the new location of the PO office?" Was that shit the most ridiculous way I ever said somethin in my whole fuckin life?

The woman adjusted her chin and smiled. "I might. You mean the post office, sir?"

She ground her teeth together and tried to keep from rolling her eyes. "No, I'm afraid it's a different meaning there for *PO*." *An it's* ma'am, *honey. Motherfuckin* ma'am!

The Indian man, who had overheard the conversation, spun around. His name tag read RAJ. "No, this person is speaking of the very large parole office that recently moved to a location just across the disgusting Gowanus Canal from here." He pointed his nose in that direction, narrowed his eyes, and said in a softer register, "I suspect that we shall be fielding such questions quite frequently from now on."

An uncomfortable moment passed. Carlotta wondered if Raj had some kind of secret prejudice against speaking to people like her. *Whatever "people like me" apposed to mean. Far's I know, I'm the only bitch who anything like me!*

"Well, Mr. Raj, since you know where it at, could you tell me how to get there from here?"

"Oh, I'm sorry! You walk out into the parking lot, take a right, and then take another right on Third Avenue, and then another right onto whatever that is, and then a final right onto Second Avenue."

I hope four rights ain't gon make a wrong.

"Are you an ex-convict?" Raj asked.

Lookit yo ass, wantin me to tell the truth! "Oh no, honey, I'm a parole officer, reporting for my first day in the new building. Why do you ask?" *Sometime I am pretty fuckin fast with this shit. Gettin over like a fat rat.*

"They are open on the holiday? Observed?"

Was it closed? Carlotta squashed her panic. "Yes, of course, we work 24-7. Emergencies don't take days off; neither do we. You know how rowdy these ex-cons can get. Why do you ask?"

"Oh, no reason. Just my stepbrother—oh, I won't go jabbering away, telling everyone his business."

Caridad swiveled her head and gazed at Raj as if a chrysanthemum had just bloomed out of his ear. Carlotta yelled "Thank you!" to the two of them as she left the desk.

In the parking lot, she dodged a Subaru and headed around the building and over the canal My man Raj was right, that shit still disgusting. An they diggin in it too. Somebody lose they wallet tryna find the Creature? More garages. Cobblestone street coming up out the asphalt—ain't too mucha that left in the city. All kinda wasteland in this here garage—an a cat?

Carlotta's journey dead-ended on the opposite side of the canal Shit, they hid the fuck outta this jwant! From there, the supermarket looked like she'd left it in Oz, sitting across the canal. She paused in front of a new building as bland as plaster Wait, this gotta be the PO, just by process a limination. The building took up the whole block, brick on the bottom, pale concrete on top, pathetic trees out front. No signs anywhere. Nothing said PAROLE OFFICE.

Farther down, Carlotta noticed a sort of loading dock. She mounted a short set of grated metal steps, almost knocking someone over as they rushed out of the nearer door, which turned out to be the exit At least there go proof that it's open today and joined the security line. Very few people were in the office, probably a skeleton crew, so the guards waved her in. The floors were covered with checkered tan and white squares of linoleum. Many twenty-foot-long rows of benches painted glossy black gleamed in the fluorescent lights. The seating reminded her of red chairs in D Block Both these type a chairs is something can't nobody fuck with too easy. Like you could take all kinda baseball bats an tire irons to it and whatnot, but ain't nothing gon break it. We was the damaged shit. She remembered one of D Block's wildest throwdowns We so broken that we done broke the shit outta some a that unbreakable furniture. She checked out the other people in the room. From that distance, most of them looked as black and anonymous as the figures on a Ped Xing sign *Honey, Ped Xing sound like a good job! Get* me *up on that sign.*

Carlotta spotted a window that made the place seem even more like a movie theater, a Plexiglas panel with two holes in it, one hole you could put your mouth up to and an arch for pushing papers. "I am supposed to be meeting with Lou DeLay," Carlotta said. The lethargic Black man behind the window shoved a clipboard with a pen attached through the arch and she signed in. "Just take a seat over there, she'll be with you shortly. I believe she's with another client right now."

Oh, that's inneresting, Lou's a she. That could be a good thing. I love that they be callin us clients, *like I'm bout to step up on a pedestal an buy my dream wedding dress or some shit.*

Carlotta sat and soon had nothing to do aside from fiddle with her fingernails and let her thoughts spiral down like dead leaves into a drain *Definitely don't wanna be thinkin too much up in here.* She cleaned her fingernails with her other fingernails, examining the red polish that didn't match her lilac ensemble. Having nothing to do kicked her memory right back into the SHU. She could hear herself breathing and started worrying that her heartbeat would stop. A toothy pack of images raced up out of the past.

Suddenly she was back there, rubbing her hands together frantically and slapping herself to fight the cold, wrapping her arms around her legs under her thin blue blanket, her body jerking, her teeth chattering like a windup skull toy. She remembered the evil worries her brain would puke up in the early morning, freaking out about the possibility of dying from AIDS, from cancer, or by the hands of the man or men about to come at her next. Which gang of convicts or COs would take the next whack? Would these particular scumbuckets finish her off? How? What would they strangle her with? Their bare hands? A torn sheet? Would she mind? Why go on living anyway? In Carlotta's worst moods, Dave's pale face appeared, interrupted by a port-wine stain around his left eye that cascaded over his cheek and temple Like the fucking Phantom of the Opera including his scariest expression, a blank stare like a great white shark taking its first bite That face was like, I just checked out the roach motel in my fucked-up head an now I'ma shove yo ass in my white cargo van an take you to location number 2, where the *truly* crazy shit gon go down.

Stop, oh God, please stop! Somebody help me! The cries reverberated in the cell, but if anyone heard them, they did not pay attention, and no one ever came to Carlotta's assistance There wasn't never no guards to guard the guards.

After she'd been through twenty minutes of hand-quivering PTSD, a brassy voice broke through the hum, shouting that old name. She clenched her palms together until her nails bit into her skin, but she refused to respond.

The loud person called herself Lou DeLay. Though a woman, she did look, comfortingly, like a man — a peculiar type of man. Lou didn't pluck her mustache. She had close-cropped, undulating hair with silver threads that dramatized its waviness, giving her head the silhouette of a crown of broccoli. She carried her compact, round body like a globe, always tilted forward, as if it were held up by a metal brace that entered her North Pole and exited through her curvy Antarctica. A suit jacket in a tight houndstooth pattern, its darts sticking up from that vast continent, completed her antique vibe This chick here look like a ballplayer from the old days, like she a catcher for the Brooklyn Dodgers, or wait, like she the umpire! Take my ass out to the ball game, yo, take my ass out with the motherfuckin *crowd*! Someone maybe a little rough and scrappy who had never used her eyes to say yes. Who had never figured out that the eyes can say yes. Or really how to speak with any body part other than a mouth.

Hearing the syllables of her deadname, Carlotta closed her eyes and breathed out. When she opened her eyes and saw the door swinging closed, though, she bounced out of her seat. She thought she might grab Lou at the door and explain herself. She remembered making her name change clear to the COs at Ithaca, so she couldn't think why it hadn't registered here, unless they wanted to keep humiliating her by remote control Which they prolly did. By the time she reached the door, it had closed and locked. Carlotta tugged at it for a second even though she knew it wouldn't budge, then banged her palm on the small square window reinforced with thin wires.

In the hallway behind the door, Lou halted and did an about-face. *Are you Dust* — she mouthed on the other side of the door.

Carlotta made a series of staccato noises and wagged her finger to silence Lou, who ran back to the threshold and flung the door open.

"I have changed my name, ma'am," Carlotta told her, extending her hand. "Carlotta Mercedes."

Lou's eyes caught fire and she practically leapt out of her jacket. "Carlotta Mercedes! Like Mercedes McCambridge?" Lou waggled her head, like a lightning bolt of happiness had zapped her face.

Someone else knew! "The very one." Talk about good signs.

"Oh my God! That's great, that's *fabulous*! My favorite thing about her is — did you know she was the voice of Pazuzu?"

"Pa Who-Who?"

"The demon!" Lou paused. When Carlotta didn't react, she rotated her wrist in the air. "From *The Exorcist*!"

"Oh! I ain't know the demon had a name, I thought he's just Mr. Demon or whatever. Pazuzu, huh? Oops, maybe we shouldn't say the name!" Carlotta covered her mouth theatrically.

"No demon would last five minutes in this joint. I'm really sorry that I called you that other name. I — that's just what I had on my sheet here, they didn't give me anything else. And geez — why would anyone who knew call you anything *but* Carlotta Mercedes?"

"I told the man at the front my real name."

"I'll take it up with him, then. Carlotta!" Lou said it a few more times, to clear the air.

The exchange lifted Carlotta's spirits; she heard the call of understanding and respect like a party across a meadow, but she hardly recognized it — she hadn't heard it in decades. Lou led her through a white door to a smaller office with multiple cubicles set up in a weird configuration. There were several stations in the room with shallow desks, each of which had a divider sticking out of the middle and a chair on either side. The chair for the PO was an office chair, the other one a metal folding chair. One of the chairs had a navy-blue suit jacket folded over the back, and one of the desks had a half-eaten hero on it. Something with onions Ooh, that smell like some shit we used to call a armpit sandwich! *Memories, light the corners of my mind*…Beige upholstery infected the room dividers and the low cubicle walls between the desks.

Lou plopped down in an ergonomic chair behind the first desk on the left, the most conspicuous one. She rocked backward, her feet kicking up from the floor, then forward again. She whacked the plastic surface with her palms. The whiteness of the lights in the drop ceiling made everybody look their worst. Plus, everybody in the joint looked like a PO This place so empty, I don't get it.

Reading Carlotta's mind, or face, Lou explained, "I'm doing a half day today. I took your case on purpose. It's slow because of the holiday, but mornings are usually dead anyway. On regular weeks, we stay open until 7 p.m. since a lot of parolees have at least one day job. With any luck, you will too." She nodded. "Thanks for getting here, Carlotta. Frankly, I thought I might have to violate you."

"Violate me?" Carlotta shouted, turning sideways, crossing her legs, and bracing, out of habit God, is this shit gonna be just like in D Block with everybody raping you like *hide your kids, hide your wife* an the COs joining in on the rapes and pretendin din't nothin happen even when you go to motherfuckers with a complaint? Shit, they be writin it in the official records: DIDN'T NOBODY RAPE NO-BODY. Or the whole fuckin system rapin you an you can't say shit? Oh right, violate. Stupid me, I forgot they use that same word.

Lou grabbed her temples and squeezed her forehead. Her small hand couldn't cover her whole face, but she had powerful fingers, like that gizmo on the end of a crane. "Lord help me! I am so used to the jargon, and no one has ever called me on that. That expression means to write you up. Violate. Everyone says it—*I am gonna have to violate you.* But you're right, it's a *very* unfortunate turn of phrase. Carlotta, I am not going to touch you."

"Oh, oh, oh, oh, oh, oh, oops," Carlotta said the entire time Lou was speaking I got my doubts bout this whole thing now, lesbian or no.

"For what it's worth, I'm one of the alphabet people too, the LGBTQIA+. I guess the beauty of it is you can say that and people still have to guess which one. Don't feel you have to tell me which letter you are."

"X," Carlotta said, vamping.

"We also have something else in common. I refuse to go by"—she whispered—"Penelope" with a frown. "Sickening, right? My parents couldn't agree on where to put a doorknob, but they both got behind that name? Fortunately, the rest of my family had the good sense, and I guess foresight, to call me Lou instead, but wait—"

"Wait what?"

"I just had a thought...I'll have to ask you about it later." Lou scrutinized Carlotta's face as if trying to read—not her mind, but her memory, something from her past.

Carlotta knew what information Lou wanted, but she didn't want to talk about it with a stranger Oh, hell no, we not goin there right off the motherfuckin bat.

"So they must have told you a lot about parole," Lou began, "and why we have it and what it's supposed to mean, right?"

"Not really, no. I mean, they said some shit, I mean stuff, but…" Carlotta demonstrated how the information had gone in one ear and out the other, making a noise like a tire deflating. She shrugged, twisted her mouth into the corner of her face, and cackled at herself. "They told me I can't drink or be round people that's drinkin. An other rules, but you could tell em to me again."

"Strategic redundancy," Lou said quietly.

Lou explained For a long-ass time an no good reason about parole, taking it all the way back to the French origin of the term and how it meant that the prisoner had given his word that he'd stay out of trouble. Back in the old days, she said, the main point of sending people to prison was to rehabilitate them, giving convicted criminals time to reflect on their crimes so they could rejoin society Society? That some rich people shit out in the Hamptons. My ass ain't never been east a Riis Beach. "Once upon a time," Lou said, "there was a prison in upstate New York" I be listenin to this fairy tale real patiently "that operated like a silent retreat. Prisoners didn't get to make any noise."

"That's a mess," Carlotta blurted. "That ain't even possible, keep a jailbird from singing? Unh-uh."

"They don't do that anymore. It was Auburn, anyway, not Ithaca."

"An you know that."

Together they went over the general rules of parole. "I'm gonna read you your stips," Lou said, "just to make sure you've heard them." Carlotta knew what they'd be like — she'd heard from inmates who came back to Ithaca — but she'd always laughed at folks who still had to follow dumb rules even on the outside Cause they wasn't me! But now she'd have her own dumb rules, so she paid attention Hold up, I can't leave the *state*? Aight, I hate Jersey anyways, but why I can't go there? What if Mary J. play the Meadowlands an my friend get freebies? Shit. I gotta get her permission to own a gun? I guess I shoulda figured on that. Least I could own one—maybe like a cute li'l Rohrbaugh R9? How I'm apposed to know who I'm talking wit that they got a criminal record? I'm apposed to axe em? I gotta let this lady into my house and my job just so she could go through my shit an axe my fam if I been doing good? Lord, don't axe *those* people. Be better if she axed motherfuckers in the street if I been doin good. She could do a urine test at any time? Carlotta sat up.

"You could do a urine test at any time? Like now?"

"Yes, like now."

Carlotta burst out laughing. "How do that even work? You got a cup in yo desk?"

"It's not a joke." Lou's face froze, and suddenly Carlotta saw that underneath her casual manner, Lou had the same hardness as the COs and cops she'd clashed with for years, the kind waiting for an infraction, ambushing you until you fucked up. Maybe she even liked it when you fucked up, because it might prove something she already thought about parolees, or people like her, or Blatinas, or whoever. "If I suspect that you're doing drugs," Lou said, "I will frog-march you to the head and drop you right there. I don't even need any proof; all I need is a hunch—I'm like Quasimodo. You will have to pee into a cup, and then if you test positive, you're back on the bus upstate quick like a bunny. I once saw it happen within an *hour*. Capisce?" She let the silence linger, staring blankly at, or maybe through, Carlotta, which had the desired effect. Then she went back to the list of stips. "You have to be at your residence by 8 p.m. every night."

Seriously? "Seriously? That is the most—"

A righteous, defensive bite entered Lou's voice, and she banged on her desk for emphasis as she spoke: "The alternative is that you go the fuck back to Ithaca, okay? We don't *have* to give a shit whether you're out of prison or not, but we do. We're trying to keep you out. You have to be on board or this isn't going to work. I actually didn't come to this job through law enforcement, you know. I studied criminal justice and social work in college and I thought I could give something back to my community, okay, and my alphabet people or whoever."

Your community? Who you even mean when you lookin at me an saying "my community"? Carlotta decided to choose her battles. "I know I ain't allowed to be in the presence a no people who drinkin alcohol or to drink alcohol myself? I'm doin that one hard, but I wanna know *why.* My beef ain't got nothin to do with me bein drunk. Much less me being *a* drunk. To my knowledge, Kaffy ain't drunk nothing neither fore he shot that lady" Plus my daddy fucked that one up for me the minute I got home.

"I think it's supposed to be a precaution? It's a special condition of your release."

"The hell that got to do with anythin, Miss Lou? Pardon my French." She paused and said, "Parole," lifting her arms like a fashion model. "You said it's a French word!"

Lou frowned and rifled through some of the paperwork in her folder. She scanned for a long time, squinting, muttering, occasionally stretching her forearms and fingers against the edge of her desk. "Oh!" she finally barked. "It's about the liquor store, Sippy Sip! The fact that it happened in a liquor store was a contributing factor. And you did a rehab program at Ithaca, didn't you?"

"Oh, for crying out loud. I wasn't never no alcoholic, I did that program cause they ain't had no other programs for me to do! Ev'body in the room thought Ise playing myself that I wasn't no alcoholic. Now, how do a holdup in a liquor store make it so you can't drink no alcohol no more? The real reason Kaffy went up in there was the money. An they don't never stop nobody who robbed nobody from using no money when they get out. They don't never stop nobody who jacked a supermarket from eatin, do they?" Carlotta fought back a smile at her own logic.

Lou almost smirked. "It's not the same thing," she said, noting that the alcohol stip wasn't standard. "I can contest it, probably, but for the time being, let's just follow the rules, no matter how weird. Believe me, I've heard of some pretty bizarre special conditions. A few years ago there was a guy in Florida who had to take his ex-wife out to Red Lobster and go bowling with her once a month. At least you can use the Internet. Some of these sex offenders, man—" Lou paused, shaking her head slightly, and then started yakking about indeterminate sentencing, how some mandatory sentences included parole.

Carlotta knew some of this. "So it come with. Like a Happy Meal."

"Like a Happy Meal. But not happy. There's not much flexibility there." Lou sighed, and then went silent for a moment. "We should really discuss your case, Carlotta. We have to make sure you don't end up in a dumpster somewhere."

Carlotta frowned and recoiled.

Lou glanced at the carpet and shook her head. "Sorry, that happened to a client of one of my colleagues last week and I can't stop thinking about it. Okay, the way this thing works, you have to really, *really* want it and be very consistent and persevere. I can only do so much. Frankly, your lateness today has me a little worried. Pardon. A *lot* worried."

"I cop to that, but I had to get some decent clothes to wear, an it had the wrong address on the sheet!" Carlotta dug into Frona's purse, tugged out the sheet, and tapped the incorrect PO address against Lou's desk. "They moved the darn office to where the heck this even at?"

"Let me see that," Lou said, swiveling the paper to her side. "Oh. Hm. Granted, there are going to be moments like that. So you should leave time for unexpected delays, right? Like me, I'm an unexpected DeLay. I've never made *that* joke before. Anyway, you have no excuses anymore." When Lou switched to gruff PO mode, Carlotta hummed under her breath.

Lou cleared her throat, coughed, and rustled some of the papers in Carlotta's file. "So next, we should schedule a home visit. I know you're in the situation you're in because nobody provided a second option. It sounds okay, but you're also living with a lot of people, and I need to know what the place is like, who the people are, where do you sleep, if you have your own space, et cetera. I'll come by later this afternoon."

Carlotta, still humming, tried not to react. "They found a spot for me," she said, "but I don't think they want me up there too long. My grandma's fine with it, but she the type a person who gon do everything for everybody. If Ise my li'l brother, she'da did the time *instead* a me. It's a whole lotta people living there, I guess. I'ma need my own space at some point. Soon."

"First things first, Carlotta." Lou's eyes glinted. "Income. You have to find some kind of a job. And I won't lie to you, it's not easy out there. The business community isn't exactly lining up around the block to read the résumés of ex-cons, okay? That goes double for people who don't conform to gender norms. They think it's too much of a liability. I'm not really supposed to do this, but I'm gonna make an exception for my alphabet people and give you a little nudge just cause I know it's so tough out there. I've got a guy, I can set you up with him. So it looks like you worked in the law library at Ithaca, that might mean you have some skills that someone might need, some clerical skills, something with books, like a bookstore? And you did laundry duty too, that's a marketable skill. Anything else?

What did you do before you went inside? And that was in—oh, wow."

"I worked at Kennedy Fried Chicken and McDonald's, and then I bagged groceries at Key Food, but I had only did that for two months before what happened happened, you know?"

"Okay. Write down whatever you've done that even seemed like work, you know, stuff you did for relatives, even. Emphasize the law library and the laundry room. Do you have access to the Internet?"

Carlotta coughed out a nervous laugh. But Lou fired a serious expression back at her. "Um," she finally managed to say, "I used TRULINCS right after it came out, but after a while I couldn't afford that shit no more. I'll be honest, I heard a lot about the Internet, I seen it here an there up at Ithaca, an since I got home, a couple a people has showed it to me on they phone, an plus I see ev'body walking round with they face glued to it on the damn street, but you already know they ain't giving out no access to no computers up in the joint like it's a handful a SweeTarts. So everything I learnt bout computers, which possibly a lot, I ain't had no chance to really *test out* or nothing. But with all the folks at home, I know I could get somebody to show me it. There ain't no kinda shortage of people in that house who could get me on the computer an help me get a job."

The tension in Lou's face settled, giving Carlotta the idea that she'd gotten the answer right. It felt to her like Lou had asked the question as a game, testing Carlotta's ability to say anything that would sound good. Lou slid a sea-green photocopy off a pile on the far side of her desk, held it in the air, and flicked it with a papery snap. She handed it to Carlotta, who reached out for it and stared until she sussed out what the document meant. At the top it sported a cartoon of a smiling white man in a suit sitting behind a desk Guess "white man at a desk" apposed to mean jobs.

There were twelve positions listed, some full-time, some part-time. Lou leaned forward, invading Carlotta's personal space enough that Carlotta could smell her hair—faintly soapy, a little waxy, more cologne than perfume—and slid her finger along the left margin, pointing out where the listings began and ended. "I advise you to take whatever offer you get, full- or part-time," Lou said. "They're not the greatest—frankly, they're not even good—but right now you just need a job, not a *good* job."

FOUR

I *need a job, need a job, need a job-job-job. Not a good-job job, just a dumbass job.* Lou said that an I keep saying it in my head until it become a li'l song, you know? Like somethin I could dance to while I'm on my way to this interview. *I think I can, I think I can.* Like I'm the Li'l Engine That Could—or Maybe Couldn't. *The Li'l Engine Who Gonna Fuck It Up.* Lou did me a good turn, she aight. She seen one a them jobs on the sheet, the boss somebody she know good enough to call up right then, make sure he in the office, an say, "I got somebody you should take a look at." The somebody being Miss Thing herself! An said what Ise about too. I ain't want her to do that part. I don't know what kinda juju she done worked on his ass, but the motherfucker said, Yes! Send the bitch down! Not the bitch, but you know. Her. Me.

They said I needed a coupla pitchers to put in with the application but Lou told me to just do passport photos at the drugstore an where it was. See, this one the only type a job where they don't mine that you got a record. This a good-ass job too! Thirteen a hour, dental, medical, vacation, sick leave—they said they gon pay you on your birthday like it's a holiday! Honest to the Lord Jesus who I don't believe in no more. Best of all, it said *paid training* on that job application. I gotta get this motha. Shit sound more like a vacation than a work job to me. I'd be on Easy Street, move outta that house next week, that place so crowded it's like living in the Atlantic-Pacific train station.

Wait — who am I kidding? Myself, that's who. Can't nobody walk out the joint after twenty-some odd years an grab a job on no first day out. That'd be stealin! But I can't be setting all my hopes on this one job — that I gotta get or I'ma die. I mean, I ain't gonna get it. But what if I did? I mean, I got to. Dude's name is Boz, sound like he some kinda ex-con hisself. Maybe that gon make him more on my side? Or less? Why do it always gotta be so much not knowin what gon happen in life?

Also there's a li'l problem. I said I could get my driver license renewed for the job, but I ain't never learnt to drive or nothing. When the hell I ever needed to drive shit? Not while I been on ice up in fucking PC or on D Block or whatever. Damn, I wish I ain't told Lou that I could drive, otherwise she wouldna got my hopes up bout this here thang, y'know? Anyhoo, I'ma just give it my best try. Could be that they also need, like, a non-driver type person to maybe deal with the wheelchairs or shit like that. I could be that person.

On the way over, I'm like, Could these people with they double strollers and these blond chilluns who came outta some kinda Gerber baby food ad get out my fucking way? But Ise nice, though, smilin when Ise thinkin it. I seened all kinda tiny li'l boutiques, too, and I'm thinkin maybe I could get my nails did or buy some new shoes, ha-ha-ha, with the gate money I shouldn't be spendin, but hell, I'ma have a job by the end of the day, so why the fuck not? Baby gots to go out on ze town after a hard day at ze work, *non*? Meet herself a rich-ass motherfucker to pay for her life an shit. Oh, I don't mean none a that — I ain't gonna say no if it happen, but it's like Grandma Frona always said: You got to "do for self." I mean, she din't never step aside to *let* nobody do for theyself, but she sure *said* the hell outta that one.

Let me tell you, every last one them stores look like it's some-body apartment, and it got a name on the front like *Amanda* or *Joaquin*, and inside it's everything painted white an only like five motherfuckin tiny shoes, one at a time, an darling, I couldn't wrap my mind around that. I guess when you got a lotta money to spend, you don't wanna be thinkin bout which style a shoe you gonna get, or the price?

So I go into one these jwants and there go Amanda herself, sittin in the back in a maxi-dress, an I know I'ma be, like, puttin my face back on after I find out how much Amanda shoes cost, but I don't want the actual designer seein my face fall off, so I say to her, I go, How much is this? an I pick up a shoe an hold it up an she goes, "It's two fifty," an take a pause an then says, "Dollars," like my ass so stupid I don't know what's the name a money or nothing bout how much shit could cost. Or I'm so poor. I nod. What, do the bitch think I'm like, "It's two dollars and fitty cent"? So I go, "Hundred," an almost busted out laughin. Then she like, "Per shoe." On the inside Ise like, *Come the fuck again?* but I just said—all calm and shit, like some Upper East Side bitch, cocked my head to the side and puffed my hair—I went, "Oh, of course. So five for the pair." An kept nodding my damn head, like just knowin how to add 250 to 250 be some kinda way to get on the inside with some rich-ass elites.

I mean, *Damn*, it be a nice shoe, too, a gold leather sandal with the heel wrapped in white leather, imported from Peru and shit, very classy, an not too sparkly to wear to this new job—or to the interview, I thought—but if I bought it at that gigantic price, I'd wanna put it in a damn jewelry box stead a wearing it or, like, coat it in plastic like a couch so I wouldn't never drip no mustard on it or nothing. Picture my ass down at Coney Island with a date, bitin into a hot dog and squirtin yellow blobs all over that bitch. Na-aah, honey, my ass ain't high class by a long shot, but it's higher class than *that*!

Meanwhile I'm sayin "it" bout the shoe, cause at that moment Ise like, There ain't no motherfucking way I could afford two a these bad boys, maybe I could just get the one an put the other on layaway? I'm just right bout to axe if they got a layaway policy an it hit me that you can't be axin shit like that at no *Amanda*, specially not to Amanda actual face.

Then some shit happen in my brain where I don't want nobody to be shamin me over no shoes, you know what I'm sayin? So it's like I got shit to prove, just like up in Ithaca. That prison mentality done snuck up on my brain like Dracula jumpin up out the coffin at 7 p.m. sharp and shit, like *Gotta get me some blood, blood, blood!* I'm like, I do got *some* money, an damn it, this America right here, I'm back out the joint an I'ma celebrate myself an reward myself for gettin through all that lockdown bullshit an stayin alive—*Ah, ah, ah, ah, stayin alive, stayin alive!*—after all, my birthday not *that* long ago, just a month an a half, I'll be damn if I'ma give *Amanda* the satisfaction a thinkin I ain't good's the next white bitch who come up in here lookin to get her hands on one got-damn two-hunnert-fitty-dollar-for-one-shoe shoes, you feel me? So Ise gon cash that check an put some money on at least one a them damn shoes just to show Amanda what's what an who who.

Carlotta whipped around to Amanda (or whoever it was) and said, "I'll be right back for these," then spent a few minutes rubbernecking up and down the block for a check-cashing joint An I mean, them shoes ain't the be-all-end-all, you know. An maybe a Access-A-Ride driver don't really wanna wear no five-hundred-dollar metallic gold shoes on the job? Scuse me, you could shut the fuck up now, please, conscience. I don't know who said you could be in my head an all up in my shit anyway. Motherfuckers gon have to start payin rent if they wanna be takin up residence in my skull. This a luxury skull right here! Made in Brooklyn, motherfucker. Two fitty for the left or the right half a *this* bitch brain.

Ain't there one a them damn places somewheres round here? Or did *Amanda* get rid of em cause they be bringin in the wrong element that been here since before her stupid ass even got borned? Maybe they closed for the holiday observed. Carlotta walked north, scanning for a place to cash a check, and spotted a storefront up the street with a sign above the door that read CHECK-O-RAMA in yellow caps What's up with that wack-ass name? Do they got Reality Check an Check-fil-A too? She jaywalked from the west side of Smith to the east, pissing off the driver of a bleating green taxicab Why the cabs green out here? What the ever-loving shit that apposed to be about? Do I got color blindness? Dag, it is hot out here what with me walking all over the motherfucking place. Mama's sweatin to the *oldies*! I love it, though, freedom! Look at me, walkin cross the street! Let me stop on this damn yellow line and do my freedom dance! Whoo! Look it — who am I? The Statue a Liberty, yass honey!

She squeegeed beads of sweat off her recently tweezed eyebrows and flicked the moisture to the pavement. The air smelled like the inside of a dog's mouth and the sun got so hot that it hurt a little but I din't care. I ain't seened the sun in so long I coulda ate it, the whole damn sun. I'ma be Blacker than Wesley Snipes tomorrow but where my fucks at? Don't got a one.

A handwritten sign on the door of Check-o-Rama said they'd be closing at 2 p.m. until Tuesday Look like I got lucky. Inside, an AC caked with greasy dust loomed above the front door, lowering the inside temperature by about one degree. Two Black people — a squat, toothless grandma and a chunky man with giant sexy lips — waited as a gnarled-looking, possibly homeless white man argued with the teller, a woman whose accent placed her heritage somewhere in the West Indies, although she looked like someone from India, her hair dark and sleek as a mink coat. Her firm deadpan attitude and business duds contrasted sharply with the messy man's high-pitched squeals, his steel-wool hair. He sported a tent-size army surplus coat raggedy enough to have fought in Vietnam by itself Hey, ain't that Nick Nolte?

After what seemed like a long time Cause it *was* a long time Carlotta got to the window and pushed her check underneath to the firm West Indian lady, who had a sticker of a Trinidadian flag in her window. Carlotta wouldn't have recognized the flag but it said TRINIDAD underneath. Just before she got to the window, another person materialized in the next space over and set up his area, a man in gold-rimmed glasses with flipped-up bifocals and long locks piled up on his head.

The Trini lady asked Carlotta to endorse the check, but Carlotta stopped cold, realizing what name they'd expect to see. She flipped the check over twice, then a third time, and when the universe didn't disappear, which might've made it possible to get what she wanted, she tried to sign with a pen connected to a bead chain on the counter. But the pen only made little scratches, no marks. She shook the pen, trying to revive it, but the ink wouldn't budge. The lady slid a fresh pen into the metal space under the teller window. Carlotta signed the check and passed it back to her; the lady let her dead eyes pass over it blankly.

By this time, the dreadlocks man had perched on his chair and snapped his bifocals into place. He squinted at Carlotta Why that motherfucker grillin me so hard? I mean, I know I look good, but you don't gotta stare. Carlotta dipped her hips and then wondered if that might seem flirtatious Oh, I could give two shits bout lookin flirty. I know Frenzy would eat this man's brain right out his head if he knew, but he ain't gonna know.

"Picture ID," the Trini woman said, though it sounded like "Pitcher high-dee" Goddamn this shit! I guess I knew this gonna happen. Carlotta opened her mouth to explain her predicament. She rifled through Frona's bag, found the laser-printed temporary ID Ithaca had issued her, and passed it to the Trini lady.

Then the brother with the locks spoke up. "Hey! Hey, bruh! Isn't you, wasn't you"—he snapped his fingers several times—"Chambers, Chambers..."

Bruh? Oh, Lorda mercy. I better cut ahead of this shit. "Yes! I *was* Chambers! It's Carlotta now! Carlotta Mercedes!" Oh, whatever the fuck. That name be the one on the damn check that I—oh, shit, I just signed it Carlotta Mercedes!—so I gotta suck it up for now. Swallow your pride, honey—just pretend like your pride be a big fat dick. "An hey, brotha, ain't you Crmph Hrbarmn?" I ain't had no idea who in creation was this man.

"You don't remember me?"

The Trini lady unfolded Carlotta's ID and turned it around in her hands. "This is not valid," she announced. "What is this?"

Carlotta shifted her attention back to the Trini lady to try to explain what happened but it came out backward.

"You don't remember me, do you?" the clerk with the locks insisted.

He sounded put out Oh my Gawd, now he gonna make a issue out this shit when it been literally decades since I seened anybody ass in this town? I been away—at the fuckin country club, you chump. Great God Amighty, Church, canst thou believe you it? Could I get a amen? Yes, a *course* I recanize you! You my brother's ex-girlfriend's social worker's babyfather's friend's bartender! How the fuck I could forget? But hold the phone, y'all! Maybe since he member me, he could vouch for me an help me get this here check cashed.

"How could I forget that purty face?" Carlotta asked.

"Apparently purty easy," the man drawled, acting butt-hurt as he shuffled papers and jingled coins around in his tray. Suddenly he flipped into bona fide attitude. "It's me, Alphonse! Alpha Dawg!"

The nickname Alpha Dawg did ring a bell, a chime from so long ago that they probably spelled it d-o-g back then Maybe one a David's friends, this bro be way too cool to be a friend a Tom's, prolly smoked a lotta ganja. She shook her memory down like a CO, but she still felt like she was squinting into a peach-colored street-light through a thick fog. Despite all the eyestrain, she couldn't figure it out until Oh, shit, he was Doodle's pot dealer going way the hell back! How on earth he membered me, must be some kinda genius, like one a them three-year-old kids that could kick your ass at chess, done memorized all the geographies a the whole world. What the hell kinda career path this motherfucker on? Not that I got no right to judge—but that's the best time to judge, when you ain't got no rights to it. Cept this shit gon be tricky. I can't really sociate myself with nobody like him or I'ma be back upstate in a New York minute. But asides from kissing up to this dude, how I'm apposed get this check cashed an get both my *Amanda* shoes?

"Oh, snap! Alpha Dawg! A *course* I member you!" Now I gotta think up a memory bout him that prove I knowed the brother but don't involve no references to no drug use…uh, I ain't coming up with nothin too fast here. "I member when Doodle and me used to, um, we'd go up to your, yeah, when you used to, you'd come to our, an we'd wait outside for you to, um, yeah!" Carlotta nodded and grinned, hoping Alphonse would get it.

The Trini clerk watched, poker-faced, like she could demolish their conversation with her eyes. Maybe she couldn't wait to enjoy rejecting Carlotta's check. She passed the temporary back to Carlotta. "I need to see some pitcher high-dee, please."

"I am sorry, ma'am, that's all I got!" Carlotta leaned against the window and then, thinking twice, down into the stainless-steel gulch under the Plexiglas. "Listen, Alphonse, could you do me a favor?" Her voice rang out against the metal down there, sounding like a robot. "Does not compute," she said quietly to test out the robot voice.

"I'm sorry—what?"

"Oh, I sound like a robot down here. Ise just kidding around. Ise thinking since you know me an everythang, you could maybe vouch for me? So I could cash this here check? Can you give him the check?"

The Trini lady, now irritated, pushed the check halfway toward her colleague and asked Carlotta to move aside—another two people had shown up on line behind her. Alphonse leaned into the lady's space; he took the check and went back. Carlotta slid to his window. He swiveled his head like an electric fan between something he was reading and something he seemed to notice about Carlotta's face. Maybe how much older she looked? Maybe he noticed the difference in gender presentation, but he suddenly shut down.

"No wonder I ain't seened you in so long!" Alphonse laughed. "How long you was up there?"

He'd figured out the issuer of the check *Shit.* She didn't care about Alphonse knowing, but the Trini woman and the people on line didn't need to know her business.

"Oh, I wasn't no inmate or nothing. I used to work up there in the kitchen, and this my severance pay for when I come back," she said through her teeth to show him she was lying *I hope he know to keep his damn mouth shut.*

The Trini clerk suddenly halted her transaction with another customer to butt in. She pointed her finger at the check like she was accusing *it* of lying. "Oh no, no, that's not de kine of check they hissue to de hemployees. Dat's de check for a, a...when dey..."

She fumbled for the right term for the kind of person she had to describe, maybe since that kind of person was right in front of her, firing mental daggers into her cheeks.

Carlotta's embarrassment contorted her face. "Formerly incarcerated *person*," she said curtly Hope she heard that *person* part.

"Oh yeah, you right, Shivana!" Alphonse said.

"That don't matter," Carlotta said. "What I need is to get it cashed. It ain't illegal to get outta prison! I mean, *damn*, that's one the most *not* illegal things going, y'all, to *not* be in no prison no more. It mean you clean, you startin over, you can't afford to be up to no good! Why don't nobody *get* that!" She sighed and raised her eyes to the ceiling for a second, as if she could talk to some god through the fluorescent lights. "Why people gotta make me feel like my ass just got sentenced?" she whispered to herself.

"Do you got a ID?" Alphonse asked.

Carlotta bit down on her tongue. She felt like kicking something. Before she could stop herself, she punted one of the poles that held up the ribbon defining the waiting line for the three people waiting at the counter. The wide base and the ribbon prevented it from falling over. It snapped up, pushed her foot backward, and almost made her fall onto the frail brown broomstick of a man who had just shown up behind her. The whole sequence of events put her in a tizzy. She muttered and tried to get her shit together. "Excuse my behavior, Alpha Dawg. It ain't becomin a no lady."

"Okay, so do you got a ID?"

Anger management. "You recanized me, though! So why do I need a ID now?"

Alphonse laughed nervously. "Oh, it ain't up to me. It's that you gotta fill out this form." He waved a packet of sheets stuck together at the top with carbon paper between them. "It's a whole mess of numbers from IDs and whatnot. It don't matter none that I know who you is. This Brooklyn, yo, it ain't Mayberry." He chuckled The fuck his problem. Fuck this motherfucker.

"Listen, this the ID I got, brotha, I need to catch a break. I just got sprung *yesterday*. That's like a birthday, so just make it a birthday present. Don't you got people that's outta Ithaca?"

"Oh, not really. My brothers all did they time up in Troy and Corinth." He mouthed the words *Me too* on the sly so that only Carlotta could see.

She raised her eyebrows. "Oh, okay. So you understand!" The career path makin sense now.

"I'm sorry. So could I see your ID?"

"Damn it, you gotta know how this work, brotha. Listen, I tried to get a name change on my DOCCS card, but it din't come through in time, so they gave me this printout wit a old pitcher on it. It don't even have my new name." She waved it in front of the booth. "That's why I axed you to hook me up, Alpha Dawg, cause you knowed me from way back, yo" I'on't even talk like this, what is wrong with me that I'm tryna get in good with this fool? I should just axe Frona to sign the damn thing over. Oh, but them Amanda shoes is fly!

Alphonse reared back and raised his eyebrows, and his hands moved to his hips for an instant. "Okay, Carlotta! I'm sorry, but I do need to see *some* form of ID before I can cash your check." He stuck the check halfway through the hole under the window.

"Here." Carlotta gave him the printout and he stared at it briefly.

"I can't accept this."

"Well, fuck this motherfuckin bullshit-ass shit, then! And fuck you too, you jive nigga!" She turned to the Trini lady. "And that's a fuck-you for you too, fucking She Monsta whatever your name!" Carlotta yanked the check from under the window and tore it, almost in half. She shouted and flung her hands around.

Alphonse taped the check, possibly holding back a laugh. "I know it's rough, m'dear, but try to keep it together!" He slipped the check into its own fresh business envelope, and Carlotta took it from him. She couldn't chill out enough to thank him, so she tucked the flap inside, folded the envelope in half, shoved it into Frona's bag, and stomped out of Check-o-Rama.

Once she was out on the hot pavement again, regrets attacked *Oh, fuck, you know what? I din't think fast enough. If he and his fam been up in Troy and now he working, maybe I coulda got me a job at Check-o-Rama. Why'd I had to go an make a goddamn scene? Damn! Damn! Damn! Carlotta, you gotta fix yourself, girl. But fuck it, I can't!* She ran at a group of pigeons. The birds tried to fly away in the tight space between Carlotta and an old lady pulling a wire shopping cart who covered her face and cursed out the pigeons in a loud, raspy voice.

In a few minutes, Carlotta stood proudly in front of Amanda again. Inside, the presumed Amanda yakked it up with two white women, one who had dyed-red hair, another with white hair that also looked dyed. Carlotta had barged in on a conversation about shoes. The ladies had brought a dog and a toddler into the shop, and both the pooch and the kid kept losing their minds the second the women focused on anything other than them. The child, possibly male but long-haired and dressed in gender-neutral colors, let out high-pitched angry squeals *Who give a fuck what it is if it gotta sound like that?* as the dyed-red mother tried to keep him from biting each of the shoes on display. Every time she tried to have the shoes conversation, he'd weep and shout "No!" at everyone. When that didn't work, he growled "Stop talking!" at least a dozen times, but the women didn't even turn.

The hound was an extraordinarily needy Bernese mountain dog. He kept looking up at the white-haired woman and brushing his giant body against her like a mega-cat. The woman chewed him out a few times for knocking over parts of the shoe display. She kept saying "Humphrey!" in a disappointed tone and shrinking back when she looked at the shopkeeper. "Humphrey, no!" Humphrey's size wouldn't have created a problem except for the size of the store, a 15-by-15-foot box further divided by a curtained-off area I don't got no idea why they need a curtain for you to try on some damn shoes, less they think it's some motherfucker round here with a foot fetish gonna peep in and get off on some naked feet. An you could see right under that curtain anyways, so it wouldn't work.

Since Carlotta couldn't cash the check, she had come back without thinking, like a rat to a trash can, but now, as she slowly twisted one side of her mouth into her cheek, watching the scene unfold, she felt ignored, disrespected. She had entered the store, the bells attached to the door had jingled, the door had closed completely again, and not one of the three ladies had so much as turned to clock her presence in the room. She remembered telling Amanda she would be back. Some generic high-energy dance music played from two white speakers on either side of the space Even the speakers gotta be white up in this racist-ass joint. Sure, the customers had a dog and a baby to fuss over, but Amanda shouldn't have let them take up her whole attention I am here! Notice me! Carlotta tried to make eye contact, but Amanda had discovered the softness of Bernese mountain dog fur. Humphrey dropped to the floor in ecstasy and rolled around, displaying his penis like he wanted a canine-human orgy.

The golden $250-for-one-shoe shoe occupied a royal spot by the door, cut by a sunbeam coming through the gathering clouds. In that striking light, it looked as gettable as a black-and-white cookie in front of a glass display case in some deli. Carlotta took a step to her left, bent her knees, and touched the shoe. She kept one hand behind her back and fixed her eyes on the chaos in front of her *My brain goin, Don't do it, honey, this ain't gonna go good. Save up from the Access-A-Rides and come back in six month, ain't no thang.* But the motherfuckin shoe insultin my ass just by sittin there. Humphrey barked and startled her. She stuck her hand in her pocket and waited, but in a second, her fingers crept out again like a spider That dog ain't barkin at me for touchin no shoe, he just enjoyin hisself. An still ain't none a these white folks noticed me neither. I could be a motherfuckin ghost.

Behind her back, her fingers did a tarantula walk over the gold-lamé shoe. An index finger slipped under the strap and flipped the shoe over into her palm. Then she did some Alvin Ailey–type move where she spun around and passed the shoe from her left to her right hand, very casually. While shoving the shoe into her crotch, halfway down into her baggy panties, she pushed open the door and crab-walked out I got the wrong size panties, but it turnt out I just needed to jack a damn shoe to make em fit! Then, trying to stay nimble My ass on some Doris Payne shit here she closed and buttoned her suit jacket enough to hide the bulge made by the shoe and hold it secure against her body, like a kilo of cocaine taped to the crotch of a drug mule.

Her breath raced Don't run, bitch, cause that gon make Amanda suspicious an run after you. They only get suspicious when Black folks be runnin somewheres, you could be Jackie Joyner-Kersee an they gon call the cops. If you run, she gon come for your ass an call the police, which I heard you could do at the same time with them cell phones, an film it too, an the whole thing, yo whole life, gon come crashin down on your ass. Humphrey gon bite you, maybe try to hump your leg to death. Yeah, you might end up dead, then they gon send your ashes up to Ithaca to do the rest a your time up in the prison. Wait at least two blocks, yes, like that. You just a regalar lady walkin down a regalar street in yo own damn neighborhood. Hello, Mr. Jones. Hello, Mrs. Smith. Lovely day, isn't it? Hot enough for you? Toodle-oo! Now pick up the pace. Where the fuck I'm goin now, though?

Carlotta patted herself down and rifled in Frona's bag with her free hand to make sure she still had all the folded tear sheets with the contact information about where to go to interview for the position That felt good—first time I patted *myself* down in a long damn time. At last, she tugged the shoe out of her crotch and stuffed it into the handbag, but it didn't quite fit. The wooden sole stuck out of the top between the hoops.

After a bum start at a chain drugstore where the photo developer didn't do passport photos and another place where nobody behind the counter knew how, Carlotta found a dry cleaner who was open, miraculously, and also, for some reason, took passport photos.

"I am getting the most out of the space!" the proprietor declared.

"Next you could put in a auto-body shop," Carlotta said as she sat down in the gray metal folding chair where all of the photographer's subjects had to plant themselves.

"Naw, there isn't enough room here to do that!" the man replied Like *I'm* the one that's being ridicalous.

"Ise just makin a joke," Carlotta said flatly, but the man didn't react What's the deal with people who don't got no kinda sense a humor at all? How they get through they life? If I had to take everything that done happened to my sorry ass serious every damn time, I would definitely be dead. I'da slit my own motherfuckin throat. The camera's flash went off The only way I know how to handle shit is to make a joke an keep movin on. What else you gon do? Try to change shit? Ain't that why our memory so bad, so that we could forget all the humiliation an pain a life, or least so we got a opportunity to do that? I *love* to forget. The flash exploded a second time Forgettin shit be like havin natural drugs up in your brain. Like if that motherfucker Dave step to me in twenty years, like, "Member how I used to do you, bitch? Member how I tore up that butt like a bad check? Member how wouldn't nobody help you, how you useta lay there for days with a bloody sheet between your legs, crying your eyes out like you was a virgin bride, then bored as shit cause you couldn't do nothing in the SHU cept cut your damn self? An Ise the only guard on duty?" I hope I could honestly say, "Who the fuck are you?" Like, memory banks erased an whatnot. Access denied, motherfucker.

The job interview would take place at an office within walking distance of Amanda, a few more blocks up Smith past Atlantic Hope they gived me the right address, this time a spot still transitioning, where richer, paler people pushed out working-class brown people who had lived there since the middle of the previous century. People had given the gray strip of municipal buildings and retail stores the generic name Downtown Brooklyn because no other neighborhood wanted it. Not even MetroTech Center, that eerie replica of a comic-book Gotham City, seemed attached to the gloomy blocks of Livingston and Schermerhorn Streets. Carlotta had seen The Nevins and some other hotels under construction at the other end of this area, but it seemed as if new residential construction had metastasized even into this area, a bona fide stumper when she flashed on what it had pushed out: second-floor African hair-braiding shops, public notaries, forgotten government offices, rubber-stamp manufacturers, and a welfare hotel pretending to be a regular hotel even with wire cages in front of the windows They wasn't fooling nobody with that shit. Why anybody wanna make this jwant all fancy?

Carlotta crossed Livingston and stopped at a cagelike contraption that suspended cars in the air, a mechanized parking lot like she had never seen before. It reminded her of a cheap roller coaster or the inside of that ride at Coney Island, the Hell Hole. On the next block she bumped into the building where her potential employer, Access-A-Ride, ran its offices. They had a skeleton crew working today, it looked like.

She sweet-talked her way past security by dropping the name Lou had written down on the job sheet. The guard insisted on calling the contact, who agreed to send her up before hearing her name. The guard didn't want to let her through without a real picture ID—he'd huffed when she showed him the passport photos—but taking her photo at the desk would have to work for the time being. "You should get a driver's license," he scolded *You* need to get out my grill, bitch. I could tell just from the way you sayin it that half the motherfuckers applying to Access-A-Ride don't got no ID an maybe not no driver license neither. But I ain't mad atcha—it means I got a shot.

She imagined the human junk streaming through the chrome gates of 130 Livingston I bet it's a heap a motherfuckers can't even drive a shoppin cart through the Key Food let alone no Access-A-Ride, maybe it's some a them folks who tried to get hired at Kennedy Fried Chicken? Whoo, they was beyond repair! Maybe some of em had also just got sprung and started on they "journey," like ev'body call it now: My reentry journey, my lockdown journey, my SIIU journey, my cold-cereal journey, my TVP journey, my fucking fatty-girl cake journey. So much people's on a goddamn journey, it's like ain't nobody never home!

The heel of the shoe she had lifted from Amanda poked partially out of the handbag. Carlotta wondered three things during the walk from the shoe store to Empire Paratransit, as they called themselves on the job sheet: (1) When I could slip into the shoe without nobody seeing me? (2) How I could keep the folks in there from seeing I ain't got but one of em? An (3) How I could work this damn shoe to get this damn job?

They asked her to sit in the reception area and wait for Boz. The office had an open plan, with a dark concrete polished floor and cinder-block walls painted the color of spoiled mayonnaise. A hefty Black worker to Carlotta's left kept adjusting both an oscillating fan and a strap on her yellow spaghetti-strap terrycloth dress. The fan sat on the floor for some reason, and every time the woman bent down to adjust it as it jerked left and right, one of the dress straps would fall to her upper arm.

After checking to make sure nobody was watching, Carlotta slid her new shoe out of the bag. She pushed the prison shoe under the chair behind her and dropped the Amanda shoe to the floor to test the glamour of her foot positions. She hid Plain Jane around the stem of the rolling chair and stuck the other foot forward Like Cinderella goin to the *ball* and imagined her entrance into Boz's personal area. She crossed her legs, letting Cinderella dangle in the air.

Of the four people in the otherwise empty office, one had a Caribbean music station blasting at their desk; on the radio a horny woman sang about needing a job applicant to drive her all over town—"Drive me!" she shouted—it sounded appropriate and inappropriate at the same time Guess they kickin back on overtime today? A different Black lady, maybe not an employee, who Carlotta could not see over the cubicle unless she stood up, was having a passionate conversation with what sounded like an ex-husband or babydaddy over childcare. She called him "nigga" so many times it sounded like his name. A couple of times she said it lovingly. Carlotta distracted herself by feeling her pride I cannot believe I got a actual interview right out the gate in a legit place. Check me the fuck out. Okay, magic shoe, work this bitch, make my ass a employed lady! They say you gotta give some to get some? Well, look at *that*, Boz. She wiggled the shoe so that the metallic fabric on the band across the arch gleamed in the murky light from the tinted window on her left. She mopped her brow with her rolled-up sleeve.

Just when she flashed the golden shoe, the receptionist escorted her farther back in the office to a cubicle where a frazzled Black man sat, beads of sweat collecting on his forehead. He had on a floral T-shirt with dark sweat stains in the pits and across the back. In his space, he cradled a folder so packed with papers that it almost couldn't close. The moment he saw Carlotta, he whapped the folder onto his desk so hard, it felt like Sweetums throwing a punch. Carlotta froze and stepped back But then Ise like, maybe if he could be so rough with a pile a papers, he done time and he gon have sympathy for me. Din't Lou say they wasn't gon care bout my record?

The receptionist introduced the man and dashed away. Boz shook Carlotta's hand limply and slumped into his chunky khaki-green office chair. He peered at Carlotta like a television I figure he starin like all them niggas in the street who can't get past what I be servin out there, like he ain't never had to interview nobody who in the life. But now he goin even past that to where it's like *Has this motherfucker ever met another human* being *before?* Did he forgot his promise to Lou? Do he know that I'm apposed to talk to his ass bout a job? Is my goddamn presence offending you, Bozzy?

The wordless stare from Boz packed enough confusion and irritation behind it that Carlotta started to think she had come to the wrong place—maybe he wasn't Boz. She rose halfway on her elbows like she'd need to get up soon before he kicked her out, but then she realized she'd have to adjust the stolen shoe to avoid his gaze and changed her mind. She angled the shoe so that it sparkled under his desk.

As if he hadn't acted flaky enough, Boz showed her his back and *then* started talking to her. "Are you going somewhere?" he finally droned in a thick, deep-voiced West Indian accent, like a father confronting a defiant daughter about to go to church in a fishnet bodysuit.

Carlotta reared back. "Is you Boz?"

"Yes."

"Lou sent me. It's about a employment? I heard her talking to you on the phone?"

"Lou? Lou who? Who Lou?" His wordplay seemed to amuse him, like he'd stirred up the bubbles in a Jacuzzi full of haughtiness. He let the front of his folder fall open and laughed with his mouth closed. Carlotta watch his shoulders shake and thought of Muttley, the snarky dog from those *Dick Dastardly* cartoons.

With a sickening rush, Carlotta thought that the folder might be full of job applications, but she couldn't tell from the angle she had.

"For that matter, who you?"

Feeling mocked and flustered, Carlotta suddenly couldn't remember Lou's last name. She thought of whapping the shoe upside the man's head. "Lou…Lou…Lou—DeLay! From the, um—" Now it's gon help my case or sink my ass if I say the PO? "From the, um, office…over on Second Avenue" If he don't get it, then it ain't no skin off my ass.

"Okay," Boz said without letting on that he understood. He rifled through a gigantic stack of papers, different from the folder, until he came to a layer of mauve sheets about three-quarters of the way down. He tugged one from that section and flicked it in Carlotta's direction. The top of the page read *ADA Transportation Assessment Application* Okay, so this a application! Good! "Okay, so this a application?" Carlotta asked.

Boz turned his neck and faced her without an expression, then turned back to his papers. Carlotta let the pilfered shoe dangle on her big toe and reached down toward it I swear to God I'ma get me some blood all over this here $250 Amanda shoe if this man don't cut it out with all the shade. What the fuck wrong with this office? It's nine hundred degrees in here—what, is the AC just broken, been broken for days? Oh, Lord!—and everybody just doin ezzackly how they please, arguin with they baby daddy all loud, throwin shade, playin they radios at full volume. A dance-hall beat had taken over; a Jamaican man with a computery voice told his girlfriend to "Sit upon de cocky" and ride it like a "jockey" Guess they tryna observe the holiday, just like my folks.

Instead of beating Boz with the shoe, Carlotta took a breath and made like she was scratching her calf. She about-faced on asking him for a pen. Instead, she snuck one from under a yellowing pile of *New York Posts* on the unoccupied desk next to his, making sure Boz wouldn't see. She stared down at the sheet of paper It been a long-ass time since I seen a job application. Okay, up here it say *New Application,* so yes, check that box. Some shit in Spanish or some yang. Chinese, too. *Please complete this application*—that sound like somethin you oughta do when you applyin for a job, sure! An this here with the pic, they wanna see them passport photos, so I'ma take em out and put em right here so I don't forget. Carlotta put the pictures on her lap and flicked them like playing cards.

Do I need information in a alternate format? In braille? No. The pen made an impression without making a mark Don't no pens be workin on the outside? so she raised it in the air and shook it, and when she put it back on the paper, a faint line of ink stuttered out Next quextion. Do I got a e-mail address? No. I'ma sign this next page an put down the date, Friday, July 3, 2015. Now here the page wit the normal questions bout yo address an everything…now the application form. How has I been travelin in the last six months? Public bus, no, subway, no, school bus, ha-ha-ha, Walkin. Taxi? The fuck goin on here? I'ma just put walkin. Aight, four. Is your disability permanent, temporary, I don't know? I ain't got no disability, so I'on't know. List which support device you use when travelin—like a cell phone? Oxygen tank, walker, scooter, service animal—what? Oxygen tank? Oh *no.* I get it. This the application for who need the service, not the motherfucker who gon be drivin the truck. What the ever-loving fuck? She took a long look at Boz's sweaty back.

"Escuse me. Mr. Boz?"

"What, child?" He continued to focus on the large pile of

photocopies, folding over the top right corner of each one, making a mark or initialing each page.

"I am apposed to be applyin for a *job* with Access-A-Ride, not the service. No disrespect to no crippled folks, but I ain't got no disabilities." Carlotta floated the piece of paper back to him. "Do you also got the application for that? Maybe in that pile a stuff?"

"Are you sure? What is going on with your shoe? That's not orthopedic?"

Now I'm pissed. Mr. Blackwell here ain't never seen no gold-lamé orthopedic shoes. That shit do not exist. She just a shady-ass li'l bumboklaat. Carlotta straightened her leg until the shoe dangled off her toe into Boz's personal space, hovering close to his lap. "Am I sure? When you ever seen a gold-lamé orthopedic shoe, Mr. Boz? You don't gotta be no fashionista to know that don't never happen — it's a good idea, though. May I please have a *job* application?"

The passport photos fell off Carlotta's lap, and when she adjusted the chair to reach down for them, she accidentally rolled the wheel over her face. Boz scanned the service application, crumpled it with one hand, and tossed it into a full garbage can. The crumpled ball fell off twice until he jammed everything down on top of it. He sent his hands on an expedition, first through the giant pile of papers in front of him, then into a rat's nest of photocopies wedged into a crevice behind a pair of coffee cups in a Greek design that read WE ARE HAPPY TO SERVE YOU, one of which had fallen over, the other of which had cold coffee in it topped with a marbled, milky skin.

Boz hadn't given her a writing surface, not even for the service application, so Carlotta cleared an area on the next desk, a junkyard of filthy three-ring binders in drab green and maroon. On the other side of the cubicles, a broken office chair sat inverted on the desk like a plastic crown. She brushed the grime off one of the binders, set it in her lap, and tested the pen out on a corner of a *New York Post*.

The application didn't spring any big surprises, just a lot of questions she knew she would need to skip. She didn't make up any lies, just decided to leave the boxes blank if she couldn't give a real answer. Then she came to the famous question—previous convictions. Without making a sound, she groaned physically. She made a faint dot in the box, hoping that Boz would not see or would get mixed up. IF SO, the next question read, PLEASE DESCRIBE Ise thinkin a writin, *Put too many cute puppies in a Easter basket* or *Convicted a sexiness in the first degree* but that shit wasn't gon fly, not even gon make nobody laugh. I'ma just put down the truth. AA & rob. I hope he think that be the name of a TV show, like it's *Pink Lady and Jeff.* Tonight on *AA & Rob,* we gon be talkin wit Mike Tyson, Martha Stewart, an Wesley Snipes, an musical guest gon be Mystikal! Now I know this shady ho ain't gonna like that only half this damn thing filled out, an I sure don't wanna axe no quextions bout what I gotta fill in and what I don't, so I'ma just hand it back and see what happen.

A fight broke out in a far corner of the room. Some frantic person got their fur rubbed the wrong way, but Carlotta couldn't pull the story out of all the raised voices. The radio launched into a song about Caribbean cooking, but after the other songs, even preparing salt fish sounded obscene. A deep voice sang, "Soak it, soak it. Soak it good."

Trying not to care, Carlotta made her face blank and smoothed the application on Boz's desk next to his big folder, then she pulled her hand away so that the page would flutter to the desk like an elm leaf falling on the tennis courts in Fort Greene Park.

Boz examined her answers and said, "Hm."

Hm. That's all you got is *Hm?* Jesus Christ Deluxe with Onions, honey, give me some better shit than *Hm!* Carlotta clamped her jaw and crossed her arms, expecting Boz to lay down a snap fight's worth of put-downs. Instead, he took a very long time to respond

I hope the stuff from the liberry gon impress him at least a little. Prolly more than my two months at Key Food. Speakin a food, my ass gettin hungry—damn, it's already 1:43! I'on't know when to feed myself without nobody tellin me no more. Boz, you shady piece a trash, just reject my ass so I could go eat!

Boz flipped the application over and combed over the whole thing twice. When he finished, he placed the paper next to his giant pile, patted it down with his fingertips, and swung around on his office chair—the most energetic thing he'd done since the interview began—so powerfully that Carlotta reared back in her own chair. "When you can start?" he asked.

Dafuq? Was this whole thing some kinda test a my patience? *Right the fuck now* is what I wanna say. But it feel like it's some shit wrong with this here li'l pitcher. He ain't say I got the job, so maybe that ain't why he axin. Maybe he basing whether or not he gon offer me the job on when I could start, an if I say the wrong day I ain't gon get it. I done heard all the horror stories bout girls who been outta lockdown four, five *years* an ain't got no job, gotta be hookin up a storm down the piers, honey. But I'ma play it cool.

"Whenever."

"Today is the holiday observed, so not today. So how about Monday?"

"Monday good."

What the fuck? Thank you, whoever! I ain't got no idea how you could get a job by fillin out half a application—maybe it *is* this magic shoe. Magine I had took the pair, they'd make me the boss!—but I ain't gon argue with nobody bout no job offer.

Boz gave her information about where to report for her first day, along with a packet about the requirements and the benefits Benefuckingfits! and explained everything, while Carlotta sat there not quite listening I'ma just take this, like Lou said, cause don't nobody know when somethin else comin along. What the fuck? Thank you, whoever! They made me boss, tho, I'd fire Boz first—clearly the motherfucker just hirin anybody off the street without no qualifications. I'd fire myself next, cause I sure as shit don't deserve none a this job. But see, honey, I got a thing for paychecks. Carlotta picked the application up, straightened her spine like a secretary in a sitcom, and wrote "Carlotta Mercedes" across the boxes labeled NAME.

FIVE

Carlotta leapt into the elevator like a drag queen doing a layup. It didn't feel real Everything them reentry case-manager bitches told me at them info sessions was completely bananas. Boz had schooled her about where to show up for work on Monday—someplace out on Atlantic Avenue also called Empire Paratransit, like the offices downtown, it said on the sheet—and shooed her out, as if he had hired her just to get her out of the way Cause obviously the only thing he care bout be puttin that li'l checkmark on every page a that giant pile a papers on what's really apposed to be his day off.

When the elevator opened to the lobby, she tried to sexify her walk on the way out and failed. Her prison shoe and her Amanda shoe had two slightly different heights, and she couldn't help subtly staggering. But eventually she put it out of her mind. She swung her hips through the glass doors and down Livingston, bypassing the crowd of sweat-glazed Black folks piling out of the buses and the filthy Macy's branch and hopping onto the B38, the B52, and the B25 buses on Fulton.

Gaining some footing, she made her way back toward the construction site that was once the Albee Square Mall and the bank building, through the former Dime Bank, past Junior's, carried along by the image of all those twinkling light bulbs, one of the few things that hadn't changed since before she went inside. In fact, they'd fixed the sign—all the bulbs worked! She had lost the other prison shoe, but she couldn't remember where and didn't care enough to retrace her steps It's like maybe I get rid a one prison shoe an gain a Amanda shoe for every prison one I lose. I could live with that! Or maybe I am simply the luckiest goddamn ho on the planet, which I know *that* ain't been the case in my life yet, so why it gon start today? I guess my ass waiting for the other shoe to drop. Which I hope it don't, less it's comin direct from *Amanda*. I'm in a damn good mood now!

Back in the childhood freedom days, Carlotta sometimes celebrated extra-special occasions with a cheesecake from Junior's, a specific type of individual cheesecake with bits of candied fruit embedded in it A motherfucking *cannoli*-ass cheesecake! Oh my Gawd! that Frona had served at her twelfth birthday party, which she counted as one of the happiest moments of her life Asides from yesterday. The getting-out part, I mean, maybe not some a that other shit that went down. An it ain't even been too many good ones since number twelve—ain't that shit sad?

So I get to Junior's an it's like a million motherfuckers lined up round the block tryna get they holiday cheesecake before closing time or something, I ain't even sure could I walk in the joint to do my lunch celebration. It seem like everybody just buggin out too—I seen some kids fightin over who shoved who an who cut in front a who, an some old man just bout fell over when his cane went out from under him, an then it's a man arguin wit the cashier bout what happened to the marble cheesecake he ordered that they ain't got an she sayin they ain't got no more marble cheesecakes in the size he want an he don't want to take two small ones instead a the big one cause it's his son birthday an his son gon have a conniption if he don't get just one cake so the cashier like, Why don't you just get one small cake? An that really make the brotha lose his shit, so I snuck in behind all that an it look like it ain't even no seats left in the dining room, tween all the white folks out with they families chompin on chicken bones an suckin out the marrow, lickin they damn fingers like they secret Black folks inside, some dreadlock brother next to em eatin a giant plate a ribs wit some red-red sauce that make it look like the motherfucker just pounced on a cow an ripped its whole skeleton apart, like he a fuckin leopard an whatnot, then a nanny with five chilluns an all of em screamin they li'l heads off. Some manager lady come out an start yellin that they closin early, in a couple hours, but din't nobody act like they heard.

I can't even see no place where no party a one could sit down cept for the lunch counter, which I really don't wanna do on account a it's a special occasion, and so I'm thinkin a maybe havin my celebration with Doodle an one or two my old friends be better than sitting at some lunch counter, long as it ain't nobody usin no drug or alcohol or nothin and they people I could sociate with an not get my Black booty sent back upstate. Maybe they wouldn't even kick me back to Ithaca an I wouldn't never see Frenzy again, have to tough out the rest a my sentence plus extra time in, like, Troy or fucking Homer, one them super-skanky-ass joints that even folks in Ithaca be talking trash about.

But just as I'm bout to turn tail, somebody get up off one them orange stools by the counter right in front of me, an I ain't proud, it's a seat, so I take it, an the lady come by an take my order. I axe her bout the old-style cheesecake—the cannoli-type cheesecake from back in the day that be so tasteable in my mind I could bite them li'l cubes a candied fruit and taste em through the sweet cheese cream, that was the *shit*, and I'm tryna get her to understand what I'm talkin bout an she like Nobody home. Like I ain't even described a thing you could do to a cheesecake on the whole planet Earth, like it ain't never been possible, like it go against the laws a science. I'm like, Cannoli. I say it real slow like she gon understand. *Can. No. Li.* I start describin them juicy bits a candied fruit an, like, a ricotta or something mixed in the cheese? She like, "I've never heard of that. We never did that. Maybe you're thinking of the Cheese-cake Factory?" Shruggin her damn shoulders. Meanwhile she ain't even half my age, prolly not even from this damn state, let alone this neighborhood — I'on't know what the Cheesecake Factory even *is* — an she gon tell *me* what cheesecake they din't used to serve up in this bitch? Na-ahh, I'on't think so. I'ma get Thing 2, he probably know bout each individual cake that done left the building since 1983. I mean, I can't call his ass, but I will once I get me a cell phone. It be nice to have one. I could maybe call somebody wit a illegal phone up at Ithaca and talk to my boo. I hope he ain't gettin into nothing new just cause I got out. My plan is we gon be together someday. Maybe me, him, an Iceman could live together — no, that ain't realistic. Down the block from Iceman. I could call Ibe too, call that nigga every day till I get him on my side, like Hi, Mama loves you. Iceman. He'd *love* that. Okay, let me stop. I gotta take a look at this menu.

A dazed-looking Black woman walked in, looking like some character cooked up by a Negro comedian from the olden times, Moms Mabley or somebody — light-colored stockings full of runs that clashed with her molasses skin, a streaky dirty-blond wig, and a big down jacket draped over her shoulders Member how it's July? It seem like she takin advantage a the crowded deli area in front, figurin ain't nobody gon notice her nutso behavior. She slipped into the lunch-counter area An I ain't never seen that as home to no sidewalk skanks, but I'm new to all this madness.

The woman turned every which way but loose, like a fly that can't find its way out of a window. She held her coat closed from the inside, delighted by the way the sleeves leapt up whenever she swerved to the left or right. Unlike many of the mainstreamed folks roaming the streets and the subways, she didn't seem upset about anything, wasn't enraged at an invisible friend, didn't harass anyone on the cheesecake line But I seened her and Ise like, *Uh-oh*. Not outta hate or nothin, just outta that thing that's like This Person Gon Cause a Ruckus or Somebody Look Like They Havin a Crisis, an they prolly gonna say some bullshit or try to fuck wit you. So I turnt away. The woman smirked and slid her feet along the terrazzo, occasionally twirling in her flats, her toes peeking out of both. Soon, still lost in a secret joke, she took a few halting paces toward the counter and let one of her sleeves brush against Carlotta's back.

I ain't even notice the first time, cause I had got so involved an frustrated with (a) the fact they ain't had the type a cheesecake I had wanted no more; (b) the attitude displayed by this ignant waitress who had no prior knowledge of the histories of cheesecakes that would help her to serve the customer who was me an the customer always right; (c) what the fuck I should order to make my celebration the best possible first-lunch-outta-prison experience, balancin how much cash I got wit what be on the menu; (d) Ise halfway thinkin I oughta just get on up outta there and go somewheres else, cause I got a rule goin where if you can't get the shit you want, don't take nothin *close* to the shit you want but not *quite*. That go for lovers too; an (e) Ise honestly feelin a li'l bit down that Ise bout to celebrate all by my lonesome, thinkin bout how my moms can't join me an my son don't get it. So I'm like, Maybe I'on't even *want* no cheesecake, maybe I should take my ass up to Kennedy Pizza Chicken on Fulton an Lafayette, see if any my friends still workin there, or maybe I could go find a coconut FrozFruit, another thing I useta love, out a bodega down DeKalb.

The second time I get hit with Miss Lady's sleeve, I turnt around and seen her and I give her the Don't-Fuck-with-Me eyes. But that chile had more issues than *Ebony* magazine an I think I know which ones. Like it wasn't no Diahann Carroll on the cover, it's OJ. She like the brotha I seened earlier, down Nevins, maybe she even livin at that same joint, his neighbor down the hall and whatnot. An she don't stop looking at me, so after a hot minute I'm like, Could I help you? An she reach her li'l hand out, a rough li'l hand, an she put it on my arm for a second an pull it back like she done put a roach on me an bout to run away, an I jump, cause I'on't know what the fuck happenin. I hate when motherfuckers touch me without permission, I *so* had it with folks just doin whatever bad shit they want to my body! An just then I membered how Glitch and Yorkie ironed my foot, an I freaked.

Then she goes, all sweet, "I touched you? I raped you."

You ain't never seened nobody grab a fork faster than what I done right then. I put that fork up to her chin like, "Get the fuck away from me, okay? Thinkin you think you raped me? You don't know what the fuck rape is, okay?"

Then I stepped back, said, "I mean, maybe you do, I'on't know your life, but you sound like you messin with me, an I can't be havin that, even though everybody fuckin with me all the motherfuckin time!" I throwed the fork down an it went *ka-ching-ting* on the floor. A coupla people turnt round an looked, but honestly not that many, cause it be so loud an unruly up in there that couldn't nobody hear nothin an didn't nothin look out the ordinary. Didn't none a the staff even notice. I thanked the great PO in the sky.

Okay, I lost it a li'l bit. But you know, while I do dig freedom more than prison—I ain't crazy or nothin—freedom be some wild shit. I mean, I love me some freedom. I love *my* freedom, but I ain't sure how much I love ev'body *else* freedom, specially not when they could pull shit on strangers like that, not knowin what gon set em off. When you out on your total own, just livin yo life like it's golden, golden, thank you, Jill Scott, an even the folks that apposed to be helpin you could seem like they out to get you, like when yo PO show up unannounced at yo doorstep or some bullshit, make you do a drug test like you seven years old an done wet yo pants?

A brawl broke out around Carlotta and the woman. Customers swiveled around to look or stepped back, trying to figure out what had happened. The waitress watched from behind the counter like a drag ball judge about to whip out a scorecard. Soon everyone had rubbernecked enough and went back, in slow motion, to the business of praying for cheesecakes and slurping soups. The manager announced the early closing time again.

Carlotta hadn't even ordered lunch, but she was done. She snatched the fork off the terrazzo from between someone's boots, put it down on the paper place mat, and pushed her way through the crowd out into the heat Feel like I'm French-kissin the back end of a vacuum out here. She almost shot across Flatbush but had to leap back onto the sidewalk because a white van jumped a light that had been red for two or three seconds. It careened down the avenue, rattling and banging over the broken asphalt like a rhino escaping from the Prospect Park Zoo.

Carlotta had five or six thoughts about where she ought to go and what she ought to do next, and finally the glowing white man on the sign said she could walk across Flatbush. She dodged between the late vehicles blocking the box. Some drivers had tried to turn; some apparently hadn't heard about red lights. A straw-hatted white girl in an SUV did a U-turn in the middle of the intersection.

Satisfying her hunger still ranked at the top of Carlotta's mental to-do list, but as she passed the dark, reflective windows of the Applebee's, she caught sight of herself in her secondhand lilac jacket and skirt, swinging her grandmother's handbag, and cringed, knowing that her look would absolutely need to change before the weekend got under way. Then she wondered if the Applebee's would make a good a place for her special occasion and immediately remembered that she didn't want to celebrate by herself *Where all my homegirls an homeboys at?* Did the high rents just push motherfuckers out to, like, Ronkonkoma? *Who even still alive from the old days?* She decided to keep walking back up DeKalb and maybe find someone to go somewhere with—at home they still had a wall phone—or ask Frona to cash that check, but maybe the banks weren't open. Maybe she could spend some of that sweet petty cash on a bigger homecoming-slash-employment hoedown tonight *I love hoedowns, honey. You can't keep a ho down.*

A monster luxury high-rise, named with an acronym that sounded like they'd ripped off a famous clothing brand, had gone up a block farther on. Carlotta stopped at its base and stared straight up but couldn't quite make out where it ended and the sky started. She lowered her head and peered into the lobby, a doorman affair with sleek finishes and a chandelier that could've been made from frozen champagne. Doom clouds went up over her head; until she saw that fancy light fixture, it hadn't dawned on her that she might not be able to afford a place in her old neighborhood even working for Access-A-Ride *My ass left town right between* Crooklyn *and* Clockers. *Negroes been talkin bout the rent goin up since* She's Gotta Have It *put that colored scene in with the nice park over there in the middle a black-and-white movie, but it din't compute, cause we just lived in that house that we owned and couldn't nobody kick our ass out. We practically housed the whole neighborhood in that bitch.*

An at first it ain't look like gentrificanation cause it was Black folks moving in. But surprise ambush!—*they was* bougie *Black folks! Frona told me they cleaned up Fort Greene and folks started callin that shit Chocolate Chelsea. It's just* Chelsea *Chelsea now*—*damn, I ain't seened so many white folks in one place since I watched a episode a* Hee Haw *on accident (an secretly kinda loved it). An these palefaces lookin damn comfortable too!*

I might gotta stay livin at home longer than I want, just to scrape up all them giant amounts a money I heard they axe for when you movin. That's if I'm lucky, cause before that they put your ass through the wringer, check the livin bejeezus out yo background, an I know when they find out I been up in Ithaca, what I been there for, an how long, that ain't gonna fly, just like the caseworkers done told me. I might have to pay, like, $800 a month for a studio with a bathtub under the kitchen sink an the commode in a closet or some shit like that. I bet Frona be okay with me stayin till I died, but I might lose my damn mind livin in that broom closet. Plus all them motherfuckin relatives!

Oh, shit, so whitey doin yoga at the funeral home now? You know it's over when they doin yoga on top a Black folks' dead bodies in Fort Greene. Bet that damn studio apartment gonna be $1,000! I hardly recanize a goddamn thing on this street. Oh, wait—that drugstore been there since forever ago. So there's one thing still here from way back when. An hold up, this fancy store with all the glass windows—I member when this was a real *shitty* bodega, had all kinda filthy broken linoleum everywhere on the floor. Look like this joint done got a million-dollar makeover from Oprah Winfrey.

As Carlotta turned at the corner of Vanderbilt, the revelation blasted through her mind that the deep thudding bass of the hip-hop that had been jiggling her insides since she'd crossed Clermont was coming from her own family's building Oh, dag! I had no idea my people be doin it up so much on ID4. This wasn't never no big deal for nobody fore I went inside. Wish they'da told my ass. An here I am comin back to celebrate my little freedom an my new job, like I'm the United States of America or some shit, an motherfuckers is all party-hardy with the Bacardi in the backyardy an whatnot.

She didn't find the downstairs gate or door unlocked and didn't think anyone would hear if she rang the doorbell, so she hoisted

Frona's key chain out of the handbag and tried almost all ten keys before she found the downstairs gate key. Then, in the musty vestibule under the stairs, she spotted two partygoers through the thin curtains on the window inside. She didn't want to repeat the key hunt, so she knocked on the door, carefully choosing the place that rattled the windows without damaging them. The windows buzzed to the beat of the song. On the other side of the door, the two had discovered each other's bodies—in the windowpane, a Black hand tugged on a pink bra strap. They ignored her. Carlotta fumbled with the key chain again, playing the same guessing game. This time her luck improved; it took only four tries. When she got the door open, the two lost their balance and almost dropped their beers. They bristled as if Carlotta had deliberately pushed them out of the way.

The woman turned out to be her sister Amber, who immediately lowered her arms, hid her beer behind her hip, and shouted in a low, sweet tone, "We wasn't doing nothing!" like someone had accused her of doing exactly what Carlotta had just witnessed.

Carlotta's attention skimmed Amber and she rolled her eyes, then turned to the scene around her, an even bigger blowout than the day before, framed by the doorway that led into the living room. The television competed with thundering hip-hop, blaring a commercial for something or someone called Lunesta, and then some sportsy music with fake trumpets. A sportscaster who also sounded fake came on some cryptic cable network—Channel 1472?—talking about race-car drivers. The aggressive growl of engines blared below his voice. An ambulance or fire truck rumbled down Vanderbilt, siren wailing at top volume. About twenty men and two or three women, nearly all of them holding beer bottles like Amber's, stood in the silvery glow of the TV, watching what looked like a rerun of a historical Indy 500, or crammed themselves onto one of a couple of ratty couches that no one had bothered to move after Tameeka's performance and the revelry that had helped Carlotta sleep better the night before.

Most of the guests paid no mind to the television, socializing, smoking, cackling, swiping chicken grease all over their phones and talking into them at the same time. A dude suddenly broke out twerking and squatted—it had to have been part of a longer conversation. Laughing people lost their balance. A few of the folding chairs from the day before still lay unfolded on their sides or flat against the parquet floor; someone had tossed the others against a far wall. Beer bottles decorated every surface a beer bottle could possibly sit on. They'd been abandoned on chairs, returned to their cardboard six-packs; they teetered on bookcases and shelves. Carlotta shook her head, thinking about how easily she could get bum-rushed back to Ithaca based on just *one* beer bottle.

She scanned the crowd for anyone familiar, checking out the men at the same time It's some lookers, but ain't none of em my type. Frenzy could dismember any a these dudes with one hand and be brushin his teeth wit the other. She also tried to find Iceman among them, but she didn't spot him. As she scoped right, into the kitchen and out to the backyard, the crowd became more female and food-focused, and dance music overwhelmed the TV. She saw deep aluminum tubs piled with fried chicken, barbecued chicken, potato salad, probably ribs, collard greens, corn bread, and something she couldn't see—okra? At least I ain't spent none a my cash down at fucking Junior's. What I was thinkin? Look like I could get *seven* lunches here for free if I wanna—which I do. This family sure done made friends wit a lotta motherfuckers since Carlotta left the scene. It would help if I recanized any a these folks. Good Lord. What *is* this? It ain't even no Fourth a no July at this point! I hope this gon be fun—natural fun, like, *Whatcha gonna do when you get outta jail? I'm gonna have some fun.* In the kitchen, people ran around in aprons—someone also wore a chef's hat—peeling potatoes into trash bins; somebody else did a funky dance to the beat of "Put Your Body in It," an oven mitt on each hand, squatting and opening the oven door to grab something that looked like a roast turkey too big for the oven.

Carlotta waded through the crowd, showing her own face An giving em angles too, honey, as she slid and tiptoed around the partiers, hoping that someone might recognize her Today gon be different? It ain't seem like it. Unlike yesterday's festivities, dominated by Tameeka's decorations, no banners lined the walls. Out of the corner of her eye, Carlotta saw the piece of paper announcing her return in a garbage can, smeared with pizza grease. Folks appeared to be in that July 4th mood, everybody pumped up to get down with Thing 1 and company Ev'body an his dog up in here an it's only the 3rd? I don't get it.

I got to the kitchen an a course there's Frona, who I recanized from her bent-over butt in front a the oven, reaching in with two mitts to get out some giant goddamn thing look like a hot tabby cat on top a cookie sheet. Ise happy to see her cause she the only person I knew in the whole place that's apposed to be my home (an the only one who could cash my damn check), so I go, "Hey, Gramma, what's all this people up in here for? An what the hell you just took out the oven?"

"Carlotta!" Frona squealed, letting the cookie sheet clang on the range. She hugged Carlotta without taking off the warm oven mitts, and when they didn't burn her, she hugged back. "This a baked Brie right here!" Frona made a show of the hot tabby cat to prove the panache of baked Brie, but with the oven mitts on, the gesture looked odd Like some kinda Black snowwoman? By the counter next to the range, she found a big sharp knife and cut into the phyllo crust Ew, it's bleedin cheese? As they talked, Frona wrestled open a bag of pita chips and spilled them randomly around the baked Brie.

"I didn't tell you this morning? Why didn't I tell you this morning? It's my friend wake!"

"Seriously?" Carlotta moved her eyes from left to right. "It don't look like nobody up in here sad bout nothing."

"I mean, you know, nowadays when somebody pass, they be having a *celebration*. Don't nobody like nobody being sad when they go. They throw you a bon voyage, a homegoing." Frona chuckled. "He loved some baked bries."

Carlotta noticed that even though people didn't have suits on, they mostly wore black. "Who died?"

"Freddy Bingham. You remember Freddy Bingham, don't you, honey? From church?"

Carlotta nodded and frowned to let Frona think she recognized the name. Frona's clarification — "From church" — clarified exactly nothing As if I ever gone to church even once two decades ago! As if I ever known nobody Frona knew from there! "Look like Freddy had a lotta lotta friends," she summed up.

"Actually, this also a early Fourth of July party too, and a birthday party for Althea's li'l girl Soraya."

The names flew past Carlotta. None of them sounded even vaguely familiar. She wondered for a moment if she had accidentally gone home to the wrong place or stumbled onto a movie set where her family was playing a bunch of strangers Reentry! Here come my space capsule out the damn sky! Whitney Houston, we have a problem!

Frona scooped hot cheese out of the dead Brie with a chip and raised it up to Carlotta's lips, blowing on it to cool it down, cupping her left hand underneath in case of falling cheese. "Have some, chile, cause when I move this out to the yard, it's gon be like I chucked a flank steak in a piranha tank!"

Carlotta blew on the hot cheese and bit down. Even the bonelike hardness of the pita chip couldn't diminish the exquisite pleasure of real, outside food. She blocked Frona with her body so that she could get access to a few more pita chips and blobs of cheesy goo Mmm, that cheese blood be kinda good! RIP Freddy!

Since the right moment to say so had not really popped up, she blurted, "I got a job!"

"You what! Right out the box?" Frona hugged her again. She raised her oven-mitted hands up to Carlotta's cheeks and squeezed hard. "You amaze me, you always have," she said. "Even when you was a little boy." She paused and added, in an almost apologetic tone, "And now that you a grown woman too. That's *really* amazing, that a li'l boy could grow up to be such a beautiful woman. But I seen that RuPaul on the TV, and she musta been a li'l Black boy who grew up to be a *white* woman, so I guess anything's possible. Maybe in a couple years you gonna be a Chinese lady! What it is? The job?"

"Grandma, you a trip. I'm gonna drive the Access-A-Ride van."

"That's so wonderful! So you learnt to drive up in Ithaca? Got yourself a license? How you do that? Wasn't you in solitary a lotta that time?"

"No, I didn't learn, but they gave me a job, so..." I can't think a nothing else you could say to finish that. "So it's their fault if I fuck it up"? "So I don't give a shit long as I'm makin money an got a job an can stay on parole good"?

"You gon be doing the dispatch, I bet."

Carlotta felt Frona chipping away at her victory and started to get annoyed. "No," she said, "they hired me to drive the van." She nodded, trying to convince herself. "But I'll do the dispatch if they need that. Hell, I'll do the *dishes*."

Frona grabbed the sides of the cookie sheet, raised it, and turned to deliver the orb out to the picnic table. "Oh!" she said. "I get it. Them people don't hire nobody who know how to drive in the first place, do they? Bet they tryna drum up mo business by runnin folks down. Well, congratulations! Lemme go put this out and then we could raise a glass. And come get me later so I can cash that check for you. I got the cash. Frona don't forget!" She left the kitchen shouting warnings about the heat of the baking tray, pushing out the back door butt-first and clicking the latch open with her elbow.

Freddy Bingham from church. Who the fuck was Freddy Bingham? An wait, no! We can't be raisin no kinda glass! That's right, I'ma have to learn how to drive. Now, how I'm gon do that on a holiday weekend when I don't even got a car to practice wit? Who do I know? Don't feel like I know nobody nowheres no more cept up at Ithaca.

She remembered something Doodle had told her years ago — that it's easier to attend a social gathering when you need things from people. Then you can waltz through the crowd from person to person with your ulterior motive in the back of your mind, figuring out how they could help you but trying not to let on that you have a need until the moment comes and you can say, "Oh! You're driving across the country next week? Can you drop my cat off in Nashville with my cousin? You would love Boodles," or whatever bizarre request. Carlotta used to think this was way shady, but Doodle had a shameless side to her that, along with her avant-garde style and natural sweetness, attracted others like a sedan bursting into flames at an intersection. Where was Doodle now, anyway? Her letters had stopped, but so had all the others Hope she ain't convicted a nothin, that would suck not to be able to hang out wit her. Now, in such a desperate moment, a time, she knew, when she had to step up her game, Doodle's dumb advice started to sound good.

Her appetite jacked by the Brie sample, she sidled over to the buffet in the next room. All the aluminum tins had sheets of plastic stretched tightly over them; a few of the warmer dishes sweated under the plastic hothouses. Though everything about this display said it was off-limits, Carlotta's hunger had gotten so intense that she thought she could just pretend she didn't know they were saving it, even if someone stepped to her and said, *Can't nobody touch this potato salad till we say a prayer for poor dead Freddy Bingham.* She did not give a shit. *She* lived in this place Can't nobody else in this room say that without lyin. I oughta fix myself a plate an sneak it up in that broom-closet bedroom just to keep away from all this goddamn dangerous beer out here. I must be the only bitch in Brooklyn who out here afraid a some fuckin Budweiser.

Once she made sure that nobody was specifically watching her or looking in her direction—she listened for people to get excited about whatever sports game was on TV—she pinched the Saran Wrap between the long nails of her thumb and index finger, peeled it up and away from the fried chicken, and told herself that she could explain by telling whoever asked that they needed to air out the wetness under there and she had volunteered out of the goodness of her heart. She raised a thick paper plate off the stack, put it next to the aluminum pan, and poked into the pile of chicken with a wooden serving spoon.

"You know we're waiting on JoAnne, dontcha?" a very unwelcome but very sexy voice breathed into her ear.

For a second she stone igged the dude, relying on the volume of the game and the music to do the work. But the voice—with a bass tone like a vibrator underneath—repeated the words, and Carlotta had to face the music. She thought about that Erykah Badu song where Erykah wants somebody to breathe on her neck Mmmmm, chile. "JoAnne who?" Carlotta regretted asking.

"Freddy's widow, JoAnne! You don't know JoAnne?"

Whoa. I ain't never seen no man had a voice that fit him so tight. I looked around and I seen everything black. This Black man with black processed hair, wearin a black suit, a black tie, an on top a that got a black eyepatch, maybe a black *velvet* eyepatch, but I couldn't quite tell in the light. Motherfucker look like he just crawled off a malt-liquor billboard. So naturally I'm all *bout that* bout that, despite the perfect man I got up in prison—maybe we could do a arrangement—but Ise disappointed cause he already all confrontational an rude, looking down on me with his voice like I ain't got no couth cause I'm eatin fore JoAnne get here. An I wanna use my feminine wiles or whatever cause I want the mofo to *like* me. Maybe there's some kinda opportunity for me with this very together, upscale brotha. He be like, *Money, money, money an mo' money*.

I switched up to my sweet tone. "Of course, JoAnne! But listen, I ain't eaten no breakfast this morning, so I'm bout as hungry as a street dog in Red Hook."

He cocked his head. "You mean those dogs chowing down on scraps of artisanal lobster from the brunch table outside the Tesla dealership right about now?"

It took Carlotta a couple of squinty thinks to catch his drift. "Oh," she said. "I been away from the city for a while" I gived him some flirty eyes, up an down an up, tryna make him think I been in, like, motherfucking Paris, France, on a modeling job, not in no damn D Block for twenty-one-ish years. "Red Hook is, like, fancy now, something?"

"Parts of it."

"Anyways, I'ma take me just one li'l chicken leg—" My voice went real high. "Knowing what I know bout JoAnne, she would want me to." I had finally put my chicken leg on a spoon but it fell off the side a the plate so I pushed it back up, ladylike as I could "My girl JoAnne always tellin folks to, like, 'Eat, Eat,' right?" I could tell he bout to disagree with what I had just said an did, so before he could say nothin I went, "Do you get to Red Hook a lot? Do you got a car in the city?" I thought Ise pretty slick cause I membered it wasn't no subways down there.

"I do have a car, actually. I live in Queens. Forest Hills."

"Really? Fascinating. Where you park it?" Ise tryna to come up with shit just to keep the motherfucker talkin, so I could keep lookin in that pretty eye, maybe get me that drivin lesson.

"Don't tell nobody, but it's really easy to park your car on the street in the outer boroughs. Some people do it in Manhattan too. You just have to know *when* to move it. In my hood, you've only got to move it once a week, and you move it *overnight*, you don't go sit in it like an idiot for an hour and a half every time they're sweeping the streets."

I can't believe I'm talkin with this man bout alternate-side parkin. This the most boringest conversation I ever had in my life. An who in life could have just one fried chicken leg an that's that? Just for the sake a not lookin bad to the friend of a lady I ain't know who husband I also ain't know who just died. The free world is bullshit. Just joking, I love it! I'm taking my freedom an puttin it in my stroll, y'all!

"And if I have to park at those moments when it's tight, I don't get frustrated, I just try to enjoy the drive, hope I get lucky. And I say my parking prayer. With the help of the Lord, I can find a space in five to ten minutes. It works." He paused and stared into Carlotta's eyes as if his story had actually proven the existence of God.

My fuckin head almost fell off my neck, I hadda try to keep from laughin so hard behind him an Jesus findin a parkin space together. I had to slam the lid down on his boring ass an change the subject. I don't know shit bout religion, I don't really believe in God no more, but I *do* know that God too damn busy to give a single fuck bout you findin a parkin space, motherfucker. No matter how cute you is. "Wow, you a expert at this. What's your name?"

"Paul. The car is a BMW."

Carlotta's eyebrows came alive. "How you could afford such a nice car?" I said it all teasing so he wouldn't get insulted. I thought, *I ain't had a day this lucky since 1993!*

Paul laughed mildly, a blood vessel in his neck throbbing as it pumped blood into his big handsome, boring-but-rich head. "It's not that nice. And I leased it when the auto industry was about to fall off a cliff. I'm a singer. Soul, a little hip-hop, quiet storm. I go by Paulie Famous, but that's not my real last name."

"So what you do for a living, then, Paulie Famous?" Something in his eyes shut off to Carlotta and he gave her a scornful look, but the added meanness boosted the needle on his sexiness into the red zone and she immediately started backtracking. "If you need to, that is. I mean, BMW, beautiful suit, nice hair…is you really famous? I been away so long, I don't know who famous in this country no more. Do people still know who Michael Jackson?" Ise lyin my face off, we had *much* TV all day up in D Block. It was tough, but we all tried to stay up on the trends an the songs.

Paul answered slowly. "Yeah, they do."

"Oh, come on, Ise joking you! I know he been dead years now!" Carlotta swatted Paul on his upper arm—an excitingly solid arm, solid but pliable, like a football. "But who famous now, aside from Beyoncé an Kanye? An Jay-Z. An Oprah. Anybody? Obama? It's like white folks can't get famous no more. They prolly mad behind that!"

He didn't respond to her musical inquiry. "It's a fair question, I guess," he said. "I'm a real estate agent. What about you? Looks like you've been abroad for a while?"

"What you mean, a woman?"

"Huh?"

"Oh! Yeah, I been away, just in another place, another country, doin my thang. I'm like a model" Well, it ain't a *total* lie. I am *like* a model. At least in my mind. "But my mama's ill—you know Paloma who live here, right? So I needed to come back and take care a her."

"Oh, I've known Paloma for years. Since before she—that's kind of you."

"It's *very* me." Carlotta put her hand on her hip and gave Paul a smoky glance. She was glad that stirring up sympathy by name-checking her ill mother had made him forget that she'd assumed singing didn't pay his rent. But she didn't get why anyone would bristle at that. She believed that unless you had a bajillion dollars and your face popped up on billboards and taxis all over New York, you weren't a celebrity. Most noncelebrities—including herself—couldn't afford their lives.

"And what is your name?" Paul asked. "I can't remember Paloma or David or Pam ever telling me about you."

"Oh, I'm nobody," Carlotta muttered, assuming that someone had mentioned that other person she had once been yet hoping that either Paul hadn't clocked her "unconventional gender identity," as her lousy lawyer had described it, or didn't care. "I ain't tryna fool nobody into thinking my ass Nicki Minaj," she'd snapped at them, "I'm just tryna be myself and look pretty, an doin a damn good job if I say so myself. This ain't bout no femme-queen realness or no butch queen up in drags, m'kay? It's called *me*. Mary's just Mary!" She had shaved as closely as possible that morning—face, legs, et cetera—and with all the stuff she'd borrowed from Frona, she'd begun to feel more real than usual Like, the song don't go *You make me feel / Mostly real*. Ithaca hardly allowed my ass a sports bra an never no panties, but them ignant motherfuckers in D Block ain't need much proof a nobody womanhood to get excited. I prolly coulda just *said* Ise a woman an that be all the femininity they need. Some a them girls ain't even need *that* much. Hell, you coulda got some niggas droolin if you just said the word *woman*. Or even, like, *wom*.

" 'I'm Nobody!' " Paul recited. " 'Who are you? / Are you—Nobody—too?' "

I wasn't gon risk coming out to this man as not borned a female if he couldn't handle what's in fronta him. He prolly known this whole time an he into people like myself. Ain't like he done high-tailed it down to Fort Greene Park or nothin, right? As Doodle used to say, the question ain't never "Do you like it Black?" or "Do you like pussy?" The right question always "Do you like *this*?" Doodle be movin her hands down her hips all slow when she said that.

"You could ask Pam if you really wanna know," Carlotta said.

"No, sorry — that's Emily Dickinson."

Dickin' who son? "Wha'? I'on't get it."

"The poet."

"Oh, so you quotin me poetry already an you ain't even showed me your Beamer?" Carlotta held out her hand, fishing for a kiss, but he twisted her fingers sideways and shook them. Carlotta wondered if he had finally clocked her and wanted out. The flirtation hung in the air. Paul seemed stunned for a second, like some far-off thought about something — maybe about whether he had parked his car in a legal parking space, or a realization about Carlotta's status — had suddenly overtaken all of his brain function. He did not reconnect for a long time, almost like Boz II. Carlotta prepared herself for him to flip out or claim that she'd done something to gross him out, some dumb screwup only college-educated sonofabitches who quoted poets in front of people they'd met five minutes before would know. She couldn't decide which would be worse So I threw out one them lines that change the subject without changing the *real* subject. Ise like, "It's so crowded and noisy in here, don't you think? I think. An I *live* here."

Paul nodded, returning to the present moment. "Yeah, I guess they're calling this a wake because there's no way you could fall asleep. You gotta stay a-*wake*."

"Oh, that's funny," Carlotta said without laughing Cause the shit was corny. "Did you find a parking space nearby?" I knew he gon love talkin bout parking an his BMW some more, so I ain't wanna lose that thread.

"It's actually just up the block. Do you want to see it?"

Ise like, "Do I want to see it?" in that voice that mean *Hell to the yes, I wanna see it, nigga!* "I thought you'd never ask. JoAnne probably won't get here for a little while, knowing her" Which I don't.

Carlotta thought of taking Paul's arm but quickly stomped on that idea; his earlier moment of blankness had put her on guard. Instead she locked eyes with him and turned her head toward the door in an elegant arc, encouraging him to turn and push through the crowd. He swiveled his massive shoulders and magically moved everyone out of the way, a wall of protection. Before she followed him to the door, she wormed her hand under the wet plastic on the chicken legs and whipped out a second one. Paul's pace didn't leave her any time to splash Tabasco on it, so she lifted the bottle from the table and stuffed everything into Frona's handbag, hiding close behind Paul's body so he couldn't see her transgression. She doubled her effort to walk right in spite of her mismatched shoes Maybe if he think he gonna fuck me like in the back seat a his car, I could get a driving lesson outta him or some money or something. Maybe I'ma need a hustle on the outside. I bet Frenzy gon be good with me doin what I need to do. Maybe I could even cut him in on the deal. I heard a people done far worse to get by on the outside. With folks that's way uglier than Mr. Paulie Famous here, too.

Once they reached the street, Paul led her fifty yards up the block, where, in the shadow of the gargantuan church, the one he said a friend of his had nicknamed Saint of All Queens, his black BMW coupe gleamed like obsidian, glossier and cleaner than any other vehicle on the block, just on the legal side of the NO PARKING ANYTIME sign. Carlotta wondered if Paul had just come back from the car wash How close do this guy be to Freddy Bingham that he gonna clean up his car for the man's wake? He ain't make it sound like they was besties or nothing.

On the garden floor of the house, the heat had felt human, but outside it felt like inhaling hot coffee. Carlotta couldn't wait to get into Paul's air-conditioned car, to feel the sweat evaporate off her forehead and out of her crotch. Another privilege of freedom—you could get out of a bad situation or a certain room just by walking to a different place This shit's like *magic*! For years I ain't had no right to complain bout no hot an cold temperatures or nothing. I forgot I could feel a way bout what make my ass uncomfortable. An now I could just get on up out the bitch an *leave*! That is crazy! I must be the damn queen a England!

Paul took a black object out of his pocket and pressed a button that made the car flash its lights and beep with a slinky metallic noise and a clunk That some Luke Skywalker shit right there. Carlotta had to keep herself from shouting like an idiot about how futuristic the car and the locks seemed to her. Probably everybody's car sounded like that now; the technology was old hat years ago. Since Paul still had no clue where she'd actually spent her make-believe modeling stint in Paris, Carlotta pretended that nothing strange had happened, even though her brain tingled with excitement like she was the first Black woman astronaut about to board a spaceship Goin to some planet without no type a discrimination an no sexist sonofabitches.

So when I got up to the motherfucker, Paul open his door an swung hisself down into that bucket seat like he Idris Elba playin James Bond. When I crossed round to the passenger side, I ran one my hands over that shiny black hood like Ise dippin my fingers into a gusher a oil that done sprung up in my backyard, singin, *Money money money money, money* like I'm the O'Jays, an Paul went bananas. He lurched out the car sayin NO! at me like Ise some kinda dog bout to take a crap on it.

He like, "The oils! The oils!"

I said, "What damn oils?"

"The oils on your hands will get on the car and damage the paint job!"

I gave him the Eye, like, *I ain't got no oils on my hands.* "My hands not dirty." Even though I know I just grabbed me some fried chicken legs.

"It isn't about dirty or not — everybody's hands have damaging oils on them. I'm sorry, I just don't want anything bad to happen to my baby." He whipped a chamois out of the glove compartment and dashed over to find Carlotta's offending fingerprints, then rubbed like Aladdin alone in his bedroom. When he got done, he made as if to kiss the roof of the car and hopped back in.

Ain't nobody who act like that deserve no car. A car apposed to be a thing you use every day to go places an get it dirty, not a replacement for your kid or your dog or some shit. If he don't want no scratches on his damn baby, he oughta keep it in a garage somewheres, not be drivin it out in motherfuckin filthy-ass Brooklyn. Maybe I shouldn't be tryna get no drivin lesson from Mr. Famous. But then how the fuck I'm apposed to learn how to drive the damn Access-A-Ride Bus fore next week? This like a gift from above — a damn fly gift, too! — an I'ma take it. This here be one them post-prison lessons they told me bout.

A man carrying a clarinet hurried up the street, mumbling to himself, and a police car blazed down DeKalb Avenue, blue and red lights flashing, blasting out a loud bloop like something from a sci-fi movie. Carlotta opened the passenger-side door, bent over, and stuck her head into the car. The car purred alive, and some generic trip-hop track immediately took over the stereo. A computer screen lit up above the AC. The tan leather interior seemed both luxurious and wasteful to Carlotta. Though she thrilled to the glamour of the ride, she bristled when she thought about how much Paul had paid for the power windows and the Bang & Olufsen stereo with razor-sharp hi-hats and thundering bass that practically put you in the recording studio next to Biggie or whoever, all this glossiness when little Black children were starving all over the country An Black sonofabitches I knew personally had died up in prison without havin did nothin but be Black in the wrong place at the wrong time. An why he so lucky, an how do he justify all this bling? She hid her indignance behind smiles and expressions of excitement and amazement—she drew air into puckered lips, she let her mouth hang open, she made a number of high-pitched squeals at a low volume with her lips pressed together. "This quite the ride, Mr. Famous!"

Paul told her what model of BMW it was, 7 Series or something, and described to her the special features of this particular line of cars and the history of Beamers, told her a lot about the diesel engine, and she couldn't hear any of what he said because she didn't care He so handsome, but he so boring! Maybe that's how his rap work, he put you to sleep wit his boringness venom an then *chomp!* She nodded slowly, pretending to appreciate what he called a "custom tortoiseshell steering wheel" Oh, shit. Did a actual tortoise had to die for him to get that? That ain't right.

When he finished his monologue about the history of the car manufacturer, he reached down to the dashboard and Carlotta saw for the first time that it had a manual transmission. She didn't think the Access-A-Ride van would have a manual transmission, and this made her rethink the driving-lesson idea But what the fuck, it gotta be better to learn this way, cause it's easier to drive a automatic, I think. It be like learnin advance math when all you need is, like, 1+1 = 2. I gon be way head a the game! "I need to learn how to drive a stick," Carlotta said dreamily.

"I could teach you. It isn't difficult at all." Paul proceeded to describe in detail the process of driving a manual transmission. From the beginning, Carlotta had no frame of reference for any of the terms he used. "Start out in neutral," he said Yes. The fuck is neutral? Is that the N? "Step on the clutch and put it in first" Step on the what an huh?

Carlotta tried not to move her face so that he would see her accept everything he said as if she had lots of experience driving things I ain't never even driven no donkey. What I'm doin thinkin I'ma know how to drive in less than twenty-four hours? As a job? Dafuq wrong wit me?

Paul put the car in gear and she watched his movements carefully, especially the twisting tendons in his hairy forearm as he pushed the jerky black knob back and forth At least if I ain't gon learn to drive, I could keep thinkin bout that arm.

After whizzing through two green traffic lights, he turned right on Myrtle and grumbled about avoiding downtown traffic. As he drove, he explained every last move and its motivation to Carlotta in real time. "So as the car slows down, you want to downshift the gears. In city driving, you're probably not gonna go above third gear, but when you come off the highway, this will come in very handy" I'm like, I prolly won't be getting on no highway in no Access-A-Ride, but think what you wanna. "I would need to find a hill to show you how to accelerate uphill once you've stopped. People think of that as the hardest thing about driving a stick, but I've never had any trouble doing it."

Carlotta couldn't help but wonder if he was flirting An also I *wanted* him to be flirtin. I wasn't gon tell Frenzy nothin less we gon gang up and take this motherfucker to the cleaners. An I hoped to the Lawd Jesus a Parallel Parking that the boring shit he was sayin meant somethin beyond what he sayin.

They passed the Sumner Houses Where they raped and killed them kids all them years ago, it was scary, Ise a kid then an they ain't caught them motherfuckers for years. Somebody told me one them guys mighta been at Ithaca an I freaked an din't sleep half that night till Ise like, They ain't at no Ithaca. They definitely nailed those motherfuckers into the dungeon at a supermax. Bet they at Southport. Carlotta let her eyes slide away from Paul's teachings and she noticed someone walking ahead on their right. It was a middle-aged woman, somewhat chunky but still lively, with gray streaks in her hair. She wore a color-blocked red and green leather dress and combat boots. The dress came to just above the knee and rose to a couple of straps on either shoulder in the same red and green pattern. It didn't look much like a summer dress. For an instant Carlotta studied the woman's back, and then recognized her bouncy, slightly limping walk Doodle! Izzat motherfuckin Doodle Frazier?

Carlotta fumbled with the power window and twisted her neck as the car passed the woman. A quick look confirmed her hunch Doodle! Oh, snap! I ain't seen that face since, like, Salt-N-Pepa was wearin door-knocker earrings! I hope she ain't no ex-con or alcoholic or nothing, but who gives a fuck. That's my girl! The window had rolled all the way down automatically by itself and the hot breath of the day blew in. Carlotta pushed half her body up out of the window while the car slowly rolled down Myrtle. Paul kept sayin, "Hey!" in staccato breaths. She shouted, loudly enough to scrape her vocal cords, "Deirdre Lynnette Frazier! Hey!"

Doodle spun around as the car passed, and her Who-the-fuck-is-yelling-at-me-from-a-car? expression developed into an Is-that-who-I-think-it-is? squint. Carlotta shouted her name, and in another couple of seconds, Doodle's face blossomed into surprise and joy. She rocked back on her heels, shrieking and hugging herself as if a magician had just whisked her dress off even after the car went farther up the street and she had to chase it.

Carlotta split her attention between shouting ecstatic greetings at Doodle and sticking her head back into the car and yelling at Paul to stop. The four cars behind the Beamer, dangerously close to one another and weaving side to side, declared their desperation to avoid getting caught at the next red light, which had just turned yellow. The Beamer squeaked through the yellow light and Paul tried to pull into a space in front of a fire hydrant but couldn't get all the way out of traffic because someone had blocked part of the space with a shopping cart full of wood beams, blue tarps, a radio, and a few torn, stained comforters. The pile in the cart might've been someone's only possessions Maybe that dude over there with the one giant dreadlock on his head an all the li'l pieces a cracker all over his beard who harassin some other brotha, but can't nobody understand what he want. Maybe that's Alternate-Side Jesus!

Just before Paulie Famous stopped the car, Carlotta leapt out, ignoring his warnings and fearful cries that Carlotta might damage the door I jumped out an grabbed Doodle an we just hugged each other an looked at each other face like, *Damn you old, how you get so old so fast?* but we knew ezzackly how. She had that same face, maybe yanked this way an that round the cheeks, still rockin them finger waves, some new dark dots over her nose and cheeks, but she mostly the same, cause Black don't crack but it do bend some. Doodle, when she calmed down, had the same expression as ever, a glint in her eyeball that said mischief Like she shoulda worn a banner around her like she in a pageant—Miss Chiff. That'd be a blip, Miss Chiff doing the kinda shit Doodle done, like putting dog doo-doo in the purse a somebody she ain't like, pushing some dude who touched her without getting no permission into the Brooklyn Museum fountain with all his clothes on, teachin her pet parrot Malcolm-Jamal to say all kinda dirty shit.

Time had probably mellowed her. You might flounce through your twenties telling off authorities, living on mayonnaise sandwiches, torpedoing all your relationships, and disrespecting everybody, but if you were still cutting up like that in your forties, that meant that you hadn't grown up or that you couldn't put the brakes on your self-harm, to the point where you might put off everyone you knew, every possible relative and ally, and wind up dying poor, despised, and alone. In Carlotta's mind, that was the worst possible fate, but she had already been there—no one had protected her from Dave, no one could have, no one *wanted* to or even expressed the desire to do so. She had never had any money, and she had put up with the kind of scorn that she couldn't even translate to describe to people who had lived their lucky regular lives entirely outside prisons. She had been alone without anything to think about except her self-destructive thoughts for longer than anyone should ever remain alone, period. So why did she suddenly consider dying poor, despised, and alone worse than living that way? Maybe she thought she deserved that fate, but Doodle didn't. It was *her* fate, and she didn't want to cut it loose that easy.

These feelings rushed through her like 3:00 a.m. traffic on the BQE, one after the other, too fast to understand. How weird to see Doodle for the first time in so long and compare her to the image in her mind that had never fallen apart, the image from before August 1993. Who had thickened her neck and cheeks, puffed up the bags below her eyes? What witch had zigzagged her white and gray wand through Doodle's hair? People said you shouldn't waste time, but time sure wasted itself, spurting and gushing all over the place like water out of a fire hydrant nobody could turn off. You could play in the spray for a while, but you would outgrow that kid stuff soon enough. The hydrant would keep going while you watched sadly through the picture window, and eventually it would start to run out and take to drizzling. Then it would go dry. And so would you.

Ise tryin not to worry if we could pick the fuck up like hadn't nothing gone down after bout twenty-one plus years an hardly no kinda contact with my girl. Plus the added fact that if I hadna went to the liquor store to buy her some damn André for her damn birthday I wouldna had to go to Ithaca in the first place. That shit wasn't gon be easy, but like with just bout everything else on that day, I hadda be like Guy Smiley an do more serious make-pretend than I ever hadda do upstate. How y'all call this freedom when can't nobody say the truth that's right in fronta they face? Sometime I gotta shake my head. Lucky for us, though, Miss Doodle checked out Mr. Famous over my shoulder cause he got out the car to try to put me back in it.

"You been home less'n a full day and you already got yourself a rich boyfriend?"

"Oh, stop it, Doodle! This Paulie Famous, he a friend of my moms an Freddy Bingham."

"Really, I knew JoAnne better," Paulie said, "I met Freddy a few times but —"

"Yeah, I heard that Freddy had died," Doodle said. "That's so sad, death, so final —"

"We just met at the wake," Carlotta told her. "He found out that I needed driving lessons so he bout to give me my first one."

"Driving lessons, oh, that's good," Doodle said. "Maybe you can give me a ride up the street as your first assignment. You have hardly changed at all."

I could not let that shit pass, but I ain't want Paul to hear, so I said real quiet an whispery, "What the shit you mean? I ain't did nothing *but* change up in that hellhole. I don't got the same name, don't got the same life — the person I was literally be dead."

"You know what I mean."

I ain't had no fuckin idea what she meant. "Oh, stop it. What kinda flaky-ass soul-essence pomade bullshit you tryna foist off on me here, girl?" I said it laughin but she knew Ise callin her out.

Doodle touched both of Carlotta's forearms, stared into her eyes, and cupped her palms against Carlotta's cheeks. A tender, penetrating smile took over her face. "Something within you remains the same, unchanged, through all these years, and I can feel that."

"Wish *I* knew what the fuck goin on in there, cause, honey, didn't nothin on the *outside* stay the same!" They gawked at each other for a while, memorizing their new faces, until Carlotta remembered the parrot. "How Malcolm-Jamal? He still sitting up on his perch goin, 'Work this pussy, work this pussy'? Did that ever help you out?"

Doodle sighed. "I'm sorry, Malcolm-Jamal has joined the ancestors. And no, I was never going to get him to ask for that on my behalf! You shut up!" They threw their heads back and shrieked.

The precious Beamer still had half its chassis sticking out into the street, so cars passing from behind had to switch into the lane of oncoming traffic. By this time, Paul had turned off the engine and put on the hazard lights. Now he locked the door with the space-age key and squeezed his beefy thighs between the car's bumper and the SUV parked in front of it.

Carlotta, just coming out of the haze of her reunion with Doodle, thought Paul might be fed up with waiting, coming to shove her back into the passenger seat. "Shouldn't we switch sides?" she asked before he could reach her.

Paul frowned. "We're gonna have the whole neighborhood in my car in a minute, aren't we?"

"No, just her. Come on! I has not seened my girl in a dog's age!"

"More like a tortoise age, honey."

"Yes! The tortoise who died so this man could have a steering wheel!"

"Nah, I'm not comfortable with that," Paul said, but soon Carlotta and Doodle, accomplices again, turned up the cajoling to a level he couldn't combat. "Okay, I'll give you the basics," he conceded, "but just for, like, a block. And if you damage my baby, you will meet Jesus."

"Least Jesus could help us find a parkin space."

Paul gave her a serious look, then unlocked and opened the passenger door. Doodle pushed the seat forward and tunneled her way toward the rear, oohing and aahing as she ran her nails above the pristine power-window buttons, the infotainment center with all the plugs and a video monitor, the genuine leather (you could smell it) seats. Even the little red seat-belt fastener held her awe for a couple of seconds.

"It's so white in here!" she kept repeating Though she prolly ruining that with her dirty li'l hands. She behaving uncool in ezzackly the way Ise tryna behave cool.

In her mismatched shoes, Carlotta wobbled in front of the car to steady herself on the hood with an oily hand. She bent forward to peer at the oncoming, swerving traffic. At a break in the stream of motorists, she hurried around to the driver's side and jumped behind the wheel, arriving breathlessly, slamming the door on the seat belt, and opening the door to free the belt. The door swung into the way of a town car whose driver leaned hard on the horn. Carlotta flinched, wrecking her already fragile confidence.

The whole time Ise thinkin bout how much this car musta costed this man, had some lambswool accessories on the front seats an a TV up in front that showed you where in the hell you was all the time, like somebody could watch you an see where you goin. Ise like, Hope I don't wreck this chariot. Why do anybody want shit this chichi? Somebody could drop a bomb on your ass if they know ezzackly where you is. I hope they don't start doin nothin like that up in Ithaca. Take the one itty-bitty slice a freedom you got an smash that shit like a cockroach under a pump, honey.

So when the lesson start, I'm like, Where that key at? Hand me the key! An Paul told me he put it inside his sock. With this Jetsons Beamer, I ain't had to turn no key. He just like, Step on the gas and push that button to do the ignition. I'm like, Is this motherfucking *Star Trek* we doing now? After the third time I got it. Paul already lookin at me out the side a his eyes, like he don't know if he shoulda 'greed to teach me this.

Behind that I just waved my hand in the air an rolled my eyes an said to Doodle, "I do not understand this new-ass modern-cars world in the slightest" Which—maybe that gave away too much, but Ise hopin it din't.

Paul sittin there tryna esplain to me to step on the clutch, which *I* always thought that's a handbag, right? I'm thinkin, what clutch? I don't see no clutch an Why you wanna step on a damn pocketbook? An then I step on the gas an gon release the clutch an that shit threw me too. Doodle seemed to know a little bit bout drivin a stick somehow, which I ain't know how she knew but then again I ain't seened her in bout fifteen years, so she coulda learnt how to be a astronaut an been up an back to Mars a couple times. So she jump in too, tryna esplain to me bout what gear an how much gas an I could not for the life of me get this vehicle goin.

Then I did this move that made the car jerk halfway off its wheels, an it sound like somethin in the motor got caught an start grindin everything down till the cogs an stuff wasn't gon be nothin but talcum powder. Paul almost kinda lost his mind at that point, thinkin I done destroyed his baby-child. He not the most patient drivin instructor, I gotta say, one star. But on the flip side, this car prolly cost more money than I ever seened in my whole life or that most normal people ever gon see less they Richie Rich, live in some giant mansion and they middle name be $. The dollars a this thing prolly coulda filled up the inside a the car an the trunk.

So I finally get it to move forward a li'l bit, an with some beginner luck it go out into the traffic, but real sudden, like a motherfucker fallin out a window—*ka-bum bum!*—and Paul tellin me what to do faster than I could possibly do it an gettin so angry he turnin red-black an every part a his face be wrinkled like he just had got borned. A bunch a times I had to power down the window an wave for motherfuckers to pass the car cause I could not go an I could not hear what nobody sayin. Doodle start pipin up wit her suggestions in a way I membered she used to do when we hung out in high school, or *not* in high school was more like where we was more often, out at Sound Factory or The Tunnel, havin a kiki on the piers, an I done that gear grindin thing again an Paul lose his shit and start shoutin at me.

He windin up like he gon put his hands on me — I'm always on the lookout for that shit, I could tell when motherfuckers bout to get physical. Frona handbag sittin right there on the divider between us, and I membered I had the hot sauce. In one swoop, like I seen folks do wit a shank up in the joint, I stopped the car, whipped that shit out, an pointed the li'l tip of the hot sauce into the man's good eye. I squeezed real hard to spread it *all* round that eyeball like my life depended on it. I got all kinda red sauce in his face and his fancy jacket. I chucked the bottle on the dash, grabbed Grandma's bag with my other hand, jumped on out the car, and booked. That sauce was real kicky too, like strip-the-paint-off-your-wall kicky.

Paul start cursin an shoutin cause it's burnin up his eyeball an he can't see nothin. The whole time I be yellin, "Doodle! Get out the car! Get out the motherfuckin car!" An it took her a second to understand what just happened an unlock the door an git runnin to where we had came from, cause Paul woulda had to turn the car round to chase us or he'da had to leave his precious Beamer behind, which he wasn't gon do in that hood in a million years. I'm pretty sure I left the car in N too, so he had to keep it from rollin into a intersection.

Next, me an Doodle runnin faster'n we know how to run, an Doodle like, "That man's a friend of Freddy Bingham, member." An all outta breath, she said, "He gon come back to the wake, in your house, that you told him you lived in, and he gonna find you, and murder you to death!"

Ise like, "Girl, he don't even know my name."

SiX

They bolted down Marcus Garvey Boulevard fast as Marcus Garvey getting kicked out of America until they'd given Paulie the slip. Carlotta bet they'd run far enough away that Mr. Famous wouldn't get his shit together fast enough to suss out where they'd gone. No way he'd track them if he had to ditch his precious Beamer in the mean streets of Bed-Stuy either. Carlotta's legs wobbled and her lopsided footwear slapped against the pavement. She was breathing heavier than a porn star and her heart felt like a gigantic waterbed with a broken frame. A blister chafed her small toe. She let her grandma's bag swing under her like an udder.

Doodle panted, bent over and worn out as they crossed Gates Avenue against the light. She put her hand on a lamppost and grabbed a garbage can to keep her balance. Carlotta was cracking up the whole time, but now the giggling turned to wheezing. She shut her engines off and leaned against a solid brick wall. A sign five feet above her head read FAMILY DOLLAR, decked out for the holiday in red-white-and-blue-striped plastic banners, but the entrance was around the corner. She wondered how the wall had stayed clean for so long — there wasn't a lick of graffiti anywhere. She hadn't seen a lot of graffiti, period Dag, it be like somebody took a giant eraser to the whole a Brooklyn. Carlotta gave Doodle a long, loving glance. She kept saying, "Oh my God, oh my God, I can't believe we done that."

Doodle pulled back her neck and said, "*I* didn't do nothing! That was all you, sugar!" Like she talkin to the judge.

This the funnest way to reunite with somebody I ever had. Damn, it almost feel like we seventeen years old again an din't none a what happened happen. We even both was able to keep runnin that fast for that long, old as our ass getting. Except — Carlotta had to own it as she listened to the two of them breathe together, and the traffic around them, a noise as uncaring as the Coney Island surf — everything *had* changed. She flashed on the punk style Doodle used to rock: vampy Day-Glo miniskirts, cat's-eye liner, maroon nails with golden decals embedded in them, her left temple shaved. Her once funky-fresh thang had evolved, matured: the skirt just above the knee and still on point, hair pulled back, nails sparkling just a smidgen. Carlotta couldn't swear she knew *this* Doodle. Did people call her something else now? Something less Junior Miss?

The joy of seeing her old friend went poof when she chewed over the fact that Doodle hadn't kept in touch after the first few years. The relationship went on, she reckoned, but maybe only in her mind. Had something similar happened with Ibe too? That man didn't favor the boy she'd dreamed of rejoining in any way. How was she going to convince him to be family with her again? Sometimes, during Carlotta's lowest moments in the SHU, Doodle's presence ramped up, and Carlotta would talk to her directly. She was one of the few friends Carlotta had remained on good terms with in her mind. At night, she would thrash with regret, wondering if she'd done something to cut her friend. Carlotta remembered an embarrassing letter she had sent Doodle, asking in two-inch-high curses why Doodle hadn't written back. The COs probably would've junked it, though cuss words didn't always raise their dander — she remembered when Beezus sent some horny love letters home to his girl, because he had read them to Carlotta in the law library "for grammar reasons" even though she kept telling him to stop. He and his girlfriend were into farting. He wrote some unforgettable smut. When he said, "I love me some hos that be farting when I hit it from behind!" she hated that she couldn't unhear it.

Carlotta and Doodle chuffed and wiped sweat off their foreheads and faces, occasionally trading a howl over what had just happened.

"Where you even get that hot sauce from, girl? Why you had it?"

"Freddy Bingham's wake happening up at Frona's. Ise lucky I could even get that because they had the food all covered in Saran Wrap, getting all steamy and uncrisp. Since when do some Negroes and Latinos wait till somebody get there to start eating? Is that some new thing from the last couple decades?"

"Oh my Lord, Carlotta. Is that really how long it been?"

"Well, if you count from when I been in custody—"

"I can't do no math in my head. Plus I don't wanna do that math." Then, in a joking voice, she asked, "So, whatcha been up to?"

Carlotta shifted against the hot brick wall, legs still bent, hands on her thighs. "Girl, you don't even know the half of it." She thought about chomping on the leftover chicken leg in Frona's handbag and thought again.

Doodle rolled her eyes, almost staring the Lord in the face, and shook her head. "And it's all my fault," she said, sincere now.

It almost offended Carlotta that Doodle, who'd cold igged her for a decade, would think she played such a big part in Carlotta's psyche Cept that she did. I saved your last letter, even though it was a whole buncha times when Ise right about to shove it down in that toilet. But damn, if the toilet paper had something written on it—even, like, a phone directory from 1949—I'da read the hell outta that too.

Carlotta took a breath. "You do not need to blame yourself. All you did was have a birthday party! Wasn't none a the rest a what happened after that none a your fault" Why the fuck I should be consolin *her* ass, please tell me? I mean, maybe she *should* take some blame if she want it. I got a whole Fresh Kills' worth a blame to dump on toppa some motherfuckers. So much of reentering society meant faking apathy and chirping the opposite of what you wanted to yell Wasn't none of these quote-unquote niceties up in the jwant!

"What happened to you all that time you was up there? I ain't heard from you for so long! I had no idea."

Carlotta wondered if Doodle's letters had stopped getting past security or if her own had never left D Block or had gotten conveniently lost I'on't know if she playin me or what, but I guess that's how it go sometime, maybe she coulda sent a letter an I coulda collect-called, but she a cheapskate so no. Ten years a not hearin from yo best friend, though—fuck, I wouldn't put it past no motherfuckin COs to hold a beef that bad. To hear Doodle say this without anyone egging her on reassured Carlotta, but since she had stopped trusting anyone at all, she wasn't betting the rent on Doodle's loyalty. Lockdown had schooled her that old friends could double-cross you at any moment Like when you the most down, they first in line to kick you in the titty. So Ise, like, cuttin my eyes at Doodle and whatnot. But same time, I had a urge to tell her everything, just spill it, like my skeleton done disappeared an I fell down an broke open an Ise just a bag a fuckin guts.

"I swear to God, they could eat you alive up in Ithaca," Carlotta said. "They some vicious sonofabitches. They'd eat they young. It prolly be healthier to eat a person than that food too." She laughed. "That shit was worse than, like—member the chicken patties at School 20 that was so hard we used to play Frisbee and saloogie wit em?"

"Yes! And it made a good puck too!"

"Magine you had to eat that every day. An worse! Best food up there be some Kit Kats and snack cakes from the commissary that motherfuckers be mushin up into a pie. Oh, chile. I spent *years* in the SHU. Literally years. The SHU, that's what they call solitary. Special Housing Unit." Already anxiety shook the space around her. She thought about Dave and suddenly saw that fat pink face, heard that car-horn voice in her ear, and remembered all the horrible things he'd barked at her. She swallowed air to still her throat How mucha this I could even say in words? "Honey, Ise in the SHU so long niggas was calling me Mother Hubbard! I know I'm laughing, but that shit's not funny."

Doodle didn't laugh. She made a face that suggested Carlotta had gone too far or crossed a line, possibly into madness.

The B15 growled up to the corner — they hadn't noticed that the brick wall was also a bus stop. The bus lumbered past the signpost and hissed. The driver pressed a few buttons and a flap moved into position at the front exit to assist a cranky woman in a wheelchair off the bus. The woman yelled at the driver for doing something wrong or rudely, Carlotta couldn't tell which. The bus waddled off — *without* a harsh cloud of soot adding another blast of heat to the heat of the already hot day Where that nasty black fog at? Did the MTA actually fix some shit to make it *better*?

"So what happened up in Ithaca?" Doodle asked. "All this time I was sure you'd get sprung early, for good behavior or something. All my other people — my cousin Isaiah, my aunt Josie — they almost all came back, and they done *much* worse shit than anything I know you done."

"Well, it's typical, I couldn't afford no lawyer, and I got me a lousy public defender — I mean, lousier than usual — what her name, Lucy something, Lucy Goosey, who she had twenty thousand other cases an zero esperience so she convinced my stupid twenty-three-years-old ass to plead guilty steada goin to trial, cause that made it easier for everybody ass cept mines, an the title a this here Lifetime TV miniseries event be *Didn't Nobody Give a Shit What Happened to Carlotta*. Plus I *did* do it, but that ain't the point. Or I didn't *do it* do it, like shootin the lady or whatever, but Ise there, an I couldn't prove I had no good intentions or nothin. So tween the lousy lawyer an the prosecutor who had some kinda thing against me, I got the maximum, honey. An I couldn't stay outta trouble. I hadda defend myself sometime. Other times I couldn't. I just couldn't." The other times crept into her mind and dragged her.

Doodle flattened her mouth and scratched behind her ear. "So, but when you went in, you had a different name and, um, I don't know, you dressed a little differently?"

"Not *that* much! Oh, that happened separate. An let me tell you, that din't help my case in the slightest, girl. But I hadda be me, couldn't be nobody else."

Doodle pursed her lips, licked them, and opened them slightly. "Is you a trans—a transv—transss—help me out here, honey. I don't know all what people like to get called now, or when, so..."

"I guess I don't got no good answers for you on that. I'm just Carlotta. That's all I got. Why people think they need more'n that? I suppose I always been Carlotta from the beginning. I mean, come on, you knew me back when! Was I Carlotta fore I had the name Carlotta or wasn't I?" She flung a hip to one side and planted her hand on it, putting forward the foot with the expensive shoe and wagging her hair slightly to emphasize her point.

"Truth be told, I ain't thought much about it then, but sure, I could see how Carlotta line up more with who you was. And is. But they kept you in the man jail?"

"Oh yes, honey. The man *prison*. An that shit wasn't no W Hotel!"

"Why they had to do that? That seem like it's a extra torture, like something you do when you *tryna* fuck somebody shit up."

Doodle's hand traveled toward Carlotta's cheek and fumbled a caress, her fingernail almost poking Carlotta in the eye. Carlotta moved the hand aside with both of hers, and the touch cleared away any lingering bits of fakeness between them.

"They don't do nothing special for *nobody*. Ain't nobody changin your bedsheets, makin little swans out the towels, puttin li'l Godiva chocolates on your bed like it's your fuckin honeymoon. Ain't nobody no individual up there, you all a number. 95F0202! That was my name. My DIN, department identification number." Carlotta sang "DIN" to the tune of an old radio commercial for a clothing store called VIM that had ripped off "Try Jah Love" by Third World. *"If you spend all year in lockdown—DIN! You will prolly have a breakdown—DIN!* member that jam?"

Doodle smirked and nodded. The sweetness of connecting through that reference sent tingles up Carlotta's thighs. She cackled and pushed herself off the hot brick wall, wiping away the sweat that had crowned her forehead since their flight from Paulie Famous, and then walked backward, beckoning Doodle, who followed automatically, toward a few shade-deficient trees farther down Marcus Garvey.

With her back still to Doodle, Carlotta let a sentence leap out of her mouth as if it had spent all day tunneling up her windpipe. "I got raped more times than I could even count." She said it with all the numbness that had strangled her in the SHU. "Almost every day. That is not a joke. Or a exaggeration. Hell, I wish it was." When she reached the scraggly tree, she turned and leaned against it and narrowed her eyes If you reject my ass behind this, Doodle, then fuck you. This the moment right here.

Doodle shot down Carlotta's glare with tenderness. She raised her arm to touch Carlotta again, without clumsiness, perhaps on the shoulder, but she was standing far enough away that she could only grasp the end of Carlotta's hair. Carlotta recoiled. Doodle raised her own hand to her ear and rubbed behind it like someone with a very specific migraine. Carlotta took a breath and prepared to cut her loose.

Doodle turned to glance at the oncoming traffic. "With me, it only happened once," she whispered.

Inside, Carlotta gasped and held her breath But, like, a course it happened to her too. Why ain't I thought a that? Women in the free world be like I was on the inside, so it's like here I am on the outside, an what gon change?

"But once is already too many times," Doodle said. "You couldn't do nothing? Report it? I know, it ain't that easy. Me, I took too long to get the police involved, because, you know, the police. And plus it was someone I thought I wanted a relationship with, at least until that night."

"When that happen, chile?" Fuckin water drippin out my left eye now like it's a damn therapy session.

"March 22, 2005. After that, I went through some times of — well, of depression after that."

"You? I can't pitcher you depressed!" The image Carlotta had kept in her mind of Doodle through her whole ordeal fell to earth like a killer crane. Maybe Doodle had ghosted her because of her own struggles, not a judgment she'd made on Carlotta I'm startin to axe myself ezzackly who wasn't there for who. I couldn't do nothin bout not bein there, though. Fuck, shit is hard!

"It's been something like ten years since you seen me, I know," Doodle said.

Hold up! Doodle's last letter was dated September something a 2005 — I memorized everything bout it on account a wasn't nothin else to do — an she ain't mention that this had happened. Meanwhile I ain't said nothin in my letters, neither. Damn, this situation tween us like when the A train you ridin on get to the Hoyt-Schermerhorn station right when you see the G train leavin, an you know it ain't gon be no G for another one hundred years.

"That's the damn truth right there," Carlotta said.

Sweat and tears now ran together down both faces We a mess. Suddenly, in a trite revelation, Carlotta saw how many black gum spots riddled the sidewalks, taking them in for the first time all at once. She wondered if there were more stars in the sky than black gum spots on the pavements of Greater New York, or than assault victims. There had to be more stars—space was infinite, and while New York felt vast to a freshly released ex-con, even one who'd grown up here, it would never feel close to infinite. The concrete, stone, and glass of the buildings looked too much like walls rising above your head. Assault victims, though…

She sighed. "They thought I changed to Carlotta so I could get out the men's area, like that big-nose motherfucker on *M*A*S*H*, which crazy cause you *can't* change from man to woman prison areas at Ithaca, they don't give nobody the *choice* to do that!" Without pausing, she switched subjects. "It wasn't always the same person. Doing it. The raping. But there was one who…a lot. One the COs. Prison guards. You get treated like you they personal prisoner…you they personal property…slavery times. An who you gonna go to that they gonna believe it's happenin? You apposed to be able to go to the COs theyselves, but when they the ones rapin you, you can't, it's like at home when shit happened and you din't go to the cops, you couldn't go to the cops, but this like you couldn't go to the cops an *also* the cops is livin in your fuckin *apartment*. Them COs just gonna call you a lyin-ass convict an that gon be that. An you get blamed for it every damn time. I mean, the outrageous shit this man, this white man, said, he couldn't shut his face the whole time, that creeped me out the most, girl. Accusin you a rapin *him*. No lie. While he doin it to you! It's like he had stole your voice an used it gainst you to keep you quiet an humiliate you an shit, like, *Help, rape! Someone help me! Get away from me, you dirty criminal!*"

Carlotta stopped giving Doodle examples, but the monologue continued in her head the way it did in most of her quiet, dark moments. *When they get you for this rape, they will keep you locked up here the rest of your life!*

Doodle grasped Carlotta's shoulders and embraced her, successfully this time. "I can't even," she said defiantly, though the words were muffled by the fabric of Carlotta's prison shirt. "I mean, I *can* imagine, but I don't want to. That shit is beyond disgusting and fucked up. You have to bring this scumbag to justice."

"Truth be told, I'm just glad to not be nowhere near Ithaca no more. I can't worry bout that right now. Mother got to put her life back together. A life she ain't never even had!"

"Honey, pardon me, but I think we both need a drink. Welcome home!" Without a pause, Doodle lunged around her and took a few bouncy steps.

Trailing behind, Carlotta clammed up for half the next block. She closed her eyes and winced a little Damn that PO! The motherfuckers know that the one thing you need more than love after almost twenty-two years in the joint is a drink an they make sure you can't get one less you willing to fuck it all up.

"I know this sweet li'l place just a few blocks up the street," Doodle said. "It's a bar and a liquor store both."

Oh, great! It prolly got a wormhole in it where they could push my ass right through back to prison. They crossed the street and passed the entrance of a fenced-in park, one that Carlotta faintly remembered but couldn't imagine in the past because of its brand-new landscaping, particularly a shiny playground done up in primary colors where little Black girls of various sizes in tight hot-pink and white polyester two-piece outfits careened past one another around brightly colored playgrounds, shrieking in mock terror. Carlotta stopped walking Stupid white people on bikes ridin up on the sidewalk behind my ass. They seemed to revel in the illegality Not even wearin no damn helmets, be makin the rents even more unaffordabler. The wind rattled the trees, and the muted chimes of a steel drum rang out from some unseen corner.

After a few more steps, Doodle turned around, noticed Carlotta lollygagging behind her, and walked back. She moved into Carlotta's personal space and frowned, her hands akimbo, defying her as a joke. "There can't be a good reason *you* don't wanna get a drink—unless you're broke. I can spot you, honey. I'm making it. Relatively."

"Hey, I don't wanna be a party pooper or nothin, but one my stips say I can't be around no alcohol or bars or liquor stores. I don't get it, cause I wasn't never no alcoholic, my cousin just shot up a lady in a liquor store is all. Ain't like I had nothin gainst liquor stores fore I went inside, you know what I'm sayin? It's just one them thangs, you know, they gotta treat you like a baby, like you still in the prison even though you out the prison." She rose a brow to hint that racism had played a part.

"Well, that kinda *is* the idea behind parole," said Doodle with a grin. "Don't worry, I get it. One of my exes got one his stupid-ass carpenter friends to cut off his monitoring bracelet and his PO found out and in *four hours* they had snatched him and throwed his ass on the bus back to Lake Placid. They Olympic-speed-skated him right back into that cell. Parole don't play."

She dug into her bra and pulled out a loose Newport and a tiny yellow plastic lighter to Carlotta's fascination How she do that without it messing up the way her titties look? Must put it under the titty. I gotta learn that trick.

"But I do need *something* to take the edge off." Doodle sighed.

She lit the cigarette and pulled deeply. Without deciding to, they walked into the park together. The warm beauty of effortless togetherness massaged Carlotta everywhere again, sparkling around her scalp.

Doodle made a show of being careful not to ash on the children's heads, capping the gesture with a theatrical grin, and half turned to Carlotta. "Do you smoke now? Whole lotta my people coming back from upstate with a nicotine jones."

"I ain't never really like it, but I don't got no stips round smokin, so maybe I oughta just do whatever shit I don't got no stips for, right? How many cigarettes you could hide in that bra, girl? You gotta teach me that trick."

An empty, sun-dappled bench sat farther inside the park, practically reaching out to them. In their half-trance, Doodle and Carlotta accepted its offer of an exclusive smoking lounge.

"You can't really smoke here," Doodle said, sitting down slowly and crossing her legs. She turned her head away from the distant eyes on the baseball diamond, people who definitely couldn't see her. "Probably won't nobody stop us, but we could get a fine. I'll just finish this quick—wanna drag?"

Carlotta took Doodle's cigarette between two fingers and inhaled, attempting to control the slight cough she let out, trying to avoid seeming like a newbie. "Luckily I got a PO who don't blend in so much. You could see that lady coming for miles. Tough li'l bull dyke."

"Oh, that's good, bull dyke, right? You can't smoke hardly nowhere no more. That's something that's changed a lot since you went inside. I member I used to go to this one club where you didn't even need to bring no smokes if you inhaled deep enough. And if you stood outside and watched them open the door, a whole giant cloud would poof out, like your mama done burnt out the element on the stove and set your dinner on fire."

They listened to the children squealing and the basketball game on the other side of the park, the heat so hot they could almost chew on it. Then, as if Doodle had just asked about Ithaca again, Carlotta's nerve cracked and she spilled the tea. "Then I cried.

Right when I got up there. I couldn't stop cryin. And that shit right there be the kiss a death, honey. Ev'body tellin me I can't be showin no weakness, but it be like my head just fulla tears an I'da had to plug up my nose to keep it all in. So I got took advantage of all the time. Don't you know some a these snide-ass motherfuckers had the nerve to nickname me Crying Game? On top a that, I got a lotta time added on."

Doodle bit her lip but said nothing, then reached out for the Newport, which Carlotta had struggled to enjoy and returned almost eagerly.

"To start with, a AA-and-rob charge carry a mandatory minimum a five years on it, an then add to that a ATM bid — ATM, that's my boo's expression for attempted murder, I'll tell you bout *him* later — Ise lookin at twenty-five to life. Lucy Goosey ain't did jack shit cause she had 365 felonies to deal with (she kept saying, 'I've got one for every day of the year') and 747 misdemeanors (based on that first joke I told her 'You could fly em away in a plane!'), her father be in hospice and she getting a divorce, all a which I hadda hear from her, like I gave a rat's ass. My girl done found herself a white man got *two* outside women, had a family wit one of em. Ise like, 'Honey, that's some next-level shit right there! You sure he not a African brother or some shit, got hisself twenty wives and shit? I know they got white folks in Africa. Three or four.' The bail set at something like what Mama brownstone woulda been worth if she'da ever renovated it an it went to the high bidder. Joe Jr. — Thing 2 — he said we *should* sell the house, bless him, but that li'l Negro was fifteen years old at the time an wasn't nobody gonna sacrifice the whole family home for Carlotta's sorry ass. So I sat up in MDC Brooklyn for a whole year, just waitin. That's round when Lucy convinced me to plead guilty stead a goin to trial, which I got mixed feelings bout to this day, cause I honestly ain't really *did* nothin cept be there when Kaffy robbed Sippy Sip, an when the sentencin finally happened, I found out Lucy did not get me no credit for no time served, so on day one in prison Ise gon be startin from scratch in terms a time. Chile, in jail I ain't cried that much, but soon's I got to Ithaca, it be like the fuckin Washington Square Park fountain up in my eyeballs, like, ksssshhhh!"

Doodle finished the cigarette and crushed it on one of the slats of the bench where someone had carved the name — or the word — CORNY. Cautiously, she picked up the thread. "So you had been serving time already, and what was — how did — "

"How did that *go*? It was the shitty beginning a the shittiest years a my life. I mean, I wrote you bout some a this. It wasn't just shitty cause it was bad, right, it was also shitty cause there was always actual shit as part a the shittiness. I mean, everything up there smell like piss and shit, cause the toilet's just right there in your cell, an ain't nothin else there an nothin to do but pee an shit. Don't but half of em work at any one time, so the shit just be sittin there waitin for a flush that ain't never gonna come, like they keepin your poops in prison too. An you keep flushin even when the damn thing don't work, thinkin that maybe at some point it gon fix itself, you all like, *Flush-flush-flush-flush-flush!* An you know the most famous thing bout prison is that the mens gon rape each other in the ass on a dime, but don't nobody never try to stop that, motherfuckers just consider it part a yo sentence. But the second-most-famous thing nobody talk about is that when you in the SHU, you go *bazack*. You like Bazack *Obama* up in that bitch. It's a thing, like not even just some people, *everybody* go out they fuckin mind at some point, an a lotta people end up chuckin they feces at some-body, not even for no reason, you could just be walkin by the wrong cell. It's like the monkey house up at the Bronx Zoo, girl, cept the monkey house cleaner an smell better, an most the monkeys, right, they tryna keep em *alive*. From the minute you in that place, you gettin a punishment in yo mind an a punishment in yo body. It take some people longer to get to that place a chuckin doo-doo at the COs, but almost everybody do. Even I did.

"Most folks on the outside think that jails and prisons is full a lazy, no-account motherfuckers. Well, that shit might be *partially* true, but put a bunch a so-called lazy, no-account motherfuckers in lockup an they *will* jury-rig the shit outta some homemade appliances an weapons an communications systems that'll blow your damn mind. It's like Nigga Google up in that bitch, honey! It's like ev'body be James Bond on a budget! 'Oh! I see you turnt your house into a vodka-distillery-slash-meth-lab overnight even though you din't pay no attention when you was in science class? Okay. Bottoms up!' It's the damn truth! Jail apposed to be transitional, but some a our asses had a long wait ahead of us anyhow. My cellmate's this brother name Aloysius who up on a weird beef that's, like, robbery an *incest*, like he had embezzled from his workplace and also he held up this female taxi driver who kept a lotta loose bills in her glove compartment, an also they said he havin a relationship with his half sister. But he tryna argue to the court that at the time he thought she's his cousin, an he kept telling any motherfucker who'd listen that in New York State it's legal to fuck your first cousin, to *marry* your first cousin too, that all his people been had told the two a them from when they was young that they's cousins an not halfsies, like they needed to cover up some shit the adults done did in the bygone days. But maybe they gonna dismiss the charge if he could prove that he ain't know?

"Anyways, this dude Al, he real good at all them kinda inventions and whatnot, had somehow turnt the toilet into a radio, I swear. Hot 97 Jams is coming out the bowl; you could see the surface a that water jigglin, like, 'This is how we do it!' So the dumbass COs at this particular jail made this *How to Deal with Prison* handbook, an on the cover it's a photocopy pitcher of a jailhouse key. An, honey, you know most a these detention centers so poor that they ain't updated nothin since 1912, so Al somehow took a chunk out the frame on the bunk bed an filed it down into a key shape that look identical to that key, cause somehow he figured out that the key in the pitcher be the master key for the whole damn jail. I watched him file that bitch down for weeks.

"He knew I had this ovah handbag, a Hermès crossbody shoulder bag — a knockoff from Canal Street, since we bein honest here — an it had a false bottom. Member that one, the pink one? They let me keep that in my house. They ain't know bout the false bottom. They let me keep that shit cause the COs an ev'body so stupid they go ezzackly by what the book say all the time, an it wasn't no rule said you couldn't have no lady handbag in no man jail — I swear, they literally went down the list with they fuckin finger, an when they ain't seen the word *handbag*, they like, 'Okay!' Plus, a crossbody style look a li'l like a military bag for a canteen or something if it ain't pink, so they prolly just unpinked it in they mind and they was good." Carlotta guffawed, wagged her hair, rolled her eyes, and coughed, then wiped her eyes free of laugh tears. "Lockdown logic!

"Al knew bout the false bottom in this Hermès bag — hard to be keeping no secrets in them small cells, your bunkie gonna know all your birthmarks, gon be able to draw the roof a your mouth from memory. Ev'body in the jail made fun a me for havin this bag, cause like I said, it was pink, an men in jail is afraid to touch or be near shit that make you not a man, an when I say *man*, I mean Paul Bunyan, Shaft, an Pablo fuckin Escobar is the only definitions of a man in that motherfucker. That's cause they know that the minute somebody figure out they not Shaft, they gonna get ass-raped harder'n Linda Blair in that movie."

Doodle sat up. "What? Didn't nobody rape Linda Blair in *The Exorcist*!"

"No, no, no, no, honey, the other one, that was on the TV. It was called, um, um—"

"Oh. As if that movie wasn't scary *enough*."

"*Born Innocent*!"

"Oh, right! I member when that came on. Mama said I couldn't stay up to watch that. But I did anyways! I regretted the hell outta that."

"So after Al got done with his key and had tested it out *very quietly* on our door late one night, he axed if he could keep it in my pink Hermès bag, an the one wise statement Thing 1 ever told me in his life was 'If somebody ever ask you to do them a favor and you can do it, you should always do it, cause you never know when you gonna need a favor back.' I mean, not like I couldna learnt that shit from a fairy tale bout a lion an a mouse or whatever, but when your daddy come up with one wise saying out all the complete bull- shit that usually be pukin out his mouth, you gotta pay attention, like, Where the hell did *that* come from? It also made me feel real powerful and sneaky as a motherfucker to have, inside that pink bag ev'body callin me all kinda faggot an bitch for carryin, the key to all a they fuckin freedoms. I coulda let every last one of em out the jail if they hadna been a asshole to me! I started struttin round like I owned the joint, an people could tell something was up, you know? Al seen me coppin a attitude, an he warnin me at night bout this one or that one who had beef with me sayin Ise actin seditty an needed puttin in my place. One a these jokers I called a pig to his face cause I saw him stuffin his whole mouth with dry minute rice from the commissary an tryna talk wit his mouth full, rice bouncin out his face like li'l maggots. He heard me call him that an took on Pig as his whole identity. Whenever he seen me after that, he be gettin up in my face goin, 'Oink-oink.' I'd just roll my eyes or what- ever, it was so tiresome. Then he got the nickname a Pig. I ain't started that, but he blamed me. Then some motherfucker I figured was him stole some rotten old potato, wrinkled, black as hell, and rubbery—like Mrs. Griffin from the colored store! Member her? I figured they had got it out the mess hall and stuck it in my shoulder bag when I wasn't lookin. But the joint be like one them computer games where you don't know what random object you pick up gon be your salvation later, so honestly, I held on to that potato, tryna figure if it could hold the key to my revenge. Like maybe I could poison that pig-ass sonofabitch with it or it could grow some funky mold that could get you high or cure a cold an I could sell the mold off the potato an make me some money. Insanity!

"But I soon figured out that whoever put the potato in had also took the key *out*. Like they's tryna balance the weight back so I wouldn't suspect nothin. To this day I ain't got no idea how they done it, cause I kept that bag with me, next to me, in my house, 99 percent a the time. They musta somehow got in my shit when I wasn't there. Witchcraft, magic tricks. Al an I ain't had no idea if they knew what that key was an what it could do, so we was terrified. I apologized to him so much my tongue almost fell out my head. I guess we shoulda seened it comin, though. We stayed up half the night the next few nights thinkin somebody gonna come in the cell and shank us to death but also tellin ourself that they too stupid to figure it out.

"For four nights, din't nothin happen, an by then we start wonderin if maybe they ain't figured out what the key was. It ain't really look like a key, just a cut-up piece a metal. But the fifth night, the first night we started sleepin at the same time, we got woke up all of a sudden in the middle a the night. At first Ise like, Holy shit, the COs puttin our ass on lockdown at three in the damn morning *again*? Then I open my eyes an it's five a these thug-ass bastards an they jump us. Us meaning me, cause they knew Al coulda had a ray gun up his keister, ev'body knew he had mad weird weapons, so they just held him back an whaled on me. Pig, who real name Booker, he one a the ringleaders a this li'l group. Al tryna get his key back, tryna figure which one of em got it, all the while Jo-Jo

Dancer, Bama, Brother Bear, and Karim attackin me. I struggled for my life, but these was some large-and-in-charge motherfuckers. People who got prison-rape fantasies need to know that *actual* prison rape ain't no kinda fantasy in no way, shape, or form, honey. That's two words don't nobody never want next to each other in they life story: *prison* and *rape*."

"I know I didn't never want to hear neither one in my story," Doodle said, pinching the fabric of her dress on each side of her breasts and agitating it in a vain effort to cool off. "Even if they wasn't put together."

"Oh Lord Yeezus, honey, this was like, you can't walk for the next three days. Like somebody could drive a Mack truck out your ass the next day. Like you just got sacked by the whole New York Giants. Like find out how much blood could come out the human body without killin it. An for what, cause I called a nigger a pig who got the nickname Pig? Please, Ise getting called all type a faggot day and night up in there, like it's my fuckin name, an the minute I call somebody called Pig a pig, it's on. What the fuck. But the physical pain don't hurt that much worse than the fact you can't do nothin bout it when it goin on, an not afterward neither. Never. This the first thing I ever done bout it right here—talk to you."

"What? Didn't nobody hear this going on and try to stop it?"

"Prolly *ev'body* heard! But it wasn't but one guard on at 3 a.m., an they was prolly on a smoke break or some shit, an meanwhile the rest of ev'body just excited that it's something happenin, anything to break up the boredom a the rest a the day, so a gang rape, hell, that's like prime-time TV to them swines. Everybody up in there ready for prime time, ain't a single Not Ready for Prime Time Playa nowhere to be found. If that particular guard had heard, I don't think he'da done nothing nohow—maybe he'da joined in. Cause the next day when I couldn't get out my cell and he come round, he ain't believed that Ise hurt bad as I was, wouldn't take my ass to the infirmary, tried to get me to snitch on the guys that done raped me, tried to make me stand up and walk, meanwhile two of em share a cell close enough to where you could prolly hear what people sayin in Al's an my cell, I can hear em chucklin, an I'm thinkin that's maybe how they knew about the key that be in the pink bag, even though me and Al kept it real quiet the whole time. Some mother-fuckers got bionic ears and whatnot.

"So I couldn't report no bunga-bunga, cause if I ratted these shitheads out, they would shank my heart to a pulp. It's like that joke where the two white explorers got took prisoner by some native peoples they was tryna gentrify out the African jungle or wherever an they gived them a choice a they punishment—said you could choose death or somethin they call bunga-bunga. So the first guy go, 'Bunga-bunga, of course!' acking like he know what it is, like it's just, I'on't know, a chicken curry. But the native peoples gather round and fuck his ass brutal in a gang rape and that's bunga-bunga. So the second dude see that, an I guess he like, *I would rather die than get ass-raped by some Negro savages*, so when they axe him to choose which one, he go, 'Death!' an the native peoples go, 'Death! By bunga-bunga!' An I *guess* they gang-rape his ass to death, but the joke don't go no farther than them sayin that. No, honey, all I could do after *my* bunga-bunga was stuff the whole roll a toilet paper up in my crack an double over on my flattress, thinkin, *At least when your butt look like 9/11 happened up in there, won't nobody be coming back for seconds* that *sloppy!* But these was some horrible pigs an I wasn't gon put nothing past em."

Doodle's eyes widened and watered; she gripped one thigh and slapped the other. "Oh, great goddess!" she muttered, her brace-lets jingling as her hand made contact with her flesh. She shook her head.

"So insteada justice, since I can't say who involved in the bunga-bungaing, the only thing them COs could do for me, like it's some big goddamn favor, is stick my ass in solitary, as if it's *me* who done something wrong on top a the something wrong ev'body think I did to be in the jail in the first place."

"Solitary is hell," Doodle intoned dreamily, looking off into the distance. "They say."

"It's the hell *of* hell is what it is. Like, axe the devil what he mos afraid a, an I bet he gon say goin to solitary in prison. Imagine you stuck inside a closet where you could put your back to one wall and touch the other wall wit your heel. Sometime you got a window if you lucky. You on TV 24-7, but it ain't no fuckin *Sonny & Cher Comedy Hour*, baby. They surveillancin yo ass, and when I say *ass* I do mean *ass*, cause you shittin an pissin an showerin out in the open for all to behold on they li'l monitors. No privacy whatsoever. You don't get no kinda human contact sometime for the whole week cept your own hand on your own body. You be lookin at your hand like, *You again?* Somebody shove a tray a crapola so-called food through your door a average a twice a day cause they do not care if you get your three squares. They'd serve you three teaspoons a pig poop they could get away with it. But the worst part is what happen to your mind when you cooped up like a — I was gonna say bear, but don't they give bears a big-ass open cage at the zoo now? We talkin here more like a parakeet cage or one them weird night animals out the World a Darkness. You member the World a Darkness at the Bronx Zoo, how they be keepin a little monkey thing with some big giant eyes inside a drawer or some shit?"

"I heard bout this crazy mad scientist up in Wisconsin?" Doodle said. "On a documentary on TV the other night? This man was torturing monkeys, puttin em in a li'l black box for, like, weeks on end! These poor monkeys. Real talk — they let white folks do any shit they want and call it science! The Whatever Foundation be like, Did y'all say monkey torture? Count us in! Here go a buncha money, white folks, now go torture us some monkeys and tell us how we can use that shit in the next war against people of color." Doodle looked at an imaginary watch. "Should be starting next week!"

"An you know they just gonna find out the obvious too! Why he hadda use a monkey to prove that shit? I coulda told him he gave me twenty dollars. Sick shit! What'd this guy find out? That solitary make you go bananas?"

"I don't know, the program came on right before I went to bed, so Ise like, 'Nope. Nah, uh-uh, I'ma be having nightmares behind this. Hard pass.' So I cut off the TV."

"Thing was, the whole thing happened right fore they finally sentenced me an sent me to Ithaca, which that's a state prison. But they call all of em 'correctional facilities.' Ain't that somethin? Sound like there gon be a secretary up there in a office got a li'l bottle a Liquid Paper she gonna dab on a typo. Correctional facility. Chile, they ain't correcting no kinda nothin in no upstate prisons, but they sure know how to *incorrect* a motherfucker. So when I got up there, they decided they was gonna keep my queeny ass in the SHU from the very start. But I hardly noticed that that happened, because I somehow got to hold on to this pink shoulder bag that I had, an I felt like it was my only friend or my mother. I couldn't hear none a that other noise.

"So for a while I'm just in this cell twenty-three hours a day, an it's just a tiny bit nicer than the one I had came from—I mean, not nicer but a li'l *bigger,* the paint be a little fresher, the walls is a color, light green, not just concrete, an I got a li'l window that if I stand on the concrete block they call my bed on my tiptoes, I could look through that window an watch a teeny-tiny fuckin stinkweed tree that had took root in the damn air shaft growin day by day.

"This stinkweed tree become like my life, the only thing I liked lookin at in my entire existence. An I knew that if I let on that Ise lookin at it, the COs gon somehow find a way to pull it up by its roots an burn it in front a my face just to destroy my spirit or my will to fight. So I kept it real quiet that Ise lookin at it. So I'm in the new SHU for maybe less than a week when I get a kite — in solitary, folks figured out how to take the threads out a bedsheet and turn it into a string that you could skid gainst the floor with some li'l weight on it so that it go under the door of other people on the ward an you could put a message or some gift a some kind inside a little package. We all did it the minute the COs wasn't walkin up and down the hallways. So I ain't been there but a week, an I am startin to get the feeling like, Oh, shit, solitary already fuckin with my brain, when some dude cross the way send me a kite. At first I'm like, Ooh, my first prison friend! But I open the li'l note an turns out he tryna sell me something he wrote down askin me do I want some m-o-l-l-y. I hadn't heard that term for a drug an Ise like, What do he mean, molly? Molly who? Molly Ringwald? He talkin bout Mexican chocolate sauce? I axed him what it was an he described it an I kinda figured out what he meant. Cause in the wayback, we called that shit GHB. But this the first time I ever heard somebody callin it molly. You know I din't do *that* much drugs fore I went in — contrary to popular belief! — but I knew that that drug did not play: only three things could happen to you you took that crap: 1) absolutely nothing; 2) you got a good high; 3) it flat-out kilt yo ass. That's two outta three possible things I don't never want from no drug I bought. Nothing or dead? Hells no. When I pay good money, motherfuckers gotta guarantee me somethin gonna happen an that it ain't gon be no all-expenses-paid trip to the morgue. But this brother convinced that he a real good salesman an had gived me a free sample — a coupla free samples — but I din't take em. I mean, I took em *from him*, but I din't put em *in me*. He kept axin me did I take it, did I take it, but I blew him off, which could be kinda hard in the SHU cause folks is always just right fuckin there, ain't nobody goin to work or takin no vacations to no goddamn Club Meds. I hid the free molly in the false bottom a my Hermès bag, even though hidin shit in there ain't gone too well for me at the jail. I'm figurin at some point it gon come in handy. The potato still in there too!

"In that whole time I'm tryna get Lucy to put me in GP because I'm startin to have some weird dreams on account a I'm trapped in solitary. I know that general population in the Ithaca Correctional Facility ain't gon be no West Indian Day Parade or nothin, but maybe I'd rather go among the people than lose my *entire* mind? I started havin this dream a lot where Ise tryna get past this six-headed dragon lady, an this other dream where somebody flushed me down the toilet, an at first I'm scared but then Ise like, *Whatever you flush down the toilet gets out the prison!* So it's a happier nightmare. Last night I had a real weird dream bout Crown Heights in '92, I think, maybe the riots? Ise a old Jewish man, and Ise wanderin round the city like a bum, lookin for some dead li'l boy, maybe his kid? I'm like wonderin if Ise apposed to be the father a the kid that got runned over an got the riots started? People throwin rocks at me the whole time, an Ise followin some other kid round, too, a young man, maybe I'm tryna get with him, but he ain't payin me no attention, like I followed him into a whorehouse an everybody in there start changin they gender back an forth, like a vogue ball somethin—"

Doodle cocked her head. "It was a little *Black* boy who got run over, and then somebody stabbed a young Jewish man. I remember that clearly. Gavin Cato was the boy's name. And the Jewish man, was, was—Yankel Rosenbaum!"

"I guess I mixed that up in my mind. If I ever knew none a that. It was a inneresting dream."

"I wonder what woulda happened if it been the other way around, like a Jewish boy got runned over and a young Black man got stabbed?"

They sat silent for a moment. Above them, a plane prepared to make the hairpin turn to land at LaGuardia, dropping low enough for them to see the logo on the stabilizer.

"Prolly the same," Doodle stated flatly.

"So even though I ain't takin this drug, I am hallucinatin—they keep the lights on in there the whole time an you stop knowin when you apposed to be asleep, so everything start to go outta whack. Even with a window, I couldn't hardly tell what time it was. An this sonofa—one the COs start passing by my cell. *Frequently.* I knew he din't like me, but he tryin real hard to pretend he do, sayin shit that make him sound like he wanna help me an be my friend but in a way that ain't had no feelings behind it. Like, I seened plenty a psychopaths on the TV, I know how they ass be actin, tryna manipulate innocent people to come in the woods, bump some lady car, an then while she lookin at the damage you done put on her fender, it's like *bam!* you whack her in the head with the tire iron. Mm-hmm. It's a mess. You could tell a whole lot by the way somebody carry theyself, and I did not like the way this nigger carried hisself. He throwed his body round like it's, I dunno, a kinda scarecrow thing that he movin with a remote control from home, you know? Real stiff, not natural, not a person you wanna see dancin, not a person you could even magine dancin without screwin your face up. He come up to the food slot an put his mouth down there near the food, prolly spittin on it, an axe me stupidness like, *How you doing today?* an actually one time he like, *What are your plans for the day?* like I'ma be like, *This afternoon I shall be taking a stroll through the royal palace gardens.* I'm thinkin, This crumbum *completamente* off his rocker. Him and his li'l pink round piggy face, got lips like a earthworm done curled up and went to sleep on his face, hair like somebody dumped glue on his head an then throwed a bale a hay at him. You could see all blue veins running through his skin, shit look like a map a all the supermax upstate prisons.

"At first Ise thinkin that even though talkin to this man make me feel like somebody had grabbed the bottom a my stomach with both hands an squeezed up my throat, I could prolly figure out how to get something from him, cause it seem like he want something from me, you know. So maybe I could sneak, like, a special privilege, a extra coupla minutes outside, a line into gettin into GP, a job workin in some part a the prison, another helping of that bean sludge they pushed through the door knowin you so desperate for some kinda food and something to do that your sorry ass would eat a pair a shoelaces if they put some damn tomato sauce on that shit. Cause even though you in solitary confinement in a fuckin prison, you still gotta figure out how to get a job and make some money, like you some kinda normal-ass businessman on the outside with a briefcase and a résumé.

"So in actuality we start playin a li'l bit of a game a chicken. He said his name Drexel, an inside I'm like, *What kinda fucking name is that?* But I already knew ev'body call this particular guy Dave, prolly cause they couldn't deal with that name neither. An later I found out that his last name be Gross. I had a lot a fun with that. Gross. I bet he the grossest one in the whole Gross family. His li'l brother, Darren, work at the ICF too, an he pretty gross, but not *that* gross. I tried to play nice with Drexel, like I would pretend to listen to all his philosophies a life, like he thought everything in your house should be organized into fuckin Ziploc bags, that you should wipe everything in your life down with bleach on accounta the toxins an germs gonna choke up your lungs, an I'm like, noddin my head, like, *Yeah, germs sho is dangerous, Dave,* meanwhile the Super Bowl a Disgustingness goin on inside my commode, it be like li'l germs down there in football uniforms goin, Hike!—plus some dude down the hall decide he gon protest how bad the Ithaca Correctional Facility treat him by flushin his toilet so much it flood the whole SHU, an less you sittin on yo bed, you gon have to wade through a inch a shit water an piss water, which Dave had did, an I guess he kept his feet clean an forgot ev'thing bout that when he walkin into the SHU? Did not make no sense whatever.

"Turnt out I been too nice. Dave ain't seem dangerous on accounta he act so weird and soft-spoken, an stupid me got used to that side a him. Usually he been the only CO on the wing, an by and by he start coming on inside my cell. Now I'm so bored and cross-eyed at this point that I put up with it, plus what I'm gon say, an to who? He ugly, but after bein in jail an prison so long, don't no looks matter to me no more. I mean, don't *nothin* matter no more. That's why men who don't be fuckin men be fuckin the fuck outta men up in there, right, cause human contact just human contact at the end a the day, something warm wit a hole that's right there an you could reach out an touch it, like if it was all squirrels with men up in lockdown, it be like, Watch out, li'l squirrel booties!"

Doodle smirked and swatted Carlotta on the arm. "You are still such a trip. Squirrels. Oh my Lord. But it's true."

"The shit happened so fast. He always talkin shit bout a girlfriend an not havin a girlfriend, an I figure he tryna say something to me about maybe I should be his girlfriend, you know how people be suggestin shit like that, hopin you gon get the hint an you gon do all the work. But I ain't paid it no mind, an I ain't had no intentions a payin it no mind, cause I wasn't innerested except as, I dunno, a squirrel buddy, an not even that, right, it be more like Ise starvin in the desert, crawlin around on my belly lookin for shit to eat, and he a cracker. Ha! I mean like a Saltine, even though the sonofabitch *was* a cracker. So I'm in the middle a answerin some dumb question he had axed me bout, I dunno, I think bout ethical somethings, like do I think a motherfucker could be a good person in a bad world, an I'm like, between Brooklyn an jail an prison, I ain't never known nothin *but* no bad worlds, so somebody better show me a good world an maybe I could answer that question an he did some martial-arts move lickety-split an violent as *hell* an suddenly he got my arms behind my back an he pins me an I'm fuckin facedown, half my face on the thin mat I sleep on and the other on the concrete platform the mat sit on, like I could feel the crease goin cross my nose an he starts sayin all kinda craziness, so fucked up I can't even—"

"You don't have to if you don't want to, Carlotta. We can leave it for another day."

"But I gotta get it out, I gotta tell somebody else or else it won'ta happened, cause won't nobody never believe me outside a you, an if I tried to press charges he would say it ain't even happened, an who the authorities gon believe? A white man CO with all the power or a Blatina convict who living as a woman? He gon be like, 'She ain't my type,' an that gon be that! When they say life's a dream, ain't that the shit talkin bout? That you know all a what happened to you, an that it's true, but ev'body else an they dog could come along with they own idea bout who you is, an all they beefs an hates an whatever an say that the shit you know's true ain't the truth an that you a fuckin liar an if it's just you against them, an they got more power than you, even though you tellin the real truth, they gonna get the world to see it like a lie."

"*Ex*-convict. Let's start calling you an *ex*-convict."

"Fine."

"And I know exactly how it feels, dear—in my case, if you know the man well enough to think that you in a relationship with him, have rolled him *many* a time, who gonna believe you when you say that this one time, something went wrong and it was rape? *He* ain't gonna believe you, that's for sure—which happened. And most people you tell not gonna believe you. I did hobble off to Killhull to get a rape kit, just in case he tried to deny it was him. But he tryna say it wasn't no different from the other times and that I consented."

"This what I'm talkin bout, girl. bout how people be twistin reality. It was so fucked up that I couldn't figure it out why he sayin what he sayin, you know? Like maybe he tryna put words in my head. Maybe he mockin my ass, addin insult to injury, you know, like these words just makin fun a what he *think* I might be thinkin an what I'd say. Maybe he think they got a secret recording goin, so if he say them things it gon keep him safe from blame? Or maybe he really *do* believe that he the victim a the rape he doin. That's what I think, cause it's the worst possible explanation for what mighta been goin on in his li'l skull. He tryna excuse hisself by sayin he gettin raped by who he rapin. He like, *I'm the victim, I'm the victim,* meanwhile you hadda be brain-dead you couldn't see he ain't no kinda victim a *nothin!*" Carlotta folded her arms and wagged her head.

Doodle's mouth went slack and she blinked like a cartoon character. "Oh, hell no. You gotta be kidding me! But actually, yeah, I understand how that kind of mentality work with a lot of men, that they think women is actually doing something to *them* that make them do the bad things they do to the women. What the fuck is that, anyways?"

"Fuck if I know."

"How long it go on?"

"The first time was at MDC for a coupla months. Then upstate, Ise in the SHU bout six years total. Not consecutive. But I don't remember all that much of it, to be honest."

"Why?"

"Oh, I forgot to say! Eventually I took the molly! Gurl, I took it *all*. An then some. The only way I could defend myself gainst a steady diet a every day gettin raped an watchin paint peel the rest a the day was to escape reality much as I could. Lucky for me I turnt out to be the kinda person who actually get a good high from molly stead a the kind who get nothin or get dead. I felt like the gods was watchin out for my ass. In fact, I hung out with the gods a lot during that time, gettin me some bottle service up in the VIP room a heaven on the top a they mountain. I had held on to my potato for a long time too. I carved a li'l face into it, like we useta do with a apple in kindergarten—member? Where you'd make a apple into a old-person face an it'd get all wrinkly when the apple dried up. Mr. Potato Face—I ain't need to do that much to the potato to give it a face, cause it already had a li'l groove that look kinda like a mouth, a sad mouth going down like this, so I just added a coupla eyeballs and nostrils with my fingernail. He kinda turnt into a idol or good-luck charm. He looked like Yoda! Sometimes I would take him out an talk to him when it wasn't nobody around, which was most a the damn time, cept people could hear you if you talked too loud, so I'd whisper to him an he'd whisper back to me. And yes—stop lookin at me like that, I know all this shit's totally weird, but Mother was on a *lotta* drugs an yes, she had lost her mind, understand, but at the time, everything made *perfect* sense to me. In fact, some a it still do make sense! He the one who told me I needed to change my name to Carlotta Mercedes an be the lady Ise meant to be. Ise like, What you talkin bout, Mr. Potato Face? But it turnt out he had also heard this same mystery story on the radio I heard when Ise a kid, scared the shit outta me, with Mercedes McCambridge in it, bout a lady who off by herself an all nervous bout somethin all the time, callin up her ex-husband and axin all kinda dumb questions, an it turns out at the end that she really inside a mental institution an the motherfuckers she talkin to is all just in her magination an it's not no real people nowhere. An you bet I felt like that up in that cell that whole time, like a lady who goin nuts and talkin to herself while she makin up all the lives a some the fake people an not wantin to deal at all with the one real person who comin into her cell to assault her and scream that she rapin him. So Mr. Potato Face told me, or I guess he *reminded* me, that the actress full name be Carlotta Mercedes Agnes McCambridge an that I should take that as my name. He's like, 'Be the woman you are.' So I listened to Mr. Potato Face, but I couldn't take that whole name on account a she had it already an still alive out there somewheres, prolly sue the hell outta me if I grabbed her whole name.

"That whole time, though, I kept puttin in requests for them to take me out the SHU an put me in GP, but instead I kept gettin more time in the SHU. I ain't completely certain bout this, but I think Dave had somethin to do with the fact that I spent so long in the SHU, like he messed with the paperwork or told somebody up the chain a command not to be botherin with me or that maybe I had assaulted him. If that's what he actually thought, I guess he felt like he could report me. I *think* that's what it is, cause when I finally got put in GP, they had just hired a new warden, a lieutenant, over Dave, who just a shift commander an ain't really had no real power cept over me an that's prolly why he decided he could do to me what he did—you know, he actually took privileges *away* from me, here I am hopin could I get something out this piece a shit an he actually petitionin to *take away* my time in the exercise yard, *take away* the li'l bag a pretzels they givin me on the daily. He'da prolly tried to take more away from me, but in solitary there ain't that damn much *to* take away, right? Like he could come to my house every night an bang on pots an pans to keep my ass awake, but that's bout as far as he could go. Meanwhile I'm already losin hundreds of sleeps on account a this bastard.

"One time I had held on to a spork, a plastic spork—one that got a buncha holes down the handle so you couldn't make it a shank—an I ain't know what Ise gonna do with a spork, an when they put us on lockdown Dave found my spork in my hidin place—not in the pink bag, but inside the mattress somewhere, an he tellin me that I'm tryna sharpen the end an use it as a shank on him even though you can't even do that with that type a spork. Meanwhile the handle ain't been touched at all, you know a lotta convicts'll melt em or file em or what have you, but it's still a intact spork, so then he's like, 'Oh, you were going to attempt suicide!' An Ise like, 'Fuck you, I'd rather kill *you* than commit suicide,' an he ain't like that comment so he put me on some kinda freaky suicide watch where they tied my ass to the bed, meanwhile I am jonesin for that molly, which I know he knew gon happen, an my supplier cross the corridor kept sendin kites hopin Ise still usin at the same rate, meanwhile I can't even lift my shoulders up off the damn mattress cause a the straps and whatnot. Mercy, mercy." Carlotta wept, but continued to talk through the weeping. "I am so sorry, Doodle, I bet you're like, 'This bitch still outta her mind,' but nobody knows this an if I die tomorrow, the way I figured Ise gonna do the whole time, an sometimes *hoping* Ise gonna, wouldn't nobody know, an it would all disappear, an that means it would keep happenin, cause when people don't know something happenin or that there's a type a person that's out there in the world, they think it don't exist, an it suffers. Honey, it suffers! Let me tell you."

Doodle stroked Carlotta's shoulder. "Well, it's—" she managed. Then, from inside her woven tote bag, her cell phone rang. She had a ringtone that sounded like an old-time desk phone, and the sound startled Carlotta, who thought for a split second that Doodle might have a magical desk phone inside her bag. Doodle fished in the bag and pulled out a dark rectangle, lit from within on one side and still ringing, and Carlotta rolled her eyes at her own gullibility. Doodle slid her thumb across the phone.

"Hello?"

The volume was loud enough that Carlotta could hear a small, tinny voice coming through. "Hello, Connie? Is that you, Connie?"

"No, sir, I think you have the wrong number."

"Ha-ha, you sound a lot like Connie. Are you sure you're not Connie?"

"No, I'm not Connie. Take care!" Doodle placed her thumb on a red dot on the screen and shoved the phone back down into the bag. A few seconds later it began to ring again, and she ignored it. "These white people always tryna tell you bout yourself, like they know anything."

"How you know he white?"

Doodle reared back, retracting her chin into her neck. "I don't know, I just know! He sound like it. Wait. That idiot just tried to tell me that I might not know if I was somebody I know I'm not! *That's* how I know."

"Oh yeah, he did do that!"

"I should've told him Connie was *dead.*"

"That would not have been the nice thing to do."

They laughed uncontrollably for a little while, but suddenly they ran out of gas and glanced around silently. An old Black man rolled a grocery cart past them filled with sparkly red, white, and blue pinwheels and acid-green glow sticks.

"You know somebody got jumped right here in this park a couple years ago," Doodle remarked. "She was, like, the girlfriend of the daughter of a friend of mine. I don't know where it happened."

Carlotta scanned the park. "Just once? This place useta look not this good. It's still dangerous?"

"It ain't like back in the day, but you never know when shit gonna go down, and it still do. Just now the real criminals, like the robber barons, is moving in, not like no small-time drug dealers, this like big-time *white* drug dealers, sumbitches who work for Pfizer."

"I ain't gonna be able to afford a apartment round here, am I? On my own, right?"

Doodle smirked, threw her head back, and laughed. "Oh, chile! You best off staying where you staying. Which I bet is back with Paloma and em, right? For free?"

"In the damn broom closet with the mice and the mold, yeah. An that's a upgrade!"

"Well, you just get a job and save your money. And move to Philly!"

"Oh, snap! I *have* a job! I'ma be driving one them Access-A-Ride buses."

"When did you learn to drive?"

"Just now! You was in the car!" Carlotta howled, throwing her head back and down between her knees and back again. She described her visit to the Access-A-Ride offices and Boz and exploded joyfully at the fact that she was supposed to start work that Monday despite not knowing how to drive and reminded Doodle that her interest in Paulie Famous had stemmed from his offer of a free driving lesson But we saw how that shit turnt out.

Carlotta suggested they go back to the house, where they could get free food and still seem pious. They left the park the way they'd gone in and walked along the Monroe Street side, where the park sported a chain-link fence along the basketball courts, twenty feet high so no basketballs could bounce over it into the street. This side of the park had fewer trees, and the sun blasted their faces for a stretch. Carlotta flattened out her hand and put it up to her forehead for a better view of the courts, where lean, sweaty, dessert-colored men (brownies, Whoopie Pies, and Nutter Butters), their hair an international buffet of texture and length (shiny bald pates, conservative fades, Jackson 5 fros), faked and dodged, their mitts swiping and grabbing, up to block, down to steal. They piled up near her and then ran away, vessels pulsing from calves to biceps, perspiring like pitchers of ice water on picnic tables.

Carlotta stopped, almost like someone about to pray, and scooped at the air for Doodle to join her. "It sure is good to see some free-range brothers after so long in the joint," she said. "Good to be free range myself!" She closed her eyes and angled her head at the searing sun, feeling the shadows of the chain links make a waffle pattern across her skin. With her eyes shut, her field of vision turned into a red wall, and she made a show of rubbing her face like the sunlight was lotion. She raked her fingers through her hair and gave it a shake.

The keening of an ambulance got louder and loomed up from

their right. It crossed on the far side of the park and zipped through the shadows of the leaves, the note it blared falling after it passed, the noise fading.

"Be careful what you wish for with these free-range brothers!" Doodle said. "Some of em be free-ranging it all over town. But I love window-shopping—specially when they got hoops on they mind and it's a giant fence between me an em. You know, I thought Ise gonna disappear at age forty, in fact Ise looking *forward* to disappearing at forty, but it turnt out a lotta these youngbloods got a mommy thang. Who knew? Well, I was shocked and appalled. After the first six. But look at those ones. They look like they need Mama to tuck em in. Aww."

Carlotta opened her eyes and scanned the basketball courts for the group Doodle had pointed out. "Oh my God," she said.

"They nice, but they ain't *that* nice. You must got on your prison goggles."

"No, that's my son."

"Ibe? Really? Which one? Oh! I ain't seen Ibe since he's itty-bitty!"

Carlotta stuck her chin out to indicate a man farther down from the ones she and Doodle had ogled. "He go by Iceman now. Said he don't want nobody calling him no place where people sellin shit secondhand."

"Which one is he? Oh, little Ibe, poor little Ibe."

Carlotta turned to Doodle more dramatically and pointed in front of her, in Iceman's general direction, using her body to block out her finger. Alone, he faced a hoop on the far side of the courts, practicing free throws with the focus of a monk. Most of his shots hit the rim or bounced against the backboard. Only two out of about twenty went in.

"Not tryna insult you or nothing," Doodle eventually piped up, "but he don't look much like your people."

"The brotha really should be playin checkers—it's that bad. He look a lot like Paloma, actually, if you get up close. An he got Jasmine's eyebrow. He play ball like Paloma too."

Doodle squinted and said, "No, you didn't," and then smiled. "But yeah, I could kinda see that." Carelessly, Doodle strolled nearer to Iceman and stopped, squaring up with him from behind the pole and the fence. She didn't catch his eye, though.

"The fuck you doin, girl?" Carlotta rooted herself, pushing the fingers of her left hand through the fence like she might climb it but careful to avoid damaging her nails. "That young man been so important to me, but he don't get it. I gotta leave this alone for a minute, you know what I'm sayin?" She tried to stop Doodle with a series of staccato barks and tell her to get clear of Iceman without making a spectacle of herself I can't even help that, cause anybody lookin at me turn my ass to a spectacle regardless.

Doodle yelled "Iceman!" a couple of times, and for a split second it was 1940 and Doodle became a housewife yelling down at a street vendor from the top floor of a brownstone.

Iceman started at her first call—he had just squatted slightly, the basketball in his palms, about to chuck it into the air, and despite Doodle's position, he didn't immediately figure out where the voice had come from. Stupidly, he looked straight up as the calls continued, as if he'd heard Jesus, then to one side, then over his right shoulder.

Doodle's voice slapped back against a concrete handball wall and a row of brownstones on Madison Street. The wall partially obscured a school that Carlotta remembered as PS 44, and she tried to remember the names of some of the kids she had known who went there Din't Skippy Johnson, who had that German shepherd that bit Marlene Tompkins, din't he go there? That girl needed ten stitches in her face, wasn't never the same. So pretty, too, fore that.

When Doodle called Iceman's name a third or fourth time, he

leaned to one side, around the pole and through the fence, and frowned at her, probably attempting to figure out both how she knew his name and whether he knew her. He palmed the ball—a red, white, and blue one *Maybe he use a special ball on the holidays* and dribbled it from one hand to the other as he ambled over to the fence *He walkin like somebody who tryna look all nonchalant, but he way too—too…chalant. I can tell his li'l ass totally chalant! How on earth am I gonna get through to this boy?*

The two spoke, but Carlotta couldn't quite hear them *Even though Ise tryin my damnedest to catch even part of it over the street noise an the airplane up there an the screechy brakes from the taxis an loud children and whatnot, plus naturally here come Mister Softee down the street blastin that fuckin song like it's in-side your skull cause you done lost your damn mind.* She tried to sing along with the ice cream truck and made a demented face, crossing her eyes, to show how dumb the song was.

The moment she pulled that bizarre expression, Doodle turned and pointed at her *Oh, perfect, like the motherfucker don't already think I be a total nutso bitch.* She assumed they had seen the crazy face, and the need to explain herself stung her in the pride. When she sidled over to them, though, they were talking about some-thing else *Good, it don't seem like neither of em noticed my weird face. But my ass already over here, so now what?* She tried to act natural.

"I just got more pressing problems to deal with, see?" Iceman was telling Doodle. "I'm in the middle of a bad roommate situation, know what I'm saying?"

He grimaced as if he had a stomachache *I know he just copping a attitude all the time an it ain't nothing else. Jasmine spoilt the shit out this li'l Negro. I member he had this stuffed bunny we useta call Mudbone, an you could tell if Mudbone fell out Ibe's bed, cause he'd make this one type a noise like a fire alarm if Mudbone drop out his* li'l arms. He ain't change that much, really. Bet he still sleepin wit Mudbone.

"One my roomies, see, I'm tryna be a good Christian man of God," Iceman said, "and he blaspheming all the time, don't believe in nothing sacred. I need to find a new place, but I'm not even sure where I'm gonna sleep tonight. Also, my roommate asked something bout my father and I told him something and he don't respect it at all, what I told him. Plus he always taking my shit. Done took my whole room!"

Carlotta put her head at an angle, throwing her hair back to uncover one ear. "What you tell him bout yo father?"

Iceman raised his hand, trying to cut Carlotta off, and that steamed her. She stepped closer to the two of them, displaying her nails and pursing her lips. She put her slick fingers through the chain link, deliberately flashing them at his eye level and wiggling them slightly to make her grandmother's nail polish twinkle.

"I told him my father *died*," he spat, meeting Carlotta's defiance with his own.

Aight, fuck you. I mean, I love you. I mean, who raised yo ass to be like this? Carlotta tilted her head in the opposite direction and nodded, steeling herself to seem completely indifferent. "In a way, that's true," she said, smirking I ain't gonna give this boy nothin. Not a thing. She stretched her fingers out and contemplated the polish. "Now, do he know bout me on his own? Behind your back? Cause, not to brag or nothin, but I am definitely good gossip, an my story too, so you can't be pretendin that the knowledge ain't got round to everybody in ten miles of Bed-Stuy. *Everybody*" I said *everybody* real slow cause I knew it gon scare him nough to make his skeleton jump out his body. "Maybe he even know you not bein truthful, son." Iceman didn't say anything, but Carlotta, sure that she had guessed correctly, got off on watching his face shudder while he tried to smother his emotions and snap back with a nasty comment through quivery lips. "I'm a li'l surprised that you not more proud a me, but that's on you."

Doodle poured out the softest version of her voice. "You have to have some sympathy for a man who's been looking for a father his whole life, though," she told Carlotta, making a delicate gesture toward Iceman with her hand. "And then..."

"An then what, he gets *me*? Is that what you bout to say? I hope y'all both know what the difference here between 'a father' an *me,* okay? That's like these motherfuckers who be calling Barack Obama 'a Black man' like he just some nigga sleeping on the damn C train an not a individual motherfucker with accomplishments up to here, covered in gold stars or whatever, done did shit that can't even no white folks do. Now, if what you want is some shit called 'a father,' then either you gonna have to change yo concept of what that mean, or you gonna have to recanize that what you see is what you get, sucka, just like Geraldine useta say." With a flourish, Carlotta slapped her hands down her flanks and shook her hips from side to side.

"So, Iceman, what are you doing for work?" Doodle blurted out.

Carlotta rested her fist on her hip and twisted her lip into a full smirk. She leveled a shady look at both of them He look like his head bout to bust open. Ha! Won that round. Gotta get him more to my side, though, put him back to bein that sweet li'l boy I member, my Beanie Baby, not no righteous wannabe.

"I'm in sales," he managed. "Got a job at this place that do a lot of telephone stuff?"

"Telemarketing?" Doodle said. "You do have a nice speaking voice."

"Thank you, ma'am. Kinda sorta. But I'm working on my rhymes."

"Wait, I thought you was tryna be a good Christian man so hard," Carlotta said. "Is you doing, like, a Christian rap?" She fluttered her hand in a circle, then regretted losing her cool But that be some crazy shit right there.

"You think can't nobody combine rap with faith? You combining a man with a woman or something, I'on't even know, so you ain't got no right to judge. Could I ask you something, straight up?"

"I don't see how I'ma stop you."

"Are you sure you my — my *parent*? I mean, no disrespect, but if you so, so, like you is, how'd you even get it up to have a child wit a woman?"

Doodle made a face like someone standing on the express track of an oncoming Metro-North train. "That *is* disrespect," she muttered at the same time as Carlotta broke out.

"You would really like it not to be true, wouldn't you? I'm sorry, Iceman, but don't nobody get to choose. My son, there is more in this life than you could think of or dream about!" Professor Brown from the law liberry useta say that all the time, told ev'body it was outta Shakespeare. She snapped her fingers in their direction. "Shakespeare said that shit too! I know, here you think I'm a ignant fool an a crook-ass tranny bitch, an it turn out I'm a genius who be quotin Shakespeare. Ain't that a blip? An shouldn't you be thankin Jesus an honorin thy mother an father more cause they the same person? Your ass got borned by immaculate conception, like you was Jesus hisself, an damn if you got no kinda appreciation for it."

Iceman swiveled toward Doodle in an attempt to cut Carlotta out of the conversation. "So you see what I'm dealing with in my life."

Carlotta strode around to Doodle's right side in order to face Iceman. "What *you* dealing with? I love it. Of course it's all bout *you*. My ass been in custody almost twenty-two years an you gotta get out your apartment cause your roomies is ungodly. I din't get to choose who gon be my roommate for the *two decades* Ise at Ithaca, an some a them niggas who my cellies — well, they'da bit *your* skinny ass in half as easy as looking at you. You'd be Fish of the Day, honey, they'd serve your ass on a platter. And I do mean *ass*." She turned to Doodle, her annoyance swelling. "Kids today!" Then she whipped back to Iceman. "I gotta say, if I'da been around to whup your ass when you was growing up, there ain't no way you'd be the insubordinate li'l beast you is today, the spoilt creature Jasmine turnt you into who can't even get a free throw in a damn basket. Let Mama come round there and show you how to shoot some hoops." Carlotta rippled her nails in front of him, pretending to wait for the pass.

Iceman lunged at Carlotta, growling that she had no right to speak his mother's name or judge him, especially not his game — what the fuck did she know about basketball? An it's true, Ise talkin *so* much smack right then. He pounced against the fence, and Carlotta and Doodle reared back a couple of feet.

Iceman leapt at them again, but the chain link bounced him back violently. He picked up his basketball and, still grumbling, launched it at them. He had probably intended to throw it at Carlotta, but it went so far off that she couldn't tell. The ball ricocheted off the fence with a sound like an armful of bracelets. The rebound hit Iceman in the shoulder and landed on his foot. Though obviously injured, he held his body and his emotions and clenched his teeth.

Carlotta and Doodle, thinking that maybe he really could go insane, inched their way down the barrier toward the next street Oh, damn, I can't believe how bad I blew it. Me an my fuckin lock-down temper just put some lighter fluid on his barbecue.

Iceman kept up his tirade, against both of them now, stumbling along and trying to dribble as he followed them down the street. He squeezed himself and the basketball through a gap where the fence ended. He followed the barrier backward, down a ramp, then forward again into the handball court, but by that time Doodle and Carlotta had picked up steam and made it to the corner. Maybe he would give up the chase?

"We not having good luck with men today," Doodle remarked.

"You call that a man?"

Carlotta tried to soften the image of Iceman smashing into the chain-link fence like a crazed pit bull by reminding herself that she had only interacted with him up until the very start of his memory, in 1997, sometime after her second anniversary in Ithaca and her name change, before Ibe's fifth birthday, on October 11. She remembered the last time she had seen him, during Jasmine's only visit upstate, on her way somewhere else, Carlotta figured then, maybe Niagara Falls, possibly with some unnamed person who had not come with her to D Block Prolly some hood thug waitin outside in a Escalade. Not that she'd've gotten jealous, except that she felt only immediate caring family should share the intimate, humiliating moments of a prison visit.

Ibe had a Megatron action figure in his lap and blabbed, in four-year-old-ese, about switching it from a robot to a dinosaur I ain't had no idea what the fuck that meant, I couldn't hardly understand his li'l kiddie voice, but ev'thing he done was so cute. The boy had stared at the Megatron with the same focus the adult version showed to his free throws. Ibe manipulated Megatron's tyrannosaurus head-arm back and forth so that it covered and uncovered the white-man head in the center Ise worried he mentally disabled, but it also seem like the situation just be real intense, so he just had to kick it with Megatron. I ain't pressed the issue. Meanwhile I been transformin my damn self.

He didn't seem too confused that his dad was different and wanted the adults to call him a new name. But Carlotta had limited resources and didn't yet know all the tricks. Her look merely raised the temperature from somewhat androgynous to rather androgynous. Jasmine appeared to take it in stride But I know she was judgin me from how she cut me off an ain't never come back, wit Ibe or without. The one moment when Ibe did look up and address

Carlotta was to say something frank and mean whose words she couldn't remember exactly Not that I would want to part of a longer phrase that got lost in the cruelty, something like *Since you're going to be here for the rest of both of our lives,* not as a question but as a given. He'd said it so casually that it didn't even sting until the next day But that damn sting still stingin right this moment. I know I shouldn't be holdin no shit gainst my own chile, but sometime a kid say some shit that make you wanna be like, *Pow! Right in the kisser!*

They had just crossed Throop Avenue and passed a nondescript grocery store when someone ran up behind them yelling An to me that's when shit gon pop, when I hear motherfuckers runnin. Carlotta jumped between the nearest vehicles, a small white delivery truck and a sedan, grabbing Doodle's arm and pulling her down. I swear I thought somebody bout to start shootin. On the outside, it's like ev'ybody gettin shot by a psycho, even some li'l kids. The hunter turned out to be Iceman, but he had only his basketball He calling me all kinda names out the Bible that I heard many times before but Doodle stood up between us so he couldn't get at me, tellin him to calm the fuck down.

But Iceman's voice couldn't match Doodle's. In the '80s, she was the lead screamer for two of the few Black punk bands in town, Young Freaks Going Wild and Desperate in a Bed and Hollywood Africans. She also knew something about keeping the peace, which must have come in handy outside clubs and in mosh pits back then But did it sound funny as all get-out for her to be yellin shit like, *I know you must be confused and hurt by this situation* louder than my son? Yes, it did. An it worked too. Iceman stashed the basketball under his arm and relaxed his stance. His disbelieving eyes slid from Doodle to Carlotta and back to Doodle.

Doodle lowered her chin and waited. "Y'all got any ideas about how to resolve this?" she asked.

Carlotta took a step backward, trying to take seriously the switch into heartfelt chat while jamming down a smirk.

Iceman wagged his head. "No," he said. "I don't see how that gon happen while this, um, while he, she…under these circumstances." He put a period on his jumbled sentence by bouncing the basketball once on the sidewalk.

"Listen, Iceman," Carlotta began. "It's my first day out. I could see that who I am don't agree wit yo lifestyle or whatever. Now, I'on't member too much from church, but I do think I heard that Christ ain't never judge nobody lest He be judged. You see where I'm comin from?"

"Not really, no."

"Cause din't that brotha be hangin wit all the kinda downtrodden folks an the hookers and whatnot?"

Iceman frowned and twisted his mouth. Doodle lifted her hands and instructed him to listen before reacting. He rolled his eyes but stayed put.

"Anyhow, if you had knew what you meant to me when Ise inside, how thinkin bout comin home an seein you literally kept me alive some days, maybe you wouldn't act so jive. I wrote to you an told you, but yo mama ain't showed you none a my letters. So I got beef with Jasmine around that, that's just how it is."

Doodle went full therapist. "Y'all are gon need to work on building your relationship. Almost from scratch, it sound like."

Iceman laughed. "That's the demon's words. I can't listen to this satanic nonsense."

"Okay, so we're talking!" Doodle chirped.

Without raising her voice, Carlotta blurted out questions as statements. "Are you fucking kidding me. Has you lost your goddamn mind," she said to Iceman, who pretended not to hear.

Doodle tried to disengage. "Y'all gonna have to find harmony at some point. But maybe we've made enough progress for today?"

"We gon leave it there?" Carlotta grabbed her head and cackled. "With my son thinkin I'm Pazuzu out *The Exorcist*?"

Doodle shrugged, addressing them both. "Y'all, this ain't really that bad. I saw way worse when I used to work at the family court downtown."

Iceman and Carlotta traded a skulky look and moved farther apart. Shaking his head, Iceman dribbled his basketball again. He turned away from them and started back toward the park.

Doodle watched him for a while with a confused expression. When he got to the corner, she shouted, "Goodbye!" like a wisecrack.

Iceman raised his eyes, admitting her existence, and then turned away. The light changed and he sauntered over the stripes of the crosswalk.

Carlotta screamed, "I love you!" and ran the other way.

SEVEN

When she caught up to Carlotta, Doodle swatted her on the arm for her sauciness and hipped her to the fact that the B52 stopped a block away, which would put them right by Carlotta's house but quick. Doodle also brought up (and then brushed off) a pain in her ankle, saying that she could walk over no problem It don't never sound convincing when people do like that. It's always like, *I can't use my foot, but it's okay if we walk seven miles* or whatever. What you apposed to do with that information? Be like, *Yeah, let's destroy your entire body knowin yo ass ain't got no health insurance?* Iceman had hoofed it toward Bedford, and Carlotta didn't reckon they would cross his righteous path again, although she suddenly caught herself grooving on her son's bad attitude Shit, he remind me a me! When they got close enough to the bus stop, there sat the bus, its doors swinging shut, the driver inching up to the red light. Carlotta and Doodle flipped out and booked over, windmilling their arms to get the driver's attention, probably giving off nutball vibes.

Fortunately, the driver saw them and had a compassion attack Musta missed a trainin day. An she a woman, an she Black, so maybe all them things, maybe who knows? The doors reopened, the hydraulic system hissed, tilting the rubber floor down. The chilly air inside tickled Carlotta's body hair, reminding her of the number one reason to take the bus in the summer. Doodle dropped her MetroCard into the tower by the driver; the machine spat it back and told her her balance. She moved to the middle of the bus, where there was only one empty seat.

For a while, Carlotta fumbled in her grandmother's bag, searching for her own MetroCard, then stuck it in the wrong way twice, setting off *boop*s of failure that made the driver, without taking her eyes off the road Or showing no human emotion whatsoever recite to her the correct way to slide it in. The bus came to the next stop, and at the same time as Carlotta's eureka moment, a thin ebony lady boarded and stepped in front of her to dunk her card into the machine like somebody dropping a yo-yo Damn, Grandma! Out of the corner of her eye, Carlotta watched Doodle lean forward in her single seat and frown, on the verge of getting up to help. Carlotta frowned back Lemme handle this. Eventually Doodle rose, the grandma took the empty seat, and somehow her friend arrived at Carlotta's side, mouth open to start a gentle lesson at the exact moment the card finally worked.

"I got this," Carlotta said. The card jumped into the space between her fingers. "That's, like, the one thing I *did* learn today."

However, the red LED display declared that Carlotta's card had a zero balance. Doodle reached into her own handbag down to the elbow.

The bus driver rolled her eyes and waved them on. "Don't worry about it." She winced.

With all the seats occupied, Doodle and Carlotta had to stand by themselves in the middle of the bus while it bounced from side to side This like a nightmare where we playin *Laverne & Shirley* crossed with *Sanford and Son,* feelin igged an judged by all these riders. Most of them wore headphones, stared deeply into their cell phones, or both, including the older woman Doodle had given up her seat for, who diddled her fingers over a loud, bright video game full of stars, sparkles, and hearts that fell from the top of the screen, exploding and disappearing What the heck that game? It's so pretty, but I can't figure none a what it's about. It look like a sugar cereal for yo eyes.

Carlotta entertained herself by pretending to look out the window while staring at other passengers' reflections, checking for anyone else who might be looking out the window. None of them were, including someone who wanted to get out at the next stop. Without raising his head from his phone, he pressed a button on a metal column that made a chime go off and lit a red sign at the front of the bus that said STOP REQUESTED It's like I been away so long that motherfuckers all done learnt a different language from me, an every time they get a second to theyself, they start messin round with that phone. Motherfuckers useta *talk* to motherfuckers, now ev'body be a zombie trapped in they own li'l world, watchin some apples blow up on a li'l portable TV.

I guess it keep some stone freaks from gettin up in your grill or playin they ghetto blasters all crunk, but don't nobody think it been nice in the wayback to say, like, hello to Mrs. Jones or Mr. Davis when they's on the way to work? I mean, I *hated* Mrs. Jones *an* Mr. Davis an their damn skank-ass children too, but it just seem crazy that it's all these folks out here with all this freedom to do any goddamn shit they want—like look out there, a whole bunch a construction goin on, there go a cute li'l park wit a whole bunch a benches, it's birds flyin, kids playin, trees everywhere—why y'all don't stop an preciate no trees? If y'all been where I been for them 7974 days, ain't seen a single damn tree cept one li'l stinkweed in solitary, you'd be out there tryna *hump* them motherfuckin trees.

Maybe that's what freedom is, the freedom to waste your fuckin freedom, to not even notice you got it till you wind up behind bars gettin your ass beat an raped by a rapist who cryin rape. Hell, I wonder how free anybody who out here pissin away they freedom anyhow? Gotta work ten jobs an still can't afford no rent, gettin kicked round by the man, gettin kicked round by your own damn man, your family up in ya face tryna tell you how to live your life all the time—Be a woman! Be a man! Wear this! Don't wear that! Watch the same fuckin TV shows I watch, even though I know they suck! Listen to the same bullshit ev'body else listenin to!—else they kick you out your broom closet, POs tryna make your whole life illegal, puttin all kinda stips up in your business, can't go in no bars, can't be round nobody drinkin, can't look at a Miller Lite ad on the motherless TV. Shit, I'ma have to be that person myself, an I ain't ezzackly down for that, but anything aboveground beat the SHU.

"Am I dressed good for a wake?" Doodle interrupted Carlotta's thoughts to ask.

Carlotta looked her over. "Doodle, you look better'n me in my stupid twenty-dollar lilac Phylicia Rashad outfit from 1985. I wouldn't worry bout that too much, honey."

"But is what I got on maybe too festive, too *happy* for a wake?"

"Chile, the way these folks carrying on up at Frona's, you could prolly wear a crotchless bodysuit outta Frederick's a Hollywood an wouldn't nobody bat a eyelash. They'd just turn the music up, honey! You should see it." Carlotta did a brief imitation of one of the guests at the wake doing a lewd dance. A lady in a headwrap glanced up from her phone and went back to her phone.

"Oh, dag, I just called you Doodle! Do anybody even still call you that?"

Doodle's laughter escalated. "Ain't nobody called me that in *decades*! I've been going by Dee from long time," she said with a sudden spasm of Jamaican flavor, though Carlotta knew she didn't have any family from the islands. "But thanks, that really took me back. To, like, Christmas of 1984 with my late auntie Thelma."

Gates Avenue had never had a strong identity Cept for when that lady kilt that girl, burnt her up in that shopping cart, an stole her baby but it had usually felt calm and quiet, mostly residential and tree-lined, with more brownstones and churches than other streets. The road was never wide enough to run buses in both direc- tions even thought it did Lord, it's frightening when the bus gotta pass somebody comin head-on but that hadn't stopped the MTA on Greene Avenue either. The trip down the street must have jogged Doodle's memory, because she described what had happened to a few of the people they knew in common who had gone on to world- wide fame and success or infamy and death.

Doodle didn't remember the baby-stealing/murder case Maybe she tryna dodge the subject altogether but when they passed St. James she mentioned that she had met Biggie a few times through mutual friends. She pointed down the block and tried to see which apartment he'd lived in, but it was too far down I met him too once, an Jay-Z an Busta Rhymes, they was all at the same school, but I did not vibe with them, they was some foolish (an also *ugly*) teen bros — back when bros was Black — always runnin round tryna impress each other wit how down they was, battlin in the streets. If they was out on Quincy doing they thang in the caveman days, I'd maybe stop an listen for a li'l bit, but Miss Thing ain't never wanna hear too mucha that nigga faggot bitch talk they throwin in there. I wasn't gon try to talk em out of it neither, cause that woulda brought too much attention to my own ass, plus the groove was ovah, so I just stood in the back an did some li'l hand claps an then went on my way to the Key Food or the CTown or wherever Ise goin. Now, if Jigga been with Bey back then, I'da paid *her* some attention. Dag, it's like I done missed the whole history a hip-hop that done growed up out my own backyard while Ise gone. Biggie got dead almost soon's I got up to Ithaca. Whatever. Who give a fuck when you got your own stars, when you got your own damn universe? Willi Ninja, Frankie Knuckles, RuPaul, Kevin Aviance. André Leon Talley, Alvin Ailey. Girlina. Mona Foot. Honey Dijon. Crystal LaBeija, Pepper LaBeija, and all the legendary children of all the legendary houses. St. Laurent. Milan. Xtravaganza. At this point prolly more of em's dead than them gangsta rap brothas too. An where the memorial paintings a they faces on the side a the damn bodegas? You know? But fuck it, I ain't tryna do no death-off.

Doodle pointed out the homes of everybody who died and how. A lot got shot. She counted on her fingers. "Member Dante from over there on Classon? Shot dead, 1996? Also Germina Wilson, Fay Richards, Illmatic Joe, Darnell Carmichael, and Eric-Lamar Montaine, who I think he got stabbed. Was that 2007? I think so because I was married then. Henrietta Guzmán, Henny, they think was poisoned by that dude, but they can't prove it and he moved out of state somewhere. Buncha people passed from AIDS—Lou Morris, George Dunbar…Norbert Sutherland. And Scottanya McCord, she OD'd. A bunch of people OD'd. LaMonte Youngman, Bussy Watson—did you know Mona Fitzgerald?—and, um, Gordon Williams. member how good he used to sing? He got into the music business with the rest of them guys and got into the drugs pretty bad, useta see him hobbling up and down DeKalb looking like the devil's chew toy. Sin and a shame. But he made an album that I think I still got on a cassette somewheres. God, we old. When Ise a kid, I used to make fun of all them old ladies and the men at the beauty shop who was always talkin bout who died, and I thought that it's cause they was old, but it turnt out a bunch of em wasn't too much older than I am now. And a hell of a lotta folks done died, too, come to think about it. Sad."

"What do you mean, you was married? I ain't heard about that!"

"Oh, I married this Nigerian cat name Ndulue Danjuma, a

musician, a real good sax player, so he could get a green card. I think Ise wife number four or something, he was always talking some yang about all the wives he already had, I never met em so I didn't know to take it serious or not. Plus he had the cash and he paid. And we got divorced at the time when we said we was gon get divorced; he kept his word. Weird about women, but mostly decent. He made some records with a French label a while back. They was good! I'll play you one when you come over. Ndu used to joke about sleeping with me, but I was all about the scratch. I mean, I thought about it for about two seconds and was like, Nah. I have to say, it wasn't a love match or nothing, but a lotta real marriages don't even go that good or last that long."

"They say sham marriages be the best marriages going."

"Well, everything was pretty much up-front. Usually it's people who using love as a excuse for all kinda bad choices and bad behavior. It made my mother real happy, like she been pretending all that time that she okay with me being single. He was Black enough for her too. We had a joke in my family that there was this one dude Mama wanted me to date named Izzy Black, cause the minute she heard Ise dating anybody, the first question out her mouth was always 'Izzy Black?'"

A masculine computer voice that sounded like it had a head cold suddenly said, "Please move away from the doors! You are standing too close to the doors!" But Doodle and Carlotta didn't move, so he kept saying it every few minutes and it made Carlotta laugh every time, which set off a chain reaction with Doodle.

Carlotta whispered that she wanted to hear him say it a hundred times. "He sound like he fly. An he got a job! Plus I could prolly marry him now, after last week."

"You're thinking about marriage now, that's interesting," Doodle said.

"I guess I still believe in love." Carlotta sighed. "An I mean love as a general thang, like friend love an home pride, not just who you sleepin wit but, like, yo family an all. I wasn't kiddin bout Ibe—I mean Iceman—when I said 'I love you.' I knew he wasn't gon like hearin it right then. But maybe it's like, I still love the li'l boy Ibe, an now I'm tryna Bogart him into lovin me back, but he different, an it don't jibe wit his Christianity values. Could be it work the other way round, too, like he loved the guy me fore I went inside, an now he can't assept Carlotta me." She batted her eyelashes. "Who he think is the devil. I bet I gotta lotta that kinda shit comin right up wit him, don't I?"

"We shall see," Doodle said.

The bus hit a bumpy patch and jostled them. Carlotta took the awkward pause that followed as a chance to tell Doodle every-thing about Frenzy, at whose name Doodle raised an eyebrow but listened calmly and nodded. Carlotta hadn't finished describing all of his wonderful qualities when they reached the bus stop closest to Frona's house, and on the short walk down Vanderbilt, past Bishop Loughlin, distinguished by its jogging track ("Biggie went there!" Doodle blurted out), and Saint of All Queens, she felt she didn't have to stop herself from gushing, that Doodle, even if she disapproved, could humor her enough that her love poked through like the sun through the clouds after a thundershower. It seemed to her at that moment that they would always remain friends, and though she knew that might not work out, Carlotta wanted to hold on to the feeling; it had the gloss of an uninterrupted, harmonious friendship. Love indeed.

Yet again, music blasted from down the street This time I know where it coming from, an I could feel it through the damn sidewalk it's so loud. I'm rollin my eyes so hard I could see my own brain.

Doodle screwed up her face, turned to Carlotta, and said, "Really?" A woman's voice kept repeating a word Carlotta couldn't quite recognize. "This that Rihanna jam, ain't it?" She sang along with it for a moment. "*Cake, cake, cake, cake, cake, cake*...it's 'Birthday Cake'!"

"So?"

"I thought this apposed to be a *wake.*"

"Frona's joint has turnt into Party Central an I can't esplain it to save my life. My grandma eighty-six years old, my mama got some real late stage a dementia and could only say one word, No — honey, you know this don't make no kinda sense, walking round here so intense? Is this a four-story disco I come back to or a nursing home? What the actual fuck? Cause if they gon party like it's 1999 all the time, I can't be stayin here not one more minute with all my damn stips. It's like I get home an it's wilder shit goin on in here than upstate!" She thought of asking Doodle if she could stay with her, but she figured she should wait for Doodle to make the offer And not enter the competition for World's Tackiest Ho.

I know you wanna bite this, Rihanna sang.

As they got closer to the house, their conversation had to stop because the music drowned them out. Carlotta unlatched the gate to the entrance under the stairs. The music paused for a couple of seconds and then the song started again. *Come and put your name on it,* Rihanna cooed.

A pair of people, probably a couple, entered the gate behind them. They had on black clothing that could've passed for mourning attire if it hadn't been velvet, like the man's suit, and didn't have shiny spaghetti straps and sequins all over it, like the woman's dress. In his right hand the man, in a bowler hat that matched his velvet suit, carried a bottle of Freixenet overhand by the neck, like he might use it as a weapon; the woman, in a black pillbox hat and fishnet veil, cradled a bouquet of white lilies in green crepe paper and plastic wrap It's like they dressed perfect for a partywake!

"Excuse me!" the man yelled at Carlotta over Rihanna. "This Frona Chambers joint? You goin' to the party?"

"Party? You mean Freddy Bingham *wake*?"

"Um, well, yes?"

Them two din't give a shit who partywake they was goin to, they just wanted to get in there no matter what. Prolly din't even know nobody in my family or Freddy Bingham's people neither.

The man cocked his head at Carlotta. "I mean, you know Freddy! Freddy didn't want nobody sad at his funeral. He was on a construction job downtown, one of these new high-rises going up on Flatbush, and you know the brother couldn't get loose without his juice — so he lost his balance and his life."

"Damn shame!" the woman shouted. "We loved him!"

Carlotta opened the gate under the stairs to let the two pass just as a group of black-clad partygoers exited, a few twirling cigarettes between their fingers, others gripping apple-shaped bottles of Red Stripe. One lady tiptoed out pinching a glass of white wine by the stem. Heavy cigarette smoke choked up the space; anyone who left the party stirred it up, but it stayed thick, almost like a curtain. Carlotta and Doodle shared a puzzled look, shrugged, and stepped into the ruckus Whoops, done broke *that* stip again.

Motherfuckers was dancin. An not no polite dancin, not no hokey-pokey, not even the hustle or nothin, it's a whole roomful a people with sweat flyin off they bodies to that cake song (that AC — way too small to deal wit the magnitude a funk), sweat cascadin off them like they was Sugar Ray Robinson an just got punched in the face in a close-up on TV, ev'body jumpin so hard you thought they's gonna break that wood floor and fall direckly into Hades. It was funky, an I mean in the old sense a *smelly*, there be this heavy locker-room stench, like a onion salad, almost stunk like D Block.

Every booty in the room had least one crotch humpin up on it. Skirts was up legs, legs was hangin off other people pelvis, panties was flappin round like flags up at Rockefeller Center, shirts was unbuttoned, white shirts was so wet you could see nipples — mens and womenses—shoes was off, bra straps was down, bras was un-hooked, drinks was spillin everywheres, people up on some chairs shakin they biggie-size badonkadonks in yo face like Bertha Butt had did her goodie an done gived birth to twenty more Butt Sisters. Wasn't nobody gainst the wall neither—you had two choices: you hadda be dancin up in there or you hadda be out the room. People was dancin in the hallways, on the sofas. I seen this girl with a behind like two hippity-hops stuck together standin on the windowsill wit her back to the crowd, shakin her groove thang like she goin to the lectric chair at midnight. I'm like, Freddy Bingham sure knowed a lotta inneresting people.

Doodle and me started kinda shimmy-shakin just so we could vibe with the crowd while we tryna make our way cross the room to where the food useta was. I'm wonderin if it's any a them wings still over there, but I can't see that far over on account a how thick the humanity be. They had turnt out the lights an pulled down the shades even though it's the middle a the afternoon. They was some *serious* party people, like I hadn't seen since long before I went inside. Even though I useta roll this same way in the yesteryears, the whole scene got me feelin all kinda claustrophobic, or just sweaty-buttophobic, till Ise tremblin a li'l bit.

The bass of the song vibrated in Carlotta's chest, rattling her like it did the window frames and unidentified knickknacks some-where between the living room and the kitchen. She went back to the buffet where she'd met Paulie Famous and found it annihilated. Doodle squeezed through the crowd and arrived at her friend's side. Carlotta smirked, thinking that while she was out there telling her story about living in the SHU, a crowd of bodacious partiers had pigged out on the whole foodscape. It looked like Crown Heights after the West Indian Day Parade.

When Carlotta took a red plastic plate in her right hand and the clawlike serving spoon in her left and scooped the leavings, she noticed a long brown hair lying across everything. Carlotta heard a guttural "Ew" from over her right shoulder, where Doodle had grabbed a blue plastic plate and stood waiting to partake of the slim pickings. "That's asgusting." Asgusting? Carlotta thought of explaining to Doodle what asgusting *really* looked like. A water bug flattened under a mystery meat burger, still twitching on the bottom half of a wet pinkish hamburger bun — *that* was asgusting. Et cetera, et cetera. Finding a human hair in the food would've improved the cuisine of D Block Hell, we'da called that a *seasoning*. But she decided not to explain I'on't need to be tellin ev'body out here what the prison experience like. They don't need to know, cause what if they start actin like I'm tellin em cause I got useta it? They gon think I still *want* hair in my food. She banged the serving claw against the side of the tin to release smaller and smaller blobs of potato salad and wiped it off on a nearby napkin.

So in the middle a all this noise an dancin an whatnot, I'm like, Where my moms at? I mean, the whole *building* can't be full a motherfuckers partyin they ass off, can it? An she ain't even enough in her right mind to be shakin her body down to the ground and singin bout cake cake cake wit all of em, much as she useta be bout that. I'm scared for her safety. I'ma take Doodle on a li'l voyage once we get what we can get out the buffet. Doodle over there holdin a dry chicken leg by her fingertips to keep from gettin messy but she like, "I'll go."

Turnt out the party was all on the first level an in the garden, an just like yesterday, soon's you get to the staircase it's dark as a sewer an quiet there. We come up out the garden level on them stairs — all the stairs in Frona's joint be creaky wooden stairs that was prolly the originals in the house an the house got built in 18-something-something, so the boots a like, Grover von Stuyvesant or whoever been up and down them stairs so many times that they worn off most the steps part an made walkin in that hall feel almost like you ridin the Cyclone back when that shit useta shake back and forth like the whole thing gon bust apart into a pile a timber, which din't that *actually* happen to the Thunderbolt? Specially once you get to the big staircase with the thick-ass banister that musta been original to the house cause you could see that almost all the paint had worn off it, an some a the steps was trick steps, meaning the whole top a the step gon flip up if you step on it the wrong way an maybe you gon lose your balance an trip an tumble down the stairs backwards an die sorta like Freddy.

I ain't seen Paloma nowhere on them first two levels, so I figure they keepin her up on the high levels out the way a all the party people. So we gone all the way up. Doodle mouth be droppin on account a she ain't been in this house for long as I been up at Ithaca, so it's crazy to her how much has changed slash how ain't nothin changed since the last time she been in the house. I shown her the broom closet at the end a the hallway an she ain't react too much to that, though Ise hopin she at least gon say somethin bout how tough it gotta be for me to live in a place like that an can I come live with her for a while an hopefully she don't be drinkin alcohol all the damn time like my folks.

Even on the fourth floor, we could kinda still hear *cake, cake, cake, cake* thumpin downstairs an all the voices an noises a the party, but the volume be way down. It sound like Rihanna be singin in a jar. One door down the hall had fresh paint on it, din't look like it belong in the same damn house, so Doodle an I look at each other like, That must be where they keepin her. Though if I'da thought bout it for a second, I shoulda listened for Pam instead, cause she be the one makin the most noise if she up there. But we ain't heard nothin. I knocked on the door with my knuckle sorta soft an then sorta loud, then I tried the doorknob, which still the real old type that look like a big diamond an it's gettin loose in the socket or whatever, an it stuck a li'l bit but then it squeaked an the door opened all slow like in a horror movie, an who be in there in the almost total dark but Thing 2.

He look like the same Joe Jr. as before, cept he bout four times the size. He look like a giant ball a clay wit a head on top. A couple empty pizza boxes and upside-down Chinese food cartons be layin on the bedspread. He got a joystick in his hand like I ain't never seen before, you gotta hold it with both hands an use your thumbs to work that mother, an it hook up to one them big-screen TVs that's stuck to the wall an almost flat, like if somebody squished a TV from when Ise a kid. That's where the weird kinda blue light in the room comin from. For a hot second, I feel like the whole brownstone be a spaceship that's bout to take off cause Joe controllin the interstellar voyage wit that high-tech keyboard.

Doodle an me opened the door all slow and polite, but Joe ain't looked up from the screen for nothin, his thumbs goin so crazy like he typin the Declaration a Independence. Some cartoony music goin *doot-doot,* an beeps and bells goin *boing-boing,* an then I—hold the fuck on, I recanize that song! That's the fuckin Mario Brothers song! How the fuck that could be what he playin? I had junior-high friends who was playin that shit, like, all the time, stead a doin they classwork. Like you could test em on math an they wouldn't know shit, but test em on Mario Brothers an they get 100 on the test an next year they the teacher. Dag, has this child been playin the same damn video game since 1993? It look ezzackly the same, like I had just traveled back in time. Wasn't them Mario Brothers apposed to be from Brooklyn?

Joe's eyes focused on the game, though he maintained a cowlike expression, his face emotionless, his mouth partially open. He didn't react, unless you could call concentrating on the little stereotype in overalls while he leapt across the screen a reaction.

"Super Mario? That's old-school," Doodle observed.

For a while all three of them didn't move, spellbound by the struggle of the plumber, which was really Joe's battle to keep the little character alive, the most basic human struggle transposed into pixels.

Finally, between levels, without looking away, after Carlotta had forgotten what Doodle had said, he growled, "No, it ain't! This bitch just came out this year. Gramma got it for me." He looked right for a second and then focused on the game again, as if slamming a door shut.

"I useta be good at this one." Carlotta sighed.

"I remember you was obsessed with it," said Doodle. "You gave all them turtles individual names."

"The turtles? Bullshit you did," Joe snapped. "Don't nobody care bout no damn turtles." He stuck out his chin at the screen as Mario kicked away a terrapin adversary. "You was out your mind you did that."

No more out my mind than what you doin, sittin on yo gigantic behind in the dark for the rest a yo natural life wit Mario an Luigi while ev'body else downstairs livin la vida loca. "Why you ain't downstairs at Freddy Bingham's wake party?" Carlotta asked.

"I don't never leave my kingdom."

Right then I clocked a funny smell in the room, like old sweaty dirty underwear and food garbage and whatnot. Somethin eggy under all of it. I had smelt it when I came on in the room, but I assepted it at first—it wasn't no worse than nothin I ever smelt in Ithaca, so the stench took a li'l while to get up my nose an start messin up my brain. Also, the depressingness of how Joe livin start to dawn on me, that it's like even though he free as a street dog, he had *chose* to sit up here all the time an not go out nowhere. The smell disgustin me an my brother startin to get me angry an maybe a li'l jealous that he could be in here puttin hisself in solitary while I'm out there tryna keep myself *outta* solitary an failin to get the fuck outta Ithaca fore I die. This dude ain't give half a fuck if he saw the sun again.

"Seriously, Joe? Kingdom?" I start wonderin where he shit an I member this the master suite, but it ain't been my parents' bedroom since 1989, when they split up, an it looked much different then.

"It's too rough out there. I tried it, but it ain't work out." He shook his head as he achieved another level. Points soared. His avatar kicked turtles into the void, shot at squids, and grabbed spinning gold coins and mushrooms, sliding down flagpoles and scuttling into castle after castle, unable to rescue the princess, whose true whereabouts remained a mystery.

Yes, something about the game and the way that Joe had dedicated himself to it had the flavor of spirituality, like he had created his own monastery where supplicants worshipped their god 24-7 through the constant search for the unattainable and pointless. Building skill at this game could not have any real-world applications; there was no chance of going pro, not even a money-making online tournament, let alone a championship. Joe didn't play against anyone. He devoted all of his time to sitting in the dark, communing with himself, avoiding the world.

"How you gon let this be your whole life?" Carlotta asked.

"You talkin like that's a *bad* thing. This my happy place, yo. Out there, it's like, I don't know, like, you look like me, don't nobody wanna give you no job, don't nobody wanna fuck you, can't afford no education or no doctors, the po-po ack like they Dr. Livingston and you a elephant, gonna shoot the fuck out your Black ass and pose for a pitcher with your head up over they fireplace, make a rug out yo skin…"

A long pause slowly filled the room, like water in a bathtub, as Joe advanced four or five levels into the game. On a couple of previous levels, he had run out of lives and had to start over. Such an avid player should've had a better game, since he played without stopping—maybe Carlotta and Doodle had screwed things up for him. It seemed like they could leave the room quietly, disappear, and igg Joe till death and it wouldn't bother him The aliens gon find his skeleton right there in five million years, watch. His hand gon be petrified to the joystick, an they gon be like, Yo, the fuck was wrong wit the human race?

Carlotta started to see Joe's game of Super Mario differently, the virtual deaths preventing a real one in the street, as if the true point of life was to rush through an endless loop of workplace accidents, probably without union backing, advancing to levels that seemed to change more than they actually did, trying to block out the monotony of that canned jingle. Joe started whistling through his teeth along with the jingle just as Carlotta thought to snap at him for making his free life into a prison. On top of feeling offended, she hated when people whistled through their teeth. Their father whistled through his teeth absentmindedly all the time Shit useta drive me crazy—it still do, no matter who doin it.

"I think Carlotta's just trying to say that it —"

"I get it, Dee—I mean I don't *get it* get it, but I get it. Y'all breakin my concentration talking all that nonsense. I just had enough of all that shit out there. Sorry to bust up the reunion, but..."

Carlotta felt as if there was more of a wake taking place in Joe Jr.'s room than downstairs I guess he got his way a dealin with shit. Or not dealin with shit. Wasn't we looking for my moms anyhow? "Joe, you know where moms at?" Gettin stuck in Joe Jr.'s Super Mario Habitrail for the rest a eternity don't fit in my plans. I got other plans for eternity. Don't know what they is, outsidea not that. But it's a start, ain't it?

"She ain't downstairs partying?"

Doodle pulled her neck backward.

"Joe, you know she ain't, you tryna be funny," Carlotta snapped.

"I ain't tryin. I *am* funny."

"Looks ain't everything, motherfucker. Where Mom at?"

"Dustin, she in a damn wheelchair, and we don't got no elevator up in here! Where you think she at? It ain't real hard to find Moms, she can't go nowheres less Pam pick her up with them body-builder arms and drag her upstairs. Don't nobody gotta axe nobody, specially not me!"

"Carlotta! It's *Carlotta*. You call me out my name again, you gonna get a shoe print in that face, Jabba the Gut."

Carlotta and Doodle used the tirade as an excuse to leave. When Doodle opened the door, a bright block of light burst into the murk.

Joe winced and shrank from the glow like a vampire in a coffin. "Man, fuck you! Fuck y'all, fuck ev'body. And shut the goddamn door!" he yelled without looking up from the game.

"Hope you enjoying the Walter Hudson lifestyle, Joe! Someday they gonna have to cut the wall open to get you outta here and bury your ass in a piano!"

"Suck my dick, you fat-shaming tranny crook!"

"I wouldn't touch that shit if I could find it," Carlotta muttered out of Joe's earshot as she shut the door, lacking the energy to continue the snap fight. But then sadness overtook her outrage.

Doodle shrugged. "Family," she said without any particular inflection.

"Ladies and gentlemen, my brother, Joseph Chambers Jr.," Carlotta said, rolling her eyes and indicating the doorway with a flourish.

She then turned back to the hall, slightly snow-blind, groping here and there for the walls to get a bead on her surroundings.

The shaft of light that cranked Joe up so much spilled through the Plexiglas bubble capping a square opening that allowed roof access. An iron ladder led up to it, challenging any hardy climber, who would then have to remove the bubble somehow when they got to the top of the ladder Is it some kinda screws up there? I'm gettin queasy just thinkin bout stickin my head up in that motherfucker. All the dust motes floating through the stairway put Carlotta in mind of a chapel, and she hardly paid any attention to the rubbery faces of shock Doodle had started making, silently expressing her amazement and horror at Joe's dedication to Super Mario, junk food, and his bed. Their eyes met, and just as Carlotta relaxed her shoulders, she heard Pam's laughter from the floor below during a break from the cake song I mean who the hell else that could be in this house, fillin up the whole space with that Jamaican voice? Sound like Geoffrey Holder in them 7Up commercials: "Noca-feen. Nevah had it, nevah will, ah-ah-ah-ah!" She tiptoed down to the next level, with Doodle close behind, still trying to scratch out her confrontation with Joe. The hot air in the stairwell stifled Carlotta enough to make her cough.

"He useta go out a lot back in the day, didn't he?" Doodle mused. "He was kind of a, like, athletic dude? Used to be good at hoops, right? Am I remembering that wrong?"

"I believe he had a football *scholarship*. Member William 'the Refrigerator' Perry? He coulda been Joe 'the Deep Freeze' Chambers. No joke."

Doodle slapped the banister lightly and shook her head.

"People change," Carlotta said, and then regretted it, like she'd blasted a sour note on a saxophone. She paused midstep and swiveled to face Doodle. "I sure as hell don't got no right to judge nobody for changin. Or maybe I just got more me, grew into myself? But I guess stupid me's always thinkin people oughta be changin for the *better*. Even when Ise in lockdown, even that whole time Ise in the SHU, I'm like, okay, one day shit's gon get better, one day. I ain't said that shit *every* day, but if I ain't had at least part a that kinda attitude, I'da just kilt myself like the first fuckin week. An my brother out here in the free world, holed up inside with Mario?

Yeah, it ain't the best for no Black mens out there—he should try life as a woman—but maybe he could save some money an go someplace easier. If that's a thing."

"You think he's depressed cause of what's going on with you guys' mom?" Doodle wondered aloud.

"No," Carlotta snapped.

"Are you?"

"Chile, I got so much to be depressed bout that I can't even get started. An I got a million things to do fore I could start feelin shit. I don't got the luxury a havin no feelings. *Feelings. Whoa, whoa, whoa, feelings.*"

Carlotta swiveled back around and continued down the staircase until the two of them entered the upstairs kitchen, an eat-in with decades of clutter and dust everywhere, even clogging the designs in the tin ceiling Joe Sr. musta let Pam use the upstairs to keep Moms out the way a all that cake nonsense, that's why we couldn't find her. Paloma sat at the far end in her wheelchair while Pam cooked what looked like fish in an inch-deep pool of hot oil and spices as smoke billowed up into the brown '70s range hood. Letters, newspapers, and magazines obscured the old plastic folding table that the Chambers half always used as a kitchen table. Carlotta remembered sitting in that same location before she went to Ithaca, though at least once a week back then, Frona or Paloma would bitch about the table still being there and pledge to buy a new one, followed by the more fundamental dirge "But with what money?" Then silence, then laziness It seem like the motto round here always been *If it's broke, don't fix it!* The fireplace ain't never worked an now it's full a yellow *New York Times*es and *Daily News*es that I don't know who ever read—David, maybe? The only way a fire gon happen is if somebody drop a cigarette in there on accident. I member that dusty glass vase wit the plastic lilies in it, I can't believe ain't nobody moved it since I been gone. So that's many years a grime. Like Mama's Colombian friend useta say, *Que gonorrea.* I member that blown-out lectric socket in the corner—din't nobody do nothin bout that? Don't nobody do nothin up in here cept Frona, an she don't seem to want nothin changin behind her back, not even that wrinkled-up blue calendar, which is—what? A kitten wit a fireman hat on? What the hell year that shit from, 1985?

Carlotta and Doodle noticed the calendar at the same moment, locked eyes, and looked at it again with much bigger eyes.

"Oh my God," Carlotta whispered. "It say October 1998" What is this, the Chambers Museum a Dust?

Carlotta swiveled her glance back to Pam and Paloma, neither of whom had sensed their presence yet. Paloma sat facing the two of them with hollow eyes. She had cocked her head to the left, her eyes focused somewhere that was nowhere. When Carlotta followed her gaze, it seemed to land on a broken cabinet just beyond Pam's head. But she realized that her mother's absent look reflected the emptiness of her mind, that very little went on in her head anymore, maybe only the word *no*. Sometime *no* is all you need, Pam had said. The root of identity. Could be English or Spanish. Everything else had slipped out. And gone where?

Pam didn't turn around. With great difficulty, she held a cell phone to her ear with her shoulder. It seemed like she couldn't hear any of the sounds around her: the sizzle of the fish in the pan, the trumpetlike news voices and urgent music of 1010 WINS blasting from a small radio on the counter, or the loud white noise of the fan she had probably turned on to capture the garlicky smoke whooshing up from the stovetop. The smoke mostly missed the intake, and the room filled with a scorchy stench that had its pleasant side, even though Carlotta also thought it could choke them to death. The open window between the counter and the kitchen table provided some relief, framing Paloma like an album-cover photo just as the afternoon sun began its extended-mix summer fade. Pam still had her nurse outfit on, and her butt quaked with every cooking movement she made, but she didn't turn around. Somehow she could hold a cell phone against her neck, cook, and talk at the same time.

Doodle and Carlotta traded a few more bemused looks. After a while, Pam turned off her phone, looked at it, and slipped it into her pocket. But she still didn't notice that Carlotta and Doodle had entered the room. It seemed as if this impasse might go on for the rest of the night unless somebody said something. Something loud.

"Hey! Mama!" Carlotta shouted, loud enough for Pam to hear, trying to sound upbeat but losing the tender feeling that had inspired her to talk. She regretted piping up until she realized that her plan had worked.

Paloma raised her head, a little sloppily and sideways-ish, but the noise could've been anything — a door slamming, an explosion, a fork falling to the floor, her long-lost daughter's greeting. For a moment Carlotta thought of Mrs. Green and her daughter and felt ashamed that she had ever disrespected them.

The greeting had alerted Pam without startling her. She shuffled around, scraping the spatula under the fish in the pan as she turned to face the visitors. The second she saw Carlotta, she perked up, pulled the spatula out of the pan, let it clatter on top of a ceramic spoon holder, opened her eyes wide, and clapped her hands before stretching her arms out for a hug and squealing. "Is Carlotta! De prodigal dawtah! An who dis, ya frien?" She leapt at Carlotta and yanked her into a bear hug, nearly smothering Carlotta's face with her big chest. Carlotta saw it coming and turned her head sideways so that she could still make eye contact with Doodle. Doodle covered her mouth, possibly to keep Pam from seeing her laugh When it come down to it, I ain't want nobody touchin me, not even nobody goin in for no hugs. I reckon I had just too much motherfuckin bad touch up in Ithaca, so to me all touching, I had a problem with it. I mean, she cool and everything, but that just don't seem to me like shit that a lady who got on a nurse cap should be doin with the people she, I guess, workin for.

Carlotta thrust out her hand to avoid the hug but then gave in and melted a little. The second she started enjoying the embrace, Pam switched gears and gave up, wiping her hands down the seams of her pants. Pam drew out a warm, close-mouthed smile, but maybe there was a blob of amusement on top Maybe to her I be the entertainment for the evening, like I'm a drag queen bout to lip-synch the blues for her ass. Doodle waved to Pam from behind Carlotta and then pulled back one of the ratty kitchen chairs. She probed its cushion before planting herself, moved aside a dark brown drinking glass, and leaned across a place mat Maybe Doodle thinking this gon be a entertainment show too.

Even with her paranoia in the red, Carlotta took Doodle's decision to park herself as a cue that she would have to attend to her mother a little bit. She threw a shady glance at Doodle and Pam as a wave of dread crested in her. She understood that there was no other way to interact with her mom than to act like a little bit of a nurse herself. She took the seat at the table opposite Doodle and leaned forward into her mother's personal space. Paloma leaned back like a stranger on the subway Do she even know who I am?

"Mama." She said it like a declaration. "It's Carlotta" I'm pointing to my own damn self like a fool. I mean, do she member that person who left so long ago an looked sorta like me, but not as much no more?

Carlotta stared intensely at her mother's face, and when her mother didn't resist or respond, scraped her chair closer to her on the floor with an unpleasant noise and took her gently by the shoulders, horrified to discover how bony they were underneath her thin white cardigan, something with lace trim, and a blouse decorated with orange blossoms in a grid. Paloma would never have worn this, Carlotta realized unhappily, if she'd had any say in dressing herself. The same went for the skirt with the ruffle around the hem, the white stockings, the shiny flats My God, Pam done dressed my mama like she a friggin grade-school chile outta Kingston. Carlotta moved in to make eye contact, but her mother's gaze focused everywhere else. She took a crack at syncing up her face with where her mother's eyes were traveling Maybe if I could tweak this shit so it *look* like a normal conversation, I could get somethin goin.

"Mama," she kept growling through her teeth, each time more frustrated than the last. "Mama!"

Doodle leaned forward and said Carlotta's name a few times.

Pam turned back to the frying pan but kept talking, her giant voice shattering the discomfort. "Oh, you won't get much outta her now. Not much happening in there!" Pam tapped her own head.

Carlotta tried not to listen. She took her mother's face in her hands and tried again to force eye contact, but staring into Paloma's eyes meant no more than staring up at the night sky, hoping for a response. She felt she could actually see a starry void in those eyes; she remembered then that eyeballs had some kind of goo inside them Usually when you be lookin at people you just look at the people, but lookin at Mama be like you just lookin at the house she useta live in. It's real painful memberin how different she was even the last time I seen her, how much she loved dancin, the dumb jokes she used to make, her funny accent, how she seemed to have this special kinda good luck that had came from her charm. People just wanted to do things for her an wit her; I bet that's why Pam doin this, too, cause it ain't like there's no shortage a old folks who need a home-health aide 24-7 even just in this damn neighborhood. This damn block.

"Nothing left but to pray fe her," Pam said/shouted.

"I ain't the prayin type," Carlotta replied. "I'm done with God."

Pam laughed from her sternum. "Don't seem to me like He done wit you!"

I ain't know what the fuck she meant by that. I'm alive? Whoopty-do, bitch.

Pam arranged a plate for Paloma. On the radio, news trumpets and keyboards sounded, and the radio man said, "You give us twenty-two minutes, we'll give you the world."

"Just got to keep her comfor-tabble," Pam said.

"It ain't nothin they got to turn this around least a little, hm?" Carlotta said, trying not to sound hopeful.

Doodle pulled her cell phone out of her purse and it lit up. She scrolled through something, pushing forward with one fingertip. The glow of the screen bathed her face in dim whitish light.

"They was working on it," Pam continued, "specially after Mr. Reagan had it, and there's some things that help some people some the time. But it ain't no miracle bout to appen. There's good days and bad days, but it don't get no better. No improvement, no!" She sounded almost cheerful.

Goddamn it, why can't Mama just snap outta this shit? Oh, I know that's a stupid thing to think or wish, but it's like she deliberately tryin not to see me, the same way I felt she didn't never see me when Ise growin up, on account a before me she had David, who got all the attention, plus I got all in her lipsticks and blouses and her platform shoes from the '70s, the "love shoes," we used to call em, and she didn't want to see no man-child a hers doin no girlie shit or shit she ain't feel was manly an you know in that Colombian culture she grew up in they all about who be the manliest macho even though most of em's four feet tall an the second you move your hip the wrong way when you five years old it's over.

She told me a story one time bout this boy from Barranquilla who dressed up as a girl with all red sequins wrapped around his waist, said his name Ramón but he said he's Ramona, she even said it happened during the big Carnival celebration so it shoulda been okay or somethin, but she told me that his papa gave him to the cuy man, the motherfucker who be on the side of the road roastin guinea pigs, that he fell into the fire and got burnt to death, and I believed her for a long time cause I was like five, then I found out that they cook em over a grill anyhow an Ise like fuck you, Mama, you lyin-ass bitch—at least in my mind I said that. Tryna scare me into wearin pants an ties an walkin butch. The fucked-up thing is that it worked for a while. An then I discovered the piers an the clubs an that was that. I bet she real happy to forget who I was. Bet she happy not to know who the fuck I am now. She always wantin me to get religion, takin me to Mass an puttin me in all that Catholic hoo-ha, makin me the worst altar boy in creation. I kept spillin stuff out the chalices an stumblin round cause a nerves. One time I tripped the priest on accident. My whole family still give me shit about that. Then I rebelled, I member, at round thirteen or fourteen when she wanna get me confirmed and I said to her face, in this room, over by that doorway to the bedroom, I said, "No, I don't want no bishop layin no kinda hands on me," and she tellin me it's gonna make my soul indelible but I thought she meant *inedible* and I'm thinkin, *The devil gonna eat my soul? That's just stupid.* So I ran on out the house. Later, when I come back, she sittin right bout where she sittin now an still cryin an I couldn't even walk all the way in the room, I just had to tiptoe round that.

It's hard when you gotta be you but other people wanna force all kinda shit on you that you don't want but they think ev'body posed to want, an what with religion an havin to pop out some grandchildren an pass on the legacy or whatever, people just tryna control the hell outta one another all the damn time. Sigh. I guess Mama want more sonofabitches to fight over the house when she and Frona gone or something—how many more she could stand? Ain't she a grandma to nough people? Maybe Iceman could come by an he could be the good grandchild, oppose to me, the prodigal dawtah.

I'm always like, Maybe I did some shit to cause this to happen, like it coulda not happened if I done all them Catholic magic rituals, an the baby Jesus coulda made it all proper an nice for her. But I bet as soon's she got the chance to put everything out her mind, including Miss Carlotta, she'da been like *yes,* get everything out that be trouble to me, get it out my brain, vacuum all that shit out. Or maybe that's more how I'd be right now if somebody stepped to me like, It'll all be okay if you wipe all the memories out your mind. I would do that, maybe. Now Mama got one foot on the other side. I wonder where she'd say she at right now? She still in her body somewheres, her soul ain't gone, but it sure ain't nobody behind them eyes.

"Mama."

Maybe if I get her to look at me it'll jog somethin in her mind. Upstanding religious lady by day, hoochie-mama party girl by night. But mostly dancin to her cumbia, not guzzlin up no sabajónes, not even during Christmas, an I'd have to school her ass to the hard drugs, she ain't never knowed nothin bout that.

"Mama? Look at me. You member me?"

Again nothin. She not even lookin in my direction when I'm talkin to her, she watchin Doodle, driftin into space. Funny, it's like I been lookin at her this whole time wonderin if she member me, but for reals, I'm like, Who this old lady wearin clothes my mama wouldn't never be caught dead in, her eyes all glassy, her head goin back an forth, not talkin? This ain't even 20 percent Mama. So who doing the not recanizin round here? Me! I'on't recanize *her*. Maybe she couldn't recanize me on accounta I ain't that same person she thought she knew when I left, but where the hell she at?

"Mama, it's me, it's..." Now what name even gonna jog her memory? I ain't gonna call my own damn self out my name. An is that shit even worth tryin? "It's Carlotta. Carlotta. Car. Lot. Ta." Carlotta turned to Doodle and attempted to make light of the situation. "I coulda told y'all this conversation wasn't gon go much a nowhere," she said.

But once it left her mouth, the joke didn't sound funny, and a long silence followed, one that seemed to fill up with something other than the silence between the three of them. Something tortured, like a sweeping lament for the death of the dying, the future demise of the healthy, the passage of endangered species, the disappearance of languages, even the passing of the day and every sort of limbo people suffer on earth. Inside her own silence, Carlotta became more sensitive to outside sounds: children crying, ambulances keening down DeKalb Avenue—*Are they in time to save that person?* she always worried—the wind rustling the leaves of the trees in the courtyard, the radio in the kitchen, other radios in other homes or passing cars. A smell like laundry detergent blew through the window. Had the party finally calmed down? But then they started up again—not the cake song, but something similar.

Carlotta searched Doodle's face for some kind of solace but instead found herself owning up to how much the distance between them had thickened. It felt as if their renewed closeness might turn out to be fake, as if each year of the fifteen since they'd last seen each other turned into a wall, an iron gate, or even that gap between two prison fences that they fill with razor wire. At Ithaca they called it the kiddie pool.

By this time Pam had cut the fish into small pieces on the plate, an old-fashioned blue one from a set Carlotta had known since childhood, etchings of New England scenes of water mills. She couldn't see which mill Pam had decided on—Baxter Grist Mill? Kenyon's? Ledyard Up-Down Sawmill?—and it grew harder to figure out after Pam put a salad down on the plate next to the dismembered fish. It didn't matter anyway. She fed Carlotta's mother, carefully showing her forkfuls of salad and fish and allowing her to clamp her mouth down over the fork.

Paloma chewed and Carlotta peered at her mother wondering who was doing the chewing Where people gone when they gone but they ain't *gone*? If it's a God out there, answer me that one, m'kay? Fuck it, you ain't home neither.

EIGHT

Carlotta had heard but not paid attention to the sound of someone clambering up the stairs, singing what sounded like "Michael Row the Boat Ashore," but she turned with a hop when Frona suddenly appeared in the doorway and multiple ambulances shrieked from one side of the neighborhood to another on their way to unluckier locations. Everyone froze, perhaps mentally measuring the distance to the tragedy. Pam even stuck her head out the window that led to the fire escape and the backyard, but apparently didn't find any helpful evidence there Prolly everybody in that damn room done had a whole buncha bad experiences round a police car, a ambulance, a fire truck, or all three, so all of us be like, Oh, shit! rememberin our shit, thinkin bout how many our people them sirens had took away. Ise memberin how Ise one them people who got took away myself.

Carlotta's grandmother shook herself free from the bewitching noises, the room went silent for a second, and then another new song bumped up from downstairs.

"Most the time you don't even notice," Frona said to no one, out of breath. "But when it's two or three at the same time..." She raised her eyebrows and moved her head from side to side, clucking her teeth.

She had a very shaky hold on a deep metal tray piled with char-edged ribs that glistened with maroon sauce, a pair of big tongs, paper plates, and an open plastic bag of red cups with a set of plastic utensils sticking up from the top one. Under her left arm she squeezed a roll of paper towels. Doodle and Pam jumped over to her side, plucking off the excess items, while Frona kept belly-aching — "I got it, I got it!" Carlotta rose and abducted the tray. She used it to push aside a couple of boxes of Christmas tree lights stacked on the kitchen table, kicking up puffs of dust in the process No, you don't got it, Miss Thing. Mrs. Thing? Grandma Thing?

Even once they'd freed her, Frona hung on to the roll of paper towels, crushing it in her palms and trying to stay cool. "I thought y'all must be starving up here, you and Pam and — "

"Grandma, you bringing that whole tray up to Joe Jr. and you know it."

"You hesh! What on earth would give you the notion that Joe — " Her attention suddenly zoomed in on Doodle. "Lord have mercy! If it ain't Miss Deirdre Frazier! Now, I remember when you was no taller than that table! How's your moms?"

"Uh, she passed," Doodle said quietly. "A few years ago, actu-ally…"

"Oh, I am so sorry to hear that! And your daddy?"

"You mean my ex-stepfather?"

"I guess that *is* what I mean, if it's like that."

"I haven't heard from him. I don't want to hear from him. I feel like everybody heard about this a while ago…" She clammed up.

Frona's eyes circled the room. After a moment she said, "Oh! Have y'all been downstairs to the party? I can't tell who there no more."

"Not yet," Carlotta said. As she spoke, Carlotta tugged a paper towel off her grandmother's roll and turned back to the table. She carefully nicked a rib by a sauce-free piece of bone, but Frona lashed out at her and smacked her hand hard enough to sting. She dropped the rib onto the plate and rubbed her hand.

"Didn't nobody say you could have none of them ribs!" Frona snapped.

Carlotta pointed at her grandmother. "They *is* for Joe Jr., isn't they?"

"I did not say nothing bout Joe, Miss Carlotta! Now, you mind your own business, please, thank you."

"Dag, I ain't seen a plate of ribs in almost twenty-two years, an here my own grandma tellin me I can't have *one*. Glad I ain't crawled across the Sahara an axed you for no glass a water."

"All right, then, take the one you touched! It got your germs on it anyways." Frona laughed Well, least I could depend on Grandma Thing for some shade. Joe up there turnin to Mount Kilimanjaro on account a all the ribs she feedin his never-goin-nowheres ass, an she worried he gonna get *my* germs. I know I been away, but for somebody who say she always thinkin bout other people, she got a habit a forgettin that Joe ain't ev'body in the whole damn world. If she keep feedin him the way she do, it won't be no room left for nobody else. Whoops. Maybe I *am* a fat-shaming ho. Least I ain't sayin that kinda shit out loud, like I woulda did upstate.

Carlotta lifted the rib again I think this the one but do I give a fuck? No, I *don't*, but before the meat arrived at her face, she paused. "Hold up. You stressin bout something, Grandma. What the heck goin on?"

"Would you mind coming with me for a second?" Frona said. Moving off without waiting for a response, she stepped into the hallway between the upstairs kitchen and the front bedroom.

David and his wife, Dwayne, had converted it into a bedroom for one of the kids. Carlotta didn't know which one—Raphael? Max?—since Dwayne had given birth to them all while Carlotta sat in the SHU, and nobody had bothered to introduce her to them, or maybe they hadn't come back from some upstate summer camp, maybe even near Ithaca It still smell like teenage-boy socks up in here, though, and it's a lotta sports books on them shelves. Look like he sleep on some kinda bed come out the wall? Frona swung the door partway shut and dug her nails into the paper towels What the hell goin on with Grandma anyways? Carlotta waggled the rib between her fingers, trying to avoid getting sauce on anything as she ate.

Frona wrinkled her sweaty forehead. "I know it's your first full day out the prison and everything, and I am very happy bout that, but I'm getting very afraid for you." Frona half whispered this warning with such fright that it almost paralyzed Carlotta—Frona's version of snake venom. "You been through hell—you don't even gotta tell nobody what done happened to you up in there for so long being like you are—so I know you don't wanna go back."

Like a idiot Ise thinkin bout the one reason I *would* wanna go back, but damn if I was gonna tell Grandma the reason be a dude name Frenzy. Or not like a idiot, like a bitch in love, but half the time a bitch in love and a idiot be the same damn bitch. Me, specifically, I'm that bitch. So I kept my mouth shut. Sound like Frona got a lot on her mind anyways.

"Now, you know that everybody down there partying and carrying on," her grandma went on, "not just cause of the holiday, but it's my old pal Freddy Bingham's wake and we gotta give him a big send-off, the kinda thing he'da enjoyed in his lifetime, right? It's a whole lot happening. So I'm tryin to make my way through the crowd with that tray and just when I get to the bottom of the staircase it's this white lady had on a kinda security-guard-type jacket? And no offense to no folks who be dressing like the other sex from what they borned, like you—and you look nice!—but she dressed like a man, with a man haircut. And I'm like, Who this person? Who invited her? Something must be up. She looking round like she don't know nobody at the party neither, like she looking for somebody in particular, so I'm like, Uh-oh. But I don't wanna assume nothing, cause that's rude. Lord knows I been on the wrong side of people assumptions my whole blessed life. So I introduce myself to her and she tell me her name, and it one them names that coulda been a man or woman name, so I ask if she want a drink, I figure that way I'ma find out if she here for the party. She brushed me off and start asking for you—*Carlotta* you—and that tipped me off that she knew you good. So I got a whole lotta crossed signals going through my mind, like I'm a switchboard operator having a bad day with Ma Bell, so I ask what it's about, and to my surprise, this lady say she your PO? Do the name Lou DeLay sound familiar to you?"

"Oh, hell yes, it certainly do!" It felt like a five-hundred-pound chunk a concrete had fell off the FDR Drive onto my skull. How I'm gonna prove to Lou that it ain't no violation of my stips goin on up in here? I'ma have to be like, What elephant? "She tryna drop me *now*? Cause that is the number two most worst possible thing to be happenin."

"Well, I didn't know where you was, so I didn't say nothing to her, and fortunately, too, because she said something bout all the dancing and drinking and carrying on, I didn't catch the whole thing, but maybe, like, it's not legal for you to live in a house where people occasionally have a party? She tugging the flaps on her jacket and snapping her suspenders like she some kinda old-timey cop or something out a Marx Brothers movie, gonna give you what for. I told her I ain't seened you but I would look for you and get back to her if I did."

"Thank you so much, Grandma. I guess that means I should leave on out the fire escape here like we useta do or somethin, that what you sayin?"

Carlotta jolted into action, half turning back toward the kitchen, but Frona thwacked her upper arm with the paper-towel roll.

"No, you ain't gon do nothing. I ain't said nothing, so — *don't*!"

"Why not?"

"Lemme finish my story and ye shall know, my child." The plastic wrapper on the paper towels made crinkling noises as Frona massaged it This driving me berserk already.

Carlotta tugged the roll out of her grandmother's hands, shouting, "Don't squeeze the Charmin!"

Frona gave her a look of surprise that faded almost instantly. Carlotta shoved the paper towels into one of the built-in bookshelves, between *The Encyclopedia of Baseball* and a jar filled with tennis balls. She made a mental note to remember that she'd left them there in case they both forgot and Raphael or Max found it and got confused.

"Miss Lou not the only one down there," Frona continued. "I gotta warn you, there's somebody *else* outside who *also* looking for you. This very good-looking man down there who say he know Paloma from long time, look like he lost one eye and the other red as a demon, he bout to pull his eyeball out his head, he rubbin it so hard. He ain't even know your name, he finds me as the owner of the house and said to me, 'I'm looking for somebody, somebody who said her name was Nobody,' and then he described a somebody who could only be you, and I said, 'I'm not sure who that is, why you looking for her?' and when he told me I said to myself, *That girl better not show her face at this li'l shindig if she know what's good for her.* Cause he said it real nice, but my intuition telling me the whole time that he literally wanna kill you dead. And I left Lou in the parlor, saying she couldn't come upstairs, but then this man decide he gonna go out in the backyard and look for you there."

"So I can't go downstairs, an I can't go out back neither."

At that point I'm saying to myself all kinda *Calm down, calm down* and *Breathe, breathe,* but I took a minute — funny how now I could have a li'l minute to think bout what I'm gon do before I jump jump jump to it, cause this time my lips wasn't gettin smashed up against no fuckin concrete wall while Ise figurin out what to do. I took my luxury minute an then I leant out into the kitchen area to see where Doodle still sittin there on the phone. I told her that our friend Mr. Famous actually *did* come back to have a chat — guess he found a parkin space! — an that we gonna have to figure out some kinda way round both him and my PO. Who knew when one them two gon figure out that I coulda gone upstairs or that Frona done lied to both of em to save my ass an keep em off my trail.

Also in that luxury minute, I started to bust some logic, an that also felt like some fancy silver-plated shit people on the outside be usin to get through they life stead a hidden shanks, long-ass finger-nails, an mad panic. I said to myself, I said, *Bitch, you could maybe face the half-blind man you almost fully blinded an tell him some bullshit bout what you done accidentally, an maybe won't much happen, but it don't seem like you could pull that kinda curveball on no PO who coming to stop you from bein round no alcohol, specially in the middle a no partywake. You can't just be like, This gigantic bunch a motherfuckers you see right here, dancin an drinkin they face off right in yo face? This ain't no party. This a wake. Which that's the truth, but who in the hell out the whole world a parole an stips an prisons gon believe that?*

So I'm figurin maybe the skylight, but Frona read my mind or I guess I looked up or something an before I even moved, she tellin me I can't go on no roof, they doin work up there, the flashing gotta be redone to stop some leaks an the whole thing a mess.

"Either you go down the stairs and face your PO like a — *person*," Frona said, "or you go out the fire escape and try to jump that fence and go next door. Grow some ovaries, my dear" Grandma could be funny sometime. But that particular thing—not so likely. It ain't like I want em neither. Imagine me with some more babies, no, thank you. It's enough tryna get Iceman back.

So I'm like, "Grandma, I'on't know what my ass ever did in life to make you think I'm bout to look some shit in the face. Asides, Paulie Famous can't send me back to no jail less he press charges, but Lou DeLay sure could. Tonight. She could do that *to-night*." The whole time I been waggin the rib bone like a magic wand, an I put it down on the table. I hauled ass over to the kitchen to where my moms was at, an Ise pullin her wheelchair out from behind the table.

At first it wouldn't go nowhere at all, like it's stuck there, an then Pam come over laughin an said, "The brakes is on, chile!" an did somethin where she kicked the brake loose.

So I tugged on the front part to pull Mama out the way an Pam helpin me an then just when I'm bout to stick my foot out onto the fire escape, I could tell from Doodle's face that she involved in somethin where she like, *I* don't gotta go down no fire escape, so, like, you on your own, chickie! Somethin like that.

So I go, "You could meet me outside later."

She look at me for a New York minute an goes, "I got to get home and feed Biscuit, that's my cat?"

But I can see a li'l hint a relief in her eyes, like the rest a what she wanna say be *An leave this crazy bitch to her fire-escape bullshit that I can get outta even if she can't.* So I gave her the I-don't-believe-you face, screwin up my lip, an said, "Don't nobody need to feed no cats regular, cause they don't never overeat. You could just put a thing in the kitchen that automatically do it." Which that's the one thing I knew bout havin a cat that I forgot I even membered up until that moment.

Doodle goes, "Right, you can do that with dry food when you go away, but I give her wet food on the daily. Yes, I spoil the shit out of her. Don't judge" So I'm like fuck this shit an start tryna yank the window up, but it's stuck. Doodle puts away her phone and stands up an says, "I'll call you!" as she walking to the door.

I yell back, "Gurl, I don't got no phone!" an I get so angry that I be channelin the Hulk or something an the window unstick itself, but by that time I think she out in the hall an din't hear what I said cause a the noise from the window bangin open an rattlin an the jams still pumpin down there. Whatever. She could call Frona. Carlotta had opened the window just enough that she could get onto the fire escape, but to do that, she had to bend herself in half, stick her torso into the opening, and twist around in a certain way Remind me a doin that dance they useta call the Worm so that she could enter the open part, while dust and paint flecks and dead insects got stuck to her clothing.

Below her, partywake guests staggered across the backyard, drinks in hands, pushing through the crowd with their chests and elbows Drink drank drunkity drunk. I'm tryna figure which a these here craniums belong to Paulie Famous. I thought it be easy — how many niggas down there gonna have a eyepatch? One. Less Freddy Bingham be friends wit Kojak. But I ain't see one single nobody that's got one.

Somehow Carlotta hadn't caught anyone's attention either, even when she climbed onto the fire escape ladder, which trembled violently and could have collapsed as she descended An maybe kilt my own ass too. But din't nobody pay no mind. That's a sign you got a good-ass party goin! Another ambulance shrieked through the neighborhood, and Carlotta paused to listen, worried that it was screaming about her future.

So when I get to the ladder an I'm bout to jump, I'm still bout seven feet off the ground, so I clench my butt, let go the sides of the ladder, an then hop backward off it, hit the ground, lose my balance, an fall backward on the legs a some hoochie girl, then on my ass. But the girl help me up an start axin me, Is you okay, you okay, as I'm brushin all the dirt an mud off all parts a my skirt, plus some the crabgrass that be growing in the cracks a the concrete I had just fell on. Only a couple people had seen an gived a shit, so I figure I'm still in the clear. My butt *hurt*, though.

Carlotta brushed the girl off and slunk over to a corner of the yard where the low branches of a tree kept her in shadow. Touching its bark, she gathered herself and scanned the backyard for Lou or Paulie, but the only face she recognized was the dude she'd mistaken for Iceman the day before Can't it be nobody out here I *wanna* see? He sauntered through the crowd, carrying two beer bottles between the fingers of one hand and yelling into the cell phone he held with the other That boy shoutin out the address a *my* home to random motherfuckers? The nerve. I oughta put a stop to that. When he reached his destination on the opposite side of the yard from Carlotta, he handed one of the beers to Iceman Oh, I shoulda known them two would be like Heckle and Jeckle. An how it is that Mr. Good Christian Man be drinkin an partyin all weekend?

Carlotta spied on the two men for several minutes, waiting for a chance to step in, mapping out what she planned to say to Iceman I figure ain't nothin gon change his mind bout me overnight, but I could speak my truth an maybe that gon get to him, like the last scene a some sitcom where it's just the two a whoever havin a heart-to-heart in the kitchen an ev'thing good tween em in two minutes. Eventually his friend excused himself, and Iceman stood alone, exposed. He peeled the slick label off his beer and turned it upside down on the bottle. Carlotta checked but still didn't see Lou or Paulie, so she cut a quick, crooked path to Iceman across the broken patio and arrived back to back with him Like I be Christie Love or some kinda spy.

"Small world, ain't it?" she said. He turned to face her. "You *musta* knowed Ise gon be here, Iceman."

"I figured, yeah, but I ain't mad atcha. My friend Carlton over there invited some industry people, an I wasn't gonna let *you* get in the way of an opportunity."

"Me? Flatterin. But you right, Mama wouldn't want that, no."

"And on the real, Ise actually looking for you, Carlotta."

I din't know what to say behind that, an I din't believe it neither, but for once I kept my mouth shut. I decided I'd let the brotha esplain this one out. Maybe he gon pologize. I nodded my head, waitin. At least he used my right name.

"I walk by faith, not by sight. Like the Bible say, we don't know what's ahead, we just gotta keep movin on, you know? And I think I been called upon to minister to you."

"Okay…coupla hours ago, son, Ise the devil and you was tryna exorcise me. You mean like that? You gon snap your fingers and turn me from devil to angel?" Carlotta lowered her chin and threw a glance at Iceman Okay, this still sucks, but I'ma just go with it.

Iceman shrugged. "Naw, I been thinking about it since then, and God musta changed my mind. The Lord works in mysterious ways, and sometimes He presents us with challenges that seem insurmountable, you know? But we gotta face them. I believe I can bring you back to the Lord. Daddy."

Carlotta put her hand to her cheek, her eyebrows rose, and she nodded. "Oh, I see what you mean wit the insurmountable!" An tween you an me, I'on't know who got more surmountin to do. "Let's get together next week and talk more."

I wanted a relationship wit him, din't I? So here go nothin. Maybe I done wished too hard for what I want. But it's somethin, an like the song go, Nothin from nothin don't leave nothin.

At that moment, Lou DeLay flew through the screen door, headed directly toward Carlotta. "I got a buncha insurmountable challenges too, Iceman," she said. "An here come one of em right now. Scuse me a minute, will you?" She ran toward Lou to make sure Iceman wouldn't get to meet her.

Carlotta was completely exposed in the center of the yard. Lou almost passed her, still searching for someone beyond her, but the sight of her client stopped her. Carlotta turned her face away and tried to use Lou's distraction as an opportunity to keep moving past her, but Lou was standing close enough that the move put Carlotta smack into her line of sight Fuck.

Lou took a step to block her exit and threw her palms out to her sides. "Carlotta—what the hell? This is the place you live in?" she shouted, looking from side to side as if she'd found out somehow that Carlotta had organized the whole partywake and had chugged at least a bottle of Henny already.

"Lou!" Carlotta barked, trying to sound like a surprised hostess. "How did you know Freddy?" she asked, and then, at a lower level, "You did know Freddy."

"Are you shitting me? I told you I was coming this afternoon for a home visit."

"You did," Carlotta said, trying not to say it as a question and give away that she'd completely blanked. "But you could still know Freddy."

"Oh, brother! No, I do not know Freddy, I don't even know who in blazes you mean, but if—"

"This his wake!"

Lou made a face like she'd sucked a lemon and put her hands on her hips. "What? In whose lopsided opinion is this a wake?"

Carlotta twisted her neck to survey the crowd. "Axe anybody here, honey."

"Don't 'honey' me. I'm your PO, not your honey. And I didn't come here to take a poll. Even if this is a wake—and maybe there's something cultural I don't know about? But even if it is, I came to see whether there's a problem with your situation, and even a Texas blind salamander could tell you that this is a big, big problem."

"What do you mean?"

"What do you mean, 'What do I mean'? You can't be around alcohol or drugs or anyone who's doing things that will knock you off track and get you sent up to Ithaca. You want to go back?"

"A course not."

"I want to help you get your life back together," Lou said, "but you have to take the initiative. I can't be here every minute of the day to make all your decisions for you, and you have to start making better life decisions than living in a place like this."

"A place like this? I grew up in this house! This ain't how it always be, it's a life celebration a this friend a my grandma's, Freddy Bingham, who died tragically."

"Carlotta, cut the crap. You don't even believe that yourself. I'm sorry to say this, but I've gotta drop you. There are so many open containers of alcohol on the premises and I can smell the drugs in the air—it's like you're living in a nightclub. You gave the parole board the impression that you had an acceptable home plan. I come in here and it's some kind of—of bacchanalian orgy going on! I've seen plenty, Carlotta, but I have never seen anything remotely like this before in terms of an unacceptable home placement. You *have* to find somewhere else to live." Lou gripped Carlotta's wrist firmly. "Where's the bathroom?"

Reluctantly, obstructed by party people, Carlotta guided Lou through the kitchen and into the hallway by the stairs to a half bathroom opposite the door to the stairs down to the subbasement. On the way, a man in a satin sweatsuit with a record-company logo on the back staggered diagonally in front of them, lost his balance, and nearly fell, but a big lady pushed him backward and he caught himself against the wall Couldja make this shit look any worse for me, brotha? Thanks but no thanks! When they got to the bathroom, they found a line ten people long going down into the subbasement. Carlotta looked at Lou, looked at the line, and pursed her lips Ise hopin she gonna just give the fuck up an go home.

"I guess we just gon have to wait," Carlotta said.

Lou leaned her hand against the wall and drummed her fingers. She eyeballed Carlotta and fumed. "Is there—" Lou stood on tiptoes and shouted over the music into Carlotta's ear. "There has to be another bathroom in this joint."

Fuck, she ain't gonna let this go. "I'm not sure we're authorized," Carlotta said.

"Don't try me, Carlotta," Lou warned. "You will not win. Either we go to the bathroom or you go to Ithaca. That's your choice."

"Follow me," Carlotta breathed. She weaved through the crowd and up to the parlor floor, lightly touching everyone's back to let them know that they needed to get out of the way, checking left and right for any debonair fellows That got a eyepatch an a attitude. Ise so sure Ise gonna run into his ass an not hers! Grandma really ain't had no up-to-the-minute intel, seem like. Wonder where that dude gone?

The crowd grew thinner after they closed the door to the garden apartment. As they passed her room, Carlotta pointed it out to Lou Ise thinkin that since it's a home visit she gon be all approvin and whatnot, but I open the door an it's like I see some lady shoes an some man shoes an some man's suit pants down by the man shoes an a lotta bumpin up an down on the mattress. Fore I even know what I'm sayin, I'm shoutin my head off. "Oh, hell no! Jesus Christ on a stick, y'all, stop fuckin in my bed an get out my room!"

I seen the man naked butt when he pull up his drawers an pants an both of em buttonin up an start frownin at *me* like, *We wasn't doin nothing! We wasn't puttin no penis in no vagina or nothin.* As if.

I stood there in the doorway so I could get a look at em and embarrass em a li'l more. I'm like, "Freddy Bingham would love this. He sure had some bumptious friends, got the nerve to be doin the Sandy Bottom Shuffle at his damn wake." When they pass me,

I'm like, "What's wrong wit y'all? Go downstairs an grieve the loss a yo friend!"

For a instant, before I seen him clear, Ise like, I hope that nigga ain't Paulie Famous, but it turnt out he's not, so I'm like, Whew. Lou standin there wit her hand on her mouth an I'm like, It is all over. Frenzy, honey, I am comin back to be yours once more an maybe forever more! Which really the only positive side a any a this, frankly. Damn, now I got "Always and Forever" stuck in my head.

"This is outrageous. People are literally having sex in the room where you're supposed to be rebuilding your life, Carlotta. Are you still going to try to convince me that this is a normal thing? A good environment to rebuild your life in? A *wake*?"

Carlotta blew out a breath. "At least they not drinkin? I don't got no stips on sex, do I? Believe what you wanna believe, Lou. Maybe they just tryna, like, say yes to life in the face a death or whatever, I dunno. You coulda axed them yourself, but they gone now. Anyways, we on our way more upstairs." Carlotta turned and left the room and creaked up the stairs. Lou followed, still aghast. "Did Boz tell you I got a job?"

"No."

"Really? Why the heck not?"

"I'm sorry, that's not what he told me at all."

Carlotta hesitated on the big staircase. "Well, what he say? Cause he told me to show up on Monday at Access-A-Rides."

"He told *me* you didn't have a driver's license. You don't, do you? And that they can't hire you to drive a van for disabled people if you don't have a license."

Carlotta leaned back against the banister with both hands supporting her like a gymnast about to do a backflip. She considered jumping but didn't I got so mad at Mr. Boz, motherfucker had the nerve to tell me I had a job, then go behind my back to my PO sayin I din't had the job fore tellin me I din't had the job hisself? Thank you, no, thank you. "*I* was honest," Carlotta spat. "Don't they need nobody to run the dispatch or whatever? I mean, don't be sociatin with that guy if he told me one thing an told you another."

"I didn't say he was a friend, I said I knew him. It could've been a matter of timing. I don't think it was malicious. Really."

My ass so mad that I be stompin up the steps like a five-year-old. We get to the upstairs bathroom door at the top of the big staircase an I go in an I'm bout to close the door but Lou stick her foot in the way.

"Not so fast," Lou said.

She push the door open an come in behind me. I'm like, What the devil, bitch? She got a messenger bag over one shoulder an she pull out a li'l plastic container the size of a one-scoop thing for a ice cream, which I know that's a urine-sample cup, so I take it out her fingers an said to her, like, Thanks, where the cap at? An she give me a screw-top cap. I turnt around.

Then she goes, "I have to see what you're doing."

"You *what*?"

"I explained this to you this morning at our meeting. Were you listening? The law requires that I make sure you aren't trying to game the system by using fake urine or someone else's urine or any other sort of deceptive method. That means I have to see what's going on. I am sorry, I imagine this is very sensitive for you as a trans person, but that's just the way it is."

"Fake urine? Where you could even *get* fake urine?"

"You'd be surprised what people can find on the internet."

I pulled up my skirt an sat down on the toilet like a proper lady an flushed. I tugged Señora Problema outta her shell—that's what I call the turtle who live in my panties but I don't never tell nobody bout that cause obviously it's crazy as fuck. But she don't wanna talk. I'm like, What's yo problem, Lady Problema? An I think like she don't want nobody lookin at her while she doin the do, you know? I mean, who the fuck do? I know I din't never like knowin the COs could see me on the closed circuit. So I shrug at Lou like, Ain't nothing happenin. An I yank my panties up an my skirt back down an cross my damn legs, even though that's kinda hard to do when you sittin on a open toilet seat. I look out the window through them pretty lace curtains at the partywake in the backyard an start growlin to myself but so Lou could hear.

I'm like, "This whole thing so goddamn humiliatin, why y'all gotta be treatin me like a infant an shit. Might's well be right back up at Ithaca, killin my number, bein with my man."

Lou iggin me, takin out her phone an lookin at her watch. She got what I'm figurin be a handheld drug tester in her other hand already, just waitin. She axed me if I maybe need a drink a water, an then damn if she don't tug a bottle a water out her bag an hand it to me.

I'm so mad, I can't even look at her. I'm like, "Nope. I'm too pissed to pee." I flushed the toilet again.

"Just imagine you're peeing on Boz's face," Lou said.

I had to laugh just a little after that, but it din't break my mood none. See, I sorta *did* had to pee, but I'm what they call pee shy. So, like, in them few times I had a cellie, I didn't hardly never pee up at Ithaca unless Ise in the shower, which that's the only time a bitch be in the cut. An in some them showers just your lower half be in the cut. An when Ise in the SHU, even though it wasn't nobody there, I knew they watchin me on *Candid Camera* all the motherfuckin time, like "Smile!" so whenever I had to go, I put my sheet or my flattress on my lap, tryna keep my rising funk from fillin up the jwant every time I took a shit or whatever, like Ise some waiter puttin a napkin in my lap at a fancy restaurant.

Lou kept holding the bottle of water out to Carlotta. "Listen, I can wait all night. I've got other clients, but none of them have ever been in as dangerous a situation as this as soon as they got on the outside. So if you want me out of your hair, I suggest you have a drink and we can wait for the moment of truth, okay?"

Carlotta stared at the water bottle for a while. The label read FIJI, and the summer-evening sun pierced the plastic, turning the bottle into a glowing brick of unflavored gelatin. The decoration below the logo, a magenta flower like a Hawaiian hula dancer might wear in her hair, reminded Carlotta that Fiji was a *place*, a tropical island so remote it sounded imaginary. She tried to picture herself there but couldn't think of any real way to go in her lifetime. Anguish threaded through her, a giant needle right up her ass, coming out of her navel. It occurred to her that the bottle itself might have come all the way from Fiji Which where the fuck is that? and the despair turned into anger Some motherfuckin plastic bottle been more places in the world in its life than me? Fuck that bottle! Do she carry that damn thing around just to make her parolees feel *more* like shit?

"Get that shit outta my face," Carlotta said. "I could pee on my own." With bear-like force, she swatted the bottle out of Lou's hand; it fell to the floor and landed by the radiator, where it spun.

Lou edged over to retrieve the water, and once she grabbed it, she stood up, leaned against the windowsill, and folded her arms, quietly waiting for Carlotta to feel the water flow. Her jaw set, she squinted at Carlotta. "Let's see it," she said.

"No," Carlotta said. "Let's *not* see it."

The staring contest continued for an entire minute. Jaws quivered. Lou stood away from the wall and let her hands fall. Carlotta flushed the toilet a third time.

"Listen," Lou said softly. "I'm on your side, Carlotta. In more ways than one. Most of the other POs, you could not say that about them. I understand what it's like to be someone who does not conform to all the gender roles and bullshit that this society puts on us. I get it. So can we just do this? I'm not getting my jollies by checking out your crotch."

Carlotta let her shoulders droop and cast her eyes down. She fiddled with the sample jar's top, twisting it open and shut. She didn't look at Lou when she spoke. "I know this home environment a problem, Lou. But if I can't be here, I'm gon be in the homeless environment out *there,* an I can't do that. I can't. I swear to you that I am not involved in none a what's goin on out there. That's some shit that my grandma—" When Carlotta heard herself say that, she grabbed her temples and squeezed Oh my God, that sound like the most ridicalous thing anybody ever said in the history a shit talk. My grandma, the party girl. Put the motherfuckin cuffs on me now. "For reals, it's a party for one a her friends who died, an I have not even *touched* none a the liquor all them fools out there imbibin like the world gon end tomorrow. So I could honestly say that you don't need to drop me cause I ain't done no drugs or no alcohols in the one day I been back. What kinda—oh, forget it." Right then I gone from twistin the cap to turnin it over onto my thigh and pressin down hard to make circles in my skin with it. Closest I could get to cuttin myself, I guess.

"I believe you—you don't seem at all fucked up. I know what that looks like. I have dropped some dudes who couldn't even unzip their pants, like, 'Can we just use the surveillance video to prove how shitfaced this guy is so I don't have to see this dude's trouser snake?' But it's not up to me. The division needs the evidence. So just pee in the cup, Carlotta. Just pee in the cup." She pulled a packet from her bag and placed it on the sink next to Carlotta, who moved her eyes toward it. "That's a moist towelette. If you don't have anything in your system, you don't have anything to worry about. I just hope you didn't breathe in too deeply at that party downstairs. Hell, I hope *I* didn't breathe in too deeply downstairs."

Carlotta hesitated and tried to take care of the problem from under the skirt, but Lou reached over and tugged the fabric up. Carlotta couldn't deal. She flushed the toilet again.

"You don't have to keep doing that," Lou said. "You're on the outside now."

The standoff lasted for ten more minutes, but instead of escalating the confrontation, Lou chatted about insubstantial things that they could agree on — the weather, the party, and, briefly, Frona and her enthusiasm Prolly she just waitin for La Problema to change her mind bout comin out her shell and givin up the golden fountain. In the end, I just couldn't hold it no more, so Ise like, Fuck it, here, she gon do her li'l flamenco dance for you or whatever. I felt it comin on so I just stuck her head in the cup for as quick a second as I could, and it turnt out she gave up more than I wanted her to, so then I pushed her down fast as fuck an pulled the cup out my crotch. I let the skirt come down over her an the rest gone in the toilet an I handed Lou the container, close to her face as I could. I know that's kinda gross but Ise tryna gross her out cause a how Ise feelin bout the whole experience.

Then it's like, What the fuck, she take some kinda medical box out her messenger bag an put it on the edge a the sink — it's one them old-time sinks, prolly not changed since the 1930s, that got a big shelf round the bowl where you could keep your soaps an shavin powder or whatever they useta use on they muttonchops an mustaches an what have you.

Lou removed a box about the size of a cell phone from her bag, mostly white, with rectangular holes in it She tookded off part the bottom a the box an it's five paper things on the end like a fork with extra prongs. She fuckin dipped that shit into the pee. I'm like, This actually yo job. Mercy, mercy me. The whole time, Lou tryna esplain ev'thing to me bout what the urinalysis — she kept calling it the UA, but to me that's United Artists, the record company who 45s I had in the '70s — what the UA test for, an all kinda legal shit I din't understand. I'm like Shut up an tell me I don't got no positive drug test. After she stuck it in the pee, she count to ten, pull it out the pee, an put it back in the box. She gawkin at the box like it's a TV.

I'm like, "I ain't did no drugs. I ain't did no drugs."

She goes, "You really have to be honest with me, Carlotta."

"I *am* bein honest!"

"The drug test doesn't lie."

"What it say? What. Do. It. *Say?*"

All a sudden, Lou din't had nothing to say no more.

"Cat got yo tongue?"

Lou puttin all her stuff back inside her bag, look like she playin for time.

I seened that kinda behavior before, so I'm like, Oh, shit, an I axe again, puttin more pressure on her. *"What it say?"*

"I can only tell you that you have tested positive."

I fell into a hole. Drugs? "For *what*? I ain't did no drugs! What drugs it said I did?"

Now she packing up all her shit, bout to just leave my ass there.

"I ain't did no drugs! Is it alcohol? Is that it?"

"I can't tell you for what. I have to take the test back to make sure it isn't a false positive—"

"Oh, it could be that. I mean, that's what it *is,* cause I din't do nothin!"

"Now, this doesn't mean that you're going back to Ithaca right now or ever, okay? You'll get a Morrissey hearing to decide whether it's a real violation. Don't worry, it doesn't mean you'll have to listen to the Smiths all day or anything. I'd want to hang myself. But you need to get out of this place and into a home environment that is not so damaging, where you won't run into drugs or alcohol and give in to temptation anymore. Can you do that for me?"

"A course, yes! But first of all, my beef don't got nothin to do with no *temptation*—to do no alcohol or no drugs. Second, I ain't had no drug problem never, period, even though I did the prison rehab.

I did some drugs, I cop to that, but it ain't never been a big — shit, you just like them folks in the rehab, think I'm in denial. But third, you ain't even tellin me what the positive be positive for!"

"I'm not arresting you! Cool your jets, Carlotta!"

"Oh. Then what you gon do?"

"I have to get this to the lab and have them make sure it isn't a false positive." She twisted the cap tightly on the urine sample and placed it in her messenger bag. "And if it isn't, I will make a decision about it then. And whether, along with the lax home environment and any other factors I find out about, this represents the kind of violation where we need to revoke you, send you back to Ithaca. I want you to make it, Carlotta. But this is not a good start. Not a good start at all. Check in with me tomorrow by 9 a.m., okay? 9 a.m. *sharp.*" Lou hunched her shoulders, turned back to meet Carlotta's eyes for a sincere moment, then glanced down. "You have two different shoes on," she said, and walked out.

The bathroom door stayed ajar. Through the noise of the party outside, Carlotta heard the stairs creaking under Lou's weight. Outside, yet another ambulance or police car howled down the avenue Lucky she ain't axe me *why* I had two different shoes on.

In the relative quiet and solitude of the bathroom, Carlotta felt that the time had come to weep Chile, all the stress done caught up to my ass. Not just the stress of thinkin Ise bout to get sent back an then not, but also thinkin that Lou maybe knew or gon figger out that I stole that shoe based on what she just said, an Ise thinkin it ain't no possible way Ise gon make it after this here setback, that that Boz motherfucker tricked my sorry ass into thinkin I had a job an Ise all happy an shit and then I find out I don't, that it gon be downhill from here, which already way down the hill, raped a thousand time by a man tellin you you rapin him, no hope for the future, positive drug test gon send me back upstate, what gon happen to my ass, that I ain't had no kinda life left to look forward

to, even outta jail, specially outta jail, where it's harder to deal with
ev'thing cause you gotta take care of it yourself an ain't nobody
tellin you where to go an what to do every damn day, which I hated
the hell outta but I guess my ass got useta that shit, an cause I
think I found an lost my best friend in the same day, that my mama
won't never know nothing in life again, let alone who the fuck I
am, that I couldn't never have no real conversation wit my father
no more, that my son a idiot who tried to cast the demon outta me
when Lord knows it ain't nobody inside me *but* the damn demon,
get rid a him an you get rid a me, an now he done a about-face
an gonna save me with Jesus — Good luck, nigga! — that everything
gon be hard hard hard for a long-ass time in the land a the free,
not hard like prison — couldn't too much be *that* hard — but still
hard hard hard in a different way. Then the weepin go all universal
an I start thinkin bout ev'body who got dead an be missing from
my hood since I went inside, an how I missed they death an they
funeral, an hell, they life too, which that's a triple tragedy — Darnell
and Germina and Illmatic Joe, Eric-Lamar an Henny, I mean, even
Biggie counted, an Ise like if I'ma count Biggie then I can't leave
out Scott La Rock an Venus Xtravaganza, Willi Smith, an a whole
ballroom fulla other people who got dead when it was AIDS everywhere, an maybe I got it now but I ain't never got tested, bet I
got it from that sonofabitch or one them other sonofabitches, then
my tears gone out to all them people from long time ago that
died in the news in a unfair way, like Yusuf Hawkins an Michael
Stewart, Eleanor Bumpurs, an then I membered me an Doodle was
talkin bout Gavin Cato and Yankel Rosenbaum, an I even felt bad
membering that white girl who got raped an killed by the preppy
dude, she ain't deserve that, don't nobody deserve none a that shit,
to get jumped an fucked an left for dead, an then it came back home
to poor Freddy Bingham, who fell off a damn scaffolding at forty
years old, younger than my ass, leavin a wife an five damn kids.

If I'da died at that age, I be dead already, wouldna had no kinda time to turn my life around, an my one kid gon try to Christianize my ass, a boyfriend, but no truly committed partner, nothing, like I hardly rolled the motherfuckin dice yet in the Game a Life, like I ain't even chose my li'l pink truck or whatever, like, I'm like, *It's too late, baby, now it's too late. Though we really did try to make it.* Then I went *ultra*-deep an was, like, thinkin bout Mrs. Dorothy Green an how none a what happened shoulda happened to nobody in that room at that time. She certainly ain't done nothin, I just had the worstest luck you could magine, an even Cousin Kaffy coulda did shit different an ended up in sports or entertainment or some shit. Din't nothin that done happened needed to happen. Life been cruel as a jive-ass pimp, just steamrolled the fuck over ev'body ass. That made me lose it on top a already losin it. And so then I'm thinkin bout what if I died, maybe kilt myself — folks useta call that "back-door parole" — an soon's I get to wherever Ise goin I gotta face, like, a tribunal a all them people who died to see if I could even get into the probation a death or if they gon send my ass back to the life I screwed up an see if I could not screw it up or at least make it not as bad, an I'm like, Fuck, it prolly ain't no better to be dead than to be doin yo time in the world or whatever, what with Biggie an Eleanor Bumpurs starin you in the face, tellin you you ain't suffered nough, not like they done, so I might's well tough shit out here. I done toughted out some worse shit in prison so maybe I could get through, but I'm still cryin an cryin, doubled over on the damn toilet, li'l tears fallin through my fingertips an down into my lap. I'm pullin the whole roll a toilet paper an it be spinnin like crazy an fall out the holder, an I pick it up an dab the roll on my face. I cry so much that, like, through the cryin I'm like, Bitch, stop feelin sorry for y'self, an then I do more weepin, I'm like, Okay, okay, feel sorry for y'self for a li'l while, you earned that shit, but cut it out in, like, five, m'kay? But I'm also cryin on account a I'm happy to be back kinda thing? An just outta so much confusion an *drama*. But then I'm like, Wait, Miss Crying Game — is you losin yo damn mind? An I stop the cryin an dabbin my face, an I take one them li'l bonus moments a time to think. I like, laugh a li'l bit an say, Okay, let me get outta this motherfucker — the motherfucker bein this house where it's a nonstop partywake. That's the first thing I gotta do to get on the right path an keep from goin back. But then I'm like, With what fuckin money am I gon leave this place? An all a sudden I member that Frona said she gon let me sign my check over to her.

Carlotta wiped her face on the sleeve of someone's bathrobe, arranged herself, and left the bathroom. Tameeka stood outside waiting, dancing in her pajamas, and two people from the party stood behind her. Carlotta could tell by their eyes that they had all heard her sobbing, but nobody did anything sympathetic or acknowledged it.

"What were you doing in there so long, Auntie Carlotta?" Tameeka asked.

This child is too too too, I know she done heard my ass. "I guess — " Carlotta said, slowly breathing out, meeting Tameeka's open gaze. "I guess Ise holdin a wake."

Carlotta peeped around the corner into the third-floor kitchen *Shoulda just stayed in there wit Mama, maybe Lou wouldna found me* and waved to Pam's back and to her mother, who sat at the kitchen table wearing her usual blank expression. Pam might have heard her blubbering in the john, but she didn't turn around. Carlotta sniffled and blew her nose into a tuft of toilet tissue she had brought out of the bathroom, crushed the paper, and leaned into the kitchen to toss the wad toward a trash can on the far side of the table *I missed, but I din't give a fuck.*

She slinked upstairs near Joe Jr.'s cave to look for her grandmother, even though she knew she wouldn't find her there — the fear of running into Paulie pushed her in the opposite direction of the party. At the top of the stairs, she put herself together, inhaled like a Hoover, and descended into Hades *Fuck, maybe it* is *a good time to talk to Iceman bout bringin me to Jesus. Positive drug test.*

Carlotta found her grandmother on the garden level, wiping off a plastic tablecloth decorated with tropical fruits in neon colors.

"You get free of them people?" her grandmother asked.

Carlotta laughed. "Yeah, Grandma, but it's always more people to get free from."

Frona remembered having found the cash to cash Carlotta's check, but they had to go all the way upstairs again to grab it from the safe-deposit box buried in her closet. That took a toll on them both Lively as Grandma be, she still eighty-six damn years old, an me, I ain't been up an down no stairs this much since twenty-two years. I signed the check over to her an she unlocked the box, which really a kind a safe with a complicated key. She pulled out more than the whole amount an I stuck out my palm for her to start countin the moneys in my hand—100!-200!-300! like on *Joker's Wild*—an my eyes was just buggin out.

So finally I'm like, "Grandma, where all this money comin from?" an she stop countin.

Grandma go, "You want the cash or no?"

I go, "Course I want it! It's my money!" even though I know most of it goin to all kinda prison fees and lawyers. "But since when you turnt into Phil Rizzuto for the Money Store?"

Frona made a sober face at Carlotta and said, "Phil Rizzuto." She put her hand that had the cash in it on her hip. "I got a reverse mortgage going," she announced As if she done outsmarted every nigga on the planet wit this whatever it was.

I ain't knowed what a reverse mortgage apposed to even be, so in my mind Ise just like, *Okay, I hope that's like a sugar daddy, maybe it's some motherfucker out there like to spoil a old lady, Lord knows it's a lotta old ladies out there deservin some good treatment from a financially secure older man.* Like me, for instance.

Frona finished counting. "Three hundred, four hundred, five hundred, thirty-five, thirty-six, thirty-seven, thirty-eight. Keep the change. And it's funny, you know that man who lookin for you who rubbing his eye out? Said his daddy work for the company that got the reverse mortgage on the house. I looked at him like, How the devil you even know that?" Frona retracted her chin toward her chest. "I don't actually believe him."

I'm lookin at all this money in my hand like I ain't never seened no money before. Which it's almost like I ain't. I roll that shit up tight an Frona gimme a rubber band to double-wrap round it an I stuff it in the pocket of the lilac skirt, which fortunately it's deep. It *is* deep! It feel like my entire life in that pocket, or the life a somebody baby or somethin, and my whole body become like a Brinks truck behind that. I thanked Frona again an gone down to my broom closet, thinkin bout how I'm gon get outta this joint.

Carlotta, still gripping the roll of bills, shut the door to her room, and it made such a pleasant, gentle click that she swung it open and closed it a few more times, letting the thrill of liberty ripple through her arms This amazin right here, that I could do this, look at me controllin a door. Here I'm at, outside the door. Now here go the door, wide the fuck open. Now I'm inside the room. Now I'ma close the door. Click. So good! Lemme go out and do that again. Oh, it's so stupid but it feel so good. What other kinda stupid shit I could do that I ain't had the chance to do all them years?

Feeling that somebody might be coming down the stairs, Carlotta pulled the door to one final time, her ear to the knob so that she could feel and hear the springiness of the bolt flicking itself into the faceplate. As her eyes adjusted to the dimming early-evening shadows, she found the light switch and flicked it, expecting to see the harsh light of the naked bulb fill the room. But instead there was an electric flash, a tiny red glow, then nothing but twilight in the space.

To her own shock, she flipped out Shit! I can't fix no fuckin light bulb! The ceiling was eleven feet high on the parlor floor — she would have to ask Frona where they stored the light bulbs and where she could find a ladder. Then she'd have to climb the ladder, replace the bulb, return the ladder, etc., etc., etc. But it only took one idiot to screw in a light bulb, like all the jokes said, and that made rebuilding her life seem harder than giving up It's like whatever look easy to the whole world gon be a bitch for my ass to get done every time I try to do for myself, an ain't nobody gon give me no kinda break on it or nothin, they gon sweat my ass more cause I'm a ex-convict an livin this here life. The light bulb might as well have been a sudden death in the family caused by her bum luck. Worst of all, the broken light would plunge her into darkness pretty soon unless she fixed all the tinier problems around it. In the light gray murk, she took a breath, lowered herself to the twisted mattress, and sat. She breathed out, lifted her legs, and kicked them, staring at her mismatched shoes I'da axed Grandma if I could borrow a pair a hers, but her feet's so *tiny*. Maybe wit this money, I could still get a nice pair downtown. She placed her hands on the mattress and hoisted herself glamorously, casting herself as Diana Ross or, on second thought, Beyoncé, or even better, some new, unique combination of the two, as if the next thing she might do, after slinking down the front steps of the brownstone in even fancier shoes than she currently had on, would be to present the next Academy Award, right there on DeKalb Avenue I'm like, What if I could just close my eyes an open em again an all my problems woulda just gone away an I could find myself before a adorin audience a all my wonderful fans. Like, Calgon, take my ass *away*!

So soon's I start dreamin my tinselly dream, I heard a *monster* ruckus bustin out downstairs. Like it's people voices shoutin louder than the music, motherfuckers screamin nasty names, then the sound a bodies slammin gainst walls, feet movin round, an furniture — furniture! — movin from one side the room to another when I know it ain't no room in the crowd for that. I heard glasses breakin, an then screamin, an somethin, like, I think it coulda been one them folding chairs clockin somebody in the head. Course I'm still pretendin to be Lena Horne as Glinda the Good Witch in *The Wiz* up in my damn fantasy, so I twinkle my hands from head to toe an I'm like, "Time to disappear, darling!" I grabbed my grandma bag that got my, like, three li'l possessions, chucked all the papers what Boz had gived me bout the job that he psyched me out on in the trash, put in my makeup kit an a scarf I borrowed from Frona, an danced my way out the front doors to the stoop, still listenin to the commotion goin wild an shakin my head.

I had took not two steps down the stairs when a *blam!* come from inside the party, then the whole motherfucker went apeshit. So, fast as my mismatched shoes could take me — guess I got used to em, whatever — I leaped down them stairs, jaywalked cross Vanderbilt, an stood over there in the bus shelter, tryna make it look like I been waitin for the bus the whole time, lookin at my wrist with no watch on it like, Where that damn bus at? Last thing on earth I need's for some sonofabitches to be arrestin my ass for some shit I ain't been nowhere nears, have to be like, Officer, Ise up in my room pretendin to be Lola Falana, I din't hear nothin, touching they shirt collar or whatever. Cause it said you can't have no contact with no law enforcement while you on parole, not even if they not arrestin you — it don't look good.

Lou right, I shoulda looked into this home situation a li'l better, maybe shit coulda worked out better if I'da gone to a halfway house or somethin, but I know that woulda had its own problems. Ain't it no place in the world where you could just be who you is, look how you wanna look, fuck who you gonna fuck, an be Black the way you be Black an don't nobody gotta give you a hard time to the point a kickin yo butt, shootin you, stabbin you, breakin yo neck wit they knee, an hangin yo ass from a goddamn tree? An if that place ain't Brooklyn, then where the fuckin fuck it at? Reckon it ain't nowheres I could get. Maybe it be, like, Fiji, an I'ma have to slap my arms together an make myself into some smoke like on *I Dream a Jeannie,* just jump in that bottle an go there.

Carlotta, out of breath, leaned against the ad panel on the bus shelter, waiting to see what would happen across the street Ise hopin the coast gon get clear, or I'on't know, somebody gon blow up the damn building like it's *The Fast and the Furious*? Every few moments, she leaned forward, checking for the bus, just in case someone watching suspected she had anything to do with the house across the street. She pictured herself as a child, sitting on the stoop and looking back at herself now *What that li'l kid gon think a me? Prolly be like, Mommy, who that crazy homeless bitch? The fuck she doin wit her life?* She laughed bitterly *Mama'd be like, That's you, queen! Suck it up!*

In a matter of minutes, sirens blared down DeKalb, this time headed to the front door of the brownstone. Carlotta held herself close to the bus shelter. When a bus lumbered up to the stop, she went around to the front of the shelter, where the driver couldn't see her *Maybe he could see the shoes, but just shoes don't mean nobody waitin for no bus.* The bus waddled into the stop, blocking her view of the brownstone. A potbellied old man from some tropical country, wearing a plaid cap and glasses, stepped out of the rear entrance, gold chains swinging inside his short-sleeved shirt, and the bus slowly chuffed down the street.

By the time Carlotta could see the house again, two police cars and an ambulance had double-parked out front, their blue and red lights bedazzling the nearest windows and the undersides of the clouds, while numerous partygoers emptied into the square concrete yard by the steps, out of the short iron gate, and onto the sidewalk, shaken, traumatized, drunk, and oblivious *Frona din't go back downstairs, I don't think, so she prolly okay. I hope din't nobody out my family have nothin happen to em, especially like that they got shot, but no way can I go find out, much's I wanna.* A few probable friends of Freddy Bingham's crossed the street to near where she stood. When they settled at the other end of the bus stop, she affected as casual an attitude as possible.

Without moving from her position by the shelter, she asked, "What happen over there, y'all? Somebody get shot?"

They said that they didn't know, and though they sounded honest, Carlotta didn't believe them These jackass chumps gotta know more'n *me*.

Almost like a response, the paramedics struggled at the stairs to bring someone out on a stretcher. Getting anything out through the garden-level entrance required a 90-degree turn and a journey up three short steps, so they had to collapse the wheels of the stretcher and tip the gurney at a steep angle that risked dumping the patient to the ground. Carlotta squinted and stood on tiptoes to see if she could recognize the victim, but she couldn't make a positive ID. It wasn't Frona and definitely not her brother You'd need somethin way bigger to get *his* ass outta there. It might've been Thing 1, but she hadn't seen him at the partywake at all. Pam had come downstairs to attend to the person on the stretcher. She stood to one side, talking, almost in the way of the paramedics.

As soon as the stretcher cleared out, the cops unrolled yards of yellow caution tape across the front steps Like they puttin up some garlands on a Christmas tree. The raising of the caution tape was a sign to Carlotta Well, it ain't no point in me tryna get back inside there tonight *now*, definitely gotta figure out some other sleepin quarters this evening.

Now that she had her money, she felt the urge to talk to Frenzy. She didn't have a phone, though, and prisoners couldn't get incoming calls. She'd need to buy a phone, write him a letter with the phone number in it, and hope that he called her. The process could take weeks An without no guarantee that he gon respond, I'm fraid to go through all that an then figger out his love ain't true. Carlotta had intended to get a cell phone since the second she left Ithaca, and now that Frona had cashed her check, she felt the urge even more pressingly. But by that hour, with the sky turning cobalt and retail outlets closing, it might not make sense to try to find the one cell phone joint open late, because it might not have good options But who give a fuck bout options when you just wanna call yo boo? The thought flooded her mind without filling it up while she watched the drama across the street. The jump-off might've passed, but she couldn't move away from the flashing scene of her childhood home invaded by a police squadron while she stood aside, shielded from the outcome. She pulled her fingers through her hair.

She thought of getting on the subway and going somewhere and remembered that the closest stop was the Clinton-Washington G train on the next block. As the paramedics loaded the stretcher into the ambulance, Carlotta got a better look at the person and still didn't recognize him Freddy Bingham friends with the whole damn neighborhood, seem like. The ambulance driver slammed the back doors shut and plopped into the front seat, revved the engine, and disappeared down the avenue. The police handcuffed certain people in the crowd and pushed them into squad cars Oh, shit, I think that motherfucker they just pulled out there is Paulie Famous, without his damn eyepatch. If they could arrest that dude, *my* sorry ass better get outta here! I'ma just find out what happened tomorrow lookin at the *Daily News*. I guess it be like, Farewell, childhood home an shit.

Carlotta entered the G train station, happy to have learned how to buy a card and pay the fare, and hulaed through the turnstile. She planned to take the G train toward Queens and switch to the Manhattan-bound L Gonna suss out some late-night wardrobe options an then try an find some old friends out by the Christopher Street piers an maybe see if I could stay with somebody or stay out all night.

Unfortunately, a ribbon of fuchsia caution tape prevented anyone from heading to the Queens-bound platform, but she didn't notice that until she had already paid and walked to the right Well, I guess I should just get on goin the other way? Maybe I could transfer at some other station like they always useta be tellin you to do but shouldn't nobody never do cause it don't never work. Here come the train, anyways.

Hearing the train rumble into the station, she trotted down to meet it and almost missed it, having forgotten that the G usually runs with only four cars in that direction I thought this mother only went to the 4th Avenue—9th Street Station! The fuck goin on? They just keep changin shit up on me. Carlotta took a seat by the window, remembering that at a certain point, the train would burst from the tunnel and go elevated, giving her a panoramic view of lower Manhattan and most of Brooklyn, from the Verrazzano to the Kosciuszko.

Before that could happen, though, the train halted at Carroll Street and loitered in the station with its doors open for longer than the usual amount of time Ugh, something wrong. Here we go. An older Chinese woman sitting across from Carlotta with a large red-and-blue-striped laundry bag between her calves, full of groceries with Chinese characters on the labels, shook herself, stood up, went to the train doors, stuck her head out, looked both ways, turned down her mouth, shrugged at Carlotta, and sat back down.

The conductor crackled onto the PA system. "No passengers, no passengers, this train is being taken out of service," he said four times.

The few people riding the train, including Carlotta, sluggishly got up from their seats or moved away from poles, trudged through the open doors, and positioned themselves in various areas of the platform.

"There's another train directly behind this one," the conductor droned.

"Bull*shit*," a freckly white woman pushing a baby carriage said to herself.

The train, now presumably empty, closed its doors and left its lonely former passengers to fend for themselves Wonder if ev'body got off—maybe some of em done stayed? I wonder what'd happen if I'da stayed on it? People still be livin on the subways. But that ain't gon look good to no PO, I know that!

A train did follow, much later than the conductor promised, and not a G. Circled with the color of fire, the letter F on the front train car roared toward Carlotta like a bad grade I got me a F on the drug test. It rushed by, ruffling her hair and outfit before rattling to a halt. Almost every time a train came into a station, she always used to wonder what would happen if she jumped in front of it I ain't never seriously considered doin that as no way a committin suicide, I had just knowed somebody who had did that, an I always wondered what that felt like, to just get slammed an have it be like, Lights out, party over, oops, outta time. But I gotta live for my boy. Maybe I could convert his ass *away* from the Lord. To who, though? Miss J. Alexander?

The doors opened, and Carlotta recalled that before she went upstate, she'd had only one rule about what to do when the MTA started running funny Take what come, don't be sittin round waitin for no right train when shit obviously fucked. With that in mind, she stepped onto the F, which was more crowded than the G, though she did find a seat across from a Black man who took up the two opposite seats. Despite the heat, he wore a ratty parka and lay unconscious, or just asleep, his clothes threadbare, a swollen foot bursting out of a disintegrating shoe that displayed his ashy skin and yellow toenails, an open sore near his heel. No one, it seemed, wanted to acknowledge his existence or get within several feet of him, so his force field extended across the subway car I'm, like, sniffin the air to make sure he ain't one them folks who got stank so bad you gotta get out the whole train car. I can't smell nothin, but maybe on account a I got used to the extra-stanky stank up in Ithaca. An there it go, right above that skanky man, the whole a Brooklyn just gettin her sequins on for the evenin, sky turnin the color a one them Popsicles, all orange an blue, li'l clouds like stuffing done come out a ripped-up pillow, an a whole buncha tall-ass buildings that I'on't know what the fuck they is. Where the sign for Kentile Floors at?

Over time, the number of passengers near herself and the Black man shrank so much that Carlotta could feel his humanity overlap with hers, her sadness for him mixing with her fear of suffering his fate and the fear of being associated with him, and at Kings Highway she got up almost involuntarily and moved to the opposite end of the train car Maybe I woulda gived him some a that money I had, but I ain't never seened the man face, for alls I know he coulda been dead, an I wasn't bout to wake nobody outta no death.

An where the fuck Ise goin, anyhow? I had got on the G goin the wrong way an now Ise on the F still goin the wrong way, done seen the nice view Ise lookin forward to but now it's like, Ugh, phone store's prolly all closed so I don't got no place to go. I sure as hell ain't gettin out nowhere near Bensonhurst. Maybe I'll just ride to the end. The yellow LED display in the window said CONEY ISLAND / STILLWELL AVENUE Coney Island...now, I ain't been *there* in a extra-long-ass time. Useta think it was Coney like Ice Cream Concy. I do got me some cash, maybe I could ride me some rides until shit blow over at home an maybe go back when it get late, see if the po-po outta there yet. Just stay the one night an figure somethin else out tomorrow. I member back when Ise a kid they useta take us down to Coney with the community-center summer day care, an on the train some li'l sumbitch puked on my leg, had the nerve to be makin fun a *me* behind that, so I smacked his li'l raggedy ass upside his head. I told him, You the puker. The puker don't get no laughin privileges. You can't be pukin on nobody an laughin at em. That ain't right. Better puke the other way next time, puker. If I saw him today, I'd call him Puker. Can't even member his real name. Shit, with that attitude, he prolly the mayor a New York City by now.

A bevy of Coney memories barged into Carlotta's brain: of turning over a cherry Italian ice to find gooey crystals below a crimson mess, like sweet blood; of shooting water into the mouth of a plastic clown in order to move a plastic racehorse down a track and getting…The fuck I ever win doin that? Anything? A giant stuffed Tweety Bird? A key chain? She remembered the tough clam strips from Nathan's even more vividly than the hot dogs, puncturing wavy French fries with wooden skewers and dipping them in bloodred ketchup What bout that funky Ferris wheel that didn't nobody never make no other one of? Wonder Wheel. Or the Hell Hole. Where the Skee-Ball at? Din't somebody used to live in the roller coaster? Or was that a movie? One time when her parents took her and her three brothers down there, she didn't want to leave, and they pretended to leave her behind But Ise old enough to call they bluff, I let em get good an far away, an Ise thinkin bout stayin, too, runnin away from home. How old I was? Seven? Stood by the cotton-candy man, watchin him twirl all the pink fluff, knowin I ain't had no money, hopin he gon take pity on me, gimme a free sample, an maybe I could live on that, sleep in the Haunted House.

Her memories reached a crescendo as the train took the usual right turn after Neptune Avenue, where, like a curtain getting pulled back, the navy blue of sky and ocean came into view between the tall apartments of Brighton Beach whose windows glowed bright orange in the sun as it very gradually set behind her. When the train doors opened at the West 8th Street — New York Aquarium stop — the walls of the station blocked the view, and stifling heat rushed in with the sounds of the beach. The noise of the surf curling onto the sand mixed with the cries of seagulls, the laughter and shrieking of children, the piercing lament of sirens, growling engines, screeching brakes, a pop song thudding from an open car window Some dude singin bout he can't feel his face?

A few minutes later, as the train moved to the terminal stop, Carlotta spotted the whimsical structures of Coney Island between the high-rises and her heart gave itself up to the seductive trap of the amusement park and its plastic promises: fun and luck, empty calories and cheap thrills, and under it all, a carnival version of history dripping with sleaze. Then, on a brick wall, she caught a glimpse of the cartoon white man with Brylcreemed hair that the park used in all its advertising, his perverted smile summing up the entire experience He grinnin like somebody down there givin the motherfucker a blowjob, but you can't see cause the drawing don't go down that far, it just be his head. His espression like, Oh yes, honey, we gonna fuck, then we gon get on a roller coaster, have a ice cream, play some attractions, go on the beach, I'ma fuck you *again*, an then I'ma snatch yo purse an yo chains an book the fuck down the boardwalk fore you even know it. An bitch, you gonna love it.

When the train got to Stillwell, Carlotta disembarked, still in a trance, and once again found herself in a place she didn't recognize I looked up like, What all they done to this motherfucker? It's like I just got out and I'm in a *Vogue* fashion spread in Paris! I member this jwant useta was sad, like they ain't done nothin to it since the Dodgers gone to LA or whatever. Now it's like some kinda Emerald Palace! Still in her Diana/Beyoncé headspace, Carlotta slunk down the stairs and outside through the pink-orange tunnel that led to Surf Avenue All these crystal ceilings an shit, shiny glass bricks an whatnot—a mural? Who they spendin all this money on this shit *for*, cause I know it ain't no Black an Hispanic folks.

At Surf Avenue, she stood kitty-corner from the original Nathan's, where people formed long lines that stretched onto the sidewalk, bathed in the red light of the neon signs outside and the yellow interiors. For a second she thought about buying a beer Just to be cunty, it'd sure be a relief after all the fuckin stips but instead bought a Coke and two hot dogs with bacon and cheese, which she then smothered in ketchup and relish from the pumps. She didn't want to miss the last few rays of the sunset The sunset! on the beach The motherfuckin *beach*! so she carefully arranged everything in the cardboard box given to her by the sister behind the counter, wadded up the change, consolidated it with the other cash, and shoved the money into her underwear. She rejoined the constant exodus to the beach, from the train station down the street past the candy shops and souvenir stores, then beyond a series of rides she had never seen before, between still more remembrances of where things had once sat Guess the Hell Hole gone, an so's the Ghost Hole or whatever they useta call that lousy haunted house right there. Wonder Wheel, my God, that bitch ain't changed in a hundred-something years. Still there. At least some shit in this fuckin city don't never get teared down an turnt to a spensive-ass condo. Shoulda landmarked that Hell Hole!

Carlotta went up the short flight of steps to the boardwalk, and after marveling at the size of the bathroom complex A fuckin castle? on the sand, she hunted up and down the boardwalk for a park bench or picnic table where she could eat in peace. Around her the city unbuttoned itself Literally, my head bout to pop off lookin at these hairy-chested niggas wit cigarette-butt nipples, holdin hands with some chunky brown ladies in they neon-pink bikini tops tryna lick a ice cream cone down an walk a dog an yell at one chile right behind em an push a stroller, meanwhile the man on his cell phone talkin some language, don't got a care in the world.

An old Russian couple stooped over their walkers and shuffled like peasants who had never left the Old Country; a tattooed pierced white boy with disks in his earlobes chatted with his Asian manga partner, who had brown streaks in their hair and mascara around their eyes; ten members of a family from India strode down the boardwalk in formation, a rainbow bomb of traditional styles and fabrics; a large lady in a Rascal wearing a nervous expression bumped over the diagonal slats in the wooden walkway; a Latino father held the hand of his kid daughter, who had on a frilly yellow bathing suit and gripped a toy bucket the same color; stout cop types, one with an Italian flag T-shirt, laughed and shared plastic cups of beer around a picnic table; closer to Carlotta, groups of spandex-clad cyclists weaved recklessly through the crowd; the lights of the rides and the restaurants winked on and glittered everywhere as the sun disappeared, like they were trying to replace it; some wig-wearing Lubavitcher ladies whose style choices made them seem like apparitions from the 1940s pushed strollers behind pudgy men in shtreimels; red, white, and blue banners flapped in front of every storefront; the smell of hot dogs, burgers, and other fryables clouded the whole area; three tall blond foreigners in Crocs took pictures of one another, trying to get the Steeplechase in the background behind their smiling faces; a middle-aged white woman in a T-shirt that read SUPREME with a flannel shirt tied around her waist almost rode her skateboard over Carlotta's toe, and when Carlotta looked down at her foot she noticed a figure through a broken slat in the wood who, once she squatted and peered into the crack, she could see was masturbating, a sight that inspired her to move off quickly, holding her thighs together; delighted screams sailed over from Astroland, the loudest from the top of the Cyclone; everywhere, hip-hop songs overlapped with salsa and pop; in the distance, a fake palm tree sprayed water over an ecstatic group of Black teenagers, including two girls with white and pink hair; on the faraway pier, Carlotta could make out the silhouettes and fishing lines of sportsmen who had probably waited all day to catch a tiny sunfish that they would have to return to the ocean; and east of the park, at JFK, where planes leapt into the sky and swooped toward the runway, a long line of aircraft approached, their lights spread out above the Atlantic like a necklace of evening stars.

No bench had any vacancies; in fact, most of them contained more people in various configurations than they'd been built to hold. The moment she noticed someone leaving half of a park bench unoccupied, Carlotta scooted toward the opening, plopped herself onto the seat, and set her food box on her knees.

She devoured her meal with only occasional pauses, during which she savored the luxury not just of the meal itself but of the surroundings and how the chaos that had intimidated her at 42nd Street just the day before now felt celebratory and blissful, not only because of the holiday But just cause my ass outside, an I could breathe in this fishy breeze that's comin off the water like I done since Ise a baby, an everywhere motherfuckers just doin whatever the fuck an havin a ball, not givin no fucks bout what nobody think a them, that they too fat, too Black, too Chinese-lookin or green (an maybe that even could be a good thing that you weird as shit, like somebody wit a reality show could come down here an discover your sideshow-ready ass, put you on national TV, an you could be makin stupid phat money).

Don't nobody down here care who you wanna fuck or whether you think God be a blue motherfucker with twenty arms or a lady with a archery set who show up in your bed like a ghost or a fuckin octopus doin a Rubik's Cube, an the thrills is cheap, but that just mean that ev'body could afford em, an ain't nobody excluded outta no fun by not havin no money, not even my boyfriend who down there whackin his joystick under the boardwalk or nobody (is that what that song bout? — *Under the boardwalk, down by the sea?*), an the weather good an it's only my ass that got nine thousand stips to worry bout, can't even talk to nobody cause they might turn out to be a convict an maybe I should move farther down this bench cause I could see people with open cans a beer an shit, or maybe it's not just me, maybe it's half these motherfuckers out here is folks that been inside, I dunno, and I'on't wanna know, I just wanna be me, I just wanna be a human fuckin person like ev'body else, without nobody tellin me not to do who I am, holdin me gainst my will, don't wanna be no statistic or no tragedy or no symbol of nothin goin wrong in society. Cause I'm what's *right*, honey, I'm what's goin *right*.

Even before Carlotta finished eating, she heard it—the loco-motive pulse of "French Kiss," a club hit she had forgotten existed despite having heard it every night she went dancing, which was almost every night, in the late summer of 1989. She reboxed her garbage and carried it with her as she walked toward the music, pausing on the way at a trash can overflowing with Nathan's boxes and soft-drink cups and teeming with yellowjackets that she had to twist her torso to avoid stirring up. Already the throbbing beat had her moving; when the synth trumpets came in, her shoulders shook by themselves. Several yards down, a DJ had cordoned off a space under a gazebo and put up a large pair of speakers on either side of it.

Closer, she found a sparse group of dancers and a few roller skaters bumping and spinning to the steady electronic thump, soon joined by the barely intelligible moans and groans that stood in for lyrics I ain't even had to think bout what Ise gon do, it was like, after all them years, my body just said, *Get down, bitch, get down!* An fore I knowed it, Ise, like, squattin and grindin my booty, twirlin my grandma bag, my hips had come unglued, an', chile, I needed to own that dance floor.

They was playin *all* the old club jams: "Push the Feeling On," "Where Love Lives," "The Anthem," "Deeper"—the Underground Diva mix, too, where Ms. Susan Clark be tearin her lungs out, not that other shit. This dude even played that one number where it sound like they singin *Don't break the fax*, an the other that go

Foam! We want some foam! that I never found out what them jams was. Hell, it wasn't nothin on this motherfucker's playlist that had came out after I went in! It's like this man knew ezzackly when time an fun had stopped for me an he decided he gon go back to that fork in the road an lemme take the other path, lemme start livin the life I coulda lived, like time gone backwards. *Last night a DJ saved my life!* I felt the glory tinglin *all* through my fuckin chakras or whatever, baby, I was like Chakra Khan out there or, better yet, Chakra *Ex*-Khan, tastin the many flavors a the night air like it be a drug that make all that negative shit that had happened *not* had happened. Why'd we treat ev'thing like it was worthless when it was really so precious, when that shit was our *lives*?

An then it's like somebody ass had some fireworks that apposed to be for the next night that I guess they rehearsin for tomorrow wit out on the beach an I din't know that's even legal but Ise like, This *my* night right here, these *my* Welcome Home, Carlotta Mercedes fireworks, an it seem like most a the folks Ise dancin with, they bout the same age as me, look like they done been through some the same shit—the drugs, the prisons, the alcohol, the AIDS—an we was feelin the joy a makin it through all that, lookin at each other like, *I see you! How you doin? Could you believe we made it?* It's *big* fireworks, too, not no damn bottle rockets and Roman candles, it's some Grucci-ass bitches, makin a giant red Afro bove my head while I'm dippin an flowin an lovin an smilin with a hundred beautiful strangers!

Then I seen this old girlfriend a mines, Minerva, who I ain't seen nor heard from the whole time Ise gone, cross the dance floor, an she wearin this flowy maxi-dress full a gold threads, some gold sandals a little like my one, an a swingy turquoise necklace. She come right over to me like it ain't no thang, like it be the day fore I went inside, like she just jumped off the wing a one them planes up there, smilin like she won the Lotto jackpot. She put her hands on my shoulders, stared in my eyeballs, said my actual name, Carlotta—like, How she even know?—an hugged the mess outta me, just like my family shoulda did.

"I heard about all kinda things that was happening up there!" Minerva shouted. "*Bad* things!"

Carlotta checked out the bump on Minerva's neck Still there, look like she ain't had none a the surgeries or nothin. But she servin some mighty real realness.

"I kept in touch with Jasmine, and I had my eye on Ibe too. I kept telling that chile to go visit you on his own once he got to the right age. It sound like shit was real hard, I can't even imagine. But I knew you was gonna make it out, girl. Ise rootin for you. You real strong, even if you don't realize it your own self. Twentysomething years, gurl. Congratulations and welcome home! Let me introduce you to some folks!"

As they moved closer to the makeshift DJ booth, Frankie Knuckles's "Workout" came on, and Minerva told Carlotta that Frankie had died of complications from diabetes a year before, just shy of sixty, and that all kinds of tributes had popped up. Nobody considered this one of them, she said, still laughing, but it would do.

The practice fireworks came to an end, leaving wispy smoke to distort the high-rises of Brighton Beach. Carlotta knew a few of the five or six people Minerva brought her over to meet, in a tangential way; they were friends of friends or relatives of people she knew, she discovered after some small talk. She knew she should've backed away But Ise like, This been a rough day, ain't nobody gonna know. An what if the drug test don't come back false? Then I'ma be fucked. Gotta live in the moment. They all had Red Stripes and Budweisers on ice in a cooler, which Carlotta tried not to notice until everyone else had an open container in their hand. Minerva handed her a Red Stripe. She stared at it like a Magic 8 Ball This one li'l bottle could change my whole future. In the instant when the drinkers put down their alcohol and returned to the dance floor, now filled with hard-core club vets from Carlotta's early years, surrounded by a rectangle of less seasoned onlookers who only occasionally stepped into the fray and without the loopy enthusiasm of the true believers, Carlotta downed the whole thing. SIGNS POINT TO YES.

The night went on, and without a safe place to stay, Carlotta thought more of using Doodle's trick for getting what you wanted out of social interactions, wondering if someone there could save her, at least for the night. But when she sized the group up, nothing seemed promising. She had sucked down more than one more Red Stripe by the time the DJ lit a joint and passed it around Why the fuck not, how many time a day Lou DeLay could drop me? I know she ain't followed me out here! She gon drop my ass every day? If she do, maybe I don't care. I already done blowed it. The test ain't gon come back negative, I musta got contact high from that damn party. Shit, did I eat a poppy seed bagel? No. But fuck it. They called it super-weed, I ain't knowed that that meant nothin cept good weed. Miss Thing been out the loop a street talk less it had came from out the joint, an some shit they say at Ithaca they only be sayin up there, an some shit they said down here din't never make it up there, it's like two countries wit they own language.

So one minute I'm dancin with these folks and havin a good-ass time, best I had in two decades. Then, over the course a, like, a hour, I start feelin woozy, like I need a drink a water, somebody gimme some seltzer or what have you, my eyes start gettin funny, like all I could see is inside a TV from the '70s with the tint knob all the way up an it's on the fritz, you could even smell how it feel like the TV bout to catch fire, an the reception sucks cause it's even up on them VHF channels — an what the fuck was ever on them channels? In the side a my eyes it's some zigzags an patterns like on a crazy bulby outfit, like I accidentally had wound up on the runway of a Comme des Garçons show with a buncha angry supermodels dressed like they come from outer space, got some green Oompa Loompa hair an puffy pillows over they face, an they start chasin me off, an after a while I ain't got no kinda idea where Ise at or where I could go or who it's safe to be hangin out wit or *nothin*.

An the next morning, when I get waked up, I'm in the motherfuckin sand wit some kid's metallic HAPPY BIRTHDAY balloon stuck in my hair, li'l shiny flakes be comin off on my skin, an it's a police officer pokin my *face* wit his goddamn baton, tellin me, It's 9:30, ma'am, wakey wakey, an my ass don't member nothin happened since the Comme des Garçons show, an I realize (1) my ass under the boardwalk, like, Oh no, maybe I hooked up with that guy I seen under here, where he at? Don't even see him; (2) my wad a cash ain't in my underwears no more or nowheres on me, an, yes, the shit gone, oh, fuck; (3) I done missed my 9:00 a.m. appointment wit Lou DeLay, no chance I'ma even get there late this time, so I'ma have to deal wit that; (4) I don't got my grandma bag neither, just to pile some shame on top a ev'thing like some Cool Whip an a li'l maraschino cherry; an (5) it come to me that if my ass talkin to the po-po, Carlotta's headed back to D Block for damn sure. Did my stupid ass really just trade almost my whole life for one night a joy? I believe I did. Here I come, Frenzy. An, oh, hell no, Dave. First, I feel like I wanna dig myself so far down in the sand the cop can't take me nowheres. But then I start laughin my ass off cause I'm like Here it is, the Fourth a July holidays, an don't you know Carlotta bout to lose *her* damn independence, gotta get on that bus goin right back up to Ithaca an it ain't even been two damn days. But honey, the free world tasted oh so sweet. Even my li'l niblet.

Ooh, honey, Miss Thing done killed her motherfuckin number! She is off paper! Din't get no extra time on top a that, but a course them scumbuckets delayed my release on accounta some bad paperwork an a staff shortage. Or so they said. But here I am on the motherfuckin bus home again! It's time for round two a Carlotta vs. the Outside World, an I got the esperience now, I know what it's like out there: it's dangerous, it's a whole lotta technological shit that you gotta get down, an social shit too, but least this time it ain't no 100,000 rules and regalations I gotta follow like Ise tryna run the Olympic hurdles up against fuckin Carl Lewis while I be on crutches. This time my ass just *out*. As in o-u-t, out. I ain't gotta be in nobody file no more. Don't gotta report to no PO, don't no Lou DeLay gotta come in the can wit me to hassle La Señora for no UA samples or United Artists or no turd samples or *nothin*. The warden gonna starve. I could drink my face off if I want. Motherfuckers could be partyin up all day and night at Grandma Frona house, shootin each other, an long's I could keep it from affectin my program to get my life together, I ain't gon end up back in D Block or no place like it. I done my damn time an then some. Paid my debt or whatever. Society sure want a whole lotta cash back from folks that ain't got no money—the fuck's that about? First off, I'ma get me a cell phone—that's prolly the first thing I shoulda did last time. Just so I could call folks an they could call me, maybe keep me outta trouble, the kinda trouble that got me sent back to Ithaca. I was hopin to get me some phone action from Frenzy but he the jivest most sometimey motherfucker out there. I wasn't even back in the jwant a week after my two days a freedom an I din't suspect nothin cause he got the poker face a death, but ev'body steppin to me like, "I hear he hookin up with some white fish in on a second-degree-murder beef." I ain't even wanna know, an when I seen him after I heard, I just looked at him how I looked at him an he knew that I knew an it was *Ovah for me, ovah for me / Darling I love you, but can't you see it's ovah for me!* Could not believe that the whole two days Ise home Ise thinkin so much that the only reason I'd ever wanna go back be that sumbitch, an it turnt out that reason ain't even been no reason! I kinda went off on him at first. Ise thinkin parole done killed my love connection or whatever, like Ise dreamin bout a ghost that ain't even exist no more. But he all like, Please, please, baby, baby, sorry, sorry, ackin like Spike in that damn movie. I mean, it din't make no sense to me, he know better than to be mixin it up with some flaky flounder, right? I just kept my ear to the ground, an one day I stepped to the fish, all innocent but tryna get information. I got me some li'l pretend conversation goin an then I brought Frenzy name into it, an soon's I said that name the dude, like, froze. Froze like I had called up the devil hisself, you know, face turnt red as a fire hydrant, start stutterin an tryna edge out the convo, backin away from me an whatnot. It gut-punched my ass, cause he looked ezzackly like I prolly do when shit come up bout Dave. An so I start thinkin that maybe it wasn't no *thang* goin on with Me and Mrs. Jones there, right, that maybe there wasn't no love connection, an instead, Frenzy had did this boy dirty. An that kinda fucked wit me cause, you know—surprise! It ain't what you thought, it's some different shit that's *worse*. An a course, I couldn't be steppin to Frenzy like, Did you do somethin to that boy they callin Goo Goo on account a he still got baby-fat cheeks? Cause snitchin, that'd get the boy in worse trouble, maybe dead. When I saw Frenzy after that, the love an the fear was both in me, like, Could he a done like that, an if I said it to him, would he snap my neck? How you could be Mr. Sweetness over here and then—I'on't even wanna go there. So I'm tryna act like I ain't suspect nothing, cause love is love, an even when it ain't real it could give you a reason to keep on keepin on. I brought it up in a kinda backhand way, like, a Could-you-magine-if-somebody sorta question, an he seem confused for reals, so that made me feel better. But I guess something kinda shattered too, cause I din't had to be all hung up on his ass no more, an maybe it be okay if I just let him go. He totally tried sayin some shit along them lines, but I did like that lady in that movie, put my hand up to his mouth like, "Don't speak! Don't speak!" We still good, ain't no beef or nothin, still kinda together, he still stickin up for me an we still kickin it now an again, but not like it usela was. An when I get to Brooklyn I gotta go back to Amanda and get me that right shoe! Oh, chile, I could not believe that when I got out this time, they gave me back some the possessions I had, like that twenty-dollar lilac suit I ain't want nohow, an underneath that, I seen that gold-lamé sandal I snatched outta Amanda and Ise like, Dafuq? The whole time I'm back up at Ithaca, Ise thinkin Amanda gon show up like the green giant goin *Fee-fi-fo-fum, where the fuck my shoe at, bitch?* Or least somebody gon figger out that I done grabbed it an nail me fo nother five years a bullshit and LOPs, but din't nobody say nothin, an then I get out this afternoon an they gimme that damn shoe back in a plastic bag. Ise laughin like, *What?* Color me surprised, honey! Oh, I been waitin on this moment more than half my life. My life could be a book. That's what Professor Brown up in the law liberry said when I told him bout all what had gone on back home, an then he say he gon help me write it too, like a "as told to" kinda thang, like I be Grace Jones or Sheila E. He axed me a million questions an be typin down all what I said like it's some important-ass shit, an the whole time I be settin the record straight on some shit, not takin no prisoners, ha-ha-ha. People in my life gon cry this thing ever come out. It gon be a wig-snatch on some folks, honey, like—whoosh! Oh *yasss,* qween! This pure freedom comin up right here, more precious than pure cocaine, I know that. I ain't had too much a this here controlled substance in next to a quar-ter of a cen-tu-ry. Dag, I spent so much time up in that bitch that to me it's like that's normal an what's out here, even though it's natural as—oh, shit, there go a deer out in them woods, right as I'm thinkin the word *natural*! Hi, deer! Yes, you natural. Watch your ass cause you right by I87 an gon get dead when some garbage truck hit yo ass! Honestly, it's like out here I ain't got no idea bout what's what no more, but I'ma get it together, you watch. I'ma get that cell phone. An a gun too, once I git some dough an a nice wardrobe together. Won't nobody mess wit me no more. I'ma a be like Pam Grier, wit razor blades hid in my Afro. Frona said it ain't nobody carryin on at the house no more cause that was just that unlucky weekend that it was both the wake and the Fourth a July parties an me comin back an ev'thing, said it been real quiet since, maybe cause all them people got arrested that night, something like twenty-five motherfuckers got took away in them squad cars, I can't even believe that shit, bet some of em wound up at Ithaca too, but I din't never see none of em, definitely not Paulie Famous. I think his dad got all kinda money an he prolly done paid his way outta jail time. I shoulda stuck with his ass, maybe he coulda paid my way out too. Maybe that's the kinda nigga I need in my life, boring but rich. You know what I'ma do? I'ma take up some real wholesome hobbies and shit when I get back, like, I dunno—knittin or somethin. I'ma make all kinda African patterns on a sweater or something, maybe you do that on a loom so maybe I gotta get a loom, which I ain't got no money for, but I bet if I ask Frona she gon say *Just use my loom, honey,* or she gon be like, *We could get you a loom down the community center,* or, *I'ma buy you a loom off this reverse mortgage that allow me to spend all the money in the world that I don't got up till the time when they come lookin for my ass,* I could make all kinda African-print clothes that shows all kinda scenes from African folktales, start me a shop, open up right next door to Amanda, be like, Hey, you recanize this shoe, ho? No, I can't do that! I can't afford nothing in life, don't got a sardine can to piss in, talkin bout I'ma open some boutiques an whatnot. But maybe! Maybe I could pologize to Paulie Famous an he could put up the money. Oh, shut up, bitch. That's right, I need to shut up and get me a goddamn job somewheres, don't know wheres. Mickey D's don't want no folks like me, maybe I could get a job at a club downtown? They got programs they told me bout, I guess, but don't none of em sound like no place nobody wanna work, but it better not be no Access-A-Ride motherfuckers tellin me I got a job that I don't got, *Boz,* hope they fired his ass an he left out that stupid building an got runned over by a Access-A-Ride van an now he just flat like a ol punching bag that done sprung a leak. Motherfucker could suck my ass! I guess Frona gon give me my mama's old room now that she out in some assisted-living situation somewheres out on Long Island, dunno why they put her all the way out there, you'd think some a these motherfuckers I'm related to might wanna go see they mama at some point before she run outta gas, which seem like it gonna be real damn soon. Maybe they just can't handle it an they want her outta they sight so they don't gotta member that Mama ain't Mama no more, like she dead but still alive, a undead zombie or a vampire, an can't nobody deal with that, I know my ass can't hardly deal with it, so Thing 1 could handle that? Like not at all, but I guess it do mean that a real room be open in the house an I guess since it's smaller than Thing 2's Super Mario Castle or happy place or whatever he call it, he don't wanna move outta that situation, but he ain't movin outta nothin at no point noways, I wonder do he even get up to go to the john no more? Maybe I need to get up an go to the john right now, can't be no worse than no prison toilet back there, Señora Problema gotta give it up to the devil down in hell right there. Pretend it's a CO. At least they lemme out on a Friday this time, won't be no point tryna get started the minute I get back, right? Cause everybody who could give you a job, they done for the weekend, I bet, so I could just get settled in the home an set some shit up an decorate Paloma room or whatever, then start worryin bout goin out an tryna get a job an reenter society—re-reenter, really! Cause that did not work out too good that first time, honey! This gon be different right here, though. *Yasss,* ho! Gonna make me some moneys. It sucked that somebody jacked all my dough that night cause I don't got hardly nothin gettin out now. Frona like, Lemme take care a you, but she got that volcano up there—*Joe Versus the Volcano,* Joe *be* the Volcano—that's like havin five mouth to feed already. I wonder who done jacked my scratch that night, I wonder if Minerva set my ass up, but why she would do that? How anybody even knowed I had all that cash anyways? Could they smell it or somethin? If somebody just outta lockdown and you seein em for the first time in who know how long, what gonna make you think that a bitch got five hundred clams in her panties? An it's some shameless motherfuckers too, takin cash that literally been up in your junk, right, takin it right outta Ms. Problema's li'l fingers, with all my sweat and funk just saturatin the hell out of it, Ise dancin so much. Maybe it fell out, maybe I just stone cold boogied it out my panties. If it got took, I hope whoever done it tryna buy some shit an the store clerk be like, *I'm sorry, sir, this money reeks a pussy. Bloomingdale policy be that we don't assept no kinda pussystank moneys. Take that shit to Macy's, gurl!* Cept they prolly *do* assept it! Prolly make it more valuable to have you some pussystank money. Only thing gonna make motherfuckers like money more than they do now. Gotta get these nails done, damn it. How long it gon be before we get to New York? Where the fuck we at? It's a damn shame, I done lived in upstate New York most a my life an ain't hardly never seen a cow, a goat, or a tree. I don't got no watch to tell what time it is, can't see nobody else phones or watches on this bus. I guess I could axe the driver but he busy wit drivin an I don't wanna be the bitch made his ass crash, an specially not on my second first day a bein out the system an wild an free in the open world again. This gon be the last day like that in her life. Not wild but you know. Free range! I definitely gotta do somethin bout my wardrobe, at least clean shit up to look presentable, not no high-fashion looks or nothin, but please get me outta this prison-issue ridicalousness an this twenty-dollar lilac suit from Gladys Knight's "I Done Gambled All My Moneys Away So Farewell" Tour or whatever, thank you very much. An my very own high-fashion makeups, finally, could look good at forty-whatever years a age, gon have to find me a sugar daddy even if I wanna buy a hot dog from the pretzel man and shit, but I'ma do what I gotta do, I mean, what else could I do, don't got no choice but to do good this time, cause it been far too long to be cavalier bout any a this shit. Ev'body else either got dead or be passin me by in one way or another, right, just by not bein in the joint you got more a life than somebody that is, an maybe you get to see your children an your boo an maybe you get to hug em an say nice shit to em, *Love you, Love you, Happy birthday,* I'on't know how them folks do. I wrote to Ibe again once Ise back in, I said all kinda *sorry*s an *love you*s an I know this time that Jasmine ain't got in the way, cause I sent it through Frona which I shoulda did in the first place, an I heard back! He just sayin stuff bout savin my soul, an Jesus said this, Jesus said that, totally tiresome, but I gotta humor the chile an go wit him. Goin to church ain't too much different than a drag ball—buncha folks on a damn stage showin out in some flowy gold-lamé getups. But I'm only gonna go if Iceman come to the club wit me. That's yo church, this my church. He in the music biz, he can't be turnin down them kinda opportunities. Frona been all good bout gettin in touch an callin on the regular since my first time out, maybe cause she know she could just talk an talk to me, an I ain't gon stop her till the warden come in and say to cut off the damn collect call cause it gettin too long, shit espensive, but she don't care. Maybe she know I'm comin back and she gon have to deal wit it, or maybe she know she gonna die, I mean, not like she got terminal cancer, but like she gonna die a natural causes eventually, an she need a confidante or somethin? Maybe she realize she can't rely on Things 1 and 2 to take care a her in ol age, they just take and take, don't know how to give nothin back. Ibe ain't told me in his Jesus letter, but Frona said he got all kinda issues goin on like he had to move out his apartment and then he been couch-surfin for a while, couldn't scrape together none a the money to get a apartment in this damn town. Like people want somethin like two month rent and then some up front, I'm like, No no no no no, I can't even pay *this* month rent, why you axin for next month an the month after that? I'on't even know if them months even gon *happen,* the way shit goin these days. I spose ventually Ise gon have to do that apartment shit myself, an this time I ain't gon have no li'l nest egg or nothin, just the sweat off my own booty. Gotta get this show on the road! People try to drag your ass down, can't be listenin to that. Gotta keep a positive attitude, can't be playin no video games all day an stayin in your kingdom! I almost had my entire life in a room for a long-ass time an I can't believe that no matter how many video games you be playin and moo goo gai pans you be eatin that you could be happy doin ev'thing in one damn room, know what I mean? I knowed a lotta folks up in the SHU, or least I passed a lotta kites wit em, an this one dude Lucas always sayin that he good, it's okay that he in solitary, an it wasn't even like me sometimes where they done it to keep him outta GP so the GP wouldn't fuck wit him but a course the guards did like Dave did wit me, an Lucas always sayin, I'm a only child so I could handle this, he said it for, like, twenty days, an then on day twenty-one, his ass turnt to a shit-throwing monkey, so much for all the crap he useta be talkin bout the Buddha, straight up this nigga be Mr. I'm So Calm Cause I Be Doin Yogas in My Goddamn Cell, *om, om, om,* ain't no place like *om,* he like, I be one with the universe and shit, can't no cages keep me inside cause my mind be free or whatever, then all a sudden he. Lost. His. Total. Mind. Like zero to sixty in a heartbeat; they hadda wrap his ass up in a turtle suit, lift the motherfucker out the SHU on a gurney, he screamin and cryin, freakin the fuck out, flooded the whole area, made a shit paintin all over the cell walls, be a shit Picasso, baby, cut hisself so much that the blood in the water be comin down the damn hall into *my* cell an I'm like, Is it any part a this motherfucker *left*? Did he done decapitate hisself? Dag. I had my moments, chile, but I ain't never flipped out on *that* tip. That's how I know it's all gon be good once I get back to the BK, to the Fort Greene, know what I'm sayin? Minerva may a fucked me over, I'on't know, hope not, but she told me she thought Ise strong an that really meant some shit to me, you know? Maybe I am—I mean I must be—it ain't ev'body could go through what I gone through wit gettin my ass kicked half my life, not bein fraid to be myself an start to live as myself in de man prison, like Pam woulda said, an havin to deal wit Dave, who still workin up there, an his skanky-ass li'l brother too, but they had moved Dave's butt outta the SHU to A Block, I heard, so I wouldna had to even look at his stupid ass even if they'da sent me back to the SHU, which they ain't, an what a relief. When they had did the re-intake, I axed them could I go to the women's part insteada back to D Block, an they's like, No. Not even gonna discuss that shit. But even if it's some dangerous motherfuckers in GP who don't like nobody who different, honey, I'd risk it for the company. Fore I went inside, you coulda never got my ass to sit down an play no checkers wit nobody, not for a apartment in Trump Tower would I done that, but now the bitch be like a checker champion! I spose I could keep goin like this with Frenzy or whatever, the motherfucker sexy as a goddamn ripe mango, but I'ma consider my options. Oh *yasss,* Qween! That motherfucker got all the superficials, know what I'm sayin? Face body dick tattoos cute li'l soul patch muscles round bubble butt lips voice hair sexy nice nape a the neck small a the back the motherfucker even had hisself some hot *earlobes,* all the superficials, but not a whole lotta the deeps. It's nice for a while, but it's a damn shame when it ain't goin nowheres. I mean, I ain't sayin it's not *fun,* but a bitch like me got places to go. An what's more, after I had gone back for them two days in July a 2015 an reconnected wit folks in Brooklyn, I started gettin more prison visits after I had came back this time, an in the room visits, where you wasn't no pheasant under glass or nothin, like when Frona came up, she could legit gimme hugs an shit, an a chocolate cake that I traded for all kinda contraband lady stuff you could use as makeup an clothes that can't nobody get in no man prison—I even found me a connection wit a woman hack, a real duck, who they put in D Block, she actually nice, I mean nice for a CO, her name Amy, she hooked me up with lipsticks and shampoos an shit, I mean nothing *great,* wasn't no MAC or no Shiseido, like the next stop for this crap prolly woulda been Dollar Tree, but it ain't like I could get picky or nothin an it was a good connection wit a person who doin a good illegal thang for me, an you can't knock that. Doodle actually made it up to Ithaca a couple times, got drove up by some folks from the hood that I ain't seened in a dog's age, honey. Maurice said he thought Ise dead, in fact, an actually I thought *he* had got killed in a fight but that turnt out as a different Maurice, which was weird cause how many Maurices it is out there? An you can't be axin nobody who come visit you in the joint like, *Nigga, ain't you dead?* That ain't polite. Doodle had got my info from Frona—naturally—sent me a letter, an I thought bout not respondin but then I got bored wit how bored Ise getting so Ise like, Fuck, you can't be holdin no grudges gainst people who more or less be on your side even if they sometimes not. An Doodle, she esplained to me one time when she come up alone, she told me all what happened to her parents and Ise like, Oh my God, chile, I can't believe that. See, first her stepfather had brung his daughters up from Barbados, they like seven and nine years old, and then a few months in, her mama caught him molestin the daughters, she knew somethin goin weird cause the daughters actin strange, like not talkin an cryin a lot, don't wanna eat nothing, won't look nobody in the eye, and Doodle mama real sharp, so she like, Some shit is up an I'ma get to the bottom of it, you know, so I'on't know how she figured out what she thought's the problem an then decide to do it, but she did a setup on Nestor an caught him in the act, but he grabbed a weapon an shot her dead. That's why Doodle call him the ex-stepfather. He at Sing Sing now, his new best friend be Son a Sam. Bad shit could happen anywheres, you know that's true. In the prison, out the prison, to the rich, to the poor, to the ain't-got-much—prolly bad shit happenin in the palace to the queen a England, but ain't nobody sayin shit bout that. Oh, you know it, honey, *yasss,* Queen! I feel bad for the queen a England. Just kidding, fuck her! But ain't nothin worse gonna happen to Miss Carlotta Mercedes, I'm leavin all the bad shit a the past in the past and movin on to my real life, that's how I'ma think a this what's comin up right here, my real life. I'ma be the queen a England my own self fore too long. All sorta opportunities gon open up to me, like now maybe folks gonna vote for some motherfuckers who could do somethin bout the bad conditions in prisons, the shit food an no heat in the winter an no AC in the summer, the fact that folks like me don't get nothin but abused, maybe if you wanna get a sex change you could get some hormones, but they still don't know where the fuck to put you in that bitch, see, ev'body think that if you a convicted criminal you don't deserve no rights to nothin an like you ain't no more'n a aminal in a cage, criminal, aminal, criminal aminal, craminal, caminal, don't nobody give a fuck aboutcha. An the more Black, the less of a fuck, an the more femme, the even less of a fuck behind that not giving a fuck, till really the amount of a fuck people be givin so small you can't even see it no more. Like microscopic amounts of a fuck. Or most likely it ain't even there. It's really just laziness, ain't it, like the less rights you think a motherfucker got, the less you think you gotta recanize that that person be a real person with a brain an feelings an children an parents, an that they lives an they struggles be real an not just some mumbo jumbo crapped out a bird's ass on your windshield. The less you think you gotta care bout another person, the less you *do* care. Gonna get me this cell phone, honey, first off. That's how you re-reenter society…now, I ain't really got no idea what's so inneresting on all these phones folks got that they gotta stick they faces in it all day, they in one place and they wishin they was some-place else, like they spend the whole time on the phone ignorin your ass that's right in the room, I seened that a li'l bit. I guess it's like havin a TV you could hold in your hand an you could talk to your friends wit an do ev'thing on an the whole world just disappear. But I need it to get my job, or my jobs. I'ma have to get a day job an a night job. You would need that to make a living in Brooklyn nowadays, honey. A secretary in a office by day an a hostess at a club by night, could be. I'ma have my pick. They always sayin how hard it is, tellin you this an that, but that's just to scare you into gettin your ass in gear, make sure you don't just be sleepin on your grandma couch all depressed cause you can't find no job an ev'body think you a degenerate motherfucker who can't get it together an you gonna be committin crimes all over em day and night. Joe ain't even had that esperience an he sittin up in his room all depressed anyways! I know he say it's too hard to be out there in life cause he a Black man, but that ain't no excuse. I useta look like Ise a Black man—that shit was hard, but it ain't never made me decide to drop the fuck outta life or whatever. An it ain't like it's some kinda picnic now! I guess I just ain't think Joe Jr. got the right idea on how to deal with the situation. You gotta get out there an *do stuff,* try to make shit work! Like RuPaul, wasn't nobody never thinkin much bout how she could conquer the world, and look what she done, least on TV, she Black and she playin a drag queen *an* a man an don't nobody got a problem with it cause it's a success. That's the shit that folks don't never argue with in this country, money an success. Hell, it's the same thing for most motherfuckers, can't had one without the other. That's what I love bout this country, shit. If you could do like her, be a Black boy who grow up to be a big star an a big success an make all kinda phat moneys dressin up like a white lady, what you couldn't do in the USA? Don't nobody got no kinda excuses. You could be a zero nothin nobody an all a sudden you wake up an you the damn president. Or, like, sometimes a motherfucker could get famous just by killin somebody, or killin a *buncha* people, you could make a name for yourself, start sellin T-shirts or place mats or hand creams wit yo name on it, like Charles Manson Steakhouse or whatever. But I ain't bout killin nobody, at least not at this point much as I has wanted to kill certain people *Dave.* But I done got too close to that death shit one time too many already, motherfuckers gettin beat to death by the COs, cons slittin each other throats, that is a world I don't never wanna see no more. An I ain't gonna! Life gon be sweet as a motherfuckin peach, I'ma bite in that peach and it gon be juicy as fuck, the juice gon be all over my face and hair, an the juice gon go up my nose an down my front an into my body, honey, just like it be with Frenzy that first time, chile, life gon be like some good sex, like with that dude Cornbread on jigs in the house an I could feel Frenzy climbing all over my back and kissing my behind like he not even Frenzy no more, he just become the idea a freedom in a human body, maybe he gon get out hisself too and we both gon be free, the warm hands a liberty caressin my thighs an openin me up with they tongue an whatnot, an Freedom, I'm a call him that now, like, Freedom Williams, Freedom gon axe me do I wanna get fucked an I'ma be like, Shit, ain't nobody ever *axed* me, motherfuckers just done jumped me an fucked me to a pulp, death by bunga-bunga or whatever, so I ain't know what to say at first, but then I'm like, inside I'm like, smilin, like I can't believe that somebody done *axed,* an that it's you, an that after all the queer streets I done walked lookin for love an findin sex, lookin for sex an findin some freakazoids who just obsessed wit me, finally it feel like somebody seen me, the real actual Carlotta me, the me *inside* me, for the first time after forty-hmm-hmm years a pain, somebody knew, somebody saw who I was an loved me for the first time, an I knew it wit my whole body an my whole brain, an, honey, I got up inside myself, an I walked through every cell a my life an I knew that wit love ev'thing gon lead somewheres good even after all the bad, so I'ma get up on all fours for Freedom, an I'ma close my eyes an relax, an open myself up to it like Ise a music box, like I be showin Freedom a li'l twirlin dancer inside a me that's made a diamonds an gold an I'm seein it myself too for the first time in a long-ass time, an I'ma say Yes honey, I do, honey I'ma say Yes motherfucker, said hell to the yes I'm sayin *YASSS.*

ACKNOWLEDGMENTS

Brendan Moroney, Clarinda Mac Low, Doug Stewart, Ben George, Jennifer Egan and David Herskovits, Helen Eisenbach, Andrew May, Gavin Edwards, Lysley Tenorio, Robbie Pollock, Griffin Hansbury, Cécile Deniard, Kalup Linzy, Anthony McFadden, Alejandro Heredia, Matthew Aaron Goodman, Lena Little, Paula Carino, Telow Baugh, Jeannine Iorio, Loyal Miles, the Edward F. Albee Foundation, the Corporation of Yaddo, MacDowell, Writers OMI at Ledig House, Christopher and Kathleen Moroney, John O'Malley, Jonathan Towers, Katherine Profeta, Nickie Osborne, Donna Frazier.

ABOUT THE AUTHOR

James Hannaham is the author of the novels *God Says No,* a Stonewall Book Award finalist, and *Delicious Foods,* which won the PEN/Faulkner Award, the Hurston/Wright Legacy Award, and was a *Los Angeles Times* Book Prize and Dayton Literary Peace Prize finalist as well as a *New York Times* and *Washington Post* Notable Book, and *Pilot Impostor,* a multigenre book of responses to the poetry of Fernando Pessoa. He lives in Brooklyn, where he teaches at the Pratt Institute, a few blocks from where his grandparents lived.